A WARRIOR'S OATH

SAGA OF THE KNOWN LANDS
BOOK SIX

JACOB PEPPERS

This is to you, Declan.
To my dinosaur-loving, car-noise-making, face-stuffing youngest son.
I love you, Deckers. I love you like you love to eat.
Or to steal your sister's toys.
But...maybe we'll talk about that later.

SIGN UP FOR THE AUTHOR'S MAILING LIST and for a limited time receive a FREE copy of *The Silent Blade*, prequel to the bestselling fantasy series *The Seven Virtues.*

Go to https://www.JacobPeppersAuthor.com to get your free book now!

CHAPTER ONE

HE WAS GOING TO DIE.

That had always been true, of course, but that truth had always been abstract, something for the future, something for another time. It had always lain on the other side of thousands of tomorrows, a million later-on's away.

But tomorrow was today, later was now, and he was out of time. *They* were out of time. Chall glanced over at Ned, and while the carriage driver's face was impressively without fear, he thought he could see knowledge of that truth in the man's eyes.

Catham was starting toward them, the bared blade of his sword in one hand, and Chall gathered what little courage he had—just enough to keep him from pissing himself—as he watched the man come.

Catham had barely taken two steps, though, when the door creaked open. Relief washed over Chall as he turned to regard the door. Priest. It had to be. The man had been looking for Catham after all. No doubt he'd followed him here and had waited to see what he'd been about, had still been waiting when he'd seen Chall and Ned taken.

All of this went through his mind in a moment, and he prepared to help

—though what help he might be with a crossbow bolt sticking out of his leg he wasn't altogether sure, particularly when he wasn't much of a fighter at the best of times.

But in the next moment, whatever hope he'd had of rescue was shattered as the door swung wide revealing not Priest or a contingent of castle guards as he'd hoped, but a person he didn't know. And while Chall didn't recognize the newcomer, it seemed clear by the unsurprised expressions of Catham and his crew that they did.

The newcomer glanced at Chall and Ned, taking in the bound, bloody men with an almost bored expression as if such sights were common to him—which, Chall supposed, given his career path as a criminal, they likely were. The man moved into the room to stand beside Catham, whispering in his ear words too low for Chall to make out.

But Chall didn't need to hear them—nor did he need to be an Empath like Ned—to note the frown on Catham's face as he listened.

"Did you tell him we've got enough?" Catham asked, sounding frustrated and angry. That was fine so far as Chall was concerned—after all, the bastard meant to kill him, so he figured it was safe to assume that what was bad for Catham was good for him and Ned.

The newcomer whispered something else, and Catham grunted, scowling in Chall's direction. "Fine," he said. "But you tell him I think it's a mistake. This sort of thing, it's best handled quickly. A man finds a snake in his yard, he can spend his time trying to figure out if it's poisonous or not, maybe get bit, maybe die for his trouble. Or he can kill the snake and settle the matter. You tell him I said as much."

The newcomer inclined his head then turned and walked out again, leaving Catham with a sour expression on his face as if he'd just eaten something that had gone off.

"Bad news, I take it?" Chall asked. "Because if it's a bad time, Ned and I can always come back later."

Catham glanced at him, grunting. "Funny. I've heard that about you, that you're funny. I've met a few funny bastards in my time, though. In my experience, they always run out of jokes pretty quickly once the bleeding starts." Catham glanced over at the man nearest him. "Take them to the back room. Less chance their screams will be heard that way."

He said it in a business-like, casual sort of way, the way another man might comment on the weather, and a chill of fear went through Chall, banishing whatever pleasure or hope he'd felt at seeing the man discomfited.

"I thought you were going to kill us," Ned said.

"Oh, we'll get around to that soon enough," Catham said, not taunt-ingly or teasingly, just as a simple statement of fact. "After all, we've got time. First, there's a few questions that need answering."

"Ask your questions, if you like," Ned said. "That doesn't mean they'll get answered."

"Oh, I don't know," Catham said, shrugging, looking bored. "I can be persuasive. Anyway, we might as well give it a try, what do you say?"

He nodded his head at the men again. Two stepped forward, grabbing Ned by either arm, and despite everything, despite the fact that he was in great pain, and in even greater danger, Chall couldn't help but be annoyed as he noted the fact that only a single man stepped forward to escort *him*.

Stupid, maybe, but there it was. First Balderath coming alone—and he *had* been alone, no matter what Maeve claimed—now this. "Just you, huh?" he asked the man beside him.

The man beside him sneered.

"It's on account of I'm injured, isn't it?"

"What the fuck are you talking about?"

Chall sighed. "Nothing. Forget it," he said as his escort—his *single* escort—led him toward the back room.

And as he stepped into that back room, as he looked once more at the table where, what felt like a lifetime ago, he had bled and quite nearly died. Where he *would* have died had it not been for Emille—Chall forgot it, too. For he found himself thinking of something else, found his anger and annoyance being replaced by fear.

He had narrowly avoided death in this room once. It seemed far too much to hope that he might do so again. He tried to tell himself that it would be okay, that it would all work out, but as accomplished of a liar as he was, he could not make himself believe it, could not escape one inevitable truth.

He was going to die.

CHAPTER TWO

HE WAS GOING TO DIE.

Cutter had come close to death before, of course. It seemed that he had spent nearly his entire life walking the line separating life from death, balanced on a dagger's edge. So far, he had survived, had faced impossible odds and yet, somehow, had prevailed. But a man could only balance for so long. If he sat and flipped a coin, perhaps it would land on heads once. Thrice. If he was lucky enough, maybe even a dozen times. But the inarguable truth was this: if he flipped it long enough, sooner or later it would come up tails. If a man courted death long enough, sooner or later, death would answer.

And so he stood beside his brother and watched as his death came.

It was all around him. It was rushing at him from seemingly every direction, bending the blades of grass as it came on, dozens of lines, all of them pointing at him and his brother.

Worse, whatever effects the bite of the wolf-like creature had had were far from gone. It felt as if the world was spinning beneath his feet, and it was all he could do to stand, to keep the Breaker of Pacts clutched in a death grip.

There would be no winning here. The coin had come up tails, that was all. He had lost his balance and his foot had come down not on the side of life, but on the side of death.

"Got a plan, Bernard?" Feledias asked, moving so that they stood back-to-back.

"Not this time, brother," Cutter said. He caught sight of eyes in the darkness, eyes that glowed in hues of lambent yellow and green and white.

He didn't know how many creatures surrounded them in the clearing, how many rushed toward them through the tall grass. They came in their hundreds, in their thousands, and as he watched them come, Cutter said a quick prayer to the gods. Not for salvation, not to be saved, for he thought that given their circumstances, perhaps that was beyond even the gods. And even if such salvation did exist, he was not worthy of it. He had earned his death, after all, countless times over the years. So he did not pray for salvation. Nor did he pray to be remembered—better for him to be forgotten, better for the world if he was.

Instead, he only prayed that he might die well, that he would keep his courage until he no longer needed it and that his enemies would mark his fall not with victory or celebration but with relief. He prayed that when his lungs gave their last breath, his enemies would not have enough left in their own to cheer.

He prayed for company to come with him into the valley of the dead.

And then, he lifted his axe, calling on what little strength he had left in him, and prepared to see to it himself.

The shadows that were the creatures, that were his enemies, rushed at him from all directions, seeming to rise like some cresting wave as they came on, a wave that would, that *could* only sweep him and his brother away underneath the force of it.

Darkness given purpose, shadows given teeth.

But Cutter had teeth of his own, a purpose of his own, not to survive but to die well, and so as that wave of creatures rushed toward him, he stood his ground, raising his axe one more time.

CHAPTER THREE

HE'D WALKED this way before.

Shadowed streets that led through darkness and deeper into it.

Buildings that crouched like gargoyles along either side of the path, seeming to regard him not with menace, but instead with malevolent welcome.

And why not? He was one of them, after all. The wayward son returned home. He had tried to be something different, something better...but he had failed. He had failed for the same reason that the fish who wishes to fly fails—because it must. The fish was a fish, after all, with no business soaring in the air. And he...he was Valden the Vicious. What made him think that he, who had spent so much time stalking the shadows, deserved to feel the light again?

Figures watched him from the shadowed alcoves of alleyways he passed, marking his progress, measuring him. But while they watched him, they did not make a move toward him, and that was no surprise. The lion lurking in the grass might pounce on the unsuspecting hare or naïve gazelle who wandered into its hunting ground, but it would not so lightly attack another of its own kind. Predator recognized predator.

So Valden walked, unmolested, through the poor district of New Daltenia, a shadow in search of other shadows. He had lost his faith, and so it was not faith he clung to but hope. The hope that, somehow, a man might travel deep enough into the darkness, might consort with shadows long enough that he would find himself stumbling into the light once more.

As he came into sight of Flo's, the brothel where he and Chall had last spoken to Nadia, Valden forced his worries, his doubts, out of his mind. There would be time later for doubt, for worry—there always was. For now, his task lay before him. Danger lay before him, and it would not do to allow himself to be distracted any more than it would serve a man to walk into a pit of vipers with his eyes closed. It wasn't a question of if that man would rouse a snake, if he would get bitten—only a matter of when.

He checked his sword to make sure it was free in its scabbard then patted his belt knife, ensuring himself it was still there. That done, he took a slow, deep breath and started toward the brothel, his eyes scanning the area around him, ready to react should any danger present itself. He didn't see anyone standing guard, but then that meant little. After all, a man did not have to see the danger for it to be there, and a crime boss such as Nadia, one of the most powerful in New Daltenia since she'd taken over for Belle, would not go unguarded. Lions might not hunt other lions, it was true, but if they were hungry enough they would do what they had to, and no sooner had someone attained any position of power than someone else started trying to figure out how to take it from them.

Certainly, there had been plenty of guards standing in their way the last time he and Chall had come here, plenty of men and women who would have been all too happy to pounce, if the order had been given.

He was more than a little surprised, then, when he made it to the brothel door unaccosted. Valden frowned, glancing around him at the city street, still empty so far as he could see. "I do not come meaning harm," he told the shadows. But the shadows, as was so often the case, did not answer.

Valden hesitated, frowning. A man, he thought, would need a good reason to step through such a door without being invited. But then it had been no small reason that had brought him here in the first place. Not a reason at all, really. A purpose. A purpose to find Catham and, in doing so, to uncover information about the reappearance of the Crimson Wolves and understand what their intentions were. Based on what he'd seen so far, he thought he knew well enough, but he hoped that in finding Catham, in speaking with the man, he might discover some means of protecting the people he cared about.

That was why he had come, after all—to protect them. Just as it was why he had not allowed Chall to accompany him. A rabbit, accompanying a lion through the savannah, might well continue unmolested thanks to its company, but then lions were hungry beasts, and Valden had thought it better not to chance it.

Chall, of course, was no rabbit—he was one of the most powerful mages Valden had ever seen, a man who possessed more courage and more honor than most people gave him credit for—himself most of all. But then those things that lurked in the darkness did not respect courage but subtlety, and they knew nothing of honor.

But it was not just thoughts of Nadia and her men that made Valden hesitate. There was something else, too. A feeling. A feeling that something lay beyond that door, that by opening it he would be stepping across a threshold from which he might not return. Silly, maybe. He had heard of people having premonitions before, of course, but he had never had one himself. Until now.

Death waited on the other side of that door. Doom waited. He knew it as well as he knew anything and never mind that he had no idea how. But his fear did not matter. *He* did not matter. What mattered was the king-dom, what mattered were his friends. He had come with a purpose and that purpose had not changed.

He opened the door.

It swung open as soon as he touched it, and he realized that it had not been latched. Which only reinforced his feeling of foreboding. After all, men did not buy safes only to place all their valuables inside and leave the door open. Neither did criminals trust in the goodness of mankind enough that they would not post guards, would not so much as even latch their door against anyone that might come uninvited.

Stepping into the brothel, Valden saw why the dozens of people inside had not challenged him as he'd approached. Namely because they were all dead. Dozens of the hardest, cruelest, most dangerous men and women in all of New Daltenia lay sprawled where they had fallen.

Valden had seen dead men before. He had seen them chopped into pieces, had seen them shot with arrows, cut down by cavalry charges. He had seen men and women pierced with blades, their throats slit, or their faces crushed by some mighty blow of mace or flail. He had seen what felt like countless soldiers, human and Fey, cut down by the Breaker of Pacts wielded by the Crimson Prince himself. And before that, he had seen plenty fall to his own blades. He had seen dead men of all shapes and sizes...

But he had never seen anything like this.

The dead men and women littering the common room had not been shot or stabbed, had not fallen to axe or sword. They had been torn apart. Pieces of them lay scattered like the limbs of broken dolls, blood staining the bodies and the floor, the tables and chairs and counter as if men had upended bucket after bucket of red paint. It was devastation, a massacre the likes of which Valden had never seen, and he had seen far more than most.

He had not prayed to Raveza, the Goddess of Temperance, in weeks, not since the prince had been sent to his death, and Valden had been unable to do anything to stop it. Not since he had decided that the gods, if they existed at all, cared nothing for mankind. Nothing he saw before him was in any danger of convincing him otherwise, yet he found himself tempted to pray anyway.

In the end, he did not. Instead, he looked around the room, trying to determine—by those pieces of broken furniture and broken bodies littering the common room floor—what had happened. And as troubling as the sight of those torn bodies was, the story his mind told him was worse.

Weapons of all sorts were scattered among the dead. Rusty swords, makeshift clubs, and knives aplenty. Examining them, Valden saw that many of those weapons were coated in blood, enough of it to show that, while whoever they'd fought might have won, they had not gotten away unscathed. Not that he would have expected them to. Any person who waltzed into the hideout of one of the city's most dangerous crime bosses and chose to take on those dozens of criminals ensconced within could, at the least, expect to shed some blood for their trouble. No, he wouldn't have expected anything less. What he *would* have expected, though, was bodies. Bodies to which the shed blood would have belonged, once upon a time.

But all of those bodies which littered the floor were Nadia's men, while the opponents they'd faced and fought were nowhere in evidence. Valden tried to imagine how many men it would take to do such a thing and all without leaving a single casualty behind.

He was still trying to imagine it when the deathly silence was broken by a soft groan. He frowned, turning and glancing at the bar, the direction from which the sound had come. Another soft groan, and he decided that whoever had made the sound was behind the bar, for those in front of it were far too dead to have made any noise.

He drew his sword.

He doubted that whoever had made the tortured, weak sound he had heard was any threat, but considering that he was standing in a room of dozens of dead who, had they known their deaths were coming, would have no doubt chosen to be somewhere, *any*where else, he thought there was no harm in being cautious.

But that caution, as it turned out, was wholly unnecessary. He stepped around the bar—and the two corpses draped over it, one who looked as if half his face had been torn off—and peered behind it, searching for the source of the groan.

A man lay sprawled in the floor behind the bar, but a single glance at his broken body—one arm had been torn completely off—and his dead-eyed stare was enough for Valden to be confident that he was not the source of the sound he'd heard.

Even as he had the thought, another groan came, a sound somewhere between a whispered gasp and a whimper. Valden walked behind the counter, toward the source of the sound, then knelt, slowly opening the door to a large cabinet built into the counter, one that sat slightly ajar.

Another whimper, this one of terror, came from inside as the door swung open to reveal a man.

It was no wonder that Valden hadn't seen him at first, for the man was curled up in the cabinet in a position that must have been terribly uncomfortable.

"*Pl-please,*" the man whimpered, "*don't...*"

"I'm not going to hurt you," Valden said, though from the blood staining the man's shirt and face he thought that someone—or, perhaps, several someones—had seen to that already.

"*I can't...I can't feel my legs,*" the man said. "*Something hit me...in the back...I think...I think maybe my legs are numb.*"

The man sounded delirious, each word an obvious struggle. Valden nodded. "Be still," he said. He slowly eased the man over from his side so that he could see his back. The man groaned in obvious pain as he did, and as he finished turning him over Valden could see why, just as he could see why the man's legs were numb. Someone had buried a dagger deep in the center of the lower part of the man's back. Blood had oozed from the wound—was still oozing, in fact—soaking his shirt and trousers in dark crimson.

"*Is...is it bad?*" the man asked.

It was. Just about as bad of a wound as a man could take and still live. At least for a little while. Valden was no healer, but he knew this—the man would never walk again. He'd seen a similar wound before, where a man's spinal cord had been severed. That one had been caused by a man getting trampled by an angry bull. He couldn't imagine the force a man might require to sever another's spinal cord with a knife, but he knew that it was a lot. He also couldn't imagine where such a man would find the strength to do it—but then, where he'd found it really didn't matter. What did was that he had.

"I've seen worse," Valden told the other man. Which was true. The part of that truth which he neglected to share, though, was the wounds he'd seen that had been worse had always been borne by dead men, the ranks of which the man would be joining soon enough, given the amount of blood he'd lost. Had he been seen to immediately, perhaps a healer might have been able to save his life, if not the use of his legs, but judging by all that he'd seen, Valden thought the man had spent at least a few hours here. What torture that must have been, wounded, hurt, waiting for his death to come, the only thing to keep him going hope that he would survive, a hope that at least some part of him must know was in vain.

"Who did this?" Valden asked.

"*Don't know...*" the dying man said, his eyes going wide and terrified at even the memory. "*Came in and just...just started killing. Liam put an arrow in 'em, I know he did...only...it didn't matter. Just pulled it out and kept... slaughtering.*"

"Who was it?" Valden asked. "City guard? A rival gang? Who?"

The man opened his mouth as if to answer, but his eyes grew wide, and he gave a slow, shuttering, rattling breath, seeming to sink in on himself. His eyes fluttered once, weakly, then closed. They did not open again.

Valden bit back a curse, rising and looking around. The last time he'd been here, he and Chall had come to Florence's together to speak to Nadia. They'd managed that much, at least, meeting with her in one of the brothel's upper rooms. She had told Valden, at the time, that if he came back, she would kill him, but then if the upper room of the brothel looked anything like the lower—and he had no reason to think otherwise—Valden thought that Nadia had plenty enough trouble on her hands without looking for more. Assuming, of course, that she was alive which, in a room full of corpses as he was, felt like quite a bit of a stretch.

He walked toward the stairs.

Two more dead men waited for him about halfway up. Clearly, they had tried to hold off whoever had come from going any further and, just as clearly, they had found no more success in doing so than those in the common room had.

Valden stepped over the bodies and continued on.

Another few steps to reach the landing, another few dead men waiting there. They had fought a tactical retreat, clearly trying to keep whoever had come from reaching someone, and it didn't take all that much guesswork to think of who that might be.

Valden moved past the corpses toward the room where Catham had brought him and Chall the last time they'd come to Florence's before the man had tried to have them killed. Valden walked up to the door where they'd spoken with Nadia—or at least would have, had there been any door left to walk up to. The frame of the doorway remained, but the door itself lay in a shattered heap several feet into the room.

Valden didn't see any of the deep gouges he would have expected to see from an axe, had someone taken it to the door. Nor did he see any dents or cracks to indicate that someone had struck it with a club or mace or some other makeshift bludgeon. Another mystery, then, to add to the growing list.

Two more dead men lay inside the room. One he didn't know, but the other Valden recognized as the big man he'd seen sharing this same room with Nadia the last time he'd come. Only, last time the man had been beating on some unfortunate soul who'd been suspected of skimming. Now, it was the man who had been beaten. One of his arms lay at an impossible angle, clearly broken, and there was a fist-sized hole in his stomach. Valden stared at that bloody, glistening hole, feeling more troubled than ever. He didn't know many things that could cause a wound like that, a hole the size of a man's fist, except...well. A man's fist.

Impossible, of course. People didn't just go around punching holes in other people's stomachs. But then, very little of what he'd seen since arriving at the brothel had made sense. He supposed there was no reason for it to start now.

He studied the two dead men, trying to get a clear understanding of what had happened—had just about decided that it was as much of a mystery as all the rest—when he noted something odd. Namely, blood. Nothing odd about that in general considering the gallons of the stuff he'd seen since entering the brothel. But it wasn't so much the blood lying on the ground that gave him pause as much as it was the *way* it lay. Not in a pool as might have been expected but in a trail, one that moved toward the back of the room.

Valden followed that trail of blood—not much, droplets, mostly—until he reached the window at the back of the room. A window that, he saw at once, had been shattered. Bits and pieces of glass still clung to the windowsill like the few remaining teeth clinging in the mouth of an old drug addict. Someone, it was clear, had used the window as a means of escape. A desperate move considering the fact that they were two stories up. A fall from such a height might not kill—though it very well might depending on how the person in question landed—but people didn't tend to go jumping out of windows for the fun of it.

He leaned forward, examining the window and peering out of it at the street below. No bodies littered the ground there, but due to the height and the darkness he was unable to tell if the trail of blood continued. He was just beginning to turn away, confident that he had learned what there was to learn, when he caught sight of something hanging from one of the remaining shards of glass.

A strand of hair. And not any hair—gray hair. Gray hair of the kind that Nadia had. It might have belonged to someone else, it was true, but then Valden didn't think so. It was a well-known fact that there were few old criminals. It, like sticking one's head in a lion's mouth for an audience, was the sort of occupation that tended to bring its participants an early death. True, he didn't know for certain that the wiry strand of gray hair belonged to Nadia, the crime boss, but then he had heard some scholars expound on the many reasons why no man knew *anything* for certain. He tended to leave them to their ramblings—there was simply too much life to live to spend time asking himself useless questions with answers that, whatever they were, could only be equally useless. It was not certainty that a man lived his life by, after all, but evidence, and the evidence suggested to him that the hair belonged to Nadia. After all, those men on the stairs and in the room had died protecting something, and the crime boss was nowhere to be seen, dead or alive.

Considering the options, he supposed it might have been possible that whoever had come had taken Nadia with them. After all, why risk battle with so many dangerous criminals if not to strike at the heart of that criminal enterprise? And why go through all the trouble of coming to this room if not to retrieve the person inside of it? He was confident, at least, that whoever had come had come with the intention of, if not killing Nadia, then taking her. But he was also confident, based on what he saw before him, that they had not managed it. At least not here.

There was the shattered window to think of, the stray gray hair clinging to one of the shards of glass. There was also the wholesale slaughter and the two dead men that pointed to it as well. After all, people didn't keep working on a task once that task was completed, and there would have been no reason for whoever had come to keep up the killing if he'd already gotten what he'd come for.

Valden tried to imagine who—or what—could have frightened the normally unflappable Nadia so much to send her diving out of a window, but his imagination was simply not up to the task.

He took a few minutes to look around the other rooms of the brothel, but they were empty. Either they had not been occupied when whatever doom had come upon Florence's came, or else those who had sheltered inside them had been left untouched and fled once the killing was done. Given the fact that Valden had been to Florence's before and it—like pretty much any brothel he'd ever visited—never had any shortage of clientele looking to make use of its services, he leaned toward the latter. Which further supported the idea that whoever had come had come for the crime boss, and when Nadia had fled, they'd had no interest in remaining.

And with that revelation, neither did Valden. He was all too happy to leave the brothel and the dead behind, moving out into the street.

Standing outside the brothel, he let his gaze travel around the street. The night seemed darker than it had before. He didn't see anyone around, and he wondered how many had walked by since the massacre had occurred, moving past the brothel without any idea of the dead that lay within it. He wondered, too, how many had entered the brothel with the intention of making use of its services only to find the dead—and then, instead of calling for the guard, had bolted.

Quite a few, he thought, given the traffic such a place might regularly elicit. Some might have been surprised that such visitors would have left the dead without bothering to call the guard and ensure that they got a proper burial. Valden, though, was not. After all, living in such a place, around such people, a person learned ways to survive, learned the unwritten rules that they needed to follow to stay safe the same way a man living in some hostile landscape would learn, if he lived long enough, the dangers, and those things which he should and should not do.

And one of those things for the crime-riddled poor district of New Daltenia was that a man—at least any man who wanted to go on breathing—was best off minding his own business, keeping his head down. Less chance of someone coming and wanting to knock it off, that way.

No, he suspected it would be some time yet before the city guard came. Likely until those bodies within started to stink badly enough that they could no longer be ignored.

Valden walked around the building toward the back side of the brothel, glancing up from time to time to gauge his progress until he judged he stood below the window through which Nadia had made her desperate escape.

He looked about the ground, kneeling to see it better in the darkness, which was only broken up by the pale glow of the moon. He couldn't see much, but he managed to make out droplets of blood. He followed them, feeling very much like a hound following a scent, staying close to the ground so as not to lose sight of them.

He didn't make it far, though, before the trail vanished. He moved back, picking it up again to be sure and then grunted as he realized that, indeed, the trail disappeared in the middle of the street. Which seemed, to him, to indicate that Nadia had jumped into a waiting carriage and made her escape. A carriage that was rather conveniently and, no doubt, intentionally placed. Valden had never made it as high up the criminal ladder as Nadia had—a fact he usually took pride in—but he was pretty confident that the position of crime boss was not a safe one. After all, there were far too many people out there—enemy and ally alike—that would have been all too happy to stick a knife in the old woman and take her place.

Which meant that, if said crime boss was clever—which Valden knew Nadia to be—then she would prepare for the not just possible but almost certain eventuality that someone or several someones would, sooner or later, make an attempt on her life.

She was gone, escaped from whoever had come for her. He did his best to ignore his frustration. He needed to find Nadia, to see what he could learn about Catham, to see if she knew where he might be found. Catham wasn't just their best lead into the Crimson Wolves and whatever they were up to—he was their only one. Which meant that he needed to speak with Nadia, a task which had just grown considerably more difficult.

Nadia's criminal enterprise had suffered a terrible blow tonight. She would be looking to lay low, to lick her wounds and plan how to get her revenge. She would no doubt have sought shelter in what was likely one of several hideouts she had throughout the city for just such an eventuality, and a hideout wasn't particularly useful if it was easy to find. Valden frowned out at the night, his mood growing darker by the moment. He had no idea where Nadia was, no idea where her bolt hole might be, nor any idea of where he might even begin to look for it.

But unfortunately, he knew someone who might.

CHAPTER FOUR

A FIST STRUCK HIM AGAIN, and Chall cried out as his already split lip split further, and the increasingly familiar taste of blood filled his mouth again. He would have fallen, had it not been for the fact that he was bound to the chair in which he sat. He hocked and spat out blood. "Sorry...about your floor," he said, making an effort to lift his head and glance beside him to where Ned sat, similarly bound. Similarly beaten. One of the carriage driver's eyes was swollen shut, and there was a line of blood working its way out of one corner of his mouth, down his face. He bared his teeth in what might have been a grin or a snarl, Chall wasn't sure.

"Don't mention it," the carriage driver said. "No use crying over... spilled blood."

"Sure you won't mind if...I do it anyway?" Chall managed. Then he was struck again, this time on the other side of the face—a slap, not a fist. Something to be grateful for, at least, though truth be told just then he was feeling pretty damned far from grateful.

"Joke all you want," Catham said, sounding almost bored. "Bran can keep this up for hours, can't you Bran?"

The man with the bloody knuckles who, for the last half hour had been using Chall and Ned as target practice for his fists, nodded. "I love it, boss."

"See that?" Catham said. "He loves it." He shrugged. "Not my sort of thing, to be honest, but you know what they say—everything ain't for everybody. Anyway, I've heard tale that if you love what you do, you'll never work a day in your life." He rose from where he was half-standing, half-sitting propped against the table where Chall had lain, fighting for his life, some time ago. All too recently, so far as he was concerned. And here he was again, not really fighting for his life but sitting and bleeding and waiting for it to end. He wondered if maybe the room was cursed. He ought to tell Ned later, when he got a chance...not that he would.

"Listen, fellas," Catham said, "it doesn't have to be this way. All this blood—as you said, it's going to wreak havoc on the floor. Blood doesn't clean out easy—take my word on that. Now, are you going to answer our questions or not?"

"You...haven't asked any...yet," Chall managed, probing his tongue around one of his teeth. Pretty sure the bastard had loosened it, but then he supposed he had bigger problems than a loose tooth.

"Okay, now that's a fair statement," Catham said. "Just thought I'd let Bran get some practice swings in first, you know how it is. Anyway, I've heard the stories about Challadius the Charmer, about how dangerous you and your companions were. Figured I'd be safe rather than sorry. It's a sign of respect, really."

"Thanks?" Chall managed.

Catham smiled pleasantly, as if they were two old friends chatting over an ale. "You really are a funny bastard. Seems the stories aren't all lies, after all. Though..." He paused, his gaze traveling up and down Chall's form, pausing at his stomach—sitting in a chair rarely helped the look of it —then grunted. "Some might have been exaggerated. Always heard you were a hand with the ladies, but then I never knew a woman to be into a man who's about as wide as he is tall."

"Turns out they like fat men more than lying criminal pieces of shit," Chall said, choosing to ignore the fact that "criminal" was the only bit of that that hadn't applied to himself more often than not. He paused as the pain in his thigh where the crossbowman had shot him pulsed sicken-ingly, and he was forced to fight back a wave of nausea. He cleared his throat, swallowing the bile there. "What can I say? They're funny like that."

Catham smiled again. "Well, I suppose that's enough chatting, don't you, Bran?"

Bran grunted—he did a lot of that, Chall had found. But then, maybe most men did a lot of grunting when they were beating another one to within an inch of his life—Chall couldn't have said. What he *could* say, though, was something he'd learned over the last half hour or so and something Bran was even then reminding him of again: being punched in the face hurt. A lot.

"Leave him alone, you piece of shit," Ned said from beside him. At least Chall thought the man still sat beside him. He could see little more than blurs past the sweat and blood in his eyes, and the man's voice sounded as if it came from a different world. Which it did, of course, for Chall was in his own world, had been taken there by this man with fists like iron. A world of pain and despair and a tooth that he was growing more and more convinced was, indeed, loose.

"Easy, now, there ain't no need for that sort of talk," Catham said. "We're all just doin' our job here. My job is to see what you know, and your job—and the fat man's job—is to...well. Tell me."

"How is he supposed to answer you when you haven't even asked a question yet?"

Catham grunted. "Well, I suppose he's not. Still, it gives Bran somethin' to do, and every fella needs somethin' to do, somethin' to keep him busy. Idle hands and all that. Isn't that right, Bran?"

The man didn't answer, and Catham sighed, shrugging. "Not much of a talker either, I'm afraid. Still, he's got other things to recommend him, a fact to which I think you both could attest."

"Just leave him alone, you bastard."

Catham shook his head slowly. "Noble, I guess. Maybe not, I don't know. It's been a while since I seen it. Not sure I'd still recognize it. Damn sure don't understand it. I've met fellas like you, over the years—not many, but a time or two. Fellas who would rather be the one getting punched than the one sitting there taking a breather. You chasin' some sort of warm and fuzzy feelin', that it?" He scratched his chin. "I saw a fella jump in front of a crossbow bolt to save his friend one time. Didn't understand that either, and if the fella was chasin' a feelin', somehow I doubt it was the one he got. Not that I've ever been shot with a crossbow bolt—I make it a point to make sure I'm on the right end of those damned things—but I haven't ever heard someone describe the feeling it gives as warm and fuzzy. What about it, mage? How's that leg of yours feeling?"

"Piss off, that's how."

"See there?" Catham said, turning back to regard the carriage driver. "Doesn't much sound warm and fuzzy to me. Anyway, even if the man *did* feel like that, he certainly didn't for long. You know, since, as it turns out, being shot in the chest with a crossbow bolt—whether to save someone else or simply because you had it coming—has pretty much the same outcome."

"There's more to life than looking out for yourself," Ned said.

"Yeah," Catham said. "Like dying. That sort of thinkin's the reason the two of you are sittin' there while I'm standin' here. If a fella is too busy worryin' about other folks, then he ain't got no time to worry about himself, and if he ain't worried about himself, then he won't be ready when the shit comes. And from me to you, friend—the shit's *always* comin'."

"Grains," Chall said. Perhaps it was foolish to drag the man's attention back to him when he'd only just found a moment's respite from being beaten, but then he'd never been called Challadius the Clever and that with good reason.

"What's that?" Catham asked.

"You said your shit's always coming. Grains. They help sometimes. Bread. I try to eat some whenever I'm hungover."

"I didn't say *my* shit," Catham said. He glanced at Ned. "He really starts to wear on you, doesn't he?"

"Forget that," Ned said. "What did you do with Val?"

"Who?" Catham asked.

"You know damn well who. Lady Valencia—where is she?"

"Oooh," Catham said, smiling. "*Val*. Now that sounds a bit familiar, doesn't it? I hope there's not problems in paradise, with you and the missus. Though I have to say, she's a bit old for you, isn't she?"

"What are you—" Ned began, but he cut off as Chall began to laugh.

He couldn't help it. Maybe he was delirious—probably he was. Probably he was a fool—certainly he was. But fool or not, delirious or not, the laughter came. Quiet at first, a low chuckle, but louder with each moment until tears of laughter were streaming from his eyes, tears to match the tears of pain he'd shed earlier.

"What's so damned funny?" Catham said, clearly not liking the laughter. After all, what sort of victim went around laughing when what they ought to be doing, Chall supposed, was whining and whimpering and begging for their life? Not that he hadn't done a bit of that in the last half hour.

"Chall, are you okay?"

This from Ned. He wasn't okay. Far from it, in fact, and he suspected that, the way the night was shaping up, he would be even further from it in a little while. But for the moment, it was all he could do to manage to stifle his laughter. The pain he felt...well, pretty much everywhere helped.

"Don't you get it?" Chall asked, glancing at the carriage driver. "He doesn't know. Which means two things—she wasn't here when these bastards showed up, that's one. The second is that his boss didn't see fit to tell him." He flashed a bloody grin. "Catham the Cautious? You ask me, they ought to call you Catham the Uninformed. Or the Untrusted, maybe."

"Does have a certain ring to it," Ned said slowly.

"Seems like maybe your boss doesn't trust you," Chall said, "though I can't imagine why. Wonder what else he's not telling you."

Catham let out an angry growl at that then stepped forward, apparently deciding that Bran had had enough fun and it was his turn. Chall thought Bran was probably a harder puncher—likely from all the practice —but then a fist in the face was still a fist in the face. His head was rocked back by the force of the blow, and the coppery taste of blood filled his mouth as he bit his cheek.

"Seems like I...touched a nerve," Chall managed.

Catham stood watching him for a moment, the anger that had overcome him slowly dissipating. "Maybe so," he admitted. "But then, I think maybe Bran and I will touch a nerve or two of yours before we finish up here. Now, enough talk. I'd say it's past time we got down to business. Let's start with an easy one—you know, since we're all friends here. How did you find out the Wolves were back?"

"I thought you said enough talk," Chall observed, stretching his jaw. It didn't feel dislocated, not quite, but it definitely felt like it was considering it.

"So I did. Suppose I'll have to speak clearly with you then, won't I? Alright—let's try this. Bran, the next time the clever mage here says something clever, I want you stick a blade in his clever leg, alright?"

"Be a pleasure," Bran said.

Chall was scared, and when he was scared, when he was in pain, he tended toward flippancy. In truth, he always tended toward flippancy, so it was all he could do to keep from asking which leg was the clever one. But he did manage it—mostly because one leg, the dumb one, probably, already had a crossbow wound, and he had little interest in getting stabbed, so that he could compare the two.

"Now then, if there won't be any more interruptions—" Catham paused, glancing meaningfully at Chall who chose for one of the first times in his life to remain silent, before going on—why don't we get back to it. I'll ask again—but not a third time—how is it you lot became aware of the Wolves' return?"

"Because of a young redheaded woman named Margaret," Chall said, seeing no reason to lie.

"Margaret?"

"That's right," Chall said, resisting the almost irrepressible urge to be sarcastic. "When someone breaks into the king's quarters and kills a serving woman, people are bound to ask questions."

"That don't explain how you come to believe the Wolves were back," Catham observed, and there was something about the man's manner, about the way he was watching Chall, that told him he already knew more about what had happened at the castle than he was letting on. Clearly, he was planning on getting as much information as he could without giving away anymore than necessary. It seemed that the man had earned his nickname after all along with a few others—mostly curses—that Chall had thought of in the last half hour. But then he thought that maybe the man wasn't just trying not to give anything away. It was also, Chall thought, a sort of test, one to see how honest Chall and Ned intended to be, maybe to decide whether or not Bran needed to bring his blade to bear after all.

"She dropped her ring," Chall said. "A signet with a wolf's head. A bit different than the usual pretty sapphire or emerald a man might expect on such a woman. Different enough to make us ask some questions. But then, you already knew that."

Catham smiled without humor. "Maybe. Still, I do love a good story, even if I have heard it before. And this story isn't done, not yet."

"What else do you want to know?" Ned asked.

Catham gave the man a smile. "How about we start with everything you know. Go from there, how'd that be?"

"Well," Chall said, "some rashes are just rashes and *other* rashes mean that a man hasn't been discerning enough with—"

"Bran."

Before Chall could say or do anything, the other man snatched the knife out of his belt as if he'd been waiting for the order and, without preamble, slammed it into Chall's thigh. Chall screamed in shock and pain, jerking against the bonds holding him to the chair, but he did not possess Cutter's strength, and the ropes held.

"Now then," Catham said as Chall devolved to whimpering in pain, "if you're all joked out—"

Chall gave a sound that was somewhere between a sob and a laugh, shaking his head.

"Something funny?" Catham asked, sounding surprised. As well he might. Chall hadn't been stabbed in the leg all that much, but he had a feeling there weren't many people who laughed after.

"I'm just...thinking," he hissed. "About what Nadia is going to...do to you. When she finds out that you...betrayed her. She didn't strike me as a... forgiving...person."

"Oh, I don't think that'll be a problem," Catham said. "My new boss, see, he doesn't much care for competition, and he isn't exactly the sort of fella that likes to handle his problems with words. He prefers a more...shall we say, direct approach. An approach that he is taking even while we sit here having our nice little chat. No, I don't expect Nadia and I will have much of a relationship after tonight. Ain't easy having a relationship with a corpse, after all."

"Wow. You really are a bastard, aren't you?" Ned asked. "The type of fella that'd betray his own mother if it served him."

Catham shrugged, clearly unbothered. "Bitch best not give me a reason. Now, enough of all that. It's past time we got down to business. I want to know everything the two of you know about the Wolves. And I want to know it now, along with who *else* knows it."

"I always wanted to fly," Ned said, "yet the gods didn't see fit to give me wings. Seems that, sometimes, life is bound to disappoint."

"Maybe that'd be true, if it was the gods standing in my way. It ain't, though. Just a fat mage and an Empath who might have chosen anything, might have *been* anything and yet chose to be a carriage driver. Maybe I couldn't convince the gods to give me wings but I'm fairly certain Bran and I can convince the two of you to tell us what we want to know. Isn't that right, Bran?"

Bran grunted obligingly, shooting Chall a grin of the sort that said that the man enjoyed his work far too much. "You know what I don't under-stand?" Chall asked in a shuddering, whimpering voice. He was finding it difficult to concentrate—he supposed being stabbed in one leg and shot in the other would do that to a man.

Catham turned to him. "Ah, the mage found his voice. Lucky us. Go on then. Regale us with your insight. Only, hurry it up, won't you? Bran does get impatient when he's interrupted at his work."

Chall did his best to push down the fear he felt. He was going to die. That much seemed obvious enough. He doubted very much if he would leave this room again. At least, not alive. Given that he was minutes—certainly no more than an hour—away from death, perhaps his curiosity about the matter that had occurred to him was a sort of desperate attempt at distracting himself. They said, after all, that curiosity killed the cat, but then if the cat was already doomed, why not be satisfied? "It's the woman," he said. "Margaret."

Catham tried to hide his expression, but he didn't quite manage it. A slight look of disgust came over him at the mention of the woman's name, and Chall was possessed of the thought that the two didn't get along. Likely both vying for favor and position, then, and he, at least, seeing her as his competition. "What about her?"

"It's just...why send her to the castle at all? She's the reason...we even know about the Crimson Wolves coming back. Had she not come to the king's quarters, had she not murdered a serving woman...we might have... gone weeks...months without knowing. So...why send her?"

"Oh, I wouldn't worry about that none, fella. The why of it don't matter, at least not to you. I'm afraid I must insist that it's going to be me asks the questions for the next little while, how'd that be? Me and Bran, of course. After that...well. Maybe you won't be so worried about all that other stuff."

It was the man's casualness that pissed Chall off. How easily he talked about his obvious intention to murder Chall and Ned. It wasn't just that it was cold-hearted—though it was. It was also that the man saw no danger at all in telling them exactly what he was going to do to them. He doubted if any man would have treated the Crimson Prince so. Even if he were bound, they would have been wary of him, for even a sheathed blade could cut, if it but slipped loose of its confines. Chall was no Prince Bernard, he knew that. But he still found himself frustrated at how little the men before him feared him. Just as he was frustrated at how much he feared them.

Chall decided something, then. He couldn't decide whether he lived or died, now. What could be done had been. What he could decide, however, was the manner in which he met that death. And he decided that he would do so standing. Figuratively, of course. He was bound to a chair and he'd been shot in one leg and stabbed in the other. For the next little while he was going to have to do all his standing from the sitting position.

"Well, I hope you two bastards got some rest," Chall said. "Because I don't feel much like answering questions. Might be I'll take some convincing."

"Chall..." Ned said, "I don't think—"

"What are they going to do, Ned?" he asked. "Kill us twice?"

"No, don't be ridiculous," Catham said, giving a soft laugh as he and Bran shared a look. "And you're right. You're dead either way. Still, if you prove difficult for us, it might be that when you get to the afterlife, you'll find that you're missin' a few fingers or toes."

"That's alright," Chall said. "I've got spares."

Catham grunted, a look of surprise and what might have been respect on his face. "Well, now. The mage has balls after all."

That felt good to hear. Ridiculous, maybe, given the situation, but that didn't change the fact that it did. At least, that was, until Catham spoke further. "Big balls," he said, glancing at Bran. "Maybe we'll start there." He looked back to Chall. "As for the rest, I appreciate your concern for us getting all tuckered out, but I wouldn't worry yourself overly much. After all, I got three boys out there that'd be more than happy to step in, should we need a breather."

"Now then, Bran. Let's see if the mage's balls are as big as I'm thinkin', how'd that be?"

The other man didn't answer, at least not with words. Instead, he drew a second knife from his tunic—the first still buried in Chall's leg—and grabbed a chair from the small table at the side of the room, dragging it in front of Chall. As he watched the man, the realization of what he intended to do to him thundering in his mind, Chall searched desperately for the courage he'd felt no more than a minute ago. He asked himself what Bernard would do in such a situation. His mind, though, would supply no answer mostly because he didn't think the prince would ever find himself in such a situation as the one Chall was now in. No, Chall was confident that whenever the prince's death finally found him, it would not be at the hands of some criminal. In fact, he had thought the prince had met that end countless times—and he with him—during the war. Yet the prince had always found a way out, a way to achieve victory even when facing the most overwhelming odds or even when in the direst situations.

Situations like a man with a sharp knife intending to use it on the last place any man would pick. But Bernard was not here now, there was no rescue coming, and so all Chall could do was to meet his end with as much dignity and courage as he could. The problem, of course, was that he'd left all his dignity and courage in his other pants.

"You put that knife down, or I'm going to kill you with it," Chall told Bran who had just sat in the chair in front of him.

The man only smiled, clearly as confident that it was an idle threat as Chall was himself. Bran slid his chair closer and was just reaching for Chall when there was a knock on the door.

"Damnit," Catham said, sounding annoyed as he glanced at Bran. "It's like the bastards wait for the perfect time." He turned to the door. "*Not now.*" A second knock came, and Catham let out an angry hiss. He rose from where he'd propped himself against the table and moved to the door.

Chall had the ridiculous thought, as the man moved to open the door, that it was the prince, come to save them, as if his thoughts had conjured him. A ridiculous, desperate thought. After all, the prince was halfway across the world, fighting for his life against untold legions of Fey. If, that was, he was alive at all, a thought that sent a fresh wave of terror through Chall. Bernard might not have been the best house guest or dinner companion, and he might have been almost as scary—and in some ways scarier—than the many threats he'd conquered, but who better to stand against the monsters threatening the world and everything Chall cared about than a man known as the Crimson Prince, a man with fangs of his own?

At any rate, when the door swung open it was not to reveal a pissed-off Prince Bernard—which was pretty much the only way the man came. Instead, it was one of the men Chall recognized as Catham's, and whatever grand notion of rescue he'd entertained vanished as convincingly as the flame of a snuffed-out candle.

"This had better be good," Catham said.

The newcomer winced, glancing between Chall and Ned then back to Catham. "It's the boss, sir. He sent a fella to fetch you—says he needs you."

"Did you tell this 'fella' that I'm busy?"

"He said this is more important. Said the boss asked for you specifically."

Catham gave a small, humorless grin. "Bet that red-headed bitch hated that," he said, confirming Chall's suspicions that there was discord between the two criminals. *Who would have thought it?*

"Can't say I know, sir. Anyway, he says you know folks, says he has need of your contacts to find..." The man hesitated, glancing at Chall and Ned. "Something he's looking for."

Something about the way the man said it made Chall think that it wasn't a some*thing* the man was talking about as much as it was a some*one,* and by the man's manner he thought that, whoever that someone was, they wouldn't be too happy when they were found.

Catham grunted. "Been lookin' to show him I'm of more use to him than that whore. This might be just the thing." He glanced at Bran. "You got this?"

"It's what I do, sir," the other man said.

"Damn but you terrify me, Bran," Catham said. "I ever tell you that?"

"Yes, sir."

Catham hesitated for a moment, glancing at Ned and Chall. "Alright, well, figure out everything they know, but try not to leave too big a mess. We don't want to risk leaving anything that points to us." He scratched his chin for a moment, thinking. "Better yet, when you're done just burn the place down." He shrugged. "A lot easier to explain a fire than two corpses who've clearly been tortured." He winked at Chall. "Got to go—duty calls and all that. Hey, but you two have a good one, alright? It's been a pleasure, but I doubt if we'll see each other again."

"You'd better hope we don't," Ned said. "I'm the sort that holds a grudge."

"Bad for your digestion, I hear," Catham said. "Anyway, we'll see if Bran can't relieve you of that burden. Bye now."

And with that, the man turned back to the newcomer. "Stay here with Bran, just in case either of these two gets a little...difficult."

"Yes, sir."

Catham shot them one more departing smile then walked through the door. The newcomer stepped through, closing it behind him and propping up with his back against it, folding his arms over his chest.

"Cautious alright," Chall said. "And clever too. The bastard."

"I can think of at least one other 'C' word that fits him well enough, if you've a mind to hear it," Ned said in a low, rumbling growl.

"Maybe later," Chall said, glancing at Bran. "Listen, man, you don't want to do this."

"Of course I want to do it."

Chall blinked. Damn. Well now that sort of cut off that conversational foray quicker than he'd expected. "Look, whatever coin they're paying you, I'm friends with the king. I'm sure we can double it."

The man only looked bored as he moved his chair closer, his knife hovering over Chall's trousers. Chall's breath was coming in shallow gasps then. "Wait, just wait, alright? If it isn't coin that does it for you, how about position? As I said, I'm friends with the king. How would you like to have your own manor?"

"Never did have much manners," Bran said, frowning. "My ma always told me so."

Chall stared, trying to decide if the man were putting him on or not. In the end, judging by the blank, humorless expression on the man's face, he leaned toward not. "No, what? No, what I mean is, how would you like to be a lord? A count, maybe? Or a duke. Lord Bran—how does that sound?"

"Sounds like a lot of work. What do I know about bein' a duke or a count?"

Chall frowned. "I mean, you could learn, couldn't you? It isn't as if—"

"Enough talk," Bran said. "The boss says to figure out everythin' you know, and I mean to."

He raised the knife over part of Chall that he had spent most of his life thinking about. Had thought about little else in truth—like most men, he supposed, only worse. That...preoccupation had certainly gotten him into some bad situations in the past and, if he were honest, the present, too. And while he liked to consider himself far grown from the man he'd once been, far removed from that cad, he was not so removed that the sight of that blade, glistening like sharpened misery, hovering over his crotch didn't send a shiver of fear through him. Fear that was enough, in fact, for him to lunge forward, his forehead leading as it struck Bran in the face.

Or, more specifically, the nose. The other man let out a strangled sound somewhere between a cry and a growl as his nose broke under the blow. His head rocked back, and he—and the chair he'd so recently dragged in front of Chall—toppled over, sprawling on the floor.

For an instant, Chall sat frozen, his forehead throbbing painfully, one of his eyes closed from the man's blood that had spattered on him when he'd hit. The headbutt had been a desperate measure—not really any thought given to it beyond protecting the part of him that made a man a man. Now, though, he had the faint glimmer of hope that they might escape and that, furthermore, *he* might be the reason for that escape.

Then, in another instant, the frozen moment thawed, and everything seemed to happen at once. Bran, from his place sprawled on the floor, let out several curses—largely impossible to understand due to the broken nose. Ned rose, still bound to the heavy wooden chair, and moved forward in an awkward hunched sort of half-walk, half-run toward the prone man, while the other man, the one who moments ago had been propped against the door, also moved forward.

Ned was faster off the mark—give him credit for that, at least. But then, with a heavy oak chair attached to him, his arms bound behind his back, it wasn't exactly a fair race. Ned rushed toward the prone Bran and managed to get one good kick in before the other man moved forward, drawing a knife. He stepped behind Chall, grabbing a fistful of his hair and jerking his head back, bringing the knife to his throat. "Not another damn move, or your friend here is goin' to be spewin' a lot more than secrets."

Ned looked back at them then froze. It would have been comical, had Chall not had a very sharp knife poised at his throat. The carriage driver stood bent over, the chair still attached, his arms tied behind his back, one leg raised from where he'd been preparing to fetch Bran another kick. He continued to stand there as the ill-used Bran groaned and climbed his way to his feet.

"Good," the man with the knife said. "Now, waddle your ass back over here and have a seat."

Ned hesitated, clearly assessing their situation and, like Chall, clearly finding that it wasn't particularly good. He shuffled back to where he'd been, easing his chair down onto the ground once more, and Chall saw that his wrists were bleeding where they'd strained against the rope.

"Now then," the man with the knife said, "one more outburst like that and—"

"Shon of a bish, I'll kill you," another voice said, and Chall turned back to see that Bran had made his way to his feet and was even now moving toward him with deadly promise in his eyes.

"Makes a man wonder, doesn't it?" Ned asked.

His tone was so casual, so conversational and at odds with the situation that everyone—even the pissed-off, bloody Bran who would certainly *not* be Lord Bran if Chall had anything to say about it—turned to regard him.

"I just mean, well, you know," Ned said, "it makes me wonder how Catham will feel about you killing us without figuring out what it was he wanted you to."

"You kicked me," Bran said. *"You shon of a bish."*

"Yes," Ned agreed, nodding. "And you tortured us and plan to kill us— I'd say that we're both shons of bishes. But that doesn't change the fact that your boss will likely be displeased if he finds out you've killed us before finding out what he wants to know."

Bran hesitated, his anger clearly at war with his common sense—not that Chall suspected the man had that much of the latter. He'd gotten a fairly good sense of Bran over the last half hour to an hour they'd spent in each other's company—far more than he would have liked, truth be told— and he didn't think the man was in danger of going into the priesthood or, as far as it went, scholarship.

Ned's argument made sense. It was logical. Well thought out. But then, Chall supposed a man didn't choose the life of a criminal because he was operating with an overabundance of forethought. Certainly Bran didn't, for the man hocked and spat, raising the blade. "He can question your corpsh, if he hash a mind to." And with that, he started toward Chall.

Chall was busy leaning back, trying to shrink in his chair, fighting for a life that was pretty much already lost, as all the living did, when there was a knock on the door and he, along with everyone else, paused to turn and regard it.

Bran let out a snarl. *"What is it?"* he shouted.

A man's muffled voice responded from the other side of the door, but in words that were unintelligible.

"What?" Bran said.

Another return call, another unintelligible garble of sound.

Bran let out a hiss. *"Watch them,"* he growled at the other man, then he started toward the door, swinging it open and clearly meaning to give whoever stood on the other side a piece of his mind. But then the person who stood on the other side had something to give him as well. Not a scolding, this, but a knife, one that lashed out, almost too quick to follow, darting into Bran's throat once, then pulling back only to dart in again.

Chall stared in shock at the unexpected attack. Bran, equally shocked and considerably more full of holes, stumbled backward, his blade falling from his fingers as both hands went to his throat, all thoughts of his anger gone in an instant.

Bran collapsed to the ground on his back, dead or well on his way, and the newcomer stepped over him, moving into the room. Chall felt another wave of shock as he realized that it was Emille, Ned's wife. If the woman felt anything at what she'd just done she didn't show it. Instead, she strode into the room as if it were just any other day. The man standing behind Chall let out a shout and charged her.

Emille waited for him to come, waited for him to lunge forward, his own knife leading. Then she stepped almost casually to the side and placed the knife in the man's chest. That's what it looked like—a placing. The same way that another might place a cup of tea on a table. A simple task that demanded little attention or effort, one that she might have done a thousand times.

But as simple as it seemed for Emille, as easy, the man himself took it considerably worse, going so far as to die. Emille pulled the blade free, and the man fell to the ground like a puppet with its strings cut. That done, Ned's wife knelt, and with two quick swipes wiped her blade clean on the dead man's shirt—he voiced no complaints—before she tucked the knife inside her tunic.

"I swear, I leave you alone for just a few minutes and look at the trouble you get up to," she said, her eyes on Ned.

Ned glanced at Chall and the two of them shared a look before turning back to regard her. The carriage driver cleared his throat. "Right, well...it's good to see you, Em. Sorry about the mess...truth to tell, we didn't expect you home so early."

"Neither did I. We got everything sorted back at the guild—at least as sorted as it can be—and Maeve thought I should come home, that you and I had some issues that needed addressing." She glanced around at the two dead men. "I can't imagine what she'll say when I tell her just how right she was. Still, I thought I might have to kill someone tonight—I just expected the person to be a bit more...bosomy."

"Wait, Em..." Ned said, looking as hurt as the two dead men lying on the floor. Well, nearly so anyway. "Are you saying, what, that you thought I was stepping out on you?"

"You've been...different, over the last few weeks. *We've* been different. I thought...maybe...I don't know, that I wasn't making you happy anymore. I thought...that maybe you wanted to be rid of me."

"Well, now that's a damned fool thing to say," Ned said, sounding angry and hurt all at once. Sounding afraid, too, Chall noted, more afraid than he had when they'd been facing certain torture and an equally certain death. "You're part of me. Shit, I'm not me without you. I'd sooner lose a leg—a fella can still walk with one leg."

"I wouldn't really call it walking..." Chall said, blinking in an effort to rid his vision of the blurriness which was increasing at a rather alarming rate.

"Fine, hopping, whatever," Ned said. "My point is, I could still get around, still go places. Without you, Em," he went on, meeting her gaze, his voice soft, "I wouldn't have nowhere to get around to, wouldn't want no place to go. Wouldn't be no point, not to any of it. Better I was a corpse than that."

"Now *that's* a damned fool thing to say," she said, but even Chall's increasingly blurry vision wasn't enough for him to miss smile that came, almost unwillingly, to her face. She started toward her husband, but he nodded to Chall. At least Chall was pretty sure he did. He'd lost a fair amount of blood and was losing a fair bit more, and it was growing increasingly difficult to...well, do anything, really, including see. The husband and wife, the room itself, in fact, had devolved into several misshapen, largely featureless blobs.

"Him first," Ned said. "He's been stabbed."

"Shot too," Chall explained in a muffled, slurred voice as the blob he took to be Emille moved toward him. "Ned barely got punched."

"Hey, I got punched," Ned said.

"Cried...like a baby," Chall lied.

Emille didn't answer—at least, not with words. Instead, the only sound she made was a hiss when she paused to look at his wounds, a hiss that Chall didn't take as a good sign. "How bad is it?" he asked.

"It's alright," Emille said. "You're going to be alright."

There was something in her voice he didn't care for, a sort of desperate urgency. "Just as long as you don't tell me to walk it off," he said. She didn't laugh. Instead, she moved to a nearby drawer and retrieved what appeared to be bandages, as well as a bottle of some opaque liquid and a needle that looked about the same size as the knife that had done the stabbing. "I don't like needles," he mumbled.

"No?" she asked as she moved back to him, pulling up the chair that Bran had so recently used before he'd caught a case of dead. "How about dying? Like that much?"

"Never tried it," he said.

She gave no clever rejoinder to that which he figured meant one of two things. Either she couldn't think of one and he had effectively won the back and forth, or she was too focused on keeping him on this side of the grave. And considering the fact that in his entire life he couldn't ever remember actually winning an argument with a woman, he thought he knew which it was and that better than he'd like.

With that in mind, Chall decided it was probably past time he changed the subject. "The men outside—"

"Won't be bothering us," Emille said. "Now be quiet and let me concentrate."

Ridiculous, of course. He figured telling him to be quiet—particularly when he was nervous—was quite a bit like telling water to dry itself up. She lifted the needle then. The rest of the world might have been blurry, but that he saw with painful clarity. Chall's mind cast itself about desperately to find something—anything—to distract him. And in its flailing, his mind settled on Lady Valencia and the fact that she was, at least so far as he'd seen, nowhere to *be* seen. "Did you see an old woman? I seem to have misplaced—"

"You wouldn't happen to be talking about a certain old *noble*woman, would you?" Emille asked. "One who is known for her vast fortune throughout all of New Daltenia and who has recently taken refuge at my and my husband's house, a certain Lady Valencia by name?"

Chall blinked, glancing at Ned who only stared at him, blob-like, before he turned back to the carriage driver's wife. "I...that is...I don't..."

"Relax, Chall," she said as she continued her work. "Ned told me everything—I'm aware of Lady Valencia, just as I am aware of everything else you and he—and Priest—have been up to in the past few days." She shook her head. "Leave you boys alone for just a little while, and there's no telling the amount of trouble you'll end up in."

Chall grunted, glancing back at Ned. "You said you didn't tell her."

"No," the carriage driver said. "I said I only told her what I needed to."

"And she needed to know everything?"

"She's my wife," the man said, as if that explained it.

"And if she decided to, to—" Chall hesitated, suddenly unable to finish, particularly since the woman he was talking about was busy trying to save his life.

"To what?" Emille asked. "Kill Lady Valencia since she was a member of the Crimson Wolves?"

Chall blinked. "That...well. Something like that."

"It may surprise you to learn this, Challadius," she said, "but we assassins, while we don't necessarily shy away from killing, are a bit more discerning than that in those we choose to murder." She shot what might have been an apologetic look at her husband. "I have no problem with Lady Valencia—if my Ned says she is a good person, then I believe him. You know, because of a little thing called trust. Maybe you've heard of it."

"Still," Chall said, frowning. "You didn't have to tell her everything. Haven't you heard the story? Three people can keep a secret as long as—"

"Two of them are dead," Emille finished. "Yes, I've heard it. And if it helps you're not so far away. Anyway, you should be glad Ned told me. If he hadn't, and if I hadn't been unable to get the idea of him and some wealthy, famous noblewoman in our home together out of my mind, I might not have come so soon. I might well have waited, come later."

"I would have been busy later," Chall said, thinking of how close they'd been to being murdered when the woman had shown up.

"I suspect that's true," she agreed.

"So you were worried that he was fooling around—what happened to all that talk of trust?"

"I trust my husband completely," Emille said, "but I'm not perfect. Now, how about you stop worrying about saving my marriage, so I can worry about saving your life?"

Chall didn't respond—mostly because he couldn't. It felt, in that moment, as if to do so required far more energy than he was capable of mustering. Instead, he took a slow, shaky breath as she did her work, and he closed his eyes, not knowing, in that moment, whether he would ever open them again.

CHAPTER FIVE

The Grand Church of Raveza's Infinite Grace and Love was considerably less impressive than its grandiose name might suggest. In truth, while pains had been taken to hide its original purpose, Valden was fairly certain it had begun its life as a warehouse for storing something. Dried and salted fish, unless he missed his guess—he'd served on a ship a long time ago as a sailor, though admittedly not for long, but it was the sort of a smell a man never forgot.

It was subtle—or, at least, as subtle as the scent of fish *could* be—but it was there nevertheless. An undercurrent of rot filling the air, tickling his nose. Valden hesitated, staring at the church, asking himself—for at least the hundredth time since leaving Florence's—if there was another way, *any* other way.

But now, like those other times, he could think of none. He was in the crime-riddled poor district of New Daltenia, and so, despite the fact that he stood before a church, in a world of sinners, only a fool might expect to treat with saints. He traveled the sewers, after all, and none knew the sewers better than the rats.

He took a slow, deep breath, steadying himself, then he walked across the street toward the church. Inside was a large room, what once would

39

have served as the warehouse's main room but what had been appropriated to fit a dozen pews, each of which looked close to falling apart. At the opposite end from which Valden stood there was a simple wooden platform upon which sat an altar where the priests of Raveza might stand and preach to visiting parishioners, regaling them with stories of Raveza's goodness, offering them comforting platitudes.

Valden knew this, for he had been one of those priests, and that not so long ago. But now he did not come as a priest, did not come as a saint but as a sinner. Just how much of a sinner remained to be seen, for he was going to find Nadia. One way or the other.

Thankfully, no priest was lecturing just then. He let his gaze travel slowly around the pews. People sat sporadically placed, about a dozen in all. Some were bent in prayer, the hopeless come in search of hope, while others were attended by men in robes that marked them as priests.

In the dim orange glow of the sconces lining the walls, Valden did not see the man he had come to find among those littering the pews, so he moved further into the church, walking slowly down the center aisle. He studied the seated men and women as he walked past, growing increasingly concerned as he still didn't see the man he'd come to speak with. He had counted on the man being here, had counted on him being able to help him find Nadia. But then the man he sought had let down countless people during the time while Valden had known him, and his would just be another name to add to the ever-increasing list.

"Good evening, friend."

Valden tensed as he spun to look to his side. He'd been so focused on examining the people in the pews, so distracted by his own worry, that he hadn't heard the newcomer approach. He scolded himself inwardly for that—men had died for less. Not every death that came upon every man was avoidable, but there was plenty that were, and no man he'd ever known had saved himself by being careless.

Still, the gray-haired man who stood before him did not look in any danger of attacking him just then. In fact, it seemed to be taking no small amount of effort for him to even stand and after another moment Valden saw why. One of the man's legs was gone beneath the knee, and he stood and walked with the help of two wooden crutches fit snugly under either arm.

The man, whose robes marked him as a priest, gave him a welcoming smile past his white beard. "Is there anything I can help you with?"

"Thank you but no, I don't need any help," Valden said.

The man, who Valden would have put in his sixties, perhaps even seventies, smiled again at that. "I hope you won't take offense if I say that if there's anything the years have taught me it's that, more often than not, it's the folks who say they don't need help that need it the most."

Valden found himself returning the smile with a small one of his own. There were some people in the world that a person just liked immediately, and he found that the man was one of those. Not the first he'd met, and one of them, once upon a time, had stuck a knife in him when his back had been turned, so while his initial impression of the man was a good one, he reminded himself not to turn his back on him anytime soon. "That may be true," he said. "Say then, that you would not be able to give me the help I require."

"Oh, I don't know," the man said. "Why don't you give me a chance? It might be I'll surprise you. So long as you don't need a partner in a race, that is," he said, waggling the capped nub of his knee for emphasis.

"I've heard people say that life is nothing more than a big race," Valden observed.

"For some," the old man agreed. "Certainly it was true for me, once upon a time, until the gods decided that I needed to slow down a bit."

Valden glanced at the man's leg and despite the fact that he had come here for a purpose, he found himself responding to the man's words with bitterness, his own soured faith coming to the fore. "If they wanted you to slow down, maybe they should have just asked instead of taking your leg."

"Maybe they did," the old priest said, smiling. "They might have yelled it, for all I know—I was never a very good listener, in my two-legged days. Anyway, in my experience the gods rarely do things halfway. Wouldn't you agree?"

Valden considered that for a moment, finally giving a small shrug. "Maybe."

The man smiled. "A man who is careful with his words, I see. They say that wise men rarely speak."

"And that fools never stop," Valden said, finishing the saying.

"Are you, then?" the old man asked.

"Am I what?"

"Are you a wise man?"

Valden considered his life as he decided what answer to give the man. It did not take long. "Closer to the fool, I'm afraid."

"But wise enough to know it," the priest said, grinning. "If only more of us possessed such wisdom. I am sure the gods are pleased to hear it."

"If they exist at all." He hadn't meant to speak the words aloud—hadn't intended to think them, in truth. But the priest did not appear offended. Instead, he only nodded slowly.

"Ah, I see," he said, nodding slowly. "A doubter."

"A realist," Valden countered.

The old man smiled. "I knew a man, once, who said that a little bit of learning took a man away from the gods and that a lot of it brought him back. Still..." He paused, watching Valden. "Perhaps I am mistaken, but I do not think that doubting the gods' existence is your problem."

"Who says I have a problem?"

"The only ones without problems are the dead," the old man said. "Anyway, in my experience, people who come here, to this place, tend to do so because they have problems that need solving. I speak with those who come here, as many as I can, and I have yet to speak to the one who came here to share how perfect his or her life was. Anyway, I think you wise enough to know that there is no thing in the world that has been created without a creator. How much less likely, then, the world itself."

"Fine," Valden said. "Maybe the gods do exist, but if they do—and I mean no offense—they are not benevolent overseers who seek our good. More like cruel children hurling rocks at a starving mongrel in the street."

The old man blinked. "Well, now, that paints a picture, doesn't it? Still, I think you lied, then."

"Lied? How?"

"I believe you did mean offense," the priest said, smiling as if to soften the impact of his words. "Not to me, perhaps, but to..." He paused, letting his gaze travel up to the ceiling. "Someone."

"And what of you?" Valden asked. "How can you be so confident that they mean well, when they let your leg be taken from you?"

The priest glanced down at his leg. "Yes, so they did. But then they saw fit to give me a spare," he finished, lifting one of his crutches and tapping it on his good leg.

"Most men prefer two."

The priest shrugged. "I was never much of a dancer, anyway. Or a runner, come to that...I've always had a particularly fine talent for sitting, though."

Valden grunted. "How can you be so happy, so content?"

The old man shrugged. "A man has to be something, doesn't he? Knowing that, it seems only a fool would choose to be unhappy when happiness is there for the asking."

"I don't know if I'd say we choose it."

"No?" the priest asked. "Then who does? The gods?"

"Maybe."

"Well, now, if that's the case, we're not really alive at all, are we? After all, I'd say it's our ability to choose—even if those choices, more often than not, are bad ones—that makes us alive."

"I know some healers who would say it is the breath in our lungs."

"Sure, or the blue in my pretty eyes, or the nails on my feet. Say you had a bit of magic. And say, with that magic, you could make a doll that looked just like a regular person. And say you could put a mechanism in that doll that could make it breathe, just like we do, talk and walk just like we do. What, then, would keep that doll from being a person? Or, put another way, am I less *me* because I lost my leg?"

Valden frowned. He'd heard similar arguments before, of course, had given similar arguments, but he'd never heard them put so succinctly, so clearly. The way the man spoke, it seemed obvious. "I understand what you're saying," he went on, "but you can't tell me that your life hasn't been more difficult with a missing leg."

"No, I can't," the priest said. "That'd be a lie, and I save my lies for my wife."

Valden raised an eyebrow at that. Admittedly, he hadn't been in a church in New Daltenia in some time, but he was still confident that their stance on abstinence—namely, that they were very, very for it—had not changed in his absence.

The old man grinned, shrugging. "Or would...if I had one. Sure, my life's been harder, but what of it? Hardship, difficulties—that's where living is done. You ask me, that's what living *is*. A man without a purpose is a sad thing, and difficulty breeds purpose. What else are any of us to do? Lie around all day? Don't the dead do the same?"

"I hope so," Valden said. "I'd be concerned if they got up and started walking around."

"Oh, I'd say there's plenty of dead men walking around," the old priest said. "They just don't know it." He wasn't smiling now. Instead, he looked sad, regretful.

"What would you suggest, then? To the dead man?"

"Oh, I'm sure that's beyond me," the old man said. "But I suppose if I were to say anything, it would be that some of the world's hardest paths lead to its prettiest places, and the only person to be pitied is the one without purpose."

Valden considered that, thinking of how to respond. He was still thinking when a door at the back of the church behind the altar opened. A woman walked out. She was young and pretty, perhaps in her early twenties with bright blond hair visible even beneath the nun's habit she wore. The woman's expression was tightly controlled, but Valden noted that her cheeks were slightly flushed, and there was a tightness to her jaw that spoke to her holding back some emotion.

Another person appeared out of the doorway behind her, a man in a priest's robes, though his were far finer than those of the old man standing in front of Valden. The ribbon draped over his shoulders and the elaborate cap perched on his head like some colorful bird marked him as the head priest. Here, then, was the man Valden had come to speak to. The man did not note him, however, did not seem to note anything at all save the

44

woman as his eyes were locked on her backside as she walked away from the door in the direction where Valden and the old priest stood.

The young woman walked up in front of the priest standing beside Valden, nodding pleasantly before curtseying before the older man. "Brother Elmer."

"Sister Olivia," the old man said, bowing his head. His gaze traveled to the head priest who was collecting one of the baskets hanging from the side of a pew where parishioners might leave donations for the church. The old priest glanced back at her. "And how are you this fine evening?"

"I'm fine, Brother Elmer, thank you for asking," she said, bowing her head.

"No problems then, Sister?" he asked. "Nothing I might help with?" He sounded to Valden, in that moment, like a father looking out for his daughter's welfare or perhaps an uncle looking after his favorite niece.

The woman's eyes shot in the direction of the head priest, then back to the old man. "Nothing I can't handle, Brother Elmer, but I thank you for your concern. Now, I'm for town—apparently we are running low on supplies. The communal wine in particular."

The old man let out a soft grunt, nodding. "I see. I will...look into the absence. Be safe in the way, Sister. The path to peace—"

"Is traveled one step at a time," she finished, flashing him a smile before curtseying again and moving past.

"Sister Olivia has been with us for a little over a month," the old man— apparently by the name of Elmer—explained as she walked away. "She has had a...difficult life, but her light is no less dim for that."

"A difficult life?"

"Suffice to say that there are those who have been taken by her and who were not satisfied by polite refusal."

Valden frowned at that, turning to regard the head priest in the distance as the man emptied out another of the donation baskets. No doubt, if asked, he would say that he was using the donations for the good of the church, but knowing him as Valden did, it would be a lie—though one, it had to be said, that would be difficult to prove. "The head priest, he meets with the priests and nuns individually?"

"Some of them," the old man said, meeting his gaze.

"I see...I know many churches in which they hold elections for the position."

"Yes," the priest said, "and others—like this one—where the head priest comes with the building."

"As in they bought the place and started the church, no doubt for noble reasons."

"No doubt," the priest agreed, giving him a small smile. "Still, while it might not be ideal, some things—like excrement, for example—are necessary and never mind that they are unpleasant."

Valden nodded. He understood that well enough, for he had only come here in the first place because he'd thought it necessary. The gods—if they existed at all—knew that he would have preferred being nearly anywhere else, likely even the Black Wood with Prince Bernard. "It's been a pleasure talking to you, Priest."

The old man smiled. "You too, stranger." He glanced in the direction of the head priest, following Valden's gaze. "Found what you were looking for, then?"

"Unfortunately," Valden said. He gave a quick bow then started in the direction of the head priest who was still emptying out the donation baskets.

The head priest was too busy looking at the coins—counting them, a very unpriestly twinkle of greed in his eyes—to notice Valden's approach.

"Funny," Valden said dryly. "You were rifling through coins that didn't belong to you the last time I saw you."

The short, fat conman glanced up distractedly from his task. "Ah yes, welcome, friend, to our church. I hope—" He cut off as his gaze reached Valden's face, his breath catching in a satisfying gasp. "V-Vicious?" he asked in a trembling voice that sounded nothing like the pompous tone he'd started with. "Is...is that you?"

"Surprised to see me, Willy?"

"I-I that is, I thought you, that is—"

"You thought I was dead, is that what you're trying to say, Willy? Valden asked. "And why would you think that, I wonder? It wouldn't have anything to do with the fact that the last time I saw you, you were standing behind two Bloody Talons, breaking into my room in the middle of the night and looking for blood?"

"*They* were looking for blood, not me," Willy said, shifting uncomfortably. "I stayed in the hallway, as you'll recall—I was just an innocent bystander."

"Who was busy counting his coins while they tried to murder me. Whatever else you are," Valden said, "you are not innocent, Willy. I think we both know that. And yes, I remember distinctly that you stayed in the hall—it is the only reason you're still alive."

The man swallowed hard. "And here I thought it was from all my good works," he said, giving a nervous titter and growing silent an instant later as Valden only stared at him. "Anyway," he went on, clearing his throat, "what uh...that is, what brings you here? Come to confess your sins? I was about to go grab a bite to eat. I don't normally take meetings myself—too busy, I'm afraid—but since we're old friends, I'd of course be happy to make an exception for you."

"Is that what we are, Willy?" Valden asked. "Old friends? And as for exceptions, I guess I wouldn't be the only one you'd be making one for today—there was the woman, too, wasn't there? The one that just left. Let me guess, the two of you old friends, too?"

"New friends, I hope," the man said, licking his lips, an expression of lust flashing across his face and making Valden want to strike him, church or not. "Though, I guess it's fair to say," the conman said, frowning after the direction the woman had gone, "that she's proving particularly...resistant to my advances."

"Only the gods know how she can resist your charm," Valden said dryly.

The conman nodded, sniffling and running an arm across his running nose, wiping snot away and causing Valden to frown in disgust. "Damned allergies," Willy said. "They've plagued me since I was a child."

"Well, I suppose we all have our challenges," Valden said. "Anyway, if the woman has any sense at all, she'll tell you to piss off."

"Pretty close," he mumbled, frowning. "Damned woman's as cold as frozen ice."

"That's the only kind of ice."

Willy grunted. "You wouldn't know it, Vicious, but it's damned hard work being a priest...wait. Come to think of it, I guess you would know it. Funny, isn't it, considering that we both come from the same place, and we both ended up priests."

"You are no priest, Willy," Valden said. Then frowned. "And neither am I."

The conman raised an eyebrow at that. "Seems like there's a story there. Care to regale an old friend?"

"Less than I'd care to stab him."

Willy sighed, shaking his head. "Between you and that ice queen, Sister Olivia, I'm not really feeling the love. I'm starved for affection is what I am."

Valden took a minute, letting his gaze travel up and down the man's ample gut where it pressed tightly against his robes. "If you ask me, you don't look starved for anything."

The fat man winced, looking down at his belly. "Sure, okay, might be I put on a couple of pounds since I saw you last."

"A couple hundred, maybe."

Willy frowned. "Didn't remember you being so funny. I guess the years have changed both of us."

"Not from where I'm standing," Valden said. "There's more of you, sure—a regrettable circumstance for anyone walking the face of the world, that—but from what I've seen you're still the same old Willy. Pulling one con or another, anything to avoid an honest day's work."

"Well, not *any*thing," Willy said. Valden said nothing, only watching him, and the fat man sighed. "Okay, fine, anything. Still, Valden, I tell you I'm not the same person I was back when you knew me. I think maybe all this playing at being a priest, a holy man, has rubbed off. That what it done to you?"

"I wasn't playing at being a priest," Valden said, again possessed of the almost irresistible urge to give the man a black eye, see how it would go with those robes of his.

"Ah, right, of course," the fat man said hurriedly, apparently picking up on how much his words had angered Valden. No surprise, really. Whatever else he was—disgusting, sickening, rage-inducing—Willy was clever. A truth Valden hated to admit but a truth just the same. After all, foolish conmen didn't tend to live very long. "Just didn't take, is all?" Willy asked.

Valden considered his time as a priest. Those had been the best years of his life, years when he'd thought he had a purpose, one beyond his own selfish gain. Yet as fine as that time had been, as cherished as his memories of it were, the truth was that they did not feel like *his* memories. It felt as if they belonged to someone else. Or, perhaps, as if those things which he had done during that time, the life he'd lived, had been nothing but a dream. A dream he would have gone on dreaming until the grave took him, if he'd been able, but then all dreams ended, sooner or later. It was the nightmares that lingered. "Something like that," he said, frowning. "But I didn't come here to talk about the past. I need your help."

The fear that had marred the fat man's face slowly changed—as Valden had suspected it might—giving way to a subtle mixture of greed and cunning. After all, to tell a man like Willy—who, out of all the world's oily, no-good conmen, was likely its oiliest—that you needed his help was like asking a bear which part of you he wanted to eat first. The bear would eat—it was what bears did, after all. It was simply their nature. In the same way, the conman would con. It was simply what he did.

"My help, is it?" Willy said, and Valden could hear the excitement in his tone, could almost see his mind working through his eyes. "Well, now, for an old friend like you, Valden, of course I am at your disposal. What can I do for you?"

Meaning, of course, How is it that I can best take advantage of you? "Not here. Your office. I'd rather not be overheard."

"Of course," the man said, bobbing his head, "as you say, old friend. Come this way."

Willy led Valden toward the back of the church and through the door he and the woman had exited minutes before. They traveled down a short, unadorned hallway to a door at the end of it. Willy paused, reaching underneath his robes and retrieving a key ring that held at least a couple of dozen keys. The man tried one and it didn't fit, then another. *"Damnit,"* the conman said in a low voice.

"I didn't think priests used such language. Particularly high priests."

Willy shot a glance back at him over his shoulder. "Yeah, well, I might have added a few keys, you know, to keep any fool with a mind to from being able to lift my keys and break in."

"Well, if it was meant to keep fools out, then I'd say you've succeeded."

"I always did appreciate your sense of humor, Valden," he said as he fished out another key, trying it with no more success than the first two. "Did I ever tell you that?"

"Did I ever tell you that if you don't hurry up and get this door open, I'm going to break it in?" Valden asked. "I've wasted enough time here already."

"Oh, don't do that, please," the fat man said, his fingers fumbling at yet another key. "How would I explain a broken door to the others?"

"That's not my problem. Anyway, I'm sure you've got a few spare lies laying around that you could foist on them."

"You know, Valden, for a man who came here seeking my help, you're being pretty hostile."

"You think this is hostile? You haven't seen anything yet, Willy."

"Right, right," the other man said, licking his lips and hurriedly thrusting another key into the lock, letting out an audible sigh of relief as it turned the latch in the door. "See, told you I'd find it. Come in, come in," he finished, ushering Valden in with a hand.

Valden frowned, hesitating. "Wouldn't happen to be two pissed off Bloody Talons waiting around the corner, would there, Willy?"

The man gave a nervous laugh at that. "Valden, don't be ridiculous. I'd never lay a trap for you."

"Particularly since you had no idea I was coming," Valden said. Still, that didn't keep him from tensing as he stepped across the threshold and into the room. Over the years, he'd met plenty of cold-blooded murderers with more morals than Willy, and the man was damned clever. It was the reason he was still breathing while so many of those who had sought his life at one time or another—probably every person in New Daltenia, certainly every one that had ever met him—weren't. Valden couldn't imagine how the man might have been aware of his coming in time to lay a trap, but then he didn't leave such things to chance. He didn't remove his hand from the knife at his waist until he'd come fully into the room and looked around, ensuring himself that it was empty save for the two of them.

Willy made his way toward a large oak desk at the back of the room, waving at a chair in front of it. "Please, have a seat—we might as well be comfortable."

Valden moved to the chair and hesitated, looking at it. It looked like a chair. Still, just because a thing looked like something didn't mean it was that. Or, at least, didn't mean it was only that. Willy looked like a priest. At least the robes he wore and his station as head priest inside a church seemed to support that idea. But if Valden were in the market for advice on how to be a better person or how to live a more fulfilled life, he would have sooner asked a mad dog for tips than consult the fat man.

"Well?" Willy said. "Are you going to sit or not? You're hurting my feelings, Valden. I almost get the impression you don't trust me."

"Which just goes to show you're not a complete fool," Valden said, and then, satisfied that the chair was safe—or, at least, as satisfied as he could be—he sat. As he did, he noted a bottle of wine sitting on the desk as well as two glasses. One, at least, which was completely full. "Seems you've been getting comfortable already."

The fat man frowned. "Trying to, anyway. That Sister Olivia is a cold one, as I believe I've mentioned. Still, she'll thaw, given time enough. I have a way of growing on people."

"Yeah," Valden said, "like a boil."

The fat man frowned. "That isn't a nice way to talk to the man you've come to asking for help. We all have to make our way in the world, Valden, me just like you, just like anybody else."

"The difference being that most people don't make their way by trampling over others, robbing them of what they have and taking advantage of them. You'll forgive me if I'm not exactly moved to compassion for your plight."

"*Most* other people," Willy said, raising an eyebrow. "But not me. Not you. After all, the Vicious I knew, he hurt plenty of people, and far more... *permanently* than I. True, I may have, on occasion, unburdened some pampered nobleman or spoiled merchant's son of their ill-gotten gains—"

"Is that how you justify it, I wonder?" Valden asked. "Do you tell yourself that those who you rob do not deserve the coin as much as you?"

"But while I might leave their pockets a little lighter," the fat man went on as if Valden hadn't spoken, leaning forward, "you, Vicious, do far more than I. Other fortunes might be made, after all, other coins procured. But a man cannot find himself another life simply for the looking. In fact, some might even consider my services a favor. After all, people rarely appreciate what they have until it's gone, and that goes doubly for the sons of rich noblemen or wealthy merchants. They're born into the riches and so have no real appreciation for them. Anyway, what need does any one man have of so much coin? I might even be said to be doing the city a service, redistributing the wealth."

"Is that how you see yourself?" Valden asked. "Some gentleman thief, solving the world's woes one theft at a time? Is that the lie you tell yourself so that you might sleep at night?"

"Maybe," the man said, frowning, his anger rising past his fear of Valden. "And what of you, Vicious? What lies do you tell yourself? Say what you will about me, but I've never killed. Can you say the same?"

"Just because you're not the one that does the deed doesn't mean you're not responsible," Valden countered, "and I am aware of more than a few men who found their deaths thanks to a whispered word from you. In fact, I was very nearly one of them."

"Those two men, they made me do that. I didn't have a choice. They would have killed me."

Valden shrugged, deciding he was bored. "Maybe. We've wasted enough time on idle chatter already. I need you to tell me where Nadia is."

"Seems the years haven't changed you so much after all, Vicious," Willy said. "Straight to the point, like always. Like an arrow seeking its target. You still practicing with that bow of yours?"

"Enough."

The man shifted, clearly uncomfortable. "Right. Right. Well, as for Nadia, I imagine she's at Florence's like always. From what I hear, nobody has a problem finding Nadia—usually their problems begin when she finds them. I've got friends that say she's even more brutal than Belle, if you can believe that."

"By friends you mean people you bribe or blackmail or extort."

"Isn't that what I said?" He shrugged. "I'd check Flo's, though don't blame me if she doesn't give you the welcome you're looking for. I hear the place is more dangerous than ever."

"You haven't been?"

"The only way I'm going to Flo's is the same as the only way I'd go to a bear's cave—dragged, kicking and screaming."

"She's not at Florence's."

Willy frowned. "Well, might be she went out, how should I know? Anyway, that's her place. Just ask anyone there, I'm sure they'll tell you where she is. If they don't stick a blade in you instead."

"Impossible—on both counts."

The conman snorted. "Look, Valden, I know you're good, but some of those bastards as work for Nadia are good too, she—"

"They're dead."

That brought Willy up short. Another, in his place, might have doubted Valden's words or might have asked some unimportant question—how they'd been killed, for example, or if he was sure. But if Willy had any talent, it was an ability to look out for himself to the exclusion of anything else, to survive, and so the question he asked was the one which most pertained to his own safety. "Who did it?"

"I don't know."

The fat man nodded, clearly already thinking it through, looking for any danger, looking too, no doubt, for any opportunity. "That's bound to shake things up a bit," he said. "And Nadia, she wasn't among the dead?"

"I wouldn't be here, if she was."

"I see," Willy said, nodding slowly. "And the reason? That you're wanting to speak to Nadia, I mean?"

"Is my own," Valden said. "Better if you don't know—less chance I have to kill you that way."

The man nodded, licking his lips nervously. "Well, everybody knows Flo's is where Nadia spends her time. If she isn't there, I'm not sure what you want from me."

"I think you know perfectly well what I want," Valden said, frowning. "Nadia escaped...whatever happened. Which means that she's fled somewhere, is hiding out, no doubt until she figures out who is responsible. I need to know where she is."

"I see," the conman said, nodding. "But what you're asking me, Vicious...it's no small thing. You see that, don't you? I mean, even if I know where she might be found—and I'm not saying I do—it seems to me that if Nadia wanted you to know her location, you would. Giving you such information—assuming I have it—might be dangerous. That is, I doubt that Nadia would thank me for it."

"I think Nadia has far bigger problems to worry about than me."

"Maybe," Willy said, "but that doesn't mean she'll see it the same way. And if she doesn't...well, odds are she'll be looking for the fella that betrayed her hideout. I've spoken with Nadia a few times, and, if I'm being honest, we didn't exactly hit it off."

"With your winning personality? I can't imagine why not."

The fat man frowned. "There you are again with the insults. My point is, Nadia might well decide to look into where you got her location from. The last thing I want is to wake up with one of her goons standing over me, getting ready to carve me a new smile. I like the one I have just fine, thank you."

"I think we both know you have plenty of safeguards in place to make sure that doesn't happen."

"Say that I do," Willy said. "So what? You want to know the truth, Vicious? Sure, I bought this warehouse and started this church because it seemed to me that religion is the biggest con of all. I just wanted a piece of it. But since I've been here, dealing with these people—some of them just as fine and good as you please—well, I like to think maybe I've become better, too. Maybe even good. Holy, even."

Valden snorted. "I've got socks that are holier than you, Willy. And however 'good' you've become, I can't imagine it's so much that you haven't been pocketing the donations I saw you collecting."

"Not all of them," the conman said defensively. "Sure, I take my cut, and why not? It's hard work being head priest—"

"Pretending to be head priest."

"My point is, I don't take all of it."

"Most, I'd wager. You certainly haven't been using it to keep the church up—it looks a couple of good stomps away from collapsing. And that's without mentioning the smell. Either way, you're stealing. The percentage you take, that's a distinction that only matters to criminals like you."

"I'm about tired of listening to you talk down to me, Vicious," the conman said. "Puts me in a mind not to help you at all. I don't much care for it."

"Then you're really going to hate what comes next, if you decide you're not going to tell me."

The man sneered at that, an expression that was a mixture of fear and anger. "All your high-minded talk, but in the end you're just another thug looking to hurt someone."

"Not looking to—*willing* to. There's a difference, though that is a distinction that will matter to me far more than it will matter to you, if I decide to stop being civil."

"Threaten me all you want—you can't make me tell you."

"I'm willing to give it a shot if you are."

The fat man swallowed at that. "Look, Vicious, there ain't no cause for us to go at each other's throats. Not us being old friends and all. I want to help you, honest—" Valden did his best to keep a straight face at the known liar saying 'honest' as if it was supposed to mean something— "only, I don't want to die doing it. And all the assurances in the world aren't going to stay the blades Nadia sends, if she chooses to."

"She won't—I won't tell her I heard it from you."

"That's no guarantee."

"There are no guarantees in this life, Willy. I'd think you'd know that by now. Well. There's one—if I leave this office without learning what I want to know, I can guarantee that I'm going to start talking to the others here. The priests, Sister Olivia—the parishioners too, of course. I think they all deserve to know who they work for and where their money's going. As you said before, we have a past, so I'm in a bit of a unique position to shed some light on the character of their head priest."

"You wouldn't do that. That would be cruel."

"Oh, Willy. It's like you don't remember me at all. Of course I'd do that. I'll do that, and I'll do far worse. Before I'm through you'll wish Nadia had sent some of her men to give you that spare smile you're so worried about. You see, it isn't just what I'm prepared to do if you don't tell me what I want to know, Willy. You made mention, earlier, of the fact that I'm an archer—that's true. I'm a fair hand with a bow. A lot of people, they think the most important thing for an archer is maybe a keen eye or a steady hand. The truth is, it's neither of those. You know what you do more than anything as an archer, a scout? You wait. That means, Willy, that I'm patient. You would not believe just how patient. But if you don't tell me what I want to know, you'll come to believe it. You'll come to understand that there are things far worse than a quick death."

That had the desired effect. The fat man's face paled as he considered the implication of Valden's words. Willy had been sitting back with his hands folded along his ample stomach, but now he put them down below the desk, out of sight, though not so fast that Valden couldn't see them tremble.

"It occurs to me, Willy, that you might have a blade hidden under there. Or, more likely, knowing you, a crossbow. I won't try to talk you out of using it, as I'm sure you'll do what you think is best. But I'll caution you, Willy—if you do use it, you had better make sure you kill me with the first shot. You won't get a second."

The fat man licked his lips and several tense seconds passed as he decided what to do, weighing his options. He was afraid, and he was right to be, for Valden had meant what he had said, and the threats he'd given had not been idle ones. That didn't make him feel proud, though, only...

ashamed. And not just ashamed but afraid. He wasn't afraid of Willy or of what the man might do. Instead, he was afraid of himself. He felt as if he were in quicksand. He had thought he'd dragged himself out of it, long ago, when he'd followed the prince, when he'd become a priest, but now he felt as if he were being sucked back in, becoming who he had once been, becoming, perhaps, who he had *always* been.

In the end, Willy sat back in his chair, seeming to deflate as he raised his hands. "Alright, Vicious. Okay. I'll tell you what you want to know."

Valden sighed, relieved that he would get a lead on where Nadia had gone and, at the same time, disappointed in himself. The real character of a man could be seen, he'd always believed, when that man was tested. Back him into a corner, threaten him or those people or things he loved, and he would show you who he really was. Certainly, Valden had done as much... and he did not like what he saw.

CHAPTER SIX

MATT DID NOT WAKE from his troubled sleep—the only kind he ever found anymore—as much as he was *pulled* from it. Dragged from it the way a willful dog might be dragged about by its leash. Only it was not a leash that pulled at him, not even a chain like that which might be used to escort a dangerous prisoner, though there was something in that which pulled him that was similar to a chain. Inevitability, he thought. Certainly it, like his life of late, was inescapable.

But what pulled him was neither chain nor leash. It was a force. A *green* force. A thought that didn't make sense, even to him, yet there was no denying it. The green pulled at him, jerked him out of his fitful slumber, and he did the only thing he could do—he woke.

Matt jerked up in his bed panting, covered in cold sweat, his skin feeling feverish. He found his gaze traveling, panicked, around his quarters, certain that someone was there, some*thing*. Some ancient, timeless being. He did not know how that creature might look, knew only that its eyes were the green of emeralds, a green so deep and complete that a man might get lost in it. He knew that well, for he thought that, somehow, he had.

He moved to sit on the side of his bed, running his fingers through hair lank with sweat. He held his hands in front of him, noting the way they trembled. He was afraid. He couldn't remember, in truth, the last time he hadn't been. And what was worse was that, if asked, he would have found it difficult to even describe what it was that scared him. There was his fear for his father and uncle, of course, the two men who were braving the many dangers of the Black Wood and that on his order and never mind that he'd been possessed by a feyling at the time.

But while his fear for them—his father, in particular—was a powerful thing, it was not the *only* thing. There were other worries, other fears. One in particular which robbed him of any but the most troubled, restless sleep. It was that he was being swallowed. Slowly consumed by some external force. It reminded him, in some ways, of how he'd felt when he'd been possessed by Emma. He felt the same helplessness as he had then, that same *inevitability* that the force, whatever it was, would overtake him, that soon there would be no *him* left and never mind that he didn't even know what that force was.

But then...that wasn't exactly true. That force, whatever it was, was green. That he knew. A green so deep it might spread and swallow the entire world until there was nothing else. No people, no land, no color at all save green.

He glanced at the small nightstand sitting beside his bed, at the two platters of unfinished food—food which he'd barely touched, truth to tell. Whatever else the last weeks had done, they had robbed him of his appetite. His gaze traveled to a small vial filled with a milky liquid, half empty, sitting near the platters. He frowned at the vial. Healer Malden's latest attempt to remedy the night terrors that allowed Matt no more than a few minutes of sleep before waking him. Matt considered reaching for it but in the end decided not to, mostly because the medicine, while it tasted of death, had proven no more useful in remedying whatever ailed him than the half dozen others which had come before it.

The urge, the *Green,* as Matt had come to think of it over the last days, pulled at him again. It was insistent, demanding and—like so many other times—Matt, feeling as if he could do nothing else, obeyed, rising to his feet.

He let his gaze travel around his quarters briefly, taking in the tousled coverlet on his bed, the sweat-soaked pillow on which his head had lain moments ago, and beyond them to the room at large. Several plates of food lay scattered around—Mistress Ophasia, the mistress of the servants, was insistent on making sure her charges brought him regular meals and never mind that he didn't eat them. Clothes, most soiled with sweat, littered the floor and furniture here and there, for while Matt suffered them to bring him food, he had not suffered them to clean his quarters no matter how much they asked.

Looking around at the room, he thought that it did not look like the sort of place where a king might live. In fact, it looked far closer to the inside of some criminal's den or poor man's hovel than it did the quarters of a king.

But while the sight of it brought a sort of shame to him—and fear, too, evidence of how far he'd fallen, the messy, untidy quarters a match for the inside of his mind—he could not focus on it for long. There was the impetus, the *need* to move, to give in to the force pulling him.

So he did.

He stepped out of his quarters. Guardsman Vorrun stood outside in the hall, along with another younger guardsman whose name he believed to be Oliver. "Vorrun," Matt said, trying for a smile but not sure if the expression ever made it to his face. "You were here last night as well. Just given up on sleep altogether, have you?"

The guardsman smiled, bowing his head. "I might say the same for you, Majesty. Going for your nightly walk?"

"Am I that predictable?"

"Of course not, Majesty," the man said, grinning. "I had you showing up five minutes ago."

Matt gave a soft laugh at that. He liked the guardsman. There was something in his demeanor that reminded him of his father, though it had to be said that Prince Bernard was a far harder man than Vorrun seemed to be.

"Angie, one of the servants, told me that the gardener has worked wonders in the king's courtyard, Majesty," the guardsman said. "Perhaps you'd like to visit it on your walk."

Matt knew the courtyard of which the man spoke, for he had been there before. He knew, also, that the king's courtyard was on the same floor as his own quarters nearer the top of the castle, and that was the exact opposite of where the force was pulling him. "Another day, perhaps," he said. "For now, I think I have a different destination in mind."

"The servants' quarters, Majesty?" Vorrun asked.

Matt gave the man a small smile. "There I am, being predictable again." It was no great surprise that the guardsman knew where he wanted to go. After all, he'd wanted to go to the same place for the last week and never mind that he had no idea *why* he wanted to go there. Only that he was driven to.

Vorrun and his companion fell into step behind Matt as he started down the castle hallway. He paid little attention to his surroundings, making his way toward the servants' quarters. Instead, his mind was—as always—focused on whatever was happening to him, focused on the fact that, whatever it was, it felt a lot like he was dying. He was sick, somehow. Perhaps it was a holdover from being possessed by the feyling, Emma—he'd decided over the sleepless nights and haunted days that that was most likely. Perhaps he was wrong. Perhaps there was some other cause. In the end, it didn't matter. What *did* was that it, whatever *it* was, was getting worse.

In the beginning, he had been able to sneak at least a few hours of decent, dreamless sleep but not anymore. Now, he dreamed. Always, he dreamed. He dreamed of men and women he had never met in places he had never been. And while he couldn't be sure, he thought that sometimes those dreams depicted people not only from a different place but from a different time, a different age. And sometimes those dreams did not depict *people* at all. Instead, his nightly journeys brought him images of the Fey, creatures of the dark, creatures who lived beneath the shadowed boughs of the great trees of the Black Wood.

He dreamed, always, and when he dreamed, he dreamed of monsters. Monsters of various shapes and sizes. He dreamed of the large and small, the beautiful and grotesque alike. He told himself, when he inevitably woke covered in sweat, stinking of fear, that they were *just* dreams and that they, like all dreams, were not real. He told himself that...but he didn't believe it.

Yes, the dreams—or the visions, whatever they might be—were getting worse. But that wasn't the only thing. There was the other bit, the bit he tried to ignore, tried to hide but which was growing increasingly more difficult to conceal. And that was this: it wasn't that he was *able* to read people's thoughts. It was that he was unable *not* to. They were always there, buzzing like beehives, and while he could maintain a certain distance, so that those buzzings were just noise, if he concentrated—and sometimes even if he didn't—that buzzing resolved itself into thoughts, into words. He had long since lost count of the number of times he replied to someone, a servant or a guard, only to discover that they had never spoken their thoughts aloud. More fuel, then, for the rumors that had begun to spread, rumors that he was insane. Mad Matthias, they called him, if only in their heads.

He thought that this, too, had something to do with the Green. The Green which had in days gone from a persuasive, nudging whisper, to a spoken entreaty, to what it was now—a demand. A demand so great that, even though he had spent the last several minutes walking and studying the floor, not really *present* in the world around him but lost—as was increasingly the case—in his own mind, when he looked up he saw that he was exactly where he wanted to go. Or, more precisely, where the Green wanted him to go.

There was no sign to mark the servants' quarters, no attendant to announce his arrival or guards to keep the riff raff out. After all, this was where what most spoiled noblemen and women thought of as "riff raff" lived. This is where they spent their time when they were not scraping before kings or bowing before lords.

Here, unlike most of the castle—he knew, for in the troubled days and weeks past he had walked nearly every inch of it—a man could hear laughing and carrying on, could hear shouting and crying, joy and anger.

He could hear *life*. And that was far better than shuffling down the haunted, silent hallways around his quarters.

Yet as much of a balm as the sounds of the servants going on with their lives might have proven, even this was not why he had come. Or, at least, he did not think so. Instead, he found his feet, largely of their own accord, moving away from the communal dining hall and kitchen where most of the sound was coming from, to the direction of the servants' sleeping quarters.

He paused at the opening to the hallway, staring down it at the doors on either side. He knew from his previous visits that the doors led to small rooms where the servants of the castle slept and stored what meager belongings they possessed.

Here, then, was his spot. The same spot he'd come to for the last three nights in a row. He almost fancied that if he looked hard enough he might see the imprint of his booted feet in the thick red carpet of the hallway. For three nights, four, including tonight, he had come here and had simply stood, not for any reason of his own but because that force, whatever it was, that pulled at him demanded that he do so. He had stood because to do anything else seemed, if not impossible, then an act of self-harm, not unlike sticking his hand purposefully into a fire or a knife into his own leg.

But today, as he stood in that familiar spot, the familiar smells and sounds of the servants' quarter washing over him, he found that the force, the Green, was not satisfied.

He began to walk.

He gave no thought to where he was going, for his thoughts on the matter, like the thoughts of a dog being led by a leash or a beast its chain, made no difference. He simply walked. He passed two or three servants as he made his way down the hall. When they noted him, their eyes went wide with shock, and they bowed and scraped, muttering apologies—as if they had anything to apologize *for*—before hurrying away.

Matt understood their surprise and felt guilty, like an intruder. After all, this was *their* place and never mind that it was situated within a castle that was, by all accounts, his. Here, in the normal course of events, they did not have to bow or apologize, to keep silent or to speak, as was required.

Here, they were their own bosses, and here they might find some peace from long, arduous lives of service. But he had come to them, had intruded on that peace. Yet while he felt guilty, he could no more change it than the mad beast, for he did not lead—he was led.

He was led down the hallway, past several closed doors and one open one in which a man and a woman stood embracing, kissing. Matt didn't know their names, but he recognized both of them as workers in the castle.

The two lovers glanced up and their faces paled as they saw him, but Matt only continued past, giving them an apologetic smile before he moved out of sight.

"There are rules against that sort of thing," the younger guardsman, Oliver, said with a frown. "There's not to be any fraternizing. With your permission, Your Highness, I'll go and see to it myse—"

"Oh, leave it," Matt said. "What's the harm? Leave them in peace, for they looked happy." *At least someone is,* he thought.

The guardsman opened his mouth as if he might speak, but a scowl from Vorrun was enough to convince him to remain silent.

Matt walked on.

He came to an intersection and turned right, traveling down another short hallway, this one having only a single door and that at its end. He glanced questioningly at Vorrun.

"Mistress Ophasia's quarters, Majesty," the man said, doing an admirable job of keeping his confusion as to why they'd come here from his tone and expression.

Matt nodded slowly, glancing back at the door. No sooner had he done so than it creaked open to reveal a young woman. He thought of her that way and never mind that she was probably four or five years his senior. The woman paused, recoiling as she nearly ran into Matt. Then she stared at him and the two guardsmen and her eyebrows nearly crawled to her hairline as she realized who he was. "M-Majesty," she said, dropping into a curtsey. "Forgive me, I, I didn't not know you were there."

"How could you?" Matt said, smiling in what he hoped was a reassuring manner. "Besides, it is I who should apologize—I am in your way."

He stepped to the side and bowed his head. "Please," he finished, gesturing to the hallway.

The girl flashed him a smile, clearly unsure of what to do. In the end, she dropped another curtsey and hurried down the hallway, ducking her head low like someone expecting a blow. Before she did, Matt saw that she was quite pretty even despite the black eye she sported.

He frowned, wondering what a servant in the castle would do to get such a nasty black eye and was still wondering when another voice spoke.

"Majesty?"

He turned to see that Mistress Ophasia stood in the doorway, unable to completely hide the confusion and surprise from her face. Confusion and surprise which was well warranted. Matt smiled at the mistress of servants. She was a short, stocky woman who looked like the world's most grandmotherly grandmother and yet, despite that—or perhaps because of it—possessed an inherent sort of authority the source of which he couldn't identify. "Hello, Mistress Ophasia. Forgive the intrusion."

"O-of course, Majesty," the woman said, "though had I known you wished to see me I would, of course, have come to your quarters. Please, what is it that I can do for you?"

"I..." Matt hesitated, his mouth open. "I don't know," he said honestly, for the truth was he had no idea why the force, why the Green, had brought him here. Only that it had.

"I...see," the woman said, clearly unsure how to answer. "Tell me, Majesty, is...is everything alright? Is there...is there something I can do?"

Can you make the dreams stop? a voice inside him asked, a desperate, scared voice that belonged to a child. *Can you make the bees go away, for I can handle little more of their buzzing? And the Green. Gods help me, the Green.* He forced a smile he did not feel. "No, of course..."

Poor lad. Poor, sweet boy, a voice spoke inside his head. It was not his voice or his thought but, he knew, Ophasia's. *It isn't fair.* "Is everything alright, Majesty?" *What they're asking of you. It isn't right.* "Can I get you a cup of tea or perhaps something else?" *You're just a boy. Just a kid.*

Matt gasped as a sudden pain shot through his head, and he brought both hands up, holding it. "I'm not...a kid," he managed.

JACOB PEPPERS

"I'm sorry, Majesty?" *Oh, you poor thing. Perhaps I'll talk to Malden. Surely there's something he can do.* "You are right, you are, of course, a man grown."

Matt gave his head a shake, feeling as if he were drowning inside his own thoughts, his own mind. Only they weren't his. He let out a desperate growl and, in another moment, the thoughts, *her* thoughts went away. He took a slow, steadying breath and raised his eyes to see Mistress Ophasia watching him, and he didn't have to be able to see into her mind to read her thoughts, not now. Matt glanced back at his guardsmen and saw that, while Vorrun controlled his expression well, his companion, Guardsman Oliver, was not so quick. Matt caught a look of what might have been disgust or suspicion before the man was able to replace it with a bland, servile expression.

He could hear the buzzing beginning again as they all reacted to his odd behavior, if only in their own minds. Desperate to distract himself, desperate to look less...well, mad, his mind cast about looking for something, *anything* to say. His thoughts landed, in another moment, on the woman who had recently left Ophasia's quarters. "The girl," he said, nearly gasped, really, like a drowning man taking his first—or perhaps his last—breath of fresh air.

"I'm sorry, Your Highness?" Mistress Ophasia asked.

"The girl," he repeated, swallowing hard, feeling like he was getting his bearings. "The one that just left."

"Diane, by name, Your Highness," the woman said. "What can I help you with regarding her? Did she do something wrong? If so, I will, of course, speak with her only—"

"No, no, it's not that," Matt said. "It's just...that is, she had a black eye."

The gray-haired woman frowned at that. "Yes, Highness. It seems that in the course of her duties Diane ran afoul of one of the castle guards. It happens, sometimes. According to what Diane told me, she and the guardsman in question happened around a corner at the same time and bumped into each other. It was unintentional, she assures me, but he did not see it that way. The guardsman took offense and chose to punish her for her lack of respect."

66

"I see," Matt said. "And the guardsman? What did he say?"

"According to Diane, he told her to get out of his way and stay out of it, Highness," the woman said, seeming surprised that he'd asked.

"No, sorry," Matt said. "What I meant was what did the guardsman say whenever you questioned him?"

"Questioned him, Your Highness?"

"Well...yes," Matt said, glancing at Vorrun then back to the older woman. "When you spoke to him about the incident? There are two sides to every story, after all, and while I do not know Diane and wouldn't presume any dishonesty on her part, it seems to me that it would be pertinent to speak with both of them."

"In a perfect world, Your Highness, I do not doubt that you would be correct," Ophasia said slowly. "But castle guardsmen do not allow themselves to be questioned by servants—even, as it happens, the mistress of servants."

Matt blinked, surprised by that. He glanced back at Vorrun who winced. "I'm afraid it's true, Majesty. Some of the guardsmen will still speak with the servants well enough, but there are a few who...well. I suppose someone with a clever tongue, like my friend Chall, might say that they take liberties. But I am not particularly clever and have never been accused of being so. I call them assholes. If you'll pardon my language."

Matt grunted. "That makes it difficult to get to the bottom of something like this then, doesn't it? And if the guard is found to be in the wrong, what happens?"

The old woman and Vorrun shared a look, and it was the guardsman who spoke. "Happens, Your Highness?"

"Right," Matt said, feeling suddenly like a fool. "To the guardsman. What happens to him, if he's found to have been abusing the servants?"

"Nothing happens, Majesty," the guardsman said.

"She is a servant, Majesty, and he is a guardsman," Ophasia said in a kind, quiet voice, as if that explained everything. And perhaps for her it did.

Matt, though, had little time for bullies. He hadn't in Brighton when he'd been a kid—and had worn more than a few black eyes because of it—

and after what he'd been through with Emma and everything else, he had even less.

"It's just the way the world works, Majesty," Ophasia said.

Matt considered that. The castle, probably the city, thought he was mad. Chall and Priest had lost trust in him, were up to something and whatever that something was he felt as if they were trying to cut him out, to exclude him. His father and his uncle were in the Black Wood, some-where, fighting for their lives. If, that was, they were still fighting at all. It seemed as if wherever he looked there was another problem he couldn't solve. But this one, this one he could.

"Maybe that was how the world worked," he told them. "But not anymore. I'll want the guardsman's name and where he's posted. I want to meet with him." He glanced at Vorrun. "You'll see to it?"

"Aye, Majesty," the man said, and though his expression was mostly controlled, Matt couldn't miss the small, admiring smile on his face. "As you say."

Matt nodded, turning back to Ophasia. "I'll want to see the girl, too. Best I hear her accounting from her own mouth. I will get to the bottom of this—there won't be any more beating of servants."

Ophasia's eyes glittered as if she were close to tears, and she bowed her head. It felt good, seeing her obvious appreciation, and for a moment, the worry and doubt and fears that had been plaguing him over the last days and weeks vanished. If the secret to happiness existed, and if it could be found, he thought it might be found, somewhere, in small kindnesses. "Yes, Majesty. And Majesty, may I just say...thank you. It means a lot that—"

"*Wait,*" he hissed, staggering as the Green suddenly rushed over him like a monstrous wave. He staggered and would have fallen had Vorrun not reached out and caught him.

"Majesty, is everything okay?" This from the guardsman, but Matt barely heard him. All of his attention was directed, was *being* directed past the mistress of servants, into her room.

Something was in there. Thrumming. Beating like some great heart, the sound of it like a siren's call, one so powerful that it seemed to shake him with its thundering pounding.

"Majesty?" Mistress Ophasia asked, her voice sounding as if it came from some great distance. "Are you well? Perhaps we should find Healer Malden, and—"

Her words turned into a cry of surprise as Matt shoved her out of the way. He never made the decision to do so, just as he'd never made the decision, an hour earlier, to wake up. Yet just like that, it seemed that he could do nothing else. The mistress of servants stumbled into the wall, and Matt moved past, growing more and more desperate by the moment, like some addict that might be found in some alleyway, scrabbling through the trash in frantic search of the poison that had consumed him.

And like that poor soul, Matt thought that, in that moment, he would have done anything to find what he searched for. He stepped into Ophasia's personal quarters, his gaze casting about, following the sound of that beating, not just a sound at all, but a *feeling*. He found his gaze traveling to a small table and mirror at the corner of the room.

He walked toward it.

A chair sat in front of the table. It was in his way, and so Matt grabbed it, casting it aside where it struck the wall and fell on the ground. There was a small jewelry box on the table. He grabbed it, throwing the small latch and opening it. A few pieces of jewelry lay inside. Matt knew little of such things, but the necklaces and earrings and one single ring all appeared, even to his untrained eye, to be of modest make, pieces that he thought most of the city's noblewomen wouldn't have been caught dead wearing.

Nothing of any note or anything remarkable among them...save one. Slowly, Matt lifted the golden chain from the box. It was a fine chain— even he could see that. He had seen similar ones adorning the necks of untold noblewomen since he'd come to New Daltenia. Back in Brighton where there had been little coin and survival had rested far more on knowledge than money, such a chain might have kept a family for a year. Here, though, in New Daltenia, such a sight was commonplace. But what *wasn't* commonplace, what drew Matt's attention and held it, was the stone hanging from it.

Not just any stone, this, but a *green* stone. An emerald, perhaps, though it didn't look like any emerald Matt had ever seen. It was the size of a child's fist, and the stone shone a vibrant green, a green he recognized well. How could he not? After all, that green had invaded his dreams, had laid siege to his mind. He knew it just as, he thought, the man who had spent decades of his life rotting in a cell could not help but recognize it. Would have done so even in darkness.

Indeed, over the last days, Matt had felt very much like a prisoner. A prisoner to his own troubled thoughts, to his own fevered dreams. And, of course...to the Green. A prisoner who could do nothing to change his fate, could only rail against it.

He had not spent decades as a prisoner, of course, but the last days had certainly *felt* like decades. But if he was a prisoner then he was a prisoner thrown into a cell for reasons he did not understand with no knowledge, even, of who had put him there. Here, then, was the first glimpse of that unseen jailer. The Green. Not in his mind, not haunting his dreams, but here, before him, in the waking world.

It was here. It was..."*This,*" he rasped, his mouth suddenly, unaccountably dry. He turned to see Mistress Ophasia moving into the room, watching him warily. Guardsman Vorrun and his companion also stepped inside, and though the older guardsman did his best to hide it, Matt could see the concern in his face. "Where did it come from?" he asked, glancing at Ophasia.

The mistress of servants blinked. "M-Majesty?"

"This necklace," Matt said, his hand shaking where he held the golden chain. "Where did it come from? Is it yours?"

She hesitated. "I...suppose you might say that, Majesty. It was given to me—or, perhaps, it might be closer to say that it was entrusted to me by Regent Weylan-dreah. He said that I might keep it so long as I never tried to sell it but kept it in my possession." She blushed, as if embarrassed. "I tried to explain to him that a woman such as myself has no business owning such a fine necklace, but he was quite insistent."

Matt blinked at that. The regent. A regent that, as it turned out, had been a feyling in disguise, one that had very nearly killed his father and his uncle, almost succeeding in a feat at which countless men and feylings had failed over the years. Of course, Mistress Ophasia, like the rest of the city—or, at least, so he hoped—had no idea of that. Chall and the others had believed—and Matt agreed—that such knowledge, that the ruler of New Daltenia itself had been a monster intent on its demise, would have caused a panic.

Ophasia suddenly paled. "Majesty, I know, that is, I heard of the Regent's...betrayal. You must know, I would never do anything to harm you or Prince Bernard or Prince Feledias. I am a loyal servant of the Known Lands, and I—"

"I know," Matt said. "I would never doubt you, Mistress Ophasia," he said, and the woman breathed a heavy sigh of relief. As well she might. While they had kept the truth of the regent's identity from the populous, they had still needed to explain his death somehow. And so a feyling intent on the destruction of the kingdom of the Known Lands had become, simply, a traitor who had meant to seize power for himself and had been killed. An easy enough lie to believe—after all, it had been done plenty of times in the past.

Matt glanced back at the emerald dangling from its chain. If indeed it was an emerald, for while it shared similarities, it seemed somehow different, somehow *more* than some inert stone, pretty or not. Even as he held it, the gem seemed to pulse with some strange, unknown power, almost as if it were alive, those pulsings the beatings of its heart. Studying it, Matt wondered what Ophasia would have thought had she known the truth, had she known the actual provenance of the necklace.

Not that he did, of course, at least not beyond the fact that the man who had given it to her had not been a man at all but a creature of the Black Wood, one intent on the destruction of the Known Lands.

"I've never worn it," Ophasia said, sounding as if she meant to defend herself. "Didn't seem right, putting so fine a piece on an old hag like myself."

Matt turned to regard her. "The beauty of this necklace would have been elevated if you had, Mistress Ophasia."

The woman's blush stripped decades from her face, and she smiled. "That is kind of you, Majesty. Still, it wasn't completely that I felt reticent. It might sound silly or superstitious but...it felt *wrong,* somehow. The necklace, I mean. At the time, I thought that feeling, that wrongness was probably just the silly fancy of an old woman's addled mind or the knowledge that I did not belong near such a piece. But now that I know of the regent's treachery, it might be that it makes more sense."

Matt nodded slowly, frowning as he turned back to the necklace, examining it. He thought he probably should have felt a similar aversion. After all, it had been the possession of a feyling intent on destroying everything and everyone he cared about. But instead, Matt found himself staring at that green, shining stone with an odd sort of fondness. It felt... familiar, almost, though he was quite sure he had never seen it before. And even the strangeness of the emerald itself—if indeed it was an emerald— was not off-putting.

It did not feel wrong, as Mistress Ophasia had put it.

It felt like the answer to a question he had not even known he had. It felt like the last, lost piece to a puzzle he'd been working on without even being aware of it.

It felt like coming home.

"Did Regent Weyldan-dreah say why he wished for you to hold on to it?"

"I'm sorry, Majesty, but no. He only stressed the importance that I not sell or be rid of it. I had no intentions of wearing it, even then, but he was regent and so, of course, I did as I was asked."

"I see," Matt said. "And did he tell you why he might return to claim it once more? What reason he might have? Or, perhaps, where it was from?" Matt didn't know much about gems; a childhood spent in Brighton where, if a family possessed a milk cow they were considered well-off, had not offered much of an education in precious stones. Still, the last few weeks of audiences and meetings with nobles and merchants had been like a crash course in such things, and he was confident that an emerald so large as the one he now held would have had a story, its origins meticulously documented so that whoever purchased or owned it might be assured of its authenticity.

"Forgive me, Majesty, but he did not say."

"A mystery, then," Matt said quietly, staring at the gem. "If you would like, Mistress Ophasia, I can take the necklace—you know, to look into it for you." He tried to sound casual, but based on the strange way the woman looked at him, he thought that he didn't quite manage it and that some of his desperate desire—no even that wasn't right—his desperate *need* to possess the necklace must have slipped either into his tone or his expression.

"Of course, Majesty," she said. "As I said, I would not presume to wear such a piece. In truth, I would be glad to be rid of it."

Matt nodded, suddenly wanting nothing more than to get away before the woman changed her mind, before she tried to lay claim to it. In that moment, he was not sure what he would have done, if she had. "Thank you, Mistress Ophasia. I bid you good night." And with that, he abruptly turned and started toward the door, cradling the necklace in both hands, pressed against his chest as if it were a small child, one he was terrified of dropping or losing.

—behaving very strangely. I do hope he is okay. That thought was from Ophasia, and he heard it as clearly as he would have had she spoken the words aloud, but hers was not the only thought that accompanied him as he moved toward the door.

There was Vorrun's voice, too. *I'd best talk to Chall about all this,* the guardsman was thinking. *He'll know what to do.* Matt wished the man luck, for he had spoken to Chall himself, only days ago, about his inability to sleep, about his strange ability to pick up on other people's thoughts and, so far at least, the mage had offered no solution.

He made it to the door and had grabbed the handle when yet another thought, this one from Guardsman Oliver, struck him.

The mad king is right, the guardsman thought. *The bastard has lost his damned mind, that's sure. Wait until I tell the fellas about this. As mad as his father, that one. Not that it matters much—the Crimson Prince is long dead by now, too busy collecting maggots to trouble anyone.*

Matt rounded on the man, fury suddenly rushing through him. "My father is not dead," he growled. "And he is not mad."

It was all he could do, in that moment, to keep from charging forward and attacking the man. For his part, Guardsman Oliver's face paled, and he looked as if he'd seen a ghost. He opened his mouth as if to speak but seemed unable to find the words.

"Majesty?" Vorrun asked, glancing between Matt and his fellow guardsman, clearly confused. "Is everything alright? Did...that is, did I miss something?"

"Perhaps you did, Vorrun," Matt said, his eyes on the other guardsman. "But I did not. I miss very little."

He became aware of the three of them watching him, became aware of the tenseness that had settled in the room so thick that a man could have cut it with a knife. He glanced down at his hands. They were no longer against his chest now, but instead in fists at his sides, and he wasn't sure whether or not he imagined that the green stone seemed to shimmer in his grip as if in response to his anger.

Anger that, even as he regarded it, began to dissipate. What was he to do? Punish Oliver for his thoughts? Besides, there was no way of knowing if they even *were* his thoughts, though Matt would have preferred to think so to the alternative. After all, if they weren't the man's thoughts then that meant that Matt was going mad in truth.

"Forgive me," Matt told the man. "I..." He trailed off then, unaware of how he might explain his abrupt outburst. Finally, he gave it up for a lost cause and glanced at Mistress Ophasia instead. "Please," he said, "do send the servant girl—Diane—to me. And the name of the guardsman. I would meet with both of them...about the incident."

They all only stared at him then, and Matt turned, hastening through the doorway and out into the hall.

And despite his hurry, he could not outrun their thoughts, thoughts that chased him down the hallway.

Something wrong—
—needs to see a healer.
Mad king, indeed.

CHAPTER SEVEN

CHALL'S EYES opened slowly and in the moment it took his lids to peel back, realization came. Realization that he was still alive—a rather nice realization, that. And a moment later a considerably less welcome one—he was in pain.

But the dull throbbing pain he felt in his thighs where he'd been shot and stabbed in turn largely vanished when his eyes came fully open, and he saw the face looming over him. Maeve's face.

"A...fine way to wake up," he rasped from a dry throat, trying a weak smile. "Unless I'm still dreaming and, if so, then it's a welcome dream."

"I'd save your flattery for the moment, Challadius," she said, frowning, "for if this is a dream, it is a dream that might well turn into a nightmare in another moment."

Chall's smile faltered at that. "What...what is it? Are you okay?"

"Am I—" she started in a shocked voice, then frowned, her eyes narrowing. "You really are a bastard, you know that? How dare you ask after me while you're lying there hurt?"

Chall hesitated. "I'm...sorry?"

He knew he was in trouble—anytime she said his full name of Challadius instead of Chall then that was pretty well a guarantee—and the look on her face did nothing to dissuade him of that notion. It was hard to read that look for sure, but it was one fraught with emotion. He had already been stabbed and shot, and it suddenly seemed likely that he was about to add beaten to the list.

Indeed, she lunged forward with shocking abruptness, and he grunted, expecting to catch a fist or an elbow—or possibly a knife. Instead, she pulled him into a tight embrace that, given the torture he'd so recently endured, was only a touch less painful than the alternative might have been.

"Thank the gods you're alright," Maeve breathed.

He was just enjoying the feel of her against him—pain or not—settling into it, when she pulled back once more, her frown well in place.

"Don't you ever go and get yourself nearly killed again, you understand me?"

"I'll do my best," he promised, and that with feeling. "Turns out, getting shot and stabbed was just about as much fun as you'd expect. You know. None."

She shook her head in frustration. "What were you thinking, doing something so foolish?"

Chall cleared his throat. "Uh...that is, which time?"

Her eyes narrowed. "There a list, then?"

"I try to keep a running tally."

"Well then how about we start with how you were so foolish as to get involved with the Crimson Wolves, not to mention Lady Valencia who used to be a member, and then go and cavort with a bunch of criminals from Priest's past without telling me?"

Chall shifted uncomfortably. Or, at least he tried to. He had been wrapped quite thoroughly in bandages—he figured some must have been close to expiring so Emille had chosen to use them up and all on him—and so his shifting amounted to little more than a nearly imperceptible wiggle underneath the coverlet draped over him. "I wouldn't say we *cavorted* per se. There was no cavorting and *certainly* no rollicking or frolicking." He glanced down at his legs. Between the blankets and the bandages, he might have thought he was no longer among the legged at all. He couldn't see the wounds, just as he couldn't see his legs, but that was alright, he guessed, for he could feel them well enough. "No cavorting," he said again, wincing, "but I suppose there might have been a bit of carrying on."

"Forgive me if I'm not in the mood for jokes, Chall," she said. "You could have died."

Judging by the look on your face, I still might. "Look, Maeve, it isn't as if I asked for all this to happen, is it? No more than you asked for Balderath the Bloodthirsty Butcher—"

"—Brutal," she said, raising an eyebrow.

"Fine, Balderath the Bloodthirsty Brutal Butcher." She gave a soft sigh at that, shaking her head, but Chall went on. "As I was saying, you didn't ask for him to come—along with those other assassins—" still a sore spot there, for *she* had warranted several while he had warranted only one escort—"but when they came, you went with them."

She frowned. "I was just doing the best I could, Chall. Trying to keep you alive, trying to keep *me* alive."

"So was I."

"And doing a damned poor job of it," she observed, glancing down at his legs to remind him of his wounds—as if he needed reminding.

"Well, we can't all be famous assassins with half a dozen knives hidden in our clothes."

"Half a dozen? You underestimate me, Chall," she said. It was meant to be a joke, but he could see the tears gathered in her eyes. Tears for him, tears that had come at the thought of him dying, tears she was holding back, he thought, as a kindness to him. Now that was a funny thing. Chall had never imagined someone might look so distraught at the idea of his death. Certainly, he knew more than a few who would celebrate it. No, he had never thought to be loved in such a way and certainly not by someone such as Maeve, a woman that was as far above him as a bird was over a worm.

She sat back, putting her hands in her lap and looking just about as scared and timid as anyone Chall had ever seen, and Maeve was not a timid woman. He reached out and took one of her hands, meeting her gaze. "You know...you know I don't do serious well, don't you, Mae?"

"I know that," she said.

"Good. Then you'll bear with me if I screw it up. You are the greatest thing that has ever happened to me. I was dead before I met you. I'd spent so long in the cold, I didn't know what it was to be warm. I was in the darkness, so deep I didn't even remember the light. Oh, I hid it behind laughs and smiles and jokes and jibes but believe me...I was in the darkness. And then you came and pulled me out of it. I can't imagine why... boredom, maybe. Some cosmic charity, you've got due. Whatever the reason, I want you to know this—I am thankful. I am thankful as only the worm can be when he has a chance, against all odds, to fly with the birds."

"Birds eat worms," she said, but the tears weren't in her eyes now but gliding down her cheeks, and there was a small smile on her face.

He smiled back. "My point is, you are everything to me." He shrugged. "You're all of it. The first thing I think of when I wake up, the last thing I think of when I lie in bed. And I want you to know that, even if I die, I count myself lucky to have known, if even for a brief moment, what it was to love and be loved by someone far greater than I deserve. After all, not every worm gets to fly. I love you, Mae. I don't know why you chose me, and I don't give it much thought, just try to appreciate every moment as much as I can, for I'm grateful for all of them."

She let out a sound somewhere between a laugh and a sob, glancing down at his bandaged form. "Even this one?"

"Even this one. I'd rather die with you, Maeve, than live with anyone else. That's the truth. I'm not looking to die. In my entire life, I've never had anywhere near as much to lose as I do now, but if I *do* die, then I'll still count myself lucky for the time I got to spend with you."

She sniffled, running her fingers across her teary eyes. "Challadius the Charmer indeed," she said. "I love you too, Chall."

She hugged him then, and he hugged her back. It was a tender, sweet moment, but it was also a moment in which certain parts of Chall's anatomy began to respond. He thought maybe he'd been a little off with the whole worm thing—pig might have been closer to the truth. Still, he'd heard it said that the heart wants what the heart wants, and he supposed the same might be said for other parts of a person's body. As they embraced, he began to softly massage her shoulders with one hand. It was a trick he'd used before, one that had a high enough success rate—about one in five, give or take—that he hadn't given it up yet.

She made a content sound at that. Not exactly an invitation, but then he figured if a fella always waited around for an invitation, he'd be doing a lot of waiting and little else. He continued to massage her as his hand traveled down her back. Just a little, then a little more until it was at the middle of her back.

She pulled back from him, raising an eyebrow, an expression on her face that told him maybe his trick wasn't quite as tricky as he thought. "You can't be serious," she said.

"Give me a few minutes, I'll show you just how serious I can be," he said, flashing her his winning smile, the smile that had melted the heart—and opened the legs—of quite a few maidens over the years.

This maiden, however, remained wholly unimpressed. "You were shot in one leg and stabbed in the other. You can't walk. Gods, Chall, you probably can't even stand."

"Don't need to," he observed, pulling her back into an embrace, massaging her shoulder again, starting the whole process over.

"And here I thought you were serious with all that bird and worm talk," she said.

"I was serious," he said. "You don't believe me, just watch me wiggle."

Someone cleared their throat.

That was odd.

It wasn't Maeve. He was sure of it. And it wasn't him—he'd been hurt, but he was pretty sure he'd know if it was. Still, he was preparing to convince himself he'd imagined it—the gods knew he'd performed under worse circumstances and with far worse partners to boot—when the sound came again.

And, this time, it was followed by a voice.

"Hate to break this up, really I do. Seems a shame after all the effort you must have put into that bird and worm bit."

Maeve sat back, then, her face flushing. For the first time, Chall paid attention to where he was. He was, he noted in a moment, back in his and Maeve's quarters at the castle. He thought surely he must have been mistaken until he saw, on the nightstand beside the bed, a familiar book, one that Maeve constantly tried to get him to read. He even noted the thin layer of dust, uninterrupted by fingerprints, that proved she had, thus far at least, failed.

Scary to think that he had been so hurt that they had come all the way back to the castle and he had never noticed. But as unsettling as that was, at least *as* unsettling was that a glance at the room's circular table showed him that he'd had an audience for his little heartfelt speech. Ned and Emille sat at the table, though in truth the table might as well not have even been there at all from the way they sat side by side, as close as they could possibly be.

"Don't get me wrong," the carriage driver said, smiling, "I like a good... what was it you called it? Oh, that's right, *wiggle*. I like a good wiggle as much as the next guy." He paused, glancing at his wife and waggling his eyebrows in an exaggerated way. Emille laughed, slapping his arm, and Ned turned back to Chall. "Only, well, I think maybe there's some stuff needs seein' to first. Besides, I reckon that healer fella—Malden, wasn't it? —will be back any minute. I'd hate for you to go through all the trouble just to be interrupted."

Chall found his face flushing hotly. He wasn't easily embarrassed— he'd made his peace with the fact that he was a cad a long time ago. Still, he found he was embarrassed now. He opened his mouth to answer and for one of the first times in his life found that he could think of nothing to say.

"Oh, don't worry about it none, fella," Ned said, grinning at his discomfort, "I reckon I'm just as embarrassed as you are."

"I doubt that," Chall managed. He cleared his throat, deciding that it was past time to change the subject. "Anyway, what are these things that need seeing to?"

The other man grinned, making it clear that he knew exactly what Chall was doing. "Well, there's your pillow talk, for one. I mean, I'm no famous womanizer, but still...all that worm talk. That works, does it?"

Chall's eyes narrowed as his face heated again. "Hey, now, there's no cause to—"

"It works," Maeve interrupted, and Chall glanced over to see her watching him. "I'll show you just how much later," she promised.

He felt his face heat for an altogether different reason at that, then he turned back to the carriage driver, giving the man a smug expression.

Ned grunted. "Huh. Well, I s'pose it pays to know your audience." His smile faded then. "Anyway, to answer your question, we still haven't heard from Val." He paused, glancing at Emille. "That is, Lady Valencia."

Emille rolled her eyes. "Ned here is convinced that if he shows any familiarity with another woman, I'll finish what those men who invaded our home started."

"Oh, come on, Ned," Chall said. "She wouldn't do that."

"I didn't say *that*," Emille said, smiling at her husband, an expression that was somehow threatening and loving all at once.

The carriage driver cleared his throat again, looking suitably nervous, so far as Chall was concerned. "Anyway, Val still hasn't shown up. She wasn't back at the house—we double-checked while you were lying around unconscious. Which means one of two things. Either she, a high-born lady with no experience in such matters, managed to first detect and then evade that bastard, Catham, and his men before they captured her, or..."

"Or she was taken," Chall said. That, of course, was the far more obvious of the two, and never mind what Catham said. After all, as Ned had intimated the woman didn't have much experience with criminals. True, she'd been part of the Wolves, but from all that she and Ned had told him hers had largely been a clerical, organizational role. A weapon's clerk might be said to be a soldier, but there was a big difference between signing off on someone checking out a weapon and using that weapon to split someone's head open. Besides which, the woman was nearly eighty, and she looked it. She wasn't exactly spry. He figured Catham and his men could have caught her easily enough at a brisk walk.

"Why would they take her, though?" Maeve asked.

"For the same reason they broke into her house to begin with," Ned said, frowning. "Val kept all the records, kept up with all the members, all those merchants and shopkeepers who helped us in one capacity or another. If anyone—anyone like Rob, say—wanted to get the Wolves goin' again, Val is the single best person in the city to make that happen."

"She struck me as a tough old bird," Chall said. "She won't do what he wants for the asking."

"That's what I'm afraid of," Ned said.

"You're saying, what?" Chall asked. "That he'd torture her?"

"Have you seen yourself?" Maeve asked.

"Okay, fair," Chall said, "but torturing two grown men is one thing— an old sweet lady, that's another...isn't it?" he asked, glancing at Ned.

The carriage driver shook his head slowly, his expression grim and getting grimmer. "I don't think so, not to Rob, at least. The Rob I once knew, he loved Val like his own mother. But the more I see, the more I think that Rob is gone. Or maybe he wasn't the man I thought he was, even back then. Whatever the case, we have to find Val. If we don't find her soon..."

He trailed off then, but then Chall thought they all understood his meaning clearly enough. If they didn't find the old woman soon, there'd be no point in finding her at all. After all, the dead were well beyond saving.

"But how would we even know where to look?" Emille asked. "It's a big city and somehow I doubt this Rob is advertising his whereabouts. As for Catham, he's well-known in the Guild for being dangerous, clever."

"Cautious, too," Chall added, frowning.

"At any rate," Emille said, turning to look at her husband, "if he or this Rob does have Lady Valencia, they won't be easy to find."

Ned nodded, frowning. "Be a damn fine time for that friend of yours, Priest, to show up."

Valden, Chall corrected in his mind, quite nearly said aloud, and then found himself frowning, sad and somehow distressed by that. He was Priest no longer. He was Valden and that only. That realization, that truth hurt. A lot. It felt to Chall as if he had lost a dear friend. Perhaps he would find him again, but he had seen Valden lately, and he was not so sure. "Why is that?" he asked, dismissing the dark thoughts.

"Well, he said he knew this Catham bastard from back in the day. Might be he'd have some line on where we might find him. Where is he, anyway? Your friend, I mean."

Chall and Maeve shared a troubled look at that. "I don't know" Chall said honestly.

"That's a shame," Ned said. "With his past, he might have been useful. Still, there's no time to waste. I wanted to hang around long enough to make sure you were...well, I won't say up and about, but still to be counted among the livin' anyways. Now that I know you don't plan on dying anytime soon, I guess I'd best get goin'. With some luck, maybe I can get a line on where those bastards took Val or, if she somehow gotten away, where she might have got away *to*." He glanced over at Emille. "You'll be okay?"

"If you will I will, as I'll be going with you," she said.

The carriage driver winced. "Em, I really don't think—"

"Don't think what, exactly?" she asked. "That I can handle it? Or is it that it's too dangerous? Need I remind you, husband of mine, that only one of us has been trained by the Assassin's Guild, and it isn't you."

Ned frowned. "It's a husband's job to protect his wife."

"Of course it is," she said. "And I'll let you—later. For now, I'm going with y—" She cut off as there was a knock on the door, and Chall hissed as his body tensing sent pain rushing through him.

"I'll get it," Maeve said, rising and starting toward the door.

"*Maeve,*" Chall blurted.

The woman turned and regarded him, and he winced. "Just...be careful, alright? I've already been shot and stabbed today—I'd rather not add killed to the mix."

"Relax, Chall," she said. "After all, what was it Emille said? Only one of us is a trained assassin." She gave him a wink then moved to the door. But despite Maeve's reassurances, Chall didn't miss the way one of her hands went into her tunic. It didn't take a genius to figure that she was grasping one of her knives, prepared to draw and use it in a moment's notice should whoever was on the other side of the door prove dangerous.

Maeve eased the door open then made a strange, shocked sound in her throat, somewhere between a grunt and a hiss.

"Maeve?" Chall asked, hissing in pain as he worked his way to a seated position. "What is it? Is everything okay? Are you alright?"

"I'm fine, Chall," she said, never turning. "Well, Ned, you said that you wanted to find some sort of lead on Lady Valencia's whereabouts, didn't you?"

"Damn right I do," the carriage driver said, and Chall could hear the worry in his voice. He recognized the look on the man's face—he'd seen it often enough to know it for what it was. The man blamed himself. That was irrational, of course, but then human beings lived on bread and water and irrationality—anyone who'd spent much time around them knew that much.

"Well, I think maybe I can help," Maeve observed from the doorway.

"Oh?" the carriage driver asked. "If you got an idea of where to start, I'd be grateful."

"I can do you one better than an idea, I think," Maeve said, then she stepped to the side, opening the door wide to reveal a familiar figure standing in the hallway.

"*Val?*" Ned said, a shock in his voice to match that he felt.

"Hello, Neddy," she said in a raspy, pained voice. The old noblewoman looked far worse than the first time Chall had met her, and *that* had been after someone had broken in her house and attempted to kill her. Her once fine dress was rumpled and torn in several places, stained with enough dirt and other, less identifiable substances that it looked as if she'd taken a roll around in a pig pen.

Her hair was tangled and loose, and she was sporting a black eye that was swollen completely shut. Something—what looked like a scrap of fabric—had been tied around one of her hands which she currently held pressed against her chest, cradled by the other. Chall saw, glancing at it, that the rag was stained with blood. The noblewoman, he also saw, only stood with the help of one of the two guardsmen accompanying her. She leaned heavily against him while the guardsman held her with an arm around her shoulders to keep her upright.

"Forgive me, Lady Maeve," one of the two guards standing behind the woman said. "She came to the front gate, asking after Lord Challadius. Normally, protocol would be that she'd wait at the gate until we verified her identity, but I thought...you know, given the state of her—"

"You were right to bring her," Maeve said. "Thank you."

The guardsman bowed. "Will there be anything else, my lady?"

Maeve glanced over at the old woman again then nodded, frowning. "Yes, if you could summon Healer Malden for us I would greatly appreciate—"

"It has already been done, my lady," the guardsman said. "Healer Malden is on his way."

She nodded. "Thank you. Please, this way." She moved to the room's table, and Ned rose, sliding a chair out for the old noblewoman before helping the guardsman to ease her down into it.

Lady Valencia let loose a pained sigh as she sat into the chair, the guardsman filing back out the way they had come.

"Gods, Val," Ned said, "what happened? We thought, that is, when we came back to the house and found those bastards waiting on us, we thought that..."

"That someone had finally laid these old bones to rest?" she asked, giving him a smile and never mind that she looked close to tears. "I'm afraid you're not..." She paused, wincing and clearing her throat. "Not going to be rid of me that easily."

"But...how did...that is..."

"How did I make it away with all my parts still in their proper places? Well..." She glanced down at her roughly-bandaged hand, cradled in her lap now. "Mostly. It would be nice to say I vanquished my foes, or perhaps that I used my own wit and cleverness to outmaneuver and elude them. The ungilded truth, however, is considerably less exciting and considerably more...dare I say it, humbling. You see, it was not skill or courage that saved me but simple dumb luck. I was sitting at your home—quite beautiful, by the way—when I'm afraid I grew bored and decided to go for a stroll—"

"*Val,*" Ned began, but the old noblewoman held up her good hand.

"I know, I know. You would scold me. Only, know that you would not say anything that I have not already said to myself in the last few hours. It was a foolish thing to do. I know that now. I think I knew it then, too, only...only I was feeling very lonely..." She paused, heaving a ragged sigh. "Many envy a noble's life, and perhaps they are right to do so, but I will say this much of it, at least—it does not prepare one for being alone. There is always someone, you see. Maids and butlers, Alder, my chamberlain. There is always someone to speak to. Only this time, of all times, this time when an old friend, a man who I once considered family, has set out to kill me that I found myself, after you all left, being alone. Completely, utterly alone."

"Val, we had to—"

"I don't blame you, Neddy," she said. "I understand that there are things that needed doing, and that you couldn't do those things while babysitting an old fool. I'm only trying to make you understand that while my decision was indeed foolish, it was also not without cause. It was for this reason that I had stepped out of your home and was a short way down the street, when the men came. I didn't think much of it, at first—men walking down the street. It's what the street is *for,* after all. It wasn't until one of them pointed in my direction and when another of them, in response, began to run at me that I realized I might be in trouble."

Emille frowned. "That's a bit odd, isn't it? I mean—" she glanced at Ned—"those men came to our house looking for the three of you. It would have been dark and so I doubt they might have recognized you immediately. It seems strange that they would set out to kill anyone in the street—not exactly discreet."

"Well, we can't all be trained assassins, love," Ned said.

Emille nodded at that, but she was still frowning, clearly thinking it over.

"And you must be Emille," the noblewoman said, giving her a warm smile. "It seems that I am not the only one of the old Wolves—though I'm left to wonder if a wolf without teeth is still a wolf at all—possessed of more than my share of luck. Neddy did not mention that you were so beautiful."

87

"Neddy has a way of not mentioning a lot of things," Emille said, glancing at her husband who pointedly avoided her gaze. "Still, I thank you for the kindness. Anyway, about the man, the one who ran after you. What happened?"

"Well, as I said before," the noblewoman said, "what happened next was mostly luck. As you might expect, at the sight of the man barreling toward me with a knife in his hand I ran—as you do when someone is running at you with the intent of killing you. But I'm afraid I was never much of a runner, even in my youth—always preferred sitting, if you want to know the truth. Still, I was determined to give it my all. He chased me down the street to an alleyway alongside a baker's—you two must quite love the smell of that. Though, just then I paid it little attention. I ran left down the alleyway—"

"I'm sorry, right, do you mean?" Emille asked.

The old woman paused, frowning. "No, no I'm quite sure it was left. Anyway, I ran left, taking the corner beside the bakery and going into the alley. The man, whoever he was, was just about stepping on my heels at that point, and I don't mind telling you that my heart was hammering in my chest like a drummer with far more enthusiasm than skill." She paused, thinking, and Chall supposed that it couldn't be easy to relive a moment like that.

"I didn't make it very far down the alley," she said, "before he was on me, grabbing me. I fought to break free and almost managed it. In the end, though, we both just went tumbling to the cobbles, and I don't mind telling you that while such stones have their place, I have decided that carpet has been one of the greatest and most underappreciated luxuries of my life." She paused, hesitating.

"Listen, Val," Ned said, "if this is too difficult, we can always do it later. It'll keep, at least for a little while and—"

"No," she said, meeting his eyes, "no, I appreciate it, Neddy, but I'm okay. Just a bit...well, addled is all. Or more addled, anyway." She glanced at Emille with a small smile. "Always so protective, our Neddy, isn't he?"

"Yes, he is," Emille said. "You were saying, about the alleyway?"

Ned glanced at his wife, a slight frown on his face. Not as if he was angry but as if she was a puzzle he was trying to solve.

For her part, Lady Valencia cleared her throat. "Right...the alleyway. Let me think for a moment...ah, yes, I've got it now. We tussled, my prospective suitor and I, and that with more alacrity than I've shown and been shown for the last thirty years or more. He was the stronger—I saw that at once. Faster too. Younger. Likely better at cards as well. But then I was motivated—I don't believe I've ever been so motivated in my life. One of his elbows fetched me a nasty blow in the eye. I'm not sure how long we fought, only that it felt like an eternity and a half. Eventually, though, the blade he held found its way into his chest. I say found its way because honestly even now I have no idea how it happened. I won't take credit for it as I was far too busy trying to not get stabbed to even consider stabbing him myself. Or himself, as it were," she finished, smiling.

"That sounds terrible," Chall said.

"Yes," the old noblewoman said, nodding slowly. "It does, doesn't it?" After a moment, she shrugged. "Still, I am alive, and so I can be nothing but grateful. The wonderful thing about the human condition, I suppose, is that no matter how dark the night gets, we quite easily forget when the sun comes again."

"Yes, quite easily," Emille agreed, and again Ned glanced at her, that puzzled frown on his face.

"The important thing is," Ned said, turning back to Lady Valencia, "that you made it out of there."

"Well, most of me," she said, glancing down at the fabric wrapped around her hands. She began to peel it back.

A part of Chall didn't want to look. Most of him didn't want to look, in fact. But then for nearly all his life, *most* of him hadn't wanted to get drunk and go whoring and acting a fool. But there was one part that always did. He figured every man had such a part, every woman, too, for that matter. It was a fool, that part, but then that was the thing about fools—they were, without fail, loud and therefore hard to ignore.

He looked.

The thin piece of stained, bloody fabric peeled back to reveal the woman's bloody hand. At least what was left of it. Someone had, apparently, taken issue with her index finger. Or, perhaps, they'd been terribly impressed with it. So impressed that they had chosen to keep it for themselves.

"He took my finger," the old woman said, staring at her wound, her voice sounding bitter and afraid for the first time since she'd arrived.

"He?" Emille asked. "Do you mean the man in the alley?"

The old woman frowned at the finger for another moment, looking very close to tears. But she raised her head to look at Emille, running an arm across her eyes. "Of course, who else?" she asked. "The knife found itself into his chest, somehow, but not before it took my finger with it. Still, I suppose I should be grateful to be alive. Just...well, it's all a bit upsetting. I suppose I shouldn't be terribly put out—after all, an old woman's fingers, like the rest of her, aren't good for much but hurting. Anyway, I've still got plenty enough to waggle disapprovingly, if I've cause. But back to the man, my would-be murderer. The knife went into his chest while we struggled. It was easier than I would have thought, but then with him on top of me as he was, he sort of landed on it, did most of the work for me. After tha—"

"Wait, he was on top?" Emille asked.

"Em, maybe—" Ned began.

"It's alright, Neddy," Lady Valencia said. "Your wife has questions, and she's right to have them. I know that had several men like my alleyway friend shown up at my house trying to kill my husband I would have had a few questions of my own. Yes, to answer you," she went on, turning to Ned's wife, "the man was on top of me at the time."

"I see," Emille said, nodding slowly.

She said no more than that, but watching her Chall thought that just because she didn't say any more didn't mean she wasn't thinking it, for there was clearly something on the woman's mind.

"After that," the noblewoman went on, "I managed to get myself to my feet—don't ask me how, for I was shaking like a leaf—and then I ran. I didn't even know where I was going at first, didn't think about it. It only mattered that I went *some*where, that I went *away*."

"So...where did you go?" This wasn't from Emille but from Maeve, and

90

Ned turned to regard her with the same sort of puzzled frown as he had his wife. "I only ask," Maeve went on, "because it's been several hours, and even the most circuitous route would not have taken you so long. Even considering..."

"My age?" the woman asked, raising an eyebrow.

Maeve gave her a small smile. "I was going to say your wounds."

"Ah, of course," Lady Valencia said, then sighed, shrugging. "To be honest, the time after that is all a bit of a blur. I guess I stumbled around the city for a while in shock and terror, sure that at any moment one of those men would find me and finish what their companion had started. In truth, I'm surprised someone didn't stop me and ask if I was okay. I must have been a sight."

"I'm not," Chall said. "People are assholes, that's all. It isn't as if they wake up and *choose* to be assholes—at least most of them. They simply are. They see a lady stumbling down the street, bloody, hurt, and they see a situation they don't want to get involved in. It's one thing to hear of tragedy, after all. It's quite another when that tragedy is standing right in front of you. It scares people, like grief and pain are sicknesses they might catch, if they get too close. So they tell themselves that they're not suited to the task, that someone else will come along, someone in a better position to help." What he didn't say—mostly because he thought the woman had been scared enough for one day— was that if someone *had* taken an active interest in her plight, they likely would have ended up making it worse for her, not better. After all, predators don't care how the gazelle got wounded, just so long as they can feast on its flesh.

She nodded, frowning. "Whatever the case, it took a while for me to get my senses back. Or at least enough of them to have a thought beyond terror. I didn't know where to go—my manse certainly isn't safe, and it seems that Ned's home isn't either. I remember you mentioning before that you stayed at the castle, and I thought it was my best hope."

"You were right to come," Ned said quickly, then winced, glancing apologetically at Chall and Maeve. Chall might have told the man not to bother—after all it wasn't as if he owned the place and thank the gods for that. He'd seen enough of kings and princes to know that being a royal wasn't all it was cracked up to be.

"Of course you were," Maeve said. "Now, I think it might be best if—" Before she could finish, there was a knock at the door. Maeve glanced around the room then moved to the door. She opened it slowly, her hand drifting inside her tunic once more, but as the door fully swung open it revealed a familiar figure standing in the hall.

Healer Malden was wearing his customary frown as he started past Maeve into the room. "What are you all part of some fool contest to see who can get hurt the most, that it?"

"If so, I'd say I'm winning," Chall said, offering the man a smile he did not return.

"Whatever else is wrong with you, Sir Challadius, it seems that your attackers did no damage to your humor." Then, in a voice almost too low to hear but not quite, "more's the pity. Now," he went on before Chall could respond, turning to Lady Valencia. "I'm assuming you are the reason I've been called?"

"Yes," Maeve answered for the noblewoman. "She was attacked."

The healer nodded, frowning at Chall. "Yes, it seems to be catching. Can you walk?" he asked Lady Valencia.

"Y-yes," she said uncertainly.

The healer nodded. "That is well. "I'm far too old to carry you."

"And I am too old to be carried," Lady Valencia said, raising an eyebrow.

The old healer grunted. "Very well, let us go to my quarters. I have more supplies there to ensure I can see to you properly."

"You don't have what you need in that bag of yours?" Chall asked, glancing at the tote the man held in one hand. "If not, why carry it?"

"For my health," the man said with such a straight face that Chall couldn't tell for sure whether he was joking or not.

"Well...sure, you would, wouldn't you?" he asked uncertainly.

Malden gave him a small smile, turning back to Lady Valencia. "Are you ready, my lady? I'll get one of the guards to assist you, if you'd like. I'm sure they'd be happy to take a break from holding down that piece of the hallway for a little while."

"That's quite alright, I think I can manage," the noblewoman said. She rose then, and despite her words she wavered, wincing in pain. Ned reached out a steadying hand, and the noblewoman glanced at him, smiling gratefully. "Before I go, I wonder...if I might stay at the castle? At least until we discover what exactly is happening and who's behind it. This is, believe it or not, the first time I've been bloodied with a man trying to kill me, and I must say I am not eager to relive the experience."

Ned glanced at Chall then, apparently deciding—rightfully so—that Maeve was the one with all the power, turned to her. Maeve nodded. "Of course, you can stay here," she told the woman. "We will figure out who is behind all of this and deal with it—I swear it."

Lady Valencia bowed her head. "It seems that, in your case, at least, the moniker holds. Maeve the Marvelous, indeed."

"This way, Lady," Malden said, stepping to the side and holding a hand out to the door. The noblewoman smiled, moving through it.

Malden paused for a moment, glancing around at each of them before his gaze settled on Chall. "Do endeavor, while I'm gone, to avoid anything sharp, won't you?"

"I guess knife juggling's out then?" Chall countered.

The old man grunted, glancing around at them again. "Well," he said, then he turned and, without another word, left.

"One can't help but wonder," Chall said after the door was closed once more, "why a man who so clearly hates people would choose to be a healer. Perhaps the torturers weren't recruiting?"

"What I wonder is why we were interrogating Val as if she were the one that attacked us," Ned said. He said "we," but by the way he was staring at his wife, Chall thought that his words were meant for her and her alone.

"Listen, Ned, it isn't that," Emille said. "I just...well, I know that she used to be your friend, but—"

"*Is* my friend," Ned countered.

"A friend who you haven't seen for what? Fifteen years?" Emille asked.

"So what?" Ned said. "So I haven't seen her in a while, so she's a criminal?"

"I never said that," his wife said. "It's just that..."

Ned sighed. "Look, Em, I should have told you sooner about Val, about all of it. I'm sorry about that—I really am. It was wrong of me. But I can promise you, Val and I are, were only *ever* just friends, nothing else. It wasn't—"

"Wait a minute," Emille said. "Do you think I'm *jealous?* Is that it?"

Ned cleared his throat, glancing at Chall for help, but Chall refused to meet his eyes. He'd gotten such looks, had heard similar tones from women before—more times than he'd like to count—and while he considered himself a loyal friend, only a fool would sign on to be a part of that if he didn't have to. "Well, I did..." the carriage driver said uncertainly, "but now, I'm thinking...that is..."

"I'm not *jealous,* Ned," she said. "The woman's thirty years older than you if she's a day. Anyway, you wouldn't be able to fool around without my knowing it."

"Good to know you trust me," the carriage driver grumbled.

Emille sighed, turning to him and taking his hands in hers where the two of them still sat at the table. "I *do* trust you, Ned. It's her I'm talking about. And it isn't even that I don't trust her, it's just that...well. Some of her story, it doesn't quite add up is all."

Ned grunted, clearly frustrated. He glanced at Chall—who still chose the coward's path of avoiding his gaze—then to Maeve. "Do you feel the same way?"

"Listen, Ned, no one is saying your friend is a bad person or anything like that, but it is true that some of her story seems a little...off," Maeve said.

"Oh?" he asked, offended. "And which part seems off to you, then? That black eye she's sporting? Just face paint, is that it? Or what about the fact that the bastard cut her finger off? Or maybe she did that to herself—you know, just for the fun of it? Maybe we can get hold of some of those torturers Chall was talking about, get them to ask her questions, how'd that be?"

"Sure," Emille said, sounding frustrated herself now, "or maybe we can ask her why she said she turned left down the alley by Sam's Bakery when you and I both well know that alley goes right."

"I don't know what difference that ma—"

"Or maybe we can ask the question of how a woman of her age has lived so long when she does things as foolish as going for a stroll along the city streets when she knows there are people hunting for her. Or perhaps she isn't a fool—perhaps she just possesses the naivety of a child, is that it?"

"Well, we can't all be assassins, can we?" Ned asked.

Emille recoiled as if he'd slapped her, looking almost physically pained at the carriage driver's words. A pain that, in another moment, turned to anger, and Chall was tempted—not for the first time since this argument had begun—to leap to his feet and run. The problem of course was that he'd been shot in one leg, stabbed in the other, and he wasn't in any danger of leaping anywhere anytime soon. Still, he hated seeing the couple at odds. Since he'd met them, he'd been impressed with how much they loved each other, how obvious that love was in every look, every word and touch. It wasn't that they constantly sat around blowing kisses at each other and competing in the age-old "I love you," "I love you more," debate. Instead it was that their love had seemed to infuse everything, was reflected in everything like the way a wood carver might make a thousand different objects but they would all still be made of wood.

To see the two of them angry made it feel to Chall as if the very ground beneath his feet had become unsteady. It was as if a man rose in the morning, stepping outside to greet the sun only to find that it had gone on holiday.

"Or here's another good question for you, Ned," Emille said, her jaw tensed. "Where's all the blood?"

"What blood?" he demanded.

"The blood from the man who attacked her," Maeve said quietly.

Ned turned to regard her with a frown. "What's that?"

"All I mean, Ned, is that I've stabbed a few people in my time—though I feel the need to say I always had a good reason. And if it happened as

Lady Valencia claims, if the man was on top of her when she stabbed him, then she would be covered in blood."

"You're joking, right?" Ned said. "I mean that...it's ridiculous. Probably she just got it mixed up, too distracted trying not to die, I'd guess, to take in all the details. But I suppose maybe later we can have her sit down and write a report about the whole damned thing, if that's what you want."

"Sure would come in handy," Emille said.

Ned frowned at his wife, but it was Maeve who spoke. "You're right, of course, Ned. Probably Lady Valencia just got the details mixed up. As you say, she had far more important things to worry about. We're not trying to say that your friend is a criminal or anything like tha—"

"Could have fooled me," Ned said.

Maeve went on as if the man hadn't spoken. "We're just trying to figure out what happened, that's all. The more we know about this Robert and his methods, the more likely we'll be able to stop him. We'll let Malden see to her, of course, but when she's alright, when she's on the mend, we'll want to question her further. Not because we think she's guilty of anything," she added quickly, "but simply because out of all the lies I was told as a child, and there were many, this one, at least, remains true: knowledge is power."

"Knowledge like whether she turned left or right?" Ned said, and Chall could hear the challenge in the man's voice.

"Yes, Ned," Emille said. "The facts matter. Which alleyway she turned down, sure, and also why she isn't covered in the man's blood. And if he was indeed on top of her, Ned, she would be."

"Well, I guess I'll just have to take your word on that," Ned said. "Not all of us can be assassins."

"No," Emille said, "or secret vigilantes bent on taking the law into our own hands."

Ned frowned. "That was a long time ago."

"Was it, Ned?" Emille asked. "Was it? Because it seems to me that whatever you and the others were doing back then, it's not finished yet."

The man hesitated at that. Chall figured he was probably having a hard time thinking of a counterpoint—mostly because there wasn't one. Robert

Palden was back—that much they all knew, for they had nearly all died at, if not his hands, then at least by his order, in the last few hours.

"I don't know why you're so defensive about this, Ned," Maeve said. "We're not trying to attack Lady Valencia—far from it. We're trying to help her, to try to help everyone in New Daltenia. Whatever the Wolves might have been once, whatever their purpose or their character, it is clear from what we've seen, from what you all have told me, that their purpose has changed and that character, though it might once have been fine, has been corrupted."

"Val's a friend," Ned said stubbornly.

"So was Robert, wasn't he?" Chall said. "Anyway, how good of a friend can she be, Ned? You haven't spoken to her in what? Fifteen years? Twenty?"

"Oh, it hasn't been that long," Ned said, glancing at his wife. He sighed, heavily. "See, Val and me—and sure, Robert, too—we weren't just...well. Coworkers. We were friends. Good friends. There was a time when we told everything to each other, shared every doubt, every fear, every triumph, too. Every bad thing and every good as passed between us. Good things," he went on, turning to look at Emille, "like a certain woman who caught a ride in my carriage, once. A certain woman who I thought—and still think, come to it—was the most amazing person I'd ever met."

Chall glanced at Maeve. "If he isn't talking about Emille, this is gonna get real awkward real fast." Maeve scowled, shushing him. Chall shushed. Not that it mattered much, for Emille didn't seem to have been paying him any mind. Instead she was looking at Ned.

"What are you saying, Ned?"

"What I'm saying is that I told Val about you. This woman I met. And had it not been for her, that's all you would have been to me. A woman I met once. As close to perfect as this world has on offer. I was scared, see. To talk to you, I mean, to pursue you...like that. And not just scared. I was...I guess maybe I was convinced—and part of me, more than a small one, still is—that you're too good for me. As far beyond me as a diamond is from the dirt it's found in."

"Or a bird is from a worm," Chall offered.

"Anyway," Ned went on as if he hadn't spoken, "point is it was Val that convinced me to give it a shot anyway. I'll never forget what she told me—she said that a man who is always focused on who he was or even who he is will never have a chance to become who he's supposed to be." He gave a small grin. "And she said that diamonds look good with a little bit of dirt on 'em."

Chall still thought his worm one was better, but judging by her face and the way she looked at her husband, Emille might have disagreed.

She took both her husband's hands in hers, meeting his gaze. "So that's why you're so defensive? Because you think that without her, without Lady Valencia, we never would have been together?"

"I know we wouldn't have," Ned said simply. "I wouldn't have had the courage without Val."

"Oh, I wouldn't be so sure, Ned," Emille said. "There's a...coworker of mine who is a fine shot with a bow. The finest I've ever seen. I've seen him hit targets with arrows at a distance so great I could barely see the stuffed dummy he aimed at. He saw it though, each time, and each time he fired the arrows made their way unerringly to his mark. As if they could do nothing else. As if they were destined to find their way there, no matter what."

Ned smiled. "Like us."

"Like us," she agreed.

"Alright," Ned said. "I guess my only question, then, is who gets to be the arrow and who's the poor stuffed bastard."

"Oh, Ned," his wife said, "I think you know that well enough."

He grunted, grinning. "Yeah, I guess maybe I do." He sighed, looking around at each of them. "I'm sorry for actin' a fool. I do that, sometimes. Most times, I guess."

"Think nothing of it," Maeve said. "I'll speak with his Majesty about Lady Valencia staying here. I don't think it should be an issue."

"You sure?" Ned asked. "I only ask because, before, we all decided it wasn't exactly safe here."

"Safer here than your place, anyway," Chall said. "Safer than hers, too."

Ned grunted. "Suppose that's true enough."

"So if Val's squared away, what's next?"

"For you?" Maeve said. "Rest. I'd say that, for the time being, at least, you're done cavorting with criminals."

"But damnit, Maeve, you know I love my cavorting," Chall said.

"Cute," she said. "I wonder if you'll make a cute corpse, too."

He winced, not sure whether to take that as a warning or a threat. Likely both. "Right. No more cavorting. But what else? That bastard Robert, not to mention that *other* bastard Catham, they're both still out there somewhere. I might not know exactly what they're up to, but I'd say it's a fair bet that whatever it is, we aren't going to like it."

"They need to be found, it's true," Ned said, frowning. "But it's a damned big city. I can do some more lookin' through the Wolves' old hide-outs, but Robert's no fool—I don't expect he'll be so stupid as to use one me or Val know about. Might be better to come at it from that other bastard's angle, then, Catham. And to that end, I think we ought to talk to that friend of yours."

"Priest, do you mean?" Maeve asked.

"He means Valden," Chall said, and again the words were out of his mouth before he was even aware he was going to speak at all.

"Fine," Maeve said, looking at him with an expression that was a mixture of sadness and disbelief. "Valden, then. Where is he anyway?"

Chall sighed, shaking his head. "I have no idea."

CHAPTER EIGHT

EVEN BEFORE VALDEN could see his destination, he could smell it. Blood and offal, rotting meat and urine. He had stood on battlefields that smelled sweeter.

That was likely why several of New Daltenia's tanneries were positioned at the edge of the city. Vital establishments, the same way that the butchers situated nearby were vital, but not establishments anyone wanted to spend any time around. Everyone loved steak, it was true, but few people wanted to be present when the cow was butchered.

Needless to say, this part of the city wasn't likely to host the next noble's ball or banquet. A place that people naturally avoided, whenever possible, a place people would, in fact, go to great lengths to avoid. Which made it just about the best place to go if you were, say, a crime boss whose organization had just suffered a terrible attack. A place to hideout, a place where if any strangers *did* come looking, they would be easy enough to spot. After all, it wasn't as if there were a bunch of innocents meandering about that one might hide among.

Of course, that didn't mean Willy had told the truth—a man like Willy only told the truth when there was no other option and sometimes not even then. There was no guarantee that there wasn't an ambush set up, waiting for Valden to stumble into it. Such an ambush was unlikely, of course—when would the man have had a chance to set it up? But unlikely didn't mean impossible. For all Valden knew, Willy had several such places in the city that he would send anyone who became a problem, like bear traps laid out and waiting to be stepped in.

Again, unlikely, but then while Willy was just about the least trustworthy person in the world—if Valden was hanging from a cliff and the conman was the only one available to save him, he'd let go and trust the cliff—the man *was* resourceful. It was the reason he was still alive when there were plenty of people in New Daltenia who would have preferred him as a corpse.

So, with that in mind, Valden took his time, walking slowly down the street. The smell seemed to grow stronger with each step he took. No place to have a pleasant stroll, but he had come here, to this place, with a purpose, to find out the truth of what was happening so that he might protect his friends. He would not be swayed from that purpose—certainly not by a foul smell nor by any trap, real or imagined.

He made his way past several tanneries to a building at the end of a dead-end street. The sign hanging from the front proclaimed it a butcher's shop, but then Valden thought that whoever had hung it had wasted their time. After all, the smell did a fine enough job of marking the place for what it was—a butcher's or, he supposed, a mass grave. Likely either would have smelled about the same.

Valden paused, staring at that shop, frowning. This, then, was the building Willy had told him about, the building where the conman priest had said Valden would find Nadia. But no guards stood out front, as Valden might have expected. Not even a homeless man or a passed-out but not truly so-passed-out drunk who might have been a concealed guard. There was nothing, no one. Only the butcher's shop in front of him, as quiet and silent as could be.

Valden hesitated but only for a moment before he walked up and knocked on the door. He waited for several seconds, and when no answer came, he knocked again.

"*We're closed,*" a voice called from inside.

Valden knocked a third time.

He heard a curse from beyond the door, some mumbled words too low for him to hear, and in another moment the door opened partway to reveal a man in a white apron, stained with blood, frowning at him. He was a big man, but out of shape, Valden saw, with a protruding belly pressing against the apron he wore and large arms that Valden thought would have once been muscle but had now largely gone to fat. "Well?" the man demanded. "What do you want then? If it's meat you're after, you'll have to wait for tomorrow. But if it's blood you're lookin' for…" He paused, glancing down at his crimson-smeared apron before meeting Valden's eyes and giving him a small grin. "Well, might be we can oblige."

"Perhaps another time," Valden said. "I've come to see her."

"The heifer what's responsible for this bit of mess on my dress, do you mean?" the man said, glancing down at his bloody apron again. "Well, now I'm afraid there's not much left of her to see."

"That's not who I mean, but then I think you know that."

The man grinned. "Sorry. Bit of butcher's humor."

"Funny, too," Valden said, watching the man.

The man watched him back for several seconds then grunted. "This 'she' you're talkin' about, the one you're tryin' to find—you sure she's in the mood to be found?"

"It seems to me that everyone can use another friend."

"That what you are, then? A friend showin' up in the middle of the night making demands?"

Valden gave a small shrug. "I'm not the one covered in blood."

The man grinned again, less an expression of amusement as much as a bearing of his teeth. "Not yet," he said. "That's the thing about walkin' into a butcher's, and *this* butcher's in particular—sometimes blood gets on a man without him meanin' for it to."

"I'll take my chances."

"You sure?" the man asked, raising an eyebrow, and Valden noted, as he did, a speck of blood on his forehead. "You seem like a nice enough fella, and some folks, well, they think they want a thing right up until they get it. Understand what I'm saying?"

"I understand," Valden said, "and I appreciate the warning, but I came here for a reason, and that reason has not changed."

The other man grunted. "Seems to me that, often times, a man's reasons get in the way of his reason, if you catch my meanin'. But, in the end, a fella is the one who decides how he'll live his life—or how he'll lose it, as the case may be." He shrugged. "You wait here—I'll check in the back, see if I misplaced this 'she' you're lookin' for, how'd that be?"

"That will be fine."

The man nodded. "And, one more thing—if you end up decidin' to leave or, well, anythin' else that requires movin', best you do it slow, alright? Wouldn't want to alarm...well. Anyone that might be watchin'."

"Alright."

The man waited another moment then sighed, giving a small shrug as if to say that he'd tried, then he closed the door.

Valden waited, but he did not watch the door. Instead, he turned, watching the street. After all, he'd spent enough time around predators to know that, more often than not, they came on their prey when it wasn't looking, when it was too distracted with something else. By the time such prey became aware of its danger, it was too late.

He could hear faint sounds of conversation from within the butcher's, too low to make out the words, too low for them to sound like anything other than inarticulate growls as the butcher spoke with someone. After a few minutes, the door opened again, and the butcher regarded him. "Sorry, fella, what did you say your name was again?"

"I didn't. But it's Valden."

The butcher blinked at that, his face paling. "That wouldn't be the same Valden used to traipse around New Daltenia some years ago, was it? The one they call 'Vicious'?"

"I am he, but I was never known for traipsing."

"No," the man said, clearing his throat. "No, I suppose not. I think, that is, I wonder if you'd wait another minute? While I...check on something?"

"Take your time," Valden said.

The man flashed him a nervous smile then the door closed again.

Valden waited.

When he'd spoken to Willy, he'd reminded the man of some of the traits scouts and archers, like Valden himself, often possessed. A keen eye was a big one, but it wasn't the only one. There was also patience. And not just patience, not just an ability to wait, but an ability to wait and remain vigilant for extended periods of time, as he did now. If Nadia was indeed inside the butcher's, she was no likely on edge—watching several dozen of her people...well, *butchered* would have no doubt had that effect. She knew Valden, they had a past, but that didn't mean that she would think that they—or he—needed to have a future. All it would take would be one word from her and death would come for him like an arrow shot from the bow of a well-trained archer.

So he waited. Vigilantly.

In less than five minutes the door opened for the third time, once more revealing the butcher. "Listen," the man said, "I'm sorry. About before, I mean. I didn't mean nothin' by it. You might not remember this, but we've met."

"Oh?"

"It was a long time ago," the butcher said, patting his protruding gut that pressed tight against the apron, "lot of pounds ago, too. You went to uh...see my brother-in-law. Had a...well, I guess you'd call it a meetin' with him."

"I see. How is he?" Valden asked, trying to be polite despite the fact that he was in a hurry and had wasted plenty enough time already trying to find Nadia.

"Well...he's dead," the man said, looking at him strangely. "Don't get me wrong—I don't blame you or hold nothin' against you, nothin' like that. I don't know what business brought you to his door, and frankly I don't give a shit. That bastard was beatin' on my sister—my nephew, too. So bad the little fella couldn't walk one time. He's far more useful as worm food than he ever was walkin' around among the livin'. Makes a man curious, though. This 'she' you came to see—you plannin' on havin' a similar conversation with her as you had with my brother-in-law?"

"I didn't come for trouble."

The man watched him for a second, as if trying to determine the truth of his words. Finally, he nodded. "Well, here's to hopin' you don't find it. If you'll follow me, I'll show you to her. Just don't mind the blood."

"I never do."

The butcher's face twitched at that, and he nodded, moving into the shop. He led Valden past shelves where different cuts and kinds of meat had been packed and preserved, ready to be sent out to various mercantiles throughout the city to a door behind the counter. The door opened up into a small room with shelves littered with what appeared to be ledgers and files. The butcher walked past these to another door at the end of the small room, opening it and stepping through. No sooner had the door swung wide than the smell of dead flesh and blood assaulted Valden's senses, washing over him like some massive wave. The butcher paused in the doorway, glancing back at him. "Good? Sometimes there's a bit of a smell—can be a little off-putting to folks who aren't used to it."

"I've dealt with worse."

The man gave him a single nod. "Right. This way then."

The butcher led him into a back room where, judging by the smell and the meat hooks depending from the ceiling, much of the bloodier business was done. The man gave him a quick nod before turning and leaving again. Valden was left standing and regarding the two men flanking the door at the back of the room. The first was a man Valden recognized from when he and Chall had visited Nadia at Florence's some time ago, before Catham had tried to have him and Chall killed. The man standing by the door had, the last time Valden had seen him, been pretending at unconsciousness, wielding a crossbow with a poisoned bolt and preparing to give Valden and Chall the last welcome they'd ever get.

Valden recognized him alright, even recognized the small crossbow dangling from his belt, though it had to be said that the jagged cut down one cheek—recent, by the look of it—and the bandaged forearm were new additions. "I never got your name last time," he said.

"Won't be gettin' it this time either," the man said. "I'm cagey that way."

"I imagine I could find it easily enough, if I had the need."

"I imagine you could," the man agreed. "So what, then? You lookin' for a friend, that it?"

"The gods know I don't need any more enemies."

"Now that is one sentiment we can agree on."

Valden nodded slowly, letting his gaze travel over the man's bandaged arm, over his bloody cheek. "Tough night?"

"Not the toughest I've had and that not by a sight. Anyway, it ain't over yet."

Valden let his gaze move to the other man. He didn't know him, had never seen him before, yet he recognized him at once—a killer. A man who, on another night, in another place, might have been the source of untold misery and pain for some unfortunate soul or souls. But not tonight. Tonight, there was a thick bandage on the side of the man's head covering his ear—not that Valden thought there was any ear left, judging by the amount of blood that had seeped through. The man stood oddly, too, hunkered over slightly, and Valden thought that as bad as the ear looked, it was far from the worst of his injuries. The men had made it away from whatever had befallen the others at Flo's, but they had certainly not done so unscathed.

They were killers—there was no telling how much pain and grief they had caused the citizens of New Daltenia. Like lions slinking in the tall grass of the savannah, here, in the city, such men were the predators, and while their potential prey hid not in warrens and burrows but in their homes, they were much the same as those always-hungry lions. But just then, Valden thought that their potential prey could rest easy knowing that for tonight, at least, their would-be hunters were far too worried about protecting their own hides to cause them any harm.

They did their best to hide it, but Valden had a lot of experience reading people, understanding them—first as a criminal and even more as a priest. And so he could see the fear in their gazes, could not help but notice the slightest tremble in the silent one's jaw. They weren't just afraid, he decided. They were terrified. Whatever they had seen at the brothel had left more than just a physical mark, that much was clear.

"I need to speak to her," he told the talker of the two.

"I don't get paid to see to what you need," the man said. "Still..." He paused, shrugging. "She said she'd see you, and the boss is the boss." He frowned slightly at his own words. A micro-expression that was gone as quickly as it had come, as was the troubled, considering look that crossed his eyes, but not gone so fast that Valden didn't note it, and not so fast that he didn't know what it meant. Nadia was the boss—for now, at least. But queens without kingdoms rarely fared well, and if a person really wanted to stab someone in the back, the best time to do it was when they were recovering from fighting someone else. Nadia and her kingdom, such as it was, was weak—Valden needed only to take in the two men she had set to guard her to know that much. And weak kingdoms, like weak creatures, drew hungry beasts.

"Come on," the man said. "The boss is this way."

He opened the door and led Valden into a small storeroom. Shelves stood on either side of the room, and a small table sat at its center, unremarkable at first glance, yet Valden found himself frowning. It sat slightly unevenly.

"Careful, fella," the talker of the two men told him. "You notice a lot. Too much, maybe. Some beasts don't bite until you see 'em."

Valden said nothing to that, only waited as the man nodded to his companion and they set about the task of lifting the table and moving it over. As they did, what had caught Valden's gaze became more obvious as the table's absence revealed what had to be the outline of a trapdoor. Whoever had built the hatch had clearly done so with an eye to concealment, and, to that end, had done a fine job, but as he had told Willy, a scout who missed things was not very useful at all and, likelier than not, destined for an early death.

The speaker of the two knelt, grabbing hold of a hinge that had been almost—but not quite—hidden, pulling it back so that part of what had been the floor opened onto a ladder. "Her Majesty will see you," he told Valden.

Valden stared down at the ladder. He couldn't see much of where it led save for that the ground below appeared to be hard-packed dirt. He met the man's gaze, trying to decide if it was a trap, for if he wasn't careful the ladder might well lead to his death. Either at Nadia's order or not—after all, the woman had already been betrayed once by Catham, it could easily happen again. That was the thing about criminals—they were not known for their loyalty.

"Well, go on then," the man said. "After you. Or do you have a thing about ladders?"

"Something like that," Valden said. He gave the man's companion a look, then he started down the ladder.

It was a short ladder and so it did not take Valden long to reach the bottom of what, as it turned out, proved to be a small cellar. A small desk sat against an earthen wall and behind that desk sat Nadia. The crime boss scowled at him over a sheaf of paper, a quill in one hand, and a small crossbow in the other. Looking at it, he saw that it was of similar make to the one her guard carried belted at his waist and one, he suspected, that bore a similar poison along its bolt tip.

"Valden," she said.

"Nadia," he said back. "Quite a welcome," he went on, glancing at the crossbow with its bolt pointed directly at him, imagining that he could see the poison glistening on its tip.

"You'll forgive me if I'm rude," the crime boss said, "but I was paid another visit recently—tonight, in fact, and that visitor was not, I'm afraid, of the friendly variety."

"I know," Valden said. "I went by Flo's."

"Not Flo's anymore," Nadia said. "Flo's dead, along with a good chunk of my crew."

"I'm sorry."

"Are you, Valden? Are you really?" she hissed, and in those few words, in the anger that flashed in her eyes, Valden could see just how much the night's events had affected her. "I only ask," she went on, "because most people, they don't think much of us. Ruffians and scoundrels, criminals all. Better off dead, they suppose." Nadia paused, apparently realizing she'd been, if not screaming, then certainly approaching it. She took a slow, deep breath, seeming to regain some small semblance of her usual, unflappable demeanor. She shrugged. "Maybe they're right. Perhaps they were not good people—shit, who am I kidding? Good people don't last long in this world of ours, even if they did somehow stumble their way in. But while they might not have been good men, they were *my* men."

"I understand."

"Do you?" she asked. "I was there, Valden—having a drink, thinking maybe to relax for a bit, if you can believe it. I *saw* what happened, what that bastard did, and I'm not sure I understand it." There was a clicking sound, and they both looked down to see that Nadia's hand which held the quill was trembling slightly, causing the instrument to tap against the desk. She let out a snarl, tossing the quill onto the desktop and spattering ink on the paper lying there.

"What a damned night," she said, shaking her head. "I tell you, Vicious, I never wanted this—to take Belle's spot. At least not most of me. Maybe there was a part of me, a small part—the fool part—that thought I could do it, that might have even been excited."

"And now?"

She looked at her hand, still trembling slightly, then clutched it into an angry fist, raising her gaze to meet his. "Now I'm just tired. And angry. And...damn but I hate to admit it, but I'm scared." In her eyes, he could see the truth of that last. "I've seen a lot in my time, Vicious. Seen men do stuff to each other that'd haunt most folks' nightmares for years. I've even done some small bit of that stuff myself. It's all about how you look at a thing, you know? Putting distance between you and it even when it's right up on you. That doesn't make sense, maybe, but that's the best way I know to explain it. Not that I guess I need to explain it to someone like you. I reckon your soul's as black as mine."

Valden said nothing to that, for it didn't seem to be needed. She sighed. "Anyway, my point is, I'm not new to this. To violence, to the darker side of the world, the one most folks never see. I've seen it—shit, I've spent most of my life living in it. I know well what a dead body looks like, the sounds it makes, just as I've tasted my own blood and that more than once. I've seen —and committed—horrors that the drunks in their taverns, telling their tales, can hardly even dream about. I have witnessed horrors so dark as to eclipse even those nightmares which haunt the dreams of the pampered nobles in their fancy manses. But I have never, Vicious, not in all my life—a life full of dark shit and little else—seen anything so dark, so terrifying as that which I saw tonight. In truth, I see it still."

"I was not there for it happening, but I saw the aftermath," Valden said. "Who was it? A rival gang?"

A sneer came across the woman's face then, but it didn't last long before it was replaced by a look of abject fear as the woman's eyes took on a distant look and she appeared to be reliving what had happened at the brothel. "I don't know who he was," she said in the sort of hushed, quiet tone a child might use when hiding under the covers with her brother or sister, both of them sure that, beyond the confines of their impromptu tent, monsters roamed. "I have never seen him before, that's the truth," she said, "and I'll tell you this, Vicious—I'm not a praying woman. I figure that the gods, if they exist, would have given up on me a long time ago. But I pray to all the gods, to any god who will listen, that I don't ever see that bastard again."

"Who do you mean? The leader of those that came?"

Nadia let out a grunting sound that was somewhere between a laugh and a sob. "He wasn't leading anyone, Vicious. There wasn't anyone to lead. Just him...gods help me, just him."

"Wait..." Valden said, confused. "Are you saying that all that I saw at Flo's, all the dead, they were the work of one man?"

"I don't know that I would call him a man," she said, and there was a tremor in her voice too, now. "A demon, maybe. Some creature sent from the pit to punish the living."

"That sounds...pretty dramatic," Valden said.

She gave him a smile without humor. "It felt pretty dramatic, too. I don't mind telling you that. Felt pretty damned dramatic watching him do what he did. You weren't there, Vicious. I was, and I'm telling you, that bastard, whoever he was, he went through my men—hard men, men with steel inside and out—like they were children out for a lark. Went at them like a lion finding himself in a nest of bunny rabbits and my, but how the fur did fly. And blood...that flew too. He didn't just kill them. He tore them apart. But then I don't have to tell you. If you were at Flo's then you know.

What he did, what he left behind, well, it isn't the sort of thing a person's likely to miss, is it?"

"No," Valden said, remembering the massacre at the brothel. "No, it isn't. But how...how is such a thing possible? No single man could do such a thing." That last statement Valden could say with some confidence. After all, he had spent years traveling and fighting with the Crimson Prince, the man who was widely regarded as the most brutal, savage, and dangerous killer to walk the face of the world, at least in recent memory and perhaps ever. And for all his incredible strength, for all his formidable will, Valden did not think that even Prince Bernard could have wreaked such havoc as he'd seen, and that even with the Breaker of Pacts in his hands. To think that a single man could have wrought such devastation was no less diffi-cult to believe than watching such a man suddenly sprout wings and fly off into the sunset.

"You don't believe me," Nadia said, watching him. She shrugged. "I can't blame you. I don't suppose I'd believe me either. After all, I've spent quite a bit of my life around killers—far more than is healthy—and none of 'em capable of what this fella did. Yet that doesn't change the fact that he *did* do it. I don't know the how, and I don't pretend to. But he did. And the lads, they didn't just stand there and let it happen, either. A fella breaks into Flo's, starts causing a problem, well they're trained to deal with that sort of thing, aren't they? Got tools for just such a job. And they used 'em. Swords and knives, crossbows, even a few chairs. They used them all. But this bastard, whoever he was, didn't care. I know a lot of those blows landed—I *saw* them land. And I also saw the son of a bitch heal from them in an instant, the wounds glowing green like some, some damned...well. I don't know. I saw him get all manner of shot and stabbed but it didn't even so much as slow him down. He just kept right on killing, butchering his way toward me."

"He came for you?"

"Oh, sure he did," she said. "That much I'm confident of, mostly because he told me. This was at first, before all the killing started. I was out having a drink, as I said, when the bastard strolled in as if he didn't have a care in the world. Gave some speech about how we were all a blight on the world. About how the world would be better off when we weren't in it. Told me that my death was just the beginning. Said that wolves were always hungry." She gave her head an angry shake. "Some nonsense like that. I figured maybe he was some fool trying to cash in on the Crimson Wolves' legacy."

Valden stared at her, his own breath quickening in his chest. "This man, what did he look like?"

She gave him a smile without humor. "You mean before he was covered in my men's blood?"

"Yes."

She considered that, shaking her head again. "Like nothing much. To be honest, he looked like a pretty good mark. Small, unassuming, some gray in his hair. Looked like he might have been a clerk, though I've never seen a clerk fight like that, never seen a clerk do the things he did." She took a slow, shuddering breath. "Never seen anybody do the things he did." She frowned. "But judging by that frown on your face, I'm thinking maybe you have."

Valden shook his head distractedly, his thoughts racing. "No, I...I haven't seen anyone do anything like that, but..."

"But you think you might know who my night-time visitor was, is that it?" she asked. "You might know the identity of my hungry wolf? Because that, Vicious, is something I would very much like to know."

"Maybe," he said.

"Then maybe, Vicious, you can tell me what you know or what you *think* you know, and you and I can remain civil."

Valden made a show of looking around the small cellar—it didn't take long. "With respect, Nadia, I don't know that you're in a position to make threats."

The woman smiled. Only, it wasn't really a smile as much as it was a simple bearing of the teeth. "Careful, Vicious. I may be backed into a corner, but then, it isn't the first time. Seems I've spent most of my life in one corner or another. And this, at least, I share with wolverines—my teeth are no less sharp because of it. And I think that you know as well as I that beasts are rarely more dangerous, rarely more fierce, than when they've nowhere left to run."

She said it convincingly, threateningly, but then Valden had seen the devastation at Flo's. A person—even a tough-as-nails person like Nadia—didn't walk away from that sort of thing unscathed. Not physically—as evidenced by the scratches and bruises she bore—and certainly not emotionally. Witnessing a massacre on that scale could not help but leave an impression. Besides, her threat was considerably less effective than it might have been even a day ago. After all, a good portion of the woman's crew of murderers lay dead. Considering what he'd seen at Flo's, the last thing she needed was another enemy. But there was another thing she hadn't mentioned about beasts backed into corners—they were unpredictable.

So, instead of pointing out her precarious position, he decided to take a different approach. "Listen, Nadia, we both have problems right now, and I'd say that, with all that's going on, the last thing we need is to be at each other's throats."

"Not when there are so many other beasties roaming around eager to take a bite, that it, Vicious?"

"Exactly."

She took a slow, deep breath. "Perhaps it is true that, considering the night's events, I am not so flush with friends that I could not use another. Tell me, Vicious, is that what we are? Friends?"

"No, not friends," he said. "But we might be allies."

She gave him a small smile, this one genuine. "You are honest, at least. I'd blame the priesthood for that failing, but then you always have been one of the few honest people who take up our trade, haven't you, Vicious?"

That didn't seem to require a response, so he gave none. She watched him for a moment then sighed. "Very well, Vicious. We will try it your way; only remember that just because the wolverine does not show its teeth, that doesn't mean it doesn't have them. And now that the pleasantries are out of the way, why don't you tell me what brings you to my door? After all, I assume that if that shit-show at Flo's didn't persuade you to drop it then it must be important."

"Yes."

"Well, go on then," she said, waving her hand. "It's been a long night, Vicious, and it doesn't look to be ending anytime soon—at least, that is, unless one of my crew makes a move, kills me, and takes my spot."

"You think they would try so soon?"

She shrugged. "I think that a wounded beast draws scavengers. Flies that'd be happy to eat shit most days but that will rouse themselves to feast, if they see an opportunity. Now, go on—tell me what's on your mind."

"Catham," Valden said.

Nadia frowned. "The Coward? What do you want with him?"

The Coward. Most knew Catham as Catham the Cautious—or, according to the carriage driver, Ned, the Clever, too. Both fit, but then so, too, did Coward. Not that many people said it, for while Catham was always careful, always cautious, people who crossed him, as a general rule, tended to end up dead shortly after. Nadia outranked him in the criminal underworld, of course, but then that didn't mean she would set herself against the man lightly. The fact that she used the unflattering moniker spoke volumes to Valden and helped inform what he said next.

He found himself thinking of Catham trying to kill him and Chall, not to mention the dead serving girl in the castle. Catham might not have done that directly, but he was definitely involved, that much was obvious, for it was clear that he was working for this Robert Palden. "You ask what I want with him?" he said, meeting her eyes. "I'll tell you—I want to kill him."

She raised an eyebrow. "Careful, Vicious, or they'll take your white robe. That sounded a lot more sinner than saint, if you ask me, and I ought to know."

"It was gray," he said.

"Sorry?"

"My robe—it was gray. Anyway, that's why I came—*he's* why I came. When we left you last, Catham tried to kill me and my companion. He very nearly succeeded. It was a good trap, neatly laid, and it was luck, not skill, that saw us clear of it." In point of fact, it had been Ned, the carriage driver, displaying that he was an Empath, a magical talent that, according to

Chall, was among the rarest in the world that had saved them, but then, ally or not, he didn't think Nadia needed to know that.

She frowned, nodding, her eyes narrowed angrily. "Yes, the Coward is always careful, and he doesn't take a step without being confident of where his stride will take him. If he moved on you, it was because he was as sure as sure could be that when the moving was done there wouldn't be any risk of you retaliating."

"Right," Valden said. "Anyway, I don't think that's all of it. He's working for the Wolves."

"The Crimson Wolves? You said something about them the last time we spoke too. Are you sure you're not just seeing ghosts, Vicious? After all, it's been nearly twenty years since the Wolves have been around. If there's any left I'd say they're fairly long in the tooth by now."

"Maybe so, but even an old wolf can bite," he countered. "But you tell me, Nadia—was it a ghost that walked into Flo's tonight?"

She frowned. "You're saying that bastard was one of these new Wolves?"

"Not a new Wolf—an old one. *The* Wolf, in fact. The one that began it all." Again, he decided to leave Ned out of it. Keeping the carriage driver's identity a secret wouldn't hurt the crime boss but not keeping it might well hurt the carriage driver.

"You mean that mad bastard that did that to my crew was one of those vigilante sons of bitches?"

"Yes."

She shook her head. "That can't be though, can it? The Wolves, they were dangerous, sure, but the man I saw, Vicious, he wasn't just dangerous. He didn't kill just to get the thing done—he enjoyed it. I'm sure I saw the mad bastard smiling and that more than once."

"The Wolves are not what they once were," he said.

She nodded grimly. "And Catham the Coward, he's somehow mixed up with this bastard, that's what you're telling me?"

"He works for him," Valden said. "Or so it seems."

She bared her teeth then, anger flashing in her eyes, and despite her dangerous situation, despite her age, Valden thought that, just then, all the caution in the world wouldn't have saved Catham if he was within her reach. "Well, that explains a few things," she said.

"Like what?"

She scowled, staring at him. "Like why so many of my operations have been failing, lately. Merchandise disappearing, *men* disappearing, and a thousand other things. Almost as if, I don't know, someone on the inside were behind it." She shook her head. "I thought it was Nate, the poor bastard I was...*speaking* with before, when you visited me at Flo's. Guess I was wrong."

"I suppose you owe him an apology then."

"Wouldn't do him much good," she said. "Some folks—priests, maybe—are all about forgiveness, all about giving people another shot. But, sad to say, in my line of work you can't afford to hand out second chances. Anyway, the types of folks I spend my time around are a long way from those penitent parishioners with their heads bowed so low they scrape the floor. If they stab you in the back once and you let it go, they're learnin' a lesson, alright, but it ain't the one you're teachin'. They won't learn not to betray you—they'll only learn to do it better. So better that, the next time, you might not see the knife until you feel it. Even if you do catch it, it don't make no difference—show weakness in my line of work, and you can bet your ass that the blade is comin'. If not from the bastard that tried you the first time, then from someone else. Let it slide, you're givin' 'em all permission, see?"

"You're saying you killed him," Valden said.

"If it's mercy you're lookin' for, Vicious, you ought to have stayed with the priests with their big churches and fancy prayers. You won't see a lot of white robes here—they don't stay clean for long."

"It was gray," he said, unable to keep the anger and disgust from his voice at the woman casually admitting that she'd killed a man who had turned out to be, if not innocent, at least not guilty of the crime for which she had condemned him and showing no remorse.

"I see that I've offended your delicate sensibilities," she said. "Well, I suppose I'll weep later. For now, though, I don't think either of us has the time to spare. If what you're sayin' about Catham is true then things are a lot worse than I thought, and there's a lot more to worry about than a few corpses."

Valden found himself frowning. He knew that he needed Nadia if he wanted to have any chance of figuring out where Catham was, what he— and thereby Robert Palden and the re-instituted Wolves—was up to. Yet despite that, he found himself angry at her casual disregard for those men and women who even now lay dead at Florence's brothel. They had been criminals, one and all, men and women who had spent their lives preying on those weaker than them, yet her easy acceptance of their deaths struck him just the same. "That's pretty cold, isn't it? Considering that those men and women died protecting you."

"What would you have me do, Vicious? Shed a few tears? Bury my head in my hands and do a bit of sobbin'? Would that make you happy? Would it put the blood back in their bodies? Put the beat back in their hearts? They're dead, that's all, and all the carryin' on in the world ain't gonna change that."

"That's it, then?" Valden asked. "Some of them, they served you for years, and that's all they get?"

"What else is there?" she said. "The dead are notoriously bad with gifts, Vicious. Spit on their grave or weep over it, you'll water the ground just the same and no difference at all to the dead. It don't matter. What *does* is that that weasel Catham knows too much. Enough that, if he's a mind to, he can make a right mess of things for me and my operations. Which means I have to be on damage control."

"Don't tell me you trusted him with important information."

She snorted. "I don't trust my own mother to do the right thing, Vicious, and she's been dead going on thirty years. Of course I didn't trust him, but that don't mean he doesn't know where some of the bodies are buried—after all, he was the one that put a lot of 'em there. He doesn't know everything, but the bastard knows enough to cause problems which means I have to tend to some matters, not least of which is hunting down that traitorous sack of shit and getting some of the lads to poke a few holes in him, see what comes out. Sorry to say that means we're goin' to have to cut this little chat of ours short. Now, if there's nothing else—"

"I'm not finished."

The woman's eyes narrowed at that, and Valden was reminded of her talk of animals backed into corners and how their teeth lost none of their sharpness. "Not yet, Vicious," she said quietly, "but you're coming damned close. This might not be much of a kingdom we're in, but you can bet your ass that I'm the queen of it. Here, I decide when we're finished, not you. Just like it's me who decides who walks out of here and who's carried—if you get my meanin'."

It would have been pretty hard to miss, but then Valden had come for a reason and he didn't mean to give it up, not yet. "Catham," he said. "I need to know where to find him."

"I imagine the same place you find any weasel—cowering in one burrow or another."

"That's not good enough."

"Careful, Vicious. I've had a long, trying night, and my patience isn't good at the best of times. There's folks that'd tell you as much...if they could."

"I need to know where Catham is—it's why I came."

"And here I thought you just came for the pleasure of my company." He only stared at her, and she frowned, raising an eyebrow. "Oh, I wouldn't worry too much on it, Vicious. Maybe things didn't go exactly how you expected when you came here, but what a fella needs to remind himself of, from time to time, is that while things might not have gone exactly his way, they could always go worse. Anyway, the truth of the matter is I don't know where that bastard Catham is, so I couldn't tell you even if I was of a mind to."

"Maybe not, but you have an idea of where to start looking. Or maybe an idea of someone that might know where he is."

"Maybe I do and maybe I don't," she said. "I don't see what difference that is to you. But if it helps you sleep, know that when I find that oily little eel, I mean to peel his skin back, see what's underneath." She finished the last in a growl and despite her calm façade—betrayed only by the slight tremor in her hands—Valden could see that she was indeed angry. Furious.

"And I wish you all the luck," he told her, "but I need to speak to him before...before you start peeling. I've got questions that need answering." Questions like why had an assassin come to the castle, sneaking around the king's quarters and murdering an innocent serving woman. Questions like why Catham had thought to kill him and Chall and what Robert Palden was planning.

"Well, we all need something, don't we, Vicious?" Nadia asked, pulling him out of his thoughts. "Like air in our lungs, say. But then it seems to me that you're askin' a whole lot without offerin' anything in return. Tell you what, how's this? You tell me where I can find that son of a bitch that wrecked Flo's, and I'll be sure to let you ask your questions of Catham before I do...well, what it is I mean to do."

"I don't know where he is."

"Then I'm afraid, Vicious, that while I do so enjoy your company, it seems we have run out of things to talk about." She glanced at the trap door, raising her voice. *"Aubrey, our visitor's ready to leave."*

The trap door opened and one of the two guards stepped down the ladder. As he did, Valden saw that it was the man he'd spoken with at the door, the one who'd refused to give him his name.

The man frowned at him as if he knew what he was thinking. "It's a boy's name, too."

"Of course," Valden said, keeping his face expressionless.

The man's eyes narrowed, then he turned to Nadia. "Want me to escort him out back, boss?"

The woman gave a small smile, her eyes traveling to Valden then back to the man. "That won't be necessary, Aubrey—the front will do well enough."

Judging by the disappointed look on the man's face, Valden thought that "the back" was code for something considerably more sinister than it sounded, and that the man had actually been asking if Nadia wanted to add one more corpse to the night's tally. Another person that wanted him dead, then—a new name to add to a list that, as far as he could tell, was growing pretty cramped. Still, he found himself dismissing the man, at least for the moment, for he had greater concerns. "The man, the one who attacked Flo's, I can't tell you where he is."

"So you've said, Vicious, now if there's nothing else—"

"But I can tell you *who* he is."

That got her attention, and Valden couldn't help but notice the gleam in her eyes, one brought on, he suspected, by thoughts of what she would do to the man when she found him. Though, if all that she had said was true and if the man really had been struck with swords and arrows and shrugged them off, he wasn't all that sure of what she *could* do. That, though, was her problem—he had more than enough of his own to see to. "You wouldn't be blowin' smoke up my skirt, would you, Vicious?" she asked. "Because I'm not in the mood to be teased."

"No teasing," he said. "I know his name."

"And you'll give it to me?"

"I'll trade it to you," he said. "For an opportunity to talk to Catham—when you find him."

She frowned. "I am not much in the mood for bargains, Vicious."

"What do you have to lose?"

"Were I you, Vicious, I would be more concerned with what *I* had to lose. Anyway, how am I to know that the name you give me will be the right one?"

"And how am I to know that you will let me speak to Catham before you deal with him?"

She gave him a sharp, dagger cut of a smile. "I suppose we'll just have to trust each other, is that it?"

"I suppose so."

She considered that for a moment then shook her head. "I could find his name on my own."

"If you could have, you would have already," he said. "He is the original leader of the Crimson Wolves, and his name has remained secret for this long, hasn't it?"

"If his name really is so hard to discover," she said, "then it begs the question, Vicious, how *you* know it."

"That isn't your concern."

She raised an eyebrow, glancing at Aubrey before looking back at him. "I could make it my concern."

Valden also looked at the man standing slightly behind him, noted the eagerness in the man's eyes, if not his expression. He thought Aubrey would have been all too pleased to hear an order to kill him. "You could," he agreed, "and I doubt I'd be able to do anything to stop you. But that won't get you his name."

"True," she said, "but then I could find it, given time enough."

"Maybe," Valden said. "I guess the question you have to ask yourself, then, is how much time you have to settle all this. How much time before one of your subordinates—or maybe more than one—decides that now is his or her time to make a move? What was it you told me earlier? Wounded animals draw scavengers, isn't that it?"

She sighed heavily. "Very well, Vicious. We'll do this your way. You tell me the name of the bastard that did for Flo's, and I'll make sure you get to have a sit down with the Coward before I finish things up with him."

Valden hesitated, wondering if he could trust her. In another moment, he dismissed the idea as useless. Of course he couldn't trust her—she wasn't the head of a band of nuns, after all. She was the leader of a criminal enterprise...at least what was left of one. He could trust her to do what she thought was best for her, that and that only. But there was another simple truth, one that was inescapable—he had no choice. He had told her that she didn't have time to waste, and that was true, but then neither did he. Catham was out there somewhere, Robert Palden, too, and the gods alone knew how many others. Out there plotting, working against the kingdom, against Matt and all the people of the Known Lands. "His name is Robert Palden. He was a clerk, once, but that was a long time ago."

She gave him a small, humorless smile. "He had the look. At least until he started murdering everybody. Any idea how the bastard is able to shrug off blows that would kill another man?"

"No," Valden said. "I'm afraid not."

She grunted, shrugging. "Well. I suppose you can't have everything. Anyway, however tough he is, whatever it is that allowed him to do it, he's not immortal, and I mean to see that for myself." She nodded at the man,

Aubrey. "Go on—get the lads and ladies lookin', will you? And see that Vicious finds his way out."

The man nodded. "Yes, boss." He glanced at Valden. "This way."

Valden started away, following the man toward the ladder, then paused, glancing back at Nadia, the woman's gaze showing that she was deep in thought, no doubt planning how she would find the man and what she would do to him when she did. "Our deal?"

The crime boss looked up at him. "I find Catham the Coward, you'll get first crack at him," she said, then bared her teeth. "But I get the last. Go on, show him out of here," she told the man who had stopped at the ladder. "And Aubrey? Just so there's no misunderstanding—show him out the front."

"Yes, boss," the man said, and Valden didn't think he imagined the disappointment in the man's tone as he started up the ladder.

Valden followed, but he did so warily, carefully. He didn't think the man would risk defying Nadia's orders, but then in a world where a man's allies were criminals and men shrugged off sword thrusts and crossbow bolts as if they were nothing, it didn't do to take things for granted.

CHAPTER NINE

THEY CAME IN THEIR DOZENS, their hundreds.

They were like dogs or wolves, but they were not dogs, were not wolves. They were far, far worse, with teeth as sharp as dagger blades and hides as thick as leather shields, eyes that blazed like lambent ghost lights in the perpetual twilight of the Black Wood.

Cutter and his brother fought back-to-back in an ever-expanding circle of corpses. He didn't know how long they had stood against the unending tide of fangs and claws, but he knew that they would not stand much longer.

They had fought for what felt like an eternity without rest or surcease. No sooner had he cut one of the creatures down than another was leaping to take its place without allowing him time enough even to take a breath.

In truth he barely knew anything at all save the rise and fall of his axe, of arms that felt as if someone had tied lead weights to them, weights that grew heavier with each swing. He was only aware of Feledias fighting behind him because of the pressure of his brother's back pressed against his, though he had no idea what shape his brother was in, for taking his attention away from the creatures rushing toward him, even for a moment, would have been certain death.

A death that was no less certain if he continued to stand and fight as he was. He was running out of strength, and he could tell from the increasing weight of Feledias on his back—his brother using him as support to keep his feet—that he was as well. Yet despite the fact that he knew that what he was doing would not work, he could not spare even an ounce of focus to consider a solution to what they faced, could spare it no more than a drowning man might, in his wild, desperate thrashing, consider just lying flat, so he might float.

He had never been known for being a thinking man, and certainly he was not in that moment. In truth, he was barely a man at all. He was an instrument. The bearer of the Breaker of Pacts. He was the lifting of the axe and the swinging of it, no more than that.

He was nothing else. There *was* nothing else...

Until there was.

One minute, Cutter was fighting for his life, unsure with each raising of the axe if he would have the strength to lift it once more until he did. The next minute, there was a sound different than the guttural growls and grunts and screeches of pain from the creatures they fought, far more alien than his own gasping, hissing, cursing pants for breath.

It was something like the rushing of a spring combined with paper tearing and suddenly a *hole* appeared in the world beside Cutter. It was as if someone had carved a chunk out of the world. He noted this out of the corner of his eye even as he brought the axe down on the latest creature to leap over the mounting wall of its dead comrades, smashing the weapon into its face and sending blood and bits of flesh and teeth flying.

Even in the numb haze brought on by his injuries and exhaustion, even in the Black Wood where strange was common and the abnormal normal, Cutter was shocked by the sudden black, jagged hole hanging in the air. He was even more shocked when something began to climb out of it.

Long, thin, pale arms stretched out of the hole, the fingers on the hands at least twice as long as those of a normal man. Even the creatures attacking Cutter froze as he, and the creatures, regarded the strange hole.

It was about the size of a man's head, but as the fingers appeared out of it, they seemed to *grab* onto the outside edges of it, stretching it as if it were fabric. The hole grew wider, bigger, until a pale gray head came out of it, beside the hands. It was a large head, half of which was taken up by bulbous, black eyes that were at least five times the size of a man's. There was no nose, as such, but two pinpricks in that pale, gray flesh, and a mouth that looked tiny in comparison to the creature's eyes.

The creature turned its large, pupilless gaze on Cutter. "*Come,*" it said in a voice that sounded like the voice of a child. "*Past waits.*"

Cutter frowned. He didn't know where that portal led, didn't much care to find out, but then he knew where remaining led. Still, he hesitated. He had done some foolish things in his life—often, he thought he had done little else—but stepping through a portal to follow some unknown, alien creature seemed like it would be in a league of its own.

"*The Gray sent us,*" the creature said in a childlike, sing-song voice.

At first Cutter couldn't think what the creature might mean, but in another moment he realized that it must be talking about the Gray Man, the feyling who was apparently Yeladrian's sire and who was also the only reason why he and Feledias had lived as long as they had.

He glanced at the portal through which the creature had appeared even as it continued to grow, revealing a long pale, too-thin body to match the spindly arms and slender fingers.

There was suddenly a chorus of growls as whatever frozen moment had overcome Cutter's attackers shattered, and they rushed toward him once more. The newcomer reached out an impossibly long finger, swirling it through the air between Cutter and the oncoming creatures, and another hole appeared, a hole through which the leaping creatures flew, screeching in what sounded like fear as they vanished inside it. That caused their fellows to hesitate, letting out mewls of uncertainty.

"Did you say something, Bernard?" Feledias panted from behind him. "Why did they stop, what is—*stones and starlight, what is that?*" his brother finished as he turned to regard the creature, half in and half out of the black hole.

"He says the Gray Man sent him," Cutter said, glancing at his brother. "He wants us to go with him."

Feledias glanced around at the hundreds of creatures surrounding them in the clearing then back at the strange, alien creature and the hole through which it had appeared. "Sure, what could go wrong?"

"You must hurry," the creature told them. *"The future comes."*

"Right," Feledias said, glancing at Cutter. "You first."

Cutter didn't want to go through that hole, that portal or whatever it was. But then he didn't much relish the idea of being killed and eaten by the demon dogs surrounding them in the clearing, so he took a deep breath and got on with it.

He stepped toward the hole, and as he did the creature moved so abruptly that he thought it meant to attack. Instead, its long-fingered hands grasped the hole and seemed to rip it open with another sound like paper tearing, and then the hole was as tall as Cutter and twice as wide displaying the creature in its fullness. It wore no more than a loin cloth, and it appeared to be at least three feet taller than Cutter's own six feet and three inches, though it was hard to tell for sure as it was hunkered down to fit in the opening. *"Must hurry,"* it told him, *"the future does not like to wait."*

"Sure, who does?" Feledias asked, glancing at Cutter expectantly.

He sighed, then before he could think better of it, stepped through the portal. There was a strange, falling sensation, similar to the feeling a man sometimes got when he fell asleep unexpectedly and woke thinking he was plummeting, his entire body reacting only for the feeling to pass a moment later. Tingles ran through his entire body, and he met what felt like resistance as he crossed through that dark opening, as if he were pushing against a thick curtain. For a moment it seemed to push against him, but then it gave way, the curtains parting, and he was through.

Cutter stumbled forward, looking around himself only to discover that he stood in the same field he'd just left a moment ago. Only...it wasn't the same. There was no army of wolf-like creatures surrounding him, but that was just the beginning. While the field appeared to be the same, all the way down to the slight rise off to his left and the woods in the distance, there was something different about it, something...dead. He had thought that the Black Wood existed in a perpetual gray twilight, but as he stood there staring at the landscape around him, he realized he'd been wrong.

For the world in which he found himself was gray in its entirety. The grass had lost its green luster, the sky its pale, faded blue. Even the distant trees, that had appeared like dark, menacing shadows before, had turned gray. It was as if the world and everything in it had been bleached of color, *drained* of it so that what remained appeared dull and lifeless, like the husk of a snake's shedded skin. Everywhere he looked was the same bland, lifeless gray.

There was a grunt from behind him, followed by a curse, and Cutter turned to see Feledias stepping out of the black portal. "Now that'll wake you up," his brother said as he hocked and spat. He grunted again, looking around them. He glanced back at the portal as the creature stepped back through and the black tear in the fabric of the world vanished. "Cheery place you brought us to."

If the creature understood his brother's sarcasm it didn't show it. It turned its large black eyes on him. *"The past is dead, and the future unborn,"* it said, the words seeming far stranger coming as they did in that lilting, sing-song child's voice.

"Dead, huh?" Feledias said. "Damn. I suppose I missed the funeral."

The creature said nothing, only continued to stare at him. Cutter's brother cleared his throat. "Right, well. I guess...thanks are in order. You know, for saving us and all."

"Gratitude is not required," the creature told him. *"The future comes, as it will, as it must."*

Feledias glanced at Cutter then back to the creature. "Well sure, it would, wouldn't it? Anyway, where are we?"

"The present past."

Feledias looked at Cutter again. "That clears that up."

"What's your name?" Cutter asked the creature.

"We are the door," the creature said in its melodic voice. *"And the latch. We are the gate and we are the key."*

"Keys, don't you mean?" Feledias said. "I mean, if it's a 'we' then it ought to be—"

"Drop it, Fel," Cutter said, then turned back to the creature. "You said the Gray Man sent you?"

"The Gray sends us where he will, and we follow. He wishes us bring you to him."

"Bring us where?" Cutter asked, holding up a hand to silence his brother who, he could feel, was preparing to say something flippant.

"The future."

"Can't we find the way ourselves?" Cutter's brother asked. "Are there signs, maybe?"

"Fel," Cutter said warningly.

"Oh, come on, brother," Feledias said. "Five minutes ago, I was sure that I was going to die, death and mutilation by demon-wolf. Now, looking around here, I'm thinking maybe I did die after all."

"Are you ready to leave?" the creature asked. *"The future is impatient to be born, and the Green will not be so easily balked. We have evaded him and his servants for the moment, but they will return."*

"Well, I was going to take my time, take in the sights," Feledias said, "but I suppose if we must hurry then who am I to argue?"

Cutter sighed, turning to the creature. "We are ready...Door."

He wasn't sure if that was the right name for the creature or not, but if it minded it didn't show it. Instead, it only inclined its head, bending its too-long, too-thin limbs and nearly touching its face to the ground before it turned. *"Come, then,"* it said. *"The future lies this way."*

And with that, the creature's arms and back seemed to unfold from where they'd been hunched together and Cutter thought that he'd been right—it was nine feet tall at the least, perhaps taller. The creature's large black eyes swiveled between the two of them then it turned and started away in a loping stride. It reminded Cutter of a time, long ago, when his father had been alive and they had lived in their homeland, not yet fled on ship to what would become the Known Lands. It was common practice for men and women to come and try to entertain the king, looking to dip their fingers into the castle coin or for some other favor. One such had brought a giant ape, the origins of which Cutter did not know, now or then. It had moved in a similar way, its great arms swinging, its knuckles nearly touching the ground as it walked inside its pen.

This creature moved like that, only its fingers could have easily touched the ground. In fact, it swayed heavily side to side as it walked and, from time to time, it would plant one hand or the other flat on the ground as if to steady itself so that it almost seemed as if it had four legs instead of two.

"Great," Feledias said from beside him, "more walking."

Cutter was weary beyond belief, aching from a dozen small wounds and some not so small ones, but he found the energy to frown at his brother. "Better than dying."

"We have to walk too far, and I suspect it will be the same thing," his brother countered. "Anyway, our new friend seems a bit top heavy doesn't he?" he asked after the creature who might or might not be named Door leaned practically sideways as it walked, propping itself on its hand and pushing off it to continue forward.

"A bit," Cutter agreed.

"Or maybe it's the wind up there. I suppose it'd blow you about like a damned—"

Cutter hissed as movement on his left caught his attention. He had not yet sheathed the Breaker of Pacts, and so he hefted it as he turned, readying himself to meet whatever it was that had caught his eye, should it attack him.

He didn't know where exactly they were, where the creature had brought them, but his first thought, as he turned toward where the movement had caught his eye, was that the wolf-like creatures had found them again.

As it turned out, though, he needn't have bothered, for the movement that had caught his eye had not been caused by one of the creatures he and Feledias had faced. Nor was it some other feyling sent by the Green Man to kill them. It was, instead, something far stranger.

"Stones and starlight, what is that?" Feledias asked from beside him.

Cutter could only shake his head as he stared at the group of translucent figures about fifty feet away from them. He could not make out any detail of them, could not have said if they were men or women, nor if they were even mortal at all or feylings. They were little more than vague blurs as they seemed to walk or glide slowly forward, so indistinct that he could barely track them with his eyes at all. He would have been convinced that they were no more than a trick of the sunlight, had there been any sunlight, but in the place of perpetual lifeless gray to which the creature had brought them there did not seem to be any sun, nor any shadow, only the gray.

"Who are they, do you think?" Feledias asked quietly as they tracked the group's progress while it moved farther away from them.

"I don't know," Cutter said.

"They are the past," a voice said, and Feledias let out a squeak of fear as they both looked up to see that Door had returned and his head was hovering above them the way an adult's might over a child as he took in the group that had drawn their attention.

"Damnit, you scared me to death," Feledias said.

The creature turned its large black eyes on him. *"You are not past yet,"* it said, a slight confusion in its sing-song voice.

"It's an expression, not—" Feledias gave his head a shake. "Never mind. Anyway, what do you mean they are the past?"

"They exist in the before."

"Then why are they here?" Feledias asked.

"This is the before," the creature said. *"This is where they exist. Now, we must hurry. The Gray wishes you to be kept safe, and the servants of the Green stalk our path still."*

Cutter frowned, turning and glancing behind them. In the expanse of field in which he stood he could see very far away, and so he thought he might catch a glimpse of their pursuers, if indeed they had pursuers, but there was nothing. "I don't see anything," he told Door.

"They do not move in the past but in the present," Door said.

"And what's to keep them from coming here?" Feledias asked. "To...to the past?"

"They might come, in time, might force open the gate between past and present, but it will take them time for it is barred and locked, and they have not the key."

"But you do," Cutter said, trying to understand the creature.

"I am the door," it said simply.

"Well, it seems to me that if we can go here and they can't, why don't we just stay here—wherever here *is*—until we get where we're going?"

"*It is not safe to remain in this place for long. We do not belong here, for we are not of the past.*"

"Don't belong here," Feledias repeated. "Well, that's the overstatement of the year." He glanced at Cutter. "Still have a few choice words for my nephew, your son, on the matter. Not that I'll likely ever get the chance to say them."

Cutter ignored his brother as best as he was able—mostly because mention of his son, Matt, and the thought that he would never see him again awakened in him a pain greater than any he had ever felt and that in a life comprised of little else. Instead, he focused on the Fey creature, Door. "What happens if we stay for too long?"

The creature turned its pupilless gaze on him. "*Any who linger too long in the past risk losing their present.*"

"I don't much like the sound of that," Feledias said.

"You mean we'll be trapped here?" Cutter asked.

"*You will not be trapped here, for you will not be you,*" Door explained with an explanation that explained, so far as Cutter could tell, nothing. "*The past is not the present, nor can it be. It is only the past.*"

Cutter frowned, and Feledias sighed. "He means we'll be dead, my axe-wielding brother."

Cutter grunted. "Right. Where are we going, then?" he asked Door.

The feyling slowly craned its long neck, turning its eyes on him once more. "*We go to the future and to do so must leave the past behind.*"

"Not too big on specifics, are you?" Feledias asked sourly.

Cutter frowned at his brother. The creature before them, while it might speak in riddles, had also just saved their lives, and he thought it probably for the best if they didn't antagonize it. He was just opening his mouth to say as much when the silence of the fields around them was broken. Cutter had not even been aware of just how thick that silence was, how complete, until it was shattered by what sounded like the distant screams of men. Distant, but no less terrible for that.

Cutter had heard such screams before, of course. Terrible, gut-wrenching shrieks of the kind brought on by men visited by some terrible anguish. He had heard such screams, had caused such screams, yet they were not the sort of thing a person got used to.

He glanced at Feledias. His brother stood stiffly beside him, staring off into the distance beyond which, somewhere, were the screamers. Feledias's face was pale, and Cutter noted that his hands were working at his sides. Feledias had heard such screams before too, had caused such screams, but it seemed that he was no more inured to them than Cutter himself.

"Those...those are the voices of men," his brother breathed. He glanced at Cutter and there was a mixture of what might have been terror and relief in his gaze. "You don't think...that is, do you think perhaps Matthias reconsidered and sent the army?"

Cutter watched his brother for a moment then glanced back in the direction of those far away screams. "I...don't know," he said, and that was the truth. But another thought came to him, one that he was not prepared to share with Feledias, not yet. If Matt had indeed reconsidered and chosen to send an expedition into the heart of the Black Wood—a mission the danger of which couldn't be overstated, that Cutter knew for he had been part of such an expedition before—then, based on the sounds, they were not faring well. If it was a rescue party come for them then it sounded like they themselves needed rescuing.

"*They are screams not from the present but from the past,*" Door observed, and this time Cutter found himself flinching, leaning his head back to look above him where the creature's face hovered.

"I don't mean to quibble, Door," Feledias said, pausing and swallowing hard at a particularly agonized howl from beyond their sight, "but they seem quite...present to me."

"*Indeed,*" the creature said. "*They are of the present past.*"

"The...present past," Cutter said.

"*The past which lies closest to our present,*" the creature explained. "*They are screams from...before. During the wars with your people. What you hear are the sounds of the prisoners which were brought back to this place. The Green*

132

insisted on...interrogating them himself. He was and remains enraged by the death of Yeladrian. He was not kind."

Cutter felt an ache in his chest at that, and he turned back to stare at the horizon, at the sound of those distant screams. Those men and women had been tortured and that terribly, that much he could hear in their cries. Despair roiled in him at those sounds, followed by anger at Shadelaresh and, lastly, anger at himself. And not just anger—shame. After all, it was he who had slain Yeladrian, he who had begun the war with the Fey in the first place, and so while his might not have been the hand that carved those screams out of those poor souls, he was still responsible. Had it not been for him, had it not been for what he'd done, they would not have been there. Yeladrian's murder had cost him, it was true, but it had cost his people far more.

He turned to regard the creature. "Can we help them?"

"The past cannot be changed," the creature said, and he did not think that he imagined a slight sound of sadness in that childlike voice. *"Nor the future. There is only the present, only the moment. And in this moment, we must go. Should we tarry too long, the past will have us, for the past is ever reluctant to allow those within to move on."*

"Well, lead on, Door," Feledias said. "Better anywhere than here."

Cutter didn't argue with that. Even the feyling seemed eager to leave, turning and starting away in its strange, loping walk.

Cutter and Feledias shared a look then followed behind him.

They traveled on in silence. Whatever else he was, Door was not much of a conversationalist. Not that Cutter could blame him for in that place of colorless gray that they walked, speaking seemed almost blasphemous, like a lewd joke told at church. Even Feledias was quiet, no small miracle that.

Cutter didn't mind the silence. He'd lived with it for a long time, after all, during his exile in Brighton. His life, then, had become a dull, gray place much like that in which he now walked.

He found himself thinking about Matt, as he walked, Matt who had been the only bright splash of color in his otherwise dull existence in those years. He thought of Matt and all the others, Chall and Maeve, and Priest, even Ned the carriage driver and his wife, Emille. He wondered if he would ever see them again. And then, as they continued, his thoughts drifted like some piece of flotsam carried on a lazy current. They walked through the past and so it was the past of which he thought. A past of which he was mostly ashamed.

As they walked, he occasionally saw other flickers of movement around them. Most, when he looked at them, vanishing altogether and those few that did not were so blurred and translucent as to be unrecognizable beyond a slight warping of air and light, like the glimmers of sunlight caught in the surface of a clear lake.

"Who did you say they were?" Feledias asked quietly, his eyes scanning the area around them, taking in the occasional flicker of light.

"They are the past," Door said, craning his long neck around to regard them while still walking forward.

"So...they're ghosts?"

Door paused. *"This is their world, not ours. In this place, it is we who are the ghosts."*

Feledias glanced at Cutter, raising an eyebrow. "You hear that, brother mine? We're ghosts."

Cutter met his brother's gaze and shrugged. "Boo."

"Oh, you can pretend to be flippant all you want, Bernard," Feledias said, "but we both know you are not the thoughtless barbarian fool you make yourself out to be. You are a wholly different kind of fool." He gave a small smile to show that it was said in jest, but Cutter found that he could not smile back. Mostly because walking through the strange place had made him think of his past, and thinking of all his mistakes, of all the terrible things he'd done, he thought that a fool was the least of what he was.

Feledias must have seen something of Cutter's thoughts in his mind, for his smile slowly faded as Door started away and they followed after. "It was only a joke, Bernard. I meant nothing by it."

"I know," Cutter said. "It was a good one."

Feledias sighed, turning back to their escort as he apparently decided it was time to change the subject. "So then, Door, where is it, exactly, that you're taking us?"

"Let it go, Fel," Cutter told his brother quietly. "Wherever we're going, it's got to be better than where we're coming from."

"Oh, I don't know, brother," Feledias said, matching his quiet tone and glancing suspiciously at the Feyling's thin back. "In my experience, things can always get worse, and while I appreciate being snatched from the literal jaws of death moments before my untimely demise—sure, sure, and yours too—I cannot help but wonder what we have been saved *for.*"

Cutter frowned. "What do you mean?"

"I *mean,* brother," Feledias said, "that a fish, plucked from the water, might think itself saved from the jaws of the shark who meant to have it for dinner...right up until it finds itself thrown on a campfire to feed a fisherman's belly."

"He said the Gray Man sent him to save us," Cutter said.

"So he said," Feledias agreed, "and the shiny bit of metal which attracts the fish might well promise a good meal, but a promise made does not mean a promise kept. Anyway, even if he *does* work for the Gray Man, what of it?"

"Now you have an issue with the Gray Man?" Cutter asked. "Because in case I need to remind you, Fel, we'd be dead if it weren't for him. He healed us, remember? Not to mention kept Shadelaresh and all the others from tearing us into pieces."

"You're right, of course," Feledias said. "He saved us, and I am quite grateful, I assure you, to have all my pieces in their proper places."

"Sure," Cutter countered, "you're full of it." He gave a small smile. "Gratitude, that is."

Feledias rolled his eyes. "All I'm saying, my not-so-clever brother, is that while I appreciate being saved, I cannot help but ask myself *why.*"

"Some people do the right thing simply because it's the right thing to do, Fel."

"Ever met these people, have you?"

Cutter's mind immediately went to Priest. Cutter himself had been their leader during the war, but in many ways he had looked to Priest, a man whose faith in the good, whose belief in doing the right thing was unshakeable. A man who had sacrificed his time and his energy, his coin and on several occasions, nearly his life, for the good of others. "Yes," he said. "I have."

Feledias frowned, as if he wanted to argue. "Then you are luckier than most. But even if you have met such a person, I would say, brother mine, that they are rare indeed. Most men do not do anything without there being something in it for them. Even good things. Perhaps *especially* good things. After all, with bad things the reward is usually obvious—I stole someone else's coin and so now I have more coin. Easier to understand than the holy man who spends his life helping the poor and the sick."

"You have a problem with helping people?"

"Not at all," Feledias said, "I only feel that such help might be considered transactional. After all, the priest *does* get something from it, does he not? Or, at least, he hopes he does. He plans for a reward just as the robber, only his reward, he believes, will not come until the next life."

"That's a pretty cynical outlook," Cutter observed.

"Look around, brother," Feledias said, waving a hand, "it is a cynical world. And in the end, the holy man is little better than the robber—both are, after all, out for their own gain."

"You're wrong," Cutter said, thinking of Valden and of himself, thinking of the differences between them. "The criminal leaves tears in his wake, the holy man smiles. They are not the same."

Feledias shrugged. "Fine, maybe they are and maybe they aren't. It makes no real difference, not unless you believe the Gray Man is a priest, and I didn't see him chanting or wearing robes. My point is, brother, that if a man keeps a tool clean and well-polished, you can bet that he means to use it, sooner or later."

"And what do you think he means to use us for, then?"

"I don't know," Feledias said quietly, shaking his head as he turned and gazed at their escort's back, "but I don't look forward to finding out."

And with that grim pronouncement hanging in the air, they followed behind the feyling.

They could do little else.

CHAPTER TEN

CHALL WOKE FEELING SIGNIFICANTLY BETTER than he had before he'd gone to sleep. Or, perhaps, passed out would have been more accurate. Either way, he felt better which just meant that he felt two steps away from death instead of one. An improvement, sure, but one that was of dubious comfort. He groaned as an ache went through his...well. Everywhere, really. He kept his eyes shut, squeezing them tighter and deciding that oblivion was more appealing, at least for the moment, than a world full of aches and pains.

He felt something, a hand, maybe, brush his leg, and that drew him back from the unconsciousness he had been settling back into. A small, tired smile came over his face. "Well, now I'll admit I might not be at my finest," he mumbled, "but I'm game if you are."

"I'm not."

Chall found himself frowning through the muddled confusion of sleep. Maeve sounded different. Her voice was deeper, gruffer. Perhaps even a little hostile. Didn't much sound like her at all in truth. In fact, it didn't even sound like a woman's voice. "Maybe some water, first," Chall said, "you've got a bit of a..." He froze as his eyes opened and he saw that it wasn't Maeve leaned over him but a far less friendly, far hairier face. One he recognized as belonging to Malden, the castle's healer.

"Fire and salt, do you think about anything else?" the healer asked.

Chall craned his neck, looking past the healer to where Maeve stood a short distance away. "Why would I?" he asked.

She sighed, shaking her head, but he saw that she was smiling, so that was alright. Even though he felt more than a little embarrassed, he told himself that at least it was only Healer Malden who'd witnessed it. Not much of a loss there. After all, it wasn't as if the old healer was one of his biggest fans anyway.

"Stones and starlight, mage, it's a wonder you don't have a small army of little ones running around the world."

Chall followed the voice and felt his face heat as he saw Ned, the carriage driver, seated at the table, leaning back in his chair and grinning widely.

Chall decided to cover his embarrassment the same way that he covered any negative emotion, including anger or fear. Sarcasm. "Who's to say I d—" He cut off, recalling Maeve's presence, and glanced over to see her watching him with a raised eyebrow. "That is...I mean..."

"I was going to say you'll live," Healer Malden said, a small smile on his face—one of the first Chall had ever seen, if not *the* first—as he glanced between Chall and the frowning Maeve. "Now, though, I'm not so sure." He turned, looking to the other side of the room. "Majesty, with your leave, I've done all I can here. Sir Challadius will recover—at least from his current wounds. With your permission, I would go and check on Lady Valencia."

Chall felt his face heat with embarrassment yet again, and he followed the man's gaze to the corner of the room where Matt sat. He was trying to think of something to defend himself, but realized in a moment that he needn't have bothered. The king of the Known Lands didn't seem to be paying attention to Malden or, indeed, the world at all. There was a distant cast to his gaze, and Chall saw his fingers toying with something in his pocket.

"Majesty?" Malden asked.

Matt blinked as if being woken from a dream and glanced over. "Sorry, Malden, what's that?"

"I asked, Majesty," the old healer said, "if I had your leave to go and check on Lady Valencia."

"Leave..." Matt said, sounding distracted, his eyes getting a distant look again.

Chall frowned. *Gods but what's wrong with the lad? Whatever it is, it's getting worse.* No sooner had the thought crossed his mind than Matt's head snapped up, his gaze suddenly clear and lucid as he stared at Chall.

"I'm fine," Matt said in an abrupt, defensive tone.

"Of...of course, Majesty," Chall said, his mouth suddenly terribly dry. "I didn't say you weren't."

"No," Matt said, sighing and shaking his head. "No, you didn't, did you?" Before Chall could say anything to that—not that he had any idea what he might say—the young man turned back to Malden. "Of course you can go, Malden. And I haven't met her but I am sure you're right, no doubt Lady Valencia is quite lovely."

"Majesty?" the healer said, his voice a mixture of confusion and embarrassment. "I never...that is..." He rose, clearing his throat and giving a bow. "Thank you, Majesty. Good day." He turned, inclining his head to the rest of the room. "Good day, all."

Chall blinked in shock. The king had told him that he could hear the thoughts of others, but the truth was he hadn't wholly believed it. How could he? But now, noting the healer's obvious embarrassment, Chall was forced to reconsider that opinion. Chall was worried about Matt...but that didn't keep him from sending a jab at the ornery healer while he had the chance. "Good day, Malden," he said. "Do tell Lady Valencia I said hello."

The old man turned and scowled at him. Chall considered telling him that if he intended to woo the noblewoman he'd do well to learn another expression. *Any* other expression would be an improvement. In the end, though, he decided against taunting the man any further. Partly because it was sort of sweet, in its way—like watching a mangy, flea-bitten, grumpy mule incline its head in the hopes of getting petted. Mostly, though, he held off any more taunts for more pragmatic reasons—namely, that

Malden was the best healer in the city and, based on how his life had been going for the last little while, Chall thought it likelier than not that he would need the man's help again sooner rather than later.

So he managed to hold his tongue until the healer, still scowling, hurried out the door, closing it behind him. "There's a love story in the making," Chall observed, saying the words with some relief, like a man who has been forced to hold his piss and is finally able to let it go.

That relief quickly faded, though, as he found himself looking at Matt. The young man already seemed to have forgotten all about the healer and Chall, about everyone else in the room, in truth. He sat with his arms propped on his knees, cradling something in both hands now. Chall caught a glimpse of a gold chain of what must have been a necklace.

Chall frowned, watching Matt toy with the necklace. To say that the boy—for in that moment, he found himself thinking of him as a boy, a lost, frightened young boy—looked troubled would have been a gross under-statement. He didn't look troubled—he looked haunted. Chall figured he understood that well enough. After all, if anyone really *could* hear the thoughts of others, those inner most secrets they whispered only to them-selves, then Chall suspected they would be privy to some disturbing things, indeed.

He glanced at Ned and Maeve, saw the two of them looking worriedly at Matt, no doubt thinking thoughts similar to his own. He realized then, for the first time, that Emille was nowhere to be seen. He was surprised by that. When he'd last been awake—before he'd passed out again—she and her husband had been so entwined together that they'd looked like one of those knot puzzles where people were given the impossible task of trying to separate one from the other. A reaction, no doubt, to the fact that one or both of them had very nearly died in the last few days.

"She left," Matt said into the tense silence, and everyone turned to regard him.

"I'm sorry, Majesty?" Chall said.

The young king's eyes shifted in their sockets, glancing at Chall from underneath his brows as he hunched over the necklace he held, but only for a moment before they shifted away again, as if it was painful for his gaze to linger on anyone for long. "Emille—she left about an hour ago. Commander Malex sent some guardsmen with her back to her and Ned's house. They mean to investigate, see what they can find out about the men. With any luck, they can figure out who one of them was and maybe that will lead us to Catham or this Robert Palden. You and Ned have been very busy these last few days," he said, a slight note of accusation in his voice and this time he met Chall's gaze and held it. He was not happy, that much was clear. "Perhaps, if you would have informed me of what was going on, I might have helped."

Chall blinked, glancing at Maeve and Ned, surprised that they had told Matt everything that had been going on. After all, he thought that the young man had more than enough on his plate, more than enough to worry about without adding more troubles to it. Maeve gave him an almost covert shake of her head, opening her mouth to speak, but Matt beat her to it.

"Ned and Maeve here have, reluctantly, filled me in about some bit of your and their activities over the last few days. The rest...well, the rest I've filled in myself."

Which meant, Chall thought, that he had read it out of their minds. That was a damned scary idea. After all, Chall had a lot of thoughts, and a lot of those thoughts weren't all that...nice. He'd been called a pervert and a lech and a thousand other things over the years—nearly all deserved—and that had been based on that small bit of his thoughts which had seeped through to the surface so that others might see it. If his mind was a room, then he figured it was one in desperate need of cleaning.

Matt gave him a small smile at that, as if he knew well what Chall was thinking—which, likely, he did. That suddenly made Chall terribly self-conscious, and he forced himself to think of Maeve to distract himself. Which wasn't hard—he rarely thought of anything else. The problem, of course, was that after a moment, his thoughts took control and, like a run away horse, sped in their own direction with abandon. Still thinking of Maeve, sure, but of how she'd been a few night's past, when darkness claimed the world and the two of them had lain in bed quietly, and then, not so quietly.

Matt winced, and Chall's eyes went wide. "Shit," he said, trying desperately to think of something else, anything else. His thoughts, casting about like a drowning man seeking something to keep him afloat, settled on grandmothers. No grandmother in particular, just old, wrinkled grandmothers. But his mind had, apparently, not completely left the filthy place it had been—in truth, it never did—which only meant that, in another few seconds, he was thinking about bedrooms and grandmothers and that only led in one direction.

Matt cleared his throat, staring at his hands where they fidgeted at the necklace, and Chall hissed. "Shit," he said again.

"About Lady Valencia," Matt blurted, the way a man might blurt out something, anything to change the subject of a particularly uncomfortable conversation. Not that there had been one, really, more just a monologue of Chall's thoughts which often made even him uncomfortable. "Malden says that her wounds were largely superficial and that she'll recover completely."

"I suspect she will," Chall said, remembering the way the man had talked about her. Or, perhaps it was closer to say the way he had thought about her. "After all, it seems to me that our Healer Malden might well see to her recovery with great...alacrity."

"You shouldn't tease him," Maeve said. "Let Malden have his fun."

"I have a hard time imagining that man having fun at all," Chall said honestly. "Still, if smiles are currency that might be spent, then I'd say he's sitting on a hoard, as frugal as that bastard is with them."

"Anyway," Matt went on, glancing between the three of them, "what are your plans now?"

"Plans, Majesty?" Chall asked.

"Yes, with Catham and this Robert Palden, with the Wolves. What's the plan?"

"Plan..." Chall said slowly. "Yes, I think I've heard the word before. I'm sure of it."

"What Chall means to say, Majesty," Maeve said, frowning, "is that we are still developing one. For one thing, we need to speak with Lady

Valencia—once she's feeling better, of course," she went on quickly, glancing at Ned.

"Oh?" Matt asked. "You think maybe she knows something about the man who attacked her that might help?"

Maeve shook her head. "I think she knows something, Majesty, though I don't think it's that."

Ned frowned. "What are you saying? Look, we've already been over this—Val's a friend. The best of friends. She isn't—"

"What I mean," Maeve interrupted, "is that she clearly knows some-thing. Why else would Robert Palden go through so much trouble to find her? Enough that he attacked her manse and then sent men to your home to hunt her down. It seems to me that Lady Valencia must know some-thing, something that endangers the Wolves and whatever their plans are. Otherwise, why waste so much time and resources trying to silence her?"

Ned frowned. "We know that already—the list. It was Val who kept all the information for all the members. He gets that, he can find all the old Wolves."

"And then what?" Maeve asked.

The carriage driver glanced between her and Chall. "What do you mean?"

"Let's say he does get the list—what does that do for him?" Maeve asked. "So he gets a list of names, maybe even where to find them. It's been more than fifteen years, Ned. That's a long time. Plenty of the people on that list will be dead. Others will have moved away, maybe even gone into hiding."

Chall grunted. "Maeve's right."

"Besides," Maeve went on, "if it was just the list that he was after why send someone here, to the castle?"

"I don't follow you," Ned said.

"The woman," Chall said as he realized just how right Maeve was and just how much of a fool he was—she tended to have that effect. "The one who killed the serving girl, the one that was skulking around Matt's quar-ters." He frowned as he remembered Catham mentioning her. "Margaret."

"That's right," Maeve said, nodding. "We wouldn't even know that the

Crimson Wolves were back if it weren't for her. They could have remained undetected for some time yet, and for secret criminal organizations—vigilante or otherwise—remaining undetected is paramount."

"So what are you saying?" the carriage driver asked. "That he doesn't want the list after all?"

"Oh no, I think he wants it alright," Maeve said. "But then men can want more than one thing, can't they? Sure, this old friend of yours, he wants the list that Lady Valencia carries, of that I am certain. But that's not all he's looking for. In fact, I would venture that it is of secondary importance to whatever drove him to send a person into the castle itself, the seat of New Daltenia's power, and risk revealing the Wolves presence once more. Not to mention the fact that he sent men to your home. No, I think he's looking for the list, but he's looking for something else, too."

"Like what?"

"I have no idea," she said, shaking her head in frustration. "But I think we need to find out. Soon. Based on what I've learned of this Robert Palden recently, if he's looking for something, I'd wager it's in all our best interests to make sure he doesn't find it."

There was a knock on the door then, and they all turned to regard it. It opened a moment later, and a familiar face poked its way in the door. Chall considered Vorrun a good friend, one of the few the years—and his antics —had left him. He and the guardsman had, once upon a time, shared quite a few ales and quite a few laughs and that on more than one occasion. Not that the guardsman looked in any danger of laughing now, as he turned to regard Matt, and though he did a good job of controlling his expression, Chall thought he could see something like worry in the man's features. "Majesty," the guardsman said, "you've a visitor. Sir Valden has returned."

Chall found himself grinning widely at that, an expression that Maeve, and even Ned shared. He had been worried about his friend ever since he'd left. After all, death at Catham's hands had very nearly found Chall and Ned, and they had been largely minding their own business. Valden had gone looking for the man.

He turned to Matt, expecting to see the young man sharing his excitement. But if Matt had even so much as heard the guard's pronouncement, he gave no sign. Instead, he only remained hunched over the necklace he cradled in both hands, studying it the way a scholar might study a particularly ambiguous passage of text, trying to understand its meaning.

"Majesty?" Vorrun said.

Matt glanced up then, rousing like someone waking from a dream and looked at the door, starting a bit when he saw Vorrun standing there and making it obvious that he had not even been aware of the guardsman's presence, so preoccupied had he been with his thoughts. "Yes, Vorrun?"

The guardsman shot a quick glance at Chall. It only lasted for an instant, half an instant, but that look communicated volumes about the man's worry for Matt. A second later he turned back to the young king. "Majesty, Sir Valden has returned and bids your leave to enter."

Matt nodded distractedly, showing none of the relief and excitement that Chall would have thought to see in him. "Sure, of course, tell him to come in," he said before beginning to study the necklace and the green emerald in his hands again.

The guardsman bowed, disappearing out of the door and a moment later Valden stepped inside the room. Despite his worry for Matt, Chall found himself grinning again. "Ah, so you are alive after all. The worms will be disappointed."

"Here's hoping they continue to be," Valden said, giving him a small smile.

"Oh, Valden," Maeve said, hurrying toward the man and wrapping him into a hug. "Stones and starlight, but I was afraid something happened to you."

"Nothing from which I won't recover," he said, giving her a smile to show that it was a joke as she released him from the embrace.

Ned moved forward then, and the carriage driver grinned as he held out his hand. "If it's alright with you, I'll settle for a handshake."

Valden nodded, taking the man's hand.

They all turned to Matt then, but the young man didn't even appear to be aware that Valden had entered the room. He was even more hunched than he had been, looking to Chall like nothing so much as a person expecting to receive a blow. His eyes were narrowed in what might have

145

been thought or concentration, and his fingers were working continuously at the necklace he held.

Chall hated silence—it was why he'd largely begun, some time early in his life, to look at it as his personal job to fill it. And he hated awkward silence most of all so when it was clear that the king wasn't going to speak, he did instead. "It's a good thing you showed up. I was just getting ready to go walking the city looking for you," he told Valden. "You know, just as soon as I could walk."

The man frowned, nodding. "Vorrun told me a little of what happened," he said. "How are you feeling?"

"Well, shit'd be an improvement," Chall said honestly.

"You would think that some people, having survived everything he recently has," Maeve said, raising an eyebrow, "might feel the need to express gratitude instead of complaints."

"I won't be able to complain when I'm dead," Chall said, "guess I'd better get it all in now." He turned back to Valden, shrugging. "Anyway, I'm alive. What of you? No fresh wounds to show us?"

"I'm afraid not," Valden said. "If it's a contest, you win."

"If it's a contest, I'd just as soon forfeit," Chall countered. "So what have you been up to then? Any luck finding Catham? Maeve's under the impression that he's looking for something, something that it'd be better for all of us if he didn't find."

Valden nodded. "That makes sense, considering the assassin that came here as well as the attack on Ned's house."

Chall frowned, annoyed that the man caught up with Maeve's reasoning so much faster than he had. But then he hadn't been shot and stabbed, had he? The bastard.

"How is Lady Valencia, by the way?" he asked, glancing at Ned.

"Val's alright," the carriage driver said, "thanks for asking."

Valden nodded. "I'm glad to hear it."

"So what have you been up to, then?" Chall asked. "Just taking your ease? Or did you find anything that can help us find that son of a bitch, Catham? I'd like to have a bit of a talk with him. The stabby kind."

"You aren't the only one," Valden said. "As for Catham, it may be that he will be found sooner rather than later, though I do not have an exact lead on his whereabouts, not yet."

"Nadia not as helpful as you would have liked then?"

"Nadia...has her own problems at the moment, I'm afraid," Valden said.

"Oh?" Chall asked. "And here I thought that all they did at Flo's was have feasts and balls."

"They won't be doing either of those things—or anything else, I suspect—at Flo's for a very long time," Valden said. "Likely ever."

Chall frowned. "What does that mean?"

Valden shot a glance at the distracted king. Chall followed his gaze only to discover that Matt was distracted no longer. Instead, he was staring directly at Valden with an intensity in his gaze that Chall could almost feel.

"You hesitate on my account," Matt said quietly. "Again, you would keep things from me."

Valden winced. "Majesty, it isn't that, it's just that—"

"But it *is* that, Valden. I know it. I know it as much as I know anything." He gave a laugh the sound of which Chall didn't care for. "I know it almost as if I could read your mind." He waved his hand. "It's fine, Valden, the ex-priest. Keep your secrets, if you can. I have little need of them." He abruptly rose then. "Let me know if I can be of service." Then, without another word, Matt moved toward the door and disappeared through it, closing it behind him.

For several seconds they all remained as they had been, staring at the door in silence. "I...I do not understand," Valden said.

"The lad is going through something, I think," Ned said.

Chall grunted. "That's an understatement. He says he thinks he can read peoples minds," he told Valden.

Valden blinked. "I...see."

"You think that's bad?" Chall asked. "Here's a worse one for you—I think he's right."

Valden's eyes opened wide at that. "You believe that he can read people's minds?"

"You happen to be thinking something, just now, about how you didn't

147

want to talk about certain things in front of Matt? Before he had his outburst?"

"Well...yes," Valden said. "But...but how would he be able to do that? Is that a gift some people have?"

"Not that I've ever heard of," Chall said.

"A holdover from being possessed by Emma, then?" Maeve asked.

They all turned to regard Chall then, looking to him for answers. The problem, of course, was that he had no answers to give them. He shook his head. "I don't know. Maybe?"

"My mother used to say you can build a bridge out of 'maybes' and 'ifs' just so long as you don't walk on it," Ned said. "You sure none of your studies back at the Academy in Daltenia didn't touch on somethin' like it?"

"Those studies that were decades ago?" Chall asked. "Look, there have been quite a few ales between now and then. Anyway, you went to the Academy too. You ever hear anything about something like that?"

"I hardly ever heard anything at all," Ned said, frowning. "I told you, they kept me sequestered away from everyone and everything."

"Chall, this is serious," Valden said. "Are you sure there's nothing? Nothing the Academy talked about that might be of use, that might explain what's happening to Matthias?"

"Anything that might help explain a man reading another's thoughts as easily as if they were a book? Easier, really, because he can do it without staining his fingers with dust or ink, without flipping so much as a page? Anything that might go into detail regarding a Fey possession when no one at the Academy even knew what the Fey were?" He realized that he'd raised his voice at the last, not out of anger as much as out of fear, fear for Matt, his friend. He gave a heavy sigh. "Yes. I'm sure."

"Then we'll have to find out some other way," Maeve said. "Perhaps Malden..."

"Perhaps Malden what?" Chall asked. "Listen, if Malden knew how to fix it, it'd be fixed already. The lad's been meeting with him for weeks now, and so far as I can tell things are only getting worse."

"So what do we do, then?" Valden asked.

Chall gave another sigh. "I don't know. Does anyone have any idea what it was he was fiddling with the whole time he was here?"

Maeve shook her head. "A necklace, it looked like to me."

"Yeah," Chall said. "A necklace that he was clutching like a woman holding tight to her virtue."

"Not any woman you'd know," Maeve said, the words coming out of her as if of their own accord, almost in a distracted, off-handed kind of way.

Chall nodded. "I'll meet with him. Try to figure out what's going on. If there is a trace of magic left over from the Feyling, Emma, then I ought to be able to detect it, if I look carefully enough. In the meantime, how did it go at Flo's?" he asked, turning to Valden.

"It didn't," Valden said, wincing. "Not really." He looked as if he might say more, but a grim expression came over his face, and he remained silent.

"We're to play a game of riddles then, is that it?" Ned asked.

"Forgive me," Valden said, "it has been a...trying night. You see, the men at Flo's—" he paused, glancing at Chall—"the ones who were there the last time we visited, you remember?"

"Better than I'd like," Chall said, grunting. "If it was up to me, I'd just as soon find a different brothel to spend my time and coin, going forward." Maeve cleared her throat. "Not that I'd go to any brothel, of course," he said quickly.

"Well," Valden said, "they're dead."

Chall frowned. "Huh? Who's dead? Someone at the brothel?"

"Everyone at the brothel," Valden said, then gave a slight shrug. "More or less. Nadia escaped. One or two others."

Chall gave a low whistle, sitting back. "I s'pose evil happens to the evil and good alike. Who was it, a rival gang, maybe? Seems to me that they would have been better off picking Nadia's crew off one at a time then coming at them in force at their place of strength." He shrugged. "But then, I suppose I'm not a criminal."

"I imagine there are a few husbands with wandering wives and a few innkeepers missing payments that might disagree with that," Maeve said, apparently not quite as over the whole brothel thing as he'd hoped.

Chall winced. "Fine, not that *type* of criminal anyway, how's that? So what about it, Pri—sorry, Valden? Was it a rival gang? Seems a lot more likely than the city guard finally deciding to rouse themselves to do something other than sit on their asses and play cards—oh, and harass the innocent while taking bribes from the guilty. Suppose there's that too."

"It wasn't a rival gang or the city guard," Valden said. "It was, I believe, Robert Palden."

Chall frowned, glancing at Maeve and Ned.

"You mean," the carriage driver said, "that you think Rob sent some men to this brothel?"

"Not...exactly," Valden said slowly, and for some reason that Chall couldn't understand the man seemed to be reluctant to go on. "I think Robert Palden went himself."

Ned grunted. "Well, that's not like the Rob I used to know. He wasn't ever much of a hands-on sort of guy—wasn't built for it, really. It's one thing for a man to have violent thoughts; it's quite another for him to be capable of that violence. Still, I s'pose a lot's changed in the last fifteen, twenty years. Why not that? I guess maybe he could have taken some of the Wolves and attacked this brothel."

"You misunderstand me," Valden said. "I don't think he took men—I think he went alone."

Chall grunted. "What do you mean alone?"

"What people usually mean, I imagine," Valden said.

Chall frowned. "The old Priest never used to be a smart ass, and he rarely lied."

"I am not the old Priest," Valden said, "but neither am I lying. According to Nadia—and the scene I came upon when entering Flo's supports this—one man took on a brothel full of dozens of criminals...and won. A man who Nadia says was somehow able to shrug off sword blows and crossbow shots as if they were nothing. A man who, based on what I saw, reveled in the violence and chaos he caused."

Ned gave a soft laugh, one that quickly dried up when Valden's face remained grim. "Look, okay, Rob's got his problems," the carriage driver said, "and I think the fella's insane, needs to be put down much the way a mad dog might be, because the dog is going to hurt others just so long as it's able. But all the madness in the world, all the hate and anger ain't goin' to stop a sword thrust."

"Maybe not," Valden said, "but Nadia said he did it just the same."

"And you believe her?" Chall asked.

"I do."

"And you think that this invincible bastard, whoever he was," Ned said, the carriage driver still not convinced, "was Rob?"

"Yes."

Chall shot a look at Maeve, saw her watching Valden with a frown on her face. "You don't think, perhaps, that this Nadia knew you were hunting Robert Palden and thought she'd blame it on him, take a chance at killing two birds with one stone? After all, I can't imagine she enjoys you coming around, knowing you're connected to the king, and I'm sure she and all the other criminals in the city have no love for one of the founding members of a vigilante group that used to hunt them."

Valden seemed to consider that for a moment, but in another he shook his head. "No. It is the type of thing she would do—Nadia has always been clever and...let's say efficient. She did not rise to the position she is in by accident. But she couldn't have given me his name in order to set us up."

"And why is that?" Ned said.

"Because she didn't have it to give. When I went to Nadia, she had no idea of the identity of the man who came upon them at Flo's. It was only after talking to her about what happened, about the man's appearance that I realized that her description matched, exactly, that you gave us of your old friend," he finished, glancing at the carriage driver.

They were silent, then, as each of them tried to think it through, tried to reconcile all that was happening. Chall found himself thinking of Prince Bernard, missing him. Not just because the man was his friend, not even because he was a powerful warrior, possibly the greatest warrior of the age. It was not their relationship or the prince's martial prowess that Chall missed, not then. Instead, it was the man's ability to simplify things. Chall had witnessed him do that, too, over the years, had watched time and time again as the prince had taken problems that seemed too big to even grasp and make them smaller, something that could be held in a man's hand, like a puzzle box waiting to be solved.

People often used the word 'simple' to describe the dim-witted, but Chall thought they were wrong to do so. The world was complicated. Home to hundreds of thousands, millions of creatures, each with their own thoughts, their own wants and desires. And in such a world, he thought that the cleverest men were those who were able to take all of that and make it simple. By doing so, the prince had, more times than Chall could count, made the unlikely likely, the impossible possible.

But Prince Bernard was not in New Daltenia. He was in the Black Wood. He could not help them. Still, as they settled in to talk of what might be done, as they searched for simple solutions to complicated problems, Chall missed him. He missed his friend.

He missed his prince.

CHAPTER ELEVEN

He walked in a field of ghosts.

He was used to ghosts, in a way, for they had followed his path for many years now. He was called the Crimson Prince for a reason, after all.

But these ghosts were different...

They were not his.

He glanced over at Feledias and saw his brother looking around them, a troubled expression on his face as he took in the figures in the field. Indistinct figures, largely featureless, some in the shapes of mortals, some not. At first, when Door had brought them to this place, those figures had been no more than motes of light, ones so faint that he could nearly have convinced himself he'd imagined them.

But the longer that they remained in the strange, featureless landscape the more *distinct* those indistinct figures became. And it was not just the figures themselves—the world around them was also becoming clearer, more *alive*. Cutter could think of it no better than that. The grass was slowly changing from the dull gray it had been to a subtle green gray. The sky, while still empty of clouds or sun, had begun to take on the faintest hint of blue, and he saw a few wisps of white inside it.

"Is it just me," Feledias said, echoing Cutter's thoughts, "or are they getting...*realer?*"

Cutter frowned, glancing around at the figures sharing the field with them. He was just about to answer when their feyling escort spoke.

"*It is not they who are changing but us,*" Door said, regarding Feledias then Cutter with his pupilless black eyes. "*This is their world, not ours. Unless we tarry too long and then, like any who spends too long in the past, we will be trapped here.*"

"What does that mean?" Feledias asked.

"*We stand now,*" Door said, and Cutter didn't think he imagined the impatience in the feyling's voice, "*with one foot in the world of the present and one in the past. Such a thing might be done for a little while, but sooner or later, each being must make a choice, to embrace the present or live in the past. And, should it refuse or neglect to make such a choice, then a choice will be made for it.*"

"I don't much care for the sound of that," Cutter said, frowning.

"And how much farther is it, then?" Feledias asked, glancing around them at the phantoms moving here and there, vague shapes still, but Cutter was not sure whether or not he imagined that they were clearer now than they had been even a few minutes ago.

"*There is no time in the past,*" Door said, "*for it exists always as it is, as it was, unchangeable.*"

Feledias glanced at Cutter, rolling his eyes before turning back to the feyling. "If it's as dangerous as you make out then why bring us here at all?"

"*The Green One's creatures had you surrounded,*" Door said. "*I thought to save you.*"

"And we're grateful," Cutter said, frowning at Feledias and wondering how he, of all people, was the one left to be diplomatic. He found himself wishing Chall was here. The man could talk his way out of anything—proof of that was in the fact that he was still walking around breathing despite a small army of husbands who would have been happy to have seen it otherwise. Yet somehow the man had managed to talk his way out of being murdered dozens of times—

certainly he wasn't quick enough on his feet to explain his many escapes. He'd talked his way out of bed past dozens of suspicious husbands and that was before one considered the dozens of women he'd talked *in* to those same beds. But Chall was miles and miles away, and so Cutter was left to do it himself.

"All he means," Cutter said, "is that if the past is really as dangerous as you say—and I believe that it is—then maybe it'd be better if we left it altogether and went back to...the present?" he finished uncertainly.

"We cannot return, not yet."

Feledias frowned. "But you just said we need to return—what of all that talk about being stuck in the past?"

"It is a real danger," Door said, *"but it is not the only one. The Green Man's minions seek us, seek you. The Unsated have been set on your trail. He has set them a task, and they will not stop in the pursuit of it until they are dead, or..."*

"Or we are," Feledias finished.

The feyling inclined his head. *"Or else one of the Blood orders it."*

"Blood, like..."

"The Green Man or the Gray. To be of the Blood is to be the purest of the Fey. The greatest among us."

"Like royalty?" Feledias asked.

Door nodded, which just went to say that the creature knew little of royalty in the Known Lands, for Cutter did not think that either he or his brother qualified as great or pure.

"They hunt you still," the feyling went on, *"and even while you are here, still they have your scent. We have evaded them, for the moment, but the Unsated will not be deterred for long, and they are not the only worry. The past presses in around us. Perhaps you feel it."*

It was Cutter's turn to frown now, for he *did* feel something, had felt it for the last half hour, perhaps more. It had started as a sort of tingling along his skin, his back and neck, but it had grown in the moments since it had first appeared. Not a tingle any longer but a strange sort of claustrophobia. He felt as if the walls were closing in on him, as if he might be crushed and never mind that there were no walls and that he'd never felt claustrophobic in his life. "I feel...something," he told the feyling.

"Me too," Feledias frowned. "I thought maybe it was gas, you know brought on by bowel-clenching terror."

"*I do not understand,*" the feyling said.

"I wouldn't worry overly much," Cutter responded. "When it comes to my brother, nobody does. Anyway, you were saying something about those hounds or wolves or whatever they were not being the worst threat?"

"*The past is almost always a far greater threat than any which might lie in a being's future, for in his past one might become lost.*"

"More of a reason, then, for us to leave this past behind now. If those damned—what did you call them, Unsated?—are on our trail anyway, why stay?"

"*We cannot,*" Door said. "*While a man might easily step back into his past, the past is not so easy to leave behind. There are only certain pathways one might take, certain...doors.*"

"And the nearest of these doors?" Cutter asked.

"*Lies far ahead. There the past meets the present and leads, as it ever will, to the future. If we make it there.*"

Cutter didn't much care for the way the creature said that, but before he could ask, Feledias beat him to it.

"Surely you've used such doors before," his brother prompted.

"*Yes,*" the feyling said. "*We have traveled the past since we were young, walked through many doors, down many paths.*"

"See?" Feledias asked, glancing at Cutter. "There's nothing to worry about."

"*But never before have we tarried so long in the past.*"

"Well, what are we waiting for then?" Feledias asked, and Cutter heard a slight breathiness in his voice, no doubt well-deserved fear when confronted by the idea of being stuck in the past. And not just any past, he thought, but that of the Black Wood, of creatures unknown and unknowable, of shadows as deep as great earthen wells. Pits into which a man might fall and find oblivion.

Then they were moving again.

Through a dark past and into a very dark, very uncertain future. But then, for Cutter at least, it seemed that that had always been true.

CHAPTER TWELVE

HE COULDN'T SLEEP.

He hated that.

It seemed to him that the older he got, the less he was able to sleep. Which was ridiculous. After all, he had far more practice at sleeping and trying to sleep now than he had ten, fifteen years ago, and he'd slept like a baby then. Almost always in someone else's bed and, quite often, with someone else's wife. Yet a guilty conscience hadn't kept him awake, that was sure.

Thinking of the past, of women and beds, Chall glanced over at Maeve sleeping beside him. A woman better than all the others, a woman far too good for the likes of him, but there she was nevertheless. Life was funny sometimes. Mostly—nearly always—its sense of humor leaned heavily into the dark, but still he couldn't help but be grateful that she was there.

Yet as comforting as her presence was, still one fact remained...

He couldn't sleep.

Partly it was because his legs seemed to be in a contest to see which one could cause him the most misery. He didn't know which one was winning, the right or the left, but what he did know was that they were each giving it their all.

But as distracting as those aches and pains were, as downright *maddening* as the itch that had settled underneath the bandages of each leg was—an itch he couldn't seem to scratch no matter how much he tried —the truth was that his legs were not the reason that he lay awake. No, what kept him awake long after any decent man should be asleep, after even the indecent ones had succumbed to drunken slumber, was an altogether different pain.

Worry for his friends.

Rare indeed were the times in Chall's life when his worry for another superseded his worry for himself, but there it was. He was worried for Priest—Valden in truth, now, or so it seemed. Chall had always leaned on him for support, finding courage in his courage, finding strength in the man's unerring belief, his *faith* that everything would be alright. Valden had always seemed almost invincible, to him, just as Prince Bernard had, though it had to be said that the two men had seemed invincible in very different ways. The prince because he destroyed anyone or anything that might hurt him before they got much of a chance and Valden because the world simply hadn't seemed able to touch him, had seemed incapable of doing him harm past the armor of faith he'd worn. But that armor was gone now, torn from him or cast aside—even now Chall was not quite sure which—and what was a priest without his faith? Just a man. And a man might be hurt, might be killed.

And of course there was Maeve to think about. He'd never met a more dangerous woman, it was true, and he figured she could take care of herself far better than he could—certainly the fact that she hadn't been shot and stabbed seemed to support that theory. But she was still only a person. She still slept, still had a back, and while it was a damned fine back, that didn't make it any less a target for a knife. And considering that she had somehow inherited leadership of a guild of assassins—people who made a practice of stabbing people in their fronts or backs or whatever part presented itself—that wasn't much of a comfort. Oh, she said she was okay, that everything was and would be fine, but then a lot of people made such assurances. They kept just right on dying anyway, though.

Then there was Prince Bernard. Prince Bernard who was somewhere in the Black Wood, facing unimaginable horrors and threats. If anyone could make it out of such a predicament, he could, but then there was no guarantee that anyone could. And that was before he considered Matt.

He had meant to see to the king before now, to try to figure out what was going on with him, but he had been distracted, mostly by almost getting killed. Still, now that he had a moment to breathe, to heal, he promised himself that he would make the time to help Matt. Not just because he was the prince's son, not even just because he was a good friend, but because he was a good *king,* and that was something the people of the Known Lands desperately needed.

With that resolution, he finally felt as though he might be able to sleep, and he closed his eyes, meaning to give it a go.

That was, of course, when there was a *creak,* and his eyes snapped wide open. He knew that creak, knew it well. It was the sound of the door opening. Maeve had asked him to look into it but he had—no doubt unsurprisingly to anyone who knew him—put it off until now. Chall turned his gaze to the door, hoping, praying that he'd imagined it. But the door swung open farther, and he gritted his teeth. "*Mae,*" he said in a whisper, hoping not to alarm the intruder, "*Mae, wake up.*"

He gave her a shake, and she replied with muttered gibberish. Chall didn't have time to wait, though, for the door opened wide to reveal a figure, little more than shadow, standing there in the darkness. *Shit,* he thought. *Shit shit shit.*

He couldn't wait for Maeve to orient herself—they'd both be dead long before then. Instead, he rolled over to the side of the bed, leaping to his feet. Or at least he meant to. The plain fact was Chall had never been much of a leaper and as it turned out being shot in one leg and stabbed in the other hadn't exactly improved matters. His full weight came down on his two injured legs, and they did the only thing they could do, given the circumstances—they folded beneath him like a couple of frozen twigs snapping in the frost.

He fell, and like all the things he'd ever done in his life, he did it without any trace of grace whatsoever. He grabbed hold of the bed's coverlet in an effort to stop his fall, but while he had been losing some weight lately—mostly because Maeve insisted on limiting his food to a miserably low degree—the coverlet never stood a chance. He fell, taking the blanket with him as he landed sprawled on the floor.

Perhaps it was the coverlet being rudely jerked off her or, perhaps, it was the manly shout that might have easily been mistaken for a pained squawk he'd given as he fell—that before the wind was so thoroughly knocked out of him. Whatever the reason, Maeve did wake up then, rolling off the bed onto the side away from the door and to her feet like it was something she practiced. A knife was in her hand. Chall didn't know where it had come from, wasn't all that sure he *wanted* to know, but he was glad she had it.

"Easy, Maeve," a voice said, "it's me."

Chall recognized that voice, or at least thought he did, and he frowned as Maeve answered. "Emille?"

"It's me," the woman repeated.

"Emille, what are—" Maeve cut off, glancing at Chall, splayed out on the floor and, he imagined, looking like a manatee waiting to be tossed a treat. "Chall, are you okay?"

"Perfect," he said, or meant to. What came out was nothing more than an unintelligible wheeze.

"Stones and starlight, let me help you to your feet." She bent over, grabbing his hand, and Chall was embarrassed by just how difficult the job was of her levering him to his feet, even as he tugged desperately at the bed with his other hand. How he felt just then, if eating less wasn't working to take the weight off, maybe he'd just give up eating altogether.

Finally, though, they managed to get him to his feet, and Chall turned to scowl at the woman in the doorway. "How dare you just barge in like that?" he demanded.

"Chall—" Maeve began.

"No, I'll handle this, Maeve," he said, holding up a hand. "Look, I don't know how you and Ned get on, but here we knock before we just barge into someone's room. Why, we might have been, you know, being intimate."

"Intimate?" Emille asked, her eyes going wide. "But you can barely walk."

"I was already in the bed, wasn't I?" he demanded. "Why would I need to walk?"

"Chall," Maeve said, "I really—"

"No, Maeve, damnit, she damn near scared the shit out of me."

"Thank the gods we didn't manage that," Emille said.

"Chall, you really ought to—"

"All I'm saying is—"

"*Chall, you're naked,*" Maeve interrupted.

Chall grunted. "What are you..." He paused, glancing down at himself. "Ah. Right. I'm naked." Admittedly, he lost a bit of steam then, grunting as he leaned over to retrieve the coverlet from the floor, wrapping it around himself. Emille wasn't grinning when he looked back at her, but he thought he could almost see the grin anyway, and he frowned. "Well, if a man can't go naked when he's in his own bedchambers when can he, you tell me that. It wasn't as if I expected company at...what time is it again?"

"A few hours after midnight," Emille supplied.

"Emille was going to check on things back at the Guild for me," Maeve explained. "I told her to come get me if she needed to."

He frowned, turning to her. "Sure, okay...fine, but what's to stop her from knocking?"

"Quite a bit, actually," Maeve countered. "Considering what's been happening in the castle lately—you know, assassins running amuck, people sneaking around, I thought it best that, if she needed me, she kept her visit secret."

"Fine I guess that makes sense," Chall said, though the truth was he wasn't all that sure it did, only sure that he was naked with nothing but a coverlet to hide it, and he'd lost most of his will to argue. "Still, you might have told me," he finished lamely.

"I'm sorry about that," Maeve said, wincing. "I meant to, honestly, but I didn't think she'd come. I only told her if it was very important and couldn't wait."

Chall glanced between the two women, his gaze finally settling on Emille. "Well? Out with it then. What's so important it got us out of bed—

some considerably more forcefully than others, I might add," he finished, frowning at Maeve.

"It's the Guild, Lady Maeve," Emille said, regarding her. "They're up to something."

"Assassins, up to something?" Chall said, still a bit sour about the whole situation. "Surely not."

A fairly biting remark, or so he thought, but the women didn't seem to agree, for if they thought anything about it at all they hid it well enough. "Who?" Maeve asked.

"I can't say for certain, Lady," Emille said, "but I believe it's Bethesa."

"Who's Bethesa?" Chall asked.

"A snake," Maeve said, frowning. "And worse, a clever one." She turned to Chall. "Will you be alright?"

"Wait, you can't mean to go."

"I don't have a choice, Chall," she said. "It might surprise you to learn, but assassins, if left alone, tend to get a bit...unruly. I've been gone too long already, only I wanted to make sure you were okay."

"I'd be a whole lot okayer if my woman wasn't planning on going back into a guild full of killers, many of which, it seems to me, wouldn't be all that put out by practicing their trade on her."

She flashed him a smile. "Do you need help getting back into bed before I go?"

"I can manage," he growled. In truth, he wasn't all that sure he could, but he'd be damned if he was going to be treated like some infant up past his bedtime, let alone risk falling again in their presence—a distinct possibility as his legs felt decidedly wobbly beneath him.

"You sure?" Emille asked, and though she kept her face straight, he thought he could hear amusement in her voice. "You seem a bit... unsteady."

"Almost as if I've been shot and stabbed," he snapped.

"Well, sure, suppose that'd do it," she said, still straight-faced. Chall had thought that Ned was a smartass, but he was beginning to think that the man had learned it from his wife.

"This is stupid," Chall said. "It's the middle of the night. Whatever it is, it'll keep until morning at least," he finished, glancing at Maeve. He was aware of the pleading in his tone but unable to do anything to stop it.

Maeve moved toward him, taking his hand in hers—at least the one that wasn't holding a knife. "Listen, Chall, I don't want to go, but—"

"Could have fooled me."

She gave a soft sigh, shaking her head. "I don't want to go," she repeated, meeting his gaze. "But we're in a precarious position right now —the truth is with Prince Bernard and Prince Feledias gone the entire kingdom is in a precarious position. The last thing we need is another problem, and believe me, the Guild is a problem waiting to happen. Assassins can't be left alone for long, or they'll get up to no good. They're a lot like children in that way."

"Sure," Chall said, "children who have been trained to kill their entire lives and who'd just as soon slit a man's throat as look at him," he said, frowning.

"Well, not quite as soon," she said, offering him a small smile, one he did not return.

"I don't want you to go," he said.

"And I don't want to leave," she said, "but I have no choice. Believe me, I'd much rather stay here and put you back to bed properly."

There was a twinkle in her eyes, one he recognized all too well—mostly because he spent pretty much every waking hour trying to summon it. "It was the naked fall from the bed wasn't it?" he said in a self-deprecating whisper so that Emille wouldn't hear.

"I've never seen anything so graceful," Maeve said, that twinkle still in her eyes, and damn if he knew what caused it. "Like a swan."

"Sure," he said, "or a drunken elephant."

She smiled. "I'll be back soon, Chall. You just make sure you're healed by then, okay?"

"Consider me healed," he said, not just to Maeve but, more, to that twinkle in her eye.

She gave a soft laugh at that. "You'll be okay," she said. "Valden is here, and you know that if you need anything while I'm gone, he'll be happy to help you."

"When it comes to Valden, I'm not sure if I know anything anymore. And as for happy, have you seen the bastard lately? I've seen some of those mopey-faced hound dogs that looked more excited about life than him. Anyway, it's not me I'm worried about. You said yourself they're a bunch of snakes and here you go, jumping into a pit of them and that without even having to be pushed."

"They are snakes," she agreed, "but even snakes might be tamed."

"I imagine there are quite a few dead men rotting in their graves that thought as much," Chall said.

She winced, then leaned forward and gave him a quick kiss. It didn't last long, just a moment, yet Chall's cheek felt cool and tingly where her lips had touched. "I'll be back soon."

"Not soon enough," he said.

She flashed him another smile, her gaze traveling him up and down, taking in his naked, partially-covered form. "If you'd like, you can be dressed just like that when I return." With that, she turned and nodded at Emille and the two started for the door.

Chall didn't like that, watching her leave. Something about it felt too... certain. Too final. "Maeve?" he blurted.

She turned back at the door.

"I love you," he told her.

She gave a small smile then. "I know," she said. "And I love you too. Now get some rest."

Then she was gone.

Chall stared at the door for several seconds, thinking dark thoughts. In another moment, he contemplated the bed, mostly because he didn't think his legs would hold him for much longer. Malden had done a fine job— whatever else the man was, such as a pain in the ass, there was no arguing that he knew his trade—but shot and stabbed was still shot and stabbed.

The bed looked comfortable, looked, just then, like pretty much the most comfortable bed he'd ever seen. But despite his words to Maeve and Emille, he didn't relish the idea of trying to climb into it. But then he didn't much care for the idea of standing there until his legs gave out beneath him—an eventuality that he thought was no more than a few minutes away.

Chall had never been the type to tackle his problems head on, always preferring to wait, to stall and procrastinate and hope that those problems took care of themselves—which they pretty much never did—but he decided that just this once he would make an exception.

ABOUT WHAT CHALL judged as two seconds or so after he had finally settled into sleep there was a knock at his door. Chall groaned. "Screw off," he grumbled, his mouth tasting foul with sleep. Then he realized that it must be Maeve returning. She'd only just left, after all, and must have come to her senses, realizing that going back to the Assassins' Guild was foolhardy at best. "*Come in,*" he called.

The door opened a moment later.

"Guess you realized I was right," he said.

"About?"

Chall frowned at the figure. Didn't much sound like Maeve. Didn't much look like Maeve either, come to it. "Valden?" he asked, surprised. "Sorry, I thought you were Maeve."

"I'm afraid not," he said. "But what was that about you being right?"

Chall shook his head sourly. "Maeve went back to the Assassins' Guild. Emille came sayin' there was some stuff needed taking care of."

"What stuff?"

"Assassin's stuff, how the shit should I know? Anyway, I thought maybe she'd realized I was right and decided not to go." He sighed. "I should have known better. Can't remember the last time she let me be right."

Valden nodded. "I'm sure that if Maeve thought it was the only choice then it was. Besides, she can take care of herself."

"Don't be a fool, Valden. Sure, she's good with a knife, one of the deadliest people I've ever known, man or woman, but none of us can take care of ourselves. It's why we just keep on dying and never mind all our efforts to the contrary."

"Is that why you are lying on the floor?" Valden asked. "An effort to the contrary?"

Chall glanced around him at the wooden floor then spared a scowl for the bed. "Say that it is," he said. Mostly because it was far less embarrassing than the truth. The truth, of course, being that he'd been unable to make it into the bed and never mind what he'd told Maeve. And so he had chosen—by default—the floor. "Anyway," he went on, deciding it best to change the subject and pausing to groan as he used the bed to pull himself to a sitting position, "what brings you here? Particularly so early in the damn morning when all decent folk—and indecent, take my word for it— ought to be sleeping."

"Morning?" Valden asked. "Chall, but it's approaching noon."

Chall frowned, glancing at the window and finding, to his shock, that the man was right. Sunlight filtered in through the glass, splashing along the floor. "Huh," he said. "So it is."

"As to your question," Valden went on, his expression growing grim, "I'm afraid something's happened."

Chall felt his breath catch in his throat at that. *Maeve. Oh, gods help me please let her be okay.* "Is it Maeve? What's happened, Valden? You have to tell me," he said, rising to his feet, managing it and never mind the aches and pains that shot through his legs. "Where is sh—"

"Maeve's fine, Chall," Valden said quickly. "Or, at least, I'm sure she is —I have not spoken to her. No, it isn't Maeve. It's Mistress Ophasia."

"The mistress of servants?" Chall asked, confused. "What about her?"

"Apparently, someone broke into her quarters."

Chall raised an eyebrow. "Oh? Well, I'm sorry to hear that. I'm sure the guards will find whoever did it, though. Anyway, if that's all, I think I'll get back to tossing and turning. If I don't count those damn sheep, who will?"

"That's not all," Valden said, and Chall paused where he'd been preparing to lie down once more. The other man winced. "There's a body."

"A body?" Chall said. "Shit. Mistress Ophasia—"

"Is fine," Valden said quickly. "At least from what I hear, though I suspect she's a bit shaken up."

"And...the body?"

"A serving girl—I didn't get her name yet," Valden said. "I'm going to find out more. Will you come?"

"Another murder in the castle? You're damn right I'm coming," Chall said. "Better than lying around here waiting for whoever it was to come back and give me a good stabbing."

"*Can* you come, though?" Valden asked.

Chall grunted. "Malden left me a walking stick," he said, jerking his head to indicate it where it stood propped against the wall. "Told me not to use it except in the case of an emergency. I'd say murder qualifies. Now, lead the way."

"Uh...Chall?"

"Yeah, Valden?"

The man looked him up and down, and Chall followed his gaze, glancing down at his naked form save the coverlet wrapped around his waist. "Ah, right," he said. "Might be I ought to put on some boots."

CHAPTER THIRTEEN

THERE WAS a knock on the door.

There had been several over the last few hours and, like those other times, Matt ignored it, just as he ignored the voice that called out "Majesty?" from beyond the door, a voice he recognized as Healer Malden. Again, the call came, and still Matt only sat as he had been, on his bed, his back against the wall, the necklace Ophasia had given him clutched in both hands.

It was rude, he knew, to not answer, but he found that he simply did not have the strength to do so. He knew that the old man was just trying to help, but he knew, also, that he could not. Matt had long since lost count of the number of concoctions they'd tried, the healer claiming that this potion or that tea would soothe Matt's mind and allow him to get some uninterrupted sleep.

None did, though. Tea or potion, nothing changed. The moment his eyes closed, and he drifted into slumber, he found himself—or perhaps it was more accurate to say *lost* himself—in the Green.

In that place, he had little sense of self beyond a panicked feeling that whatever he was, whatever he *had been* was being swallowed, consumed by the Green. It was at once a terrible, horrifying feeling and, somehow at

168

the same time, a comforting one. Horrifying because it was a thing over which he had no control, one which grew stronger no matter what he did and comforting because when he was inside the Green, when *it* was inside of *him,* he did not, for one of the few times in his life, feel alone.

Perhaps the only time. He thought that, maybe, humans were always at least a little lonely. How could they be anything else? After all, even those who had many friends, much family that they cared for and who cared for them, could not be truly, *fully* known, just as they could not truly, *fully* know another. To do that, another would have to live inside their head, to know each thought and whim as it occurred, to understand the origin of such thoughts, the purpose of such whims, and even the man himself could not say as much. No one knew anyone else, then, not really, not even a man himself. Perhaps *particularly* not a man himself.

But the Green knew him.

That was the scary, comforting part. But what was even more unsettling was that *he* was beginning to know *it.* The necklace had a lot to do with that, he thought, the necklace which even now he held in a tight grip. He opened his hands and looked at it again, at the green stone. Sometimes, he thought that if he looked closely enough, if he was still enough, he could see *storms* raging within that green. Flickers of lightning, shifting of dark clouds. Other times, though, like now, it seemed like nothing more than a stone. Empty.

Or no, that wasn't right, not *empty.* Sometimes, the stone spoke to him and sometimes it didn't, that was all. And for the moment, at least, the stone, the Green was silent.

Until it wasn't.

Matt was standing even before the knock came, moving toward the door. He did not pause to get dressed, for he was dressed already. He rarely bothered changing into sleeping clothes now. What was the point when he rarely slept?

He opened the door just as the newcomer had raised their fist to knock. "Hi Chall," he said. "Valden," he went on, nodding to the second man. "What is it?" he asked. "What's happened to Ophasia?"

The two men shared a look, frowning. In another moment they turned back to Matt. "Forgive me, Majesty, but did someone come and inform you?" Chall asked. "I was under the impression that you had not been answering your door for some time and that you did not know." Chall glanced at Vorrun and the second guard standing with him as if for confirmation, but the two men remained standing resolute, like statues, saying nothing, betraying nothing.

"News travels fast, I suppose and bad news worse of all," Matt said, picking up more from the men's errant thoughts even as they stood there. He wouldn't say as much, though, for already they were staring at him as if he were crazy. If he had told him that he had known they were coming even before they turned down the hall then he would likely end up locked in some cell. Perhaps that would even be for the best, but prisoners, so far as he knew, were not allowed jewelry, and he would not let them take the necklace from him.

He could not.

"How is Mistress Ophasia?" Matt asked.

"We're...not sure," Chall said. "We're going now, if—"

"Of course," Matt said. He saw that Chall was looking at his hands where he still gripped the necklace, and he pulled out the chain and draped it over his own neck, trying to appear casual when the truth was he felt anything but. "Lead on," he told the mage.

Chall looked as if he wanted to say something, likely to *ask* something, but thankfully he decided to let it go, and in another moment they were moving.

CHALL DID his best to avoid glancing worriedly at Matt as they walked or at Valden to see if he, too, was as concerned as he was himself. Mostly because he knew that, if he did, the lad would not miss it—he did not miss much these days, seemingly privy to knowledge he had no way of possessing, such as the fact that something had happened at Mistress Ophasia's. Chall and Valden had come to tell him of it, yet he seemed to already know more than they, and how was that possible when Vorrun had told Chall that the king had not opened his door to anyone, including Healer Malden, for over a day? How was that possible? Unless, of course, the king really *could* read people's thoughts.

What about it, lad? Chall asked in his own head. *You there? You listening?*

He abruptly paused in the hallway, spinning quickly to look back at Matt, to catch the young man's reaction. Matt stared at him, a small smile of what might have been dark amusement on his face. Did Chall imagine the look of knowledge in the young man's eyes, or had he actually heard his thoughts?

"Everything okay, Chall?" Matt asked, raising an eyebrow at him.

"Fine, Majesty," Chall said, watching the young king's face. "Only, I thought I saw a bee, and Valden is deathly allergic."

"No, I'm not," Valden said from beside him.

"No, maybe not," Chall said, still watching Matt, "but you could be. Anyway, it appears to have been a false alarm." He was aware of Matt watching him, a small smile on the king's face. Left with nothing else to do, Chall turned and started down the hallway again, just as confused and unsure now as he had been.

It took them nearly fifteen minutes to reach the servants' quarters. When they did, Chall could not help but notice that there were four guards stationed at the hall leading deeper into where the castle's servants lived.

Years ago, Chall had been involved in more than a few trysts with buxom serving wenches or ones with certain glimmers in their eyes—or sometimes just with ones that had a bit of free time. So he was well aware that guards were not normally situated at the hall. After all, the whole point of guardsmen was to stop crimes and what crime might be committed in such a place? Not theft, surely, for most of the men and women in the servant's quarters had very little to steal. What could you take from such a person when the only thing of value they had was their lives? The answer was an obvious one.

"With your leave, Majesty," Vorrun said, "we will remain here—the hallway has been cleared."

"Of course," Matt said in a distracted mumble. Chall frowned, glancing over at the king to find him squinting, one ear turned toward the hallway the way a man might do if he were struggling to hear a distant sound.

Chall shared a look with Valden. "Majesty," he said, "is—"

"This way," Matt said, frowning, then he started forward.

That left Chall and Valden with nothing to do but follow, and so they did, moving down the hallway but not before Chall glanced at the guards who'd been stationed at the hall, trying to determine, by their demeanor, what had happened. He couldn't tell much, but he didn't think any of them were in any danger of breaking into song and dance anytime soon.

Halfway down the hall, they came upon Commander Malex who stood talking quietly to Mistress Ophasia. The woman was weeping quietly, and the commander was talking in a low whisper, clearly trying to offer comfort. Commander Malex turned at their approach, and he bowed to Matt, the mistress of servants sketching a hasty curtsey a moment later.

"Majesty," Malex said.

"Commander Malex," Matt said, nodding even as he turned to the woman. "Mistress Ophasia," he said quietly, "are you alright?"

"I-I'm unharmed, Majesty," the woman responded.

"That is not what I meant," Matt said, and for perhaps the first time since Chall had met him at his quarters—for the first time likely in days—the young king seemed all the way there, completely present and in the moment, as he focused on the older woman. He took her hands in his, waiting until she met his eyes. "I'm sorry," Matt told her. "I truly am."

The woman looked at him with unmistakable gratitude and then began to sob again, her forehead going into Matt's shoulder. The young man put his hand on her back, holding her, offering what comfort he could, and in that moment Chall was as proud of him as, he believed, any father might have been of any son, as proud as any citizen might be of their king.

Something was going on with Matt, that was true, but beneath that troubled, worried, distracted exterior was still the same young man Chall had met what felt like a lifetime ago in the Black Wood. A young man who was kind, perhaps even to a fault, who thought deeply and felt deeply. A young man who did not shy away from a hard thing because it was hard, who seemed to inherently understand something that it had taken Chall a lifetime to learn: that, more often than not, the hard thing was also the right thing.

Whatever else the young man was, whatever other problems he faced, there was no denying this—he was his father's son. His father who, while he was known across the kingdom for his physical strength, was respected by those who knew him not for his ability to crush skulls—although he could and had on more than one occasion—but instead his strength of character, his strength of *will*. A solid presence, one that told his allies, without saying anything at all, that everything would be okay, that he would *make* it okay.

Matt had that same quality, that same will. Chall had caught inklings of it before, several times, but he had never seen it so fully realized as he did now.

He felt it, and a quick glance at Valden showed that he felt it too. The man's default seemed to be cynicism lately, but just then he didn't appear cynical. Instead, for the first time in a very long time, he did not look as if he'd eaten something sour, or perhaps as if he expected life to offer little else besides pain and sadness. Instead, he looked...hopeful.

Matt did not offer empty platitudes to the woman as many might have in his place and here, too, he was similar to his father, for Prince Bernard was not known for his speech and that with good reason. The man rarely said more than was necessary and never something he did not mean or believe, even when doing so might offer comfort. Chall knew this, for he had long since lost count of the occasions when he'd wished the man had. Some thought him cold and hard for that—and sometimes he was, if he thought cold and hard was what was needed—but say this for Prince Bernard and, apparently, for his son: no one ever needed to wonder if he was being honest.

Finally, the old woman pulled back, gazing at Matt with grateful eyes, and Chall decided that if she had not been loyal to him before, she was now. There was respect and admiration in her gaze as she spoke. "Thank you, Majesty."

Matt inclined his head. He glanced farther down the hall, in the direction of Mistress Ophasia's quarters, then back to the old woman. "We will have questions, but they need not be answered now, if you don't feel up for it."

The woman took a deep, shuddering breath, making an obvious effort to compose herself. "No, it...it's okay, Majesty. I want to help, if I can."

"Very well," Matt said, "but if at any time it becomes too much...know that you are more important than your answers."

She gave him a teary smile then. "Thank you, Majesty. Your...I hope you will not think me out of line if I say that we—the kingdom, I mean—are lucky to have you."

Matt gave her a smile at that, but there was something odd about it. "Thank you, Mistress Ophasia." He turned to Commander Malex and gave a nod. "Best we'd go and see."

"Of course, Majesty," Malex said, starting down the hall. They followed, and the moment Ophasia turned away the king's expression changed. Chall saw, then, what it was about the young man's smile that had struck him as strange. It had been fake. In fact, the look on the king's face in response to the old woman's words about the kingdom being lucky to have him was not a smile but, unguarded, a grim wince that seemed very close to shame.

Looking at his face, Chall was reminded that often the worst wounds a man suffered were invisible to those around them, yet they bled just the same. As they walked down the hallway past the rooms of the other servants, Chall noted several standing in their doorways. They bowed low as Matt passed but not quickly enough for Chall to miss the worried expressions on their faces.

The door to Mistress Ophasia's rooms was at the end of the hall, and as they approached Chall saw that it had been left open.

"Diane is inside?" Matt asked quietly.

Commander Malex turned, clearly surprised. "Forgive me, Majesty, but I was not aware that you had been informed."

"Say that I have," Matt said.

The commander nodded. "Yes, Majesty—she's inside."

Matt frowned grimly at the door. "Show me."

"Of course—this way, if you will, Majesty," Commander Malex said. "Only, I would watch your step. It...it is a bit of a mess."

As they started filing through the door, Chall turned to Valden. "Diane? How does he know her name? We're the one that told him about it, and *we* don't know."

Valden shook his head slowly, staring after Matt. "Come on."

There were just about a thousand things Chall would have rather done than walk in that room, but the others were already moving inside. He considered begging off, telling them his legs were hurting terribly—no lie there. But he knew even as he had the thought that he wouldn't. His friends were going inside, so he was going inside. He heaved a sigh, gathering what courage he possessed—tattered, frayed scraps ready for the trash heap—and stepped inside.

Chall had never been inside the mistress of servants' quarters before, but he had been in a few of the servants' themselves, in his time—late night trysts or, sometimes, early day trysts, depending on when the mood and, more importantly, the opportunity struck. And so he knew that the room was bigger than that of the other servants, though it was a far cry from a king's quarters and not so large that he couldn't take it all in with one quick sweep of his gaze.

A bed sat against the wall, the sheets and coverlet immaculately made, the corners tucked in. No doubt Mistress Ophasia had made it herself, and who finer to do it than the one who taught all the other servants how?

There was a small desk against the wall opposite the bed, but Chall barely noticed it. Instead, his attention caught on the corpse splayed out in the middle of the floor. It was always off-putting seeing dead bodies—Chall had seen enough to know—but in the incredibly tidy, perfectly kept and maintained rooms of the mistress of servants it seemed almost profane, almost sacrilegious.

Chall didn't enjoy looking at or even being around dead bodies and never mind that anyone looking at the course of his life couldn't help thinking otherwise. The fact was, he'd seen plenty of dead people. Far too many. Sometimes it seemed to him he'd seen far more of the dead than he had of the living.

But he had rarely seen anything so shocking as the dead woman. She lay sprawled on her stomach near the room's center. Judging by the crimson streaks running across the floor, she'd tried to crawl away from her attacker. Judging by the gouges in the wood floor and the splintered, jagged nails that Chall could see where her hands were even now stretched toward the door, she had tried hard.

Not that it had done her any good. Whoever had come upon the woman had had no intention of letting her go. Chall didn't stop to count, but at a guess he thought there were at least a few dozen stab wounds dotting the woman's body, her back and legs and arms, maybe as many as fifty. Someone had gone at her with a knife—maybe several someones, by the look of it. From the number of wounds, Chall thought there could have been as many as half a dozen attackers.

He swallowed, trying to force down his rising gorge. It went, if reluctantly. "Do we know how many there were?" he asked quietly. "There had to have been, what? At least three, maybe more?"

"We...do not believe so," Commander Malex said.

Chall frowned. "So what *do* you believe?" He turned away from the body, feeling a great sense of relief as he did. "And how have we not found the bastards who did this? From the looks of it, they ought to be covered in blood."

"Bastard," Commander Malex said.

"Wait a minute," Chall said, "are you saying..."

"Healer Malden just left a few minutes ago," Malex said. "He examined the...the body, and—"

"*Diane,*" Matt said, his voice a low growl, and Chall couldn't tell if the king sounded more like he was going to shout in anger or cry in grief. Both, maybe. "*Her name was Diane.*"

"Of course, Majesty," Commander Malex said, bowing his head. "Healer Malden, he examined...Diane, and said that, based on the wound patterns and their similarity he believed that there was only one attacker."

"One person?" Valden asked, and even though he spoke quietly Chall could hear the surprise—surprise to match his own—in the man's voice.

"So Healer Malden believes," Commander Malex said.

"Not a person," Matt said, his voice thick with emotion. "A monster. Anyone who would do this...they could only be a monster."

Chall had no intention of disagreeing and, judging by the silence that followed the king's words, no one else did either. Just as well, as based on the expression of angry challenge on Matt's face, Chall thought anyone who disagreed would have quickly regretted it. He understood Matt's frustration and his angry reaction, for he had done the same many times. Sometimes, when circumstances left a man feeling angry but he couldn't express his anger to the person or thing responsible, he found himself expressing it to those nearest him instead.

"I was supposed to meet her," a voice said, and they all turned to see Mistress Ophasia. The old woman had stopped just inside the doorway, apparently unwilling or unable to come any farther than that. Chall had known her for some time, and although they'd never been close, she'd always struck him as formidable. And not just that—steady. She, along with Healer Malden, Commander Malex, and some few others were the anchors upon which the smooth running of the castle rested.

But, just then, the woman looked anything but steady. Not that Chall could blame her. If he'd walked in his quarters to discover a body as mutilated as the one lying on the ground before them—*Diane,* he reminded himself, *her name's Diane*—he would have been unsteady too. Likely he would still be clinging to the room's ceiling like a cat with its claws sunk in. Or weeping in the corner, maybe.

"What was the meeting about?" Valden asked.

"Nothing that might have led to...to this," Mistress Ophasia said. "At least, I do not believe so. Only..." She paused, glancing at Matt. "I was meeting with her about what we discussed the other day, Majesty, regarding her...encounter with the guardsman—the one we spoke about. I was going to talk to her, as you requested, about meeting with you. She was...afraid."

"I see," Matt said quietly, and although his expression was difficult to read, Chall thought he heard something in the young man's voice, some terrible grief or pain lying just beneath the surface of those two simple words.

"I had meant to be here before she arrived," Ophasia went on, tears gathering in her eyes, "but th-there was an issue in the kitchen I had to deal with, and I was running behind. H-had I been here on time, perhaps Diane would..." She broke into a sob then, the tears streaming out of her eyes. She buried her head in her hands, shaking with her grief.

Chall glanced at Valden, expecting the man to step forward, as he had a thousand times before, to offer comfort as he had a thousand times. But the man only stared at her, a pained expression on his face. He noted Chall's look and winced in what might have been apology.

Chall found himself growing angry at the man. Perhaps it was misplaced anger—the same way that Matt had been angry a moment ago, his frustration driving him to lash out at anything or anyone. But misplaced or not, it was there just the same, and based on the surprise that came over Valden's face, something of it must have shown in Chall's expression.

In the end, he found himself stepping forward, embracing the old woman. "It is not your fault," he said. "Had you been on time, there would have been two bodies lying on the floor instead of one. The type of person who would...the type of person who would do something like this wouldn't have been dissuaded by your presence."

She shuddered against his chest and nodded. "Th-thank you, Sir Challadius. You are...you are kind."

Chall had been called a lot of things before, but he wasn't sure kind had ever been one of them. Wasn't sure, either, that it ought to be, but that didn't keep him from feeling nice at hearing it. At least, that was, until he glanced at the floor and saw the body lying there once more.

"Sh-she should not have even been here," Mistress Ophasia said quietly. "Had I not asked her to come, she would have been safe in her rooms."

Chall wanted to disagree. He even entertained, briefly, the idea that whoever had killed the serving girl had done so because they had something against her for some reason. After all, to stab someone dozens of times like they had, it seemed to Chall that they had to have had something against her. It would have been tiring work.

But then, a glance around the room at the drawers of the bureau, all ripped out, their contents dumped on the ground, a look at the closet and desk which had suffered a similar treatment argued against that. Whoever had come had been looking for something, that much was obvious. Less obvious, though, was what that something might be. Still, there was the mistress of servants to think of just then. "It's not your fault," he told her.

Not much, maybe, but it was the best he could think of just then.

"Chall's right," Matt said, studying the body with a hard, grim stare. "It's not your fault. It's mine."

"Majesty—" Chall began.

Matt raised a hand, silencing him as he turned to Commander Malex. "The person responsible for this—where are we at on finding him?"

Commander Malex winced. "I have men combing the castle now, Majesty, searching. Whoever it is, whoever did this, Healer Malden assures me that he couldn't have done it without getting blood on himself or his clothes. We will find him."

"Unless he has already left the castle," Valden said.

"It is...unlikely," Commander Malex said. "According to Healer Malden, we found the body only minutes after the crime was committed."

Mistress Ophasia gave a fresh sob at that, and the commander winced before going on. "Malden said he didn't believe the perpetrator could have made it out of the castle by the time we found her. At least not without someone noticing."

"And did they?" Chall asked. "Notice, I mean?"

Commander Malex shook his head. "I have already spoken with the guards on duty at the front of the castle, as well as the gate. No one has gone past them in the last several hours save for Lady Maeve."

"Maeve left the castle?" Matt asked, glancing at Chall.

"She had...business in the city, Majesty," he said. The sort of business, he thought, that might well end up with someone being stabbed—that was one of the primary functions of assassins, after all. Not that it was likely that an assassin was responsible for the dead woman lying before them. The sorts of people the Guild employed were efficient, trained killers, unemotional, detached. The person who had done this to the serving woman had not been focused on efficiency, or at least it didn't seem so to him.

"I see," Matt said. He turned back to Commander Malex. "And they are sure? No one else left?"

"No one, Majesty," Malex said.

"So what, then?" Chall asked. "Either the bastard is invisible, or else he somehow managed to climb over the castle walls or out a window, maybe?" He shook his head, frustrated.

"There's another option," Valden said quietly, and they all turned to him.

"Oh?" Chall asked.

The man nodded. "It may be that the attacker hasn't left at all, that he is still in the castle, somewhere."

"I don't much love the sound of that," Chall said.

"You really believe that? That he's still in the castle, I mean?" Matt asked, frowning.

Valen shrugged. "I do not know, Majesty. There is simply no way of knowing."

"Oh, gods help us," Mistress Ophasia sobbed.

"Majesty, if you approve," Commander Malex said, "perhaps it would be better if Mistress Ophasia got some rest."

"Of course," Matt said, still staring at the body. "Ask Vorrun to find her the most secure room we have. Place a guard outside, then you go and find this man, whoever he is. And when you do," he went on, finally turning away from the body and meeting the commander's gaze, "you let me know first."

Chall stared at the grim set of the young king's jaw, at the coldness in his eyes, and again he saw something of the young man's father in him. It wasn't just his father's will, it seemed, that Matt had inherited, but his anger, his fury, too.

"Yes, Majesty," Commander Malex said, a slightly troubled expression on his face as he bowed then offered his arm to Mistress Ophasia. The older woman took it and in another moment they were heading out the door and down the hall.

Only when they were gone did Chall speak. "Who would do such a thing?" he asked. "I mean...okay, maybe they did come to rob her, but this..." He glanced at the body then pulled his gaze away again. "This is different. This wasn't just theft."

"I agree," Valden said. "Furthermore, why come here at all?"

"What do you mean?" Matt asked.

"All I mean, Majesty," Valden said, "is that if our thief, whoever he is, really only meant to steal valuables, then there are far better places in the castle to do it than the servants' quarters. It seems to me, then, that if our thief chose to rob Mistress Ophasia it was because he came looking for something specific."

"Like what?" Chall asked.

Valden shook his head. "I don't—"

"I have to go," Matt blurted.

Chall turned to him. "Majesty, is everything alright?"

"Fine," Matt said in a tone of voice that was, Chall thought, pretty damned far from fine. "I just...I have to go."

Then, before either of them could say anything else, Matt turned and walked out the door, not quite running but not all that far from it either.

Chall turned to Valden. "What was that about?"

"I don't know," Valden said, staring at the door through which Matt had exited a moment before. "Something is wrong with Matthias, I think."

"Yeah?" Chall asked. "Well, that seems to be going around, doesn't it?"

"Something is on your mind, I take it," Valden said.

"You're damn right something's on my mind," Chall snapped. "Quite a few somethings, in fact. Like, for example, the fact that my woman is, even now, at a guild full of people who kill *other* people for a living. They could have been anything—bakers maybe. But they *chose* to kill people instead. Or how about the fact that Prince Bernard is gone to the Black Wood when we, when the *kingdom,* need him most? But if that isn't enough for you, then what about how his son has something—something serious, I think—going on with him? And then, of course, there's the body lying at our feet and the fact that someone is running around the castle poking holes in people for reasons I can't begin to imagine."

"I'll admit, things are—"

"I'm not finished," Chall said, holding up his hand for silence. "You were right in what you were going to say, things *are* bad. But then in my experience they often are. I can handle bad—the gods know I've handled it nearly my whole life. I've faced the bad over and over again. But this time, this time's different. This time, Bernard's gone, Maeve too, and Matt might as well be. This time I'm alone."

Valden frowned at that. "You're not alone, Chall. I'm here."

"Are you?" he said. "Are you, really? Because if you ask me, Valden you haven't been here for some time now. Sure, you're going through the motions, maybe, but that's about it. You're like a puppet, just walking around, doing things, not really caring. Damnit, it's all going to shit, can't you see that? All of it. I don't need a puppet. I need my friend. The one who used to always know the thing to say, the thing to do. The one who believed everything was going to work out. The one who believed it so much that he made *me* believe it. I want, I *need* my friend back. I don't need Valden the Vicious. I need Priest."

The other man studied him for several seconds, then, finally, spoke. "I don't think he exists anymore," he said quietly. "And if he does...if he does, I don't know where to find him."

Chall nodded, feeling suddenly very close to tears, in that moment. Strange, maybe, but there it was. "Well, when you do, why don't you let me know?" he said. "Because I miss him. I miss my friend. And you know what? The world sure could use some more priests." He glanced down at the dead woman. "I think it's got more than its share of killers already."

Then, with that, he turned and left, unable to stay in the room with the dead any longer. One of them still drew breath, it was true, but Chall thought he was dead just the same and it would take a miracle to revive him.

The problem, of course, he thought as he walked out the door, was that in New Daltenia just then, grief and tragedy were in abundance, while miracles...

Well, miracles were in short supply.

CHAPTER FOURTEEN

MATT STUMBLED away from Mistress Ophasia's quarters, away from the others, his breath ragged, his mind a storm of grief and rage and terror and shame and a thousand other emotions, far too many to identify and understand. His guard walked behind him, the man's troubled thoughts at his behavior only adding to the din reverberating inside his head. The guard was meant to keep him safe from any threat, yet Matt felt pursued just the same. And not just pursued...he felt haunted.

Emma was no longer in his mind. The feyling had possessed him, once, had made of him little more than a prisoner inside his own head. He remembered how he'd felt then. Helpless. Afraid. Weak. Like a child crying in the darkness, begging for help with no help coming.

Emma was no longer in his mind. He knew that, for he had defeated her himself—in a way that he even now didn't really understand. Yet he felt haunted just the same. Only it wasn't the feyling that haunted him, not now. It was his own conscience.

It seemed that everywhere he turned, there was nothing but pain, nothing but grief, and that unending. He clutched at the green stone underneath his nightshirt as if it were a magic talisman, found some small comfort in it. He wasn't sure why the stone's touch reassured him, only that it did.

But even the reassurance the emerald offered was not enough to keep back the despair pervading his thoughts as he fled the servants' quarters. As he fled Chall and Valden and their worried looks, their worried thoughts, but most of all fled from the corpse lying on the floor of Mistress Ophasia's quarters.

Not a corpse, he told himself viciously. *Diane.* Diane, the woman who he had meant to help. Only he had never got the chance. And it seemed to him that no sooner had he decided to help her than the world had chosen to use her as an example, to visit some terrible tragedy upon her if for no other reason than to show him that he could do nothing, that he *was* nothing.

As he'd stared at the woman's body, he'd felt angry, furious, but more than that he'd felt guilty. It was a guilt that had grown heavier and heavier with each minute he'd spent in Mistress Ophasia's quarters until it had felt almost impossible to draw a breath. And so he'd run. He had never made a conscious choice to do so. He'd ran simply as a reaction in the same way that a man, touching a hot hearth would jerk his hand away, his body seeking to avoid that pain even before his mind understood it for what it was.

But that running had done him little good. Like the man who realizes too late the heat of the stone hearth, he had been burned already. Burned, *seared* by the vision of the dead woman lying in a pool of her own blood, a sight that he was confident would haunt what little troubled sleep he managed if he managed any at all. Not that he could sleep just then.

"Back to your quarters, Majesty?"

Matt nearly started at the sound of the guardsman's voice, and he realized that he'd been standing still for the last several minutes. He turned to regard the guardsman. Normally, two of them would have escorted Matt wherever he went, but as Vorrun was currently on the errand of finding a safe place for Mistress Ophasia, there was only the one man. Matt couldn't remember his name and that bothered him.

"I'm sorry, Guardsman..."

"Patrick, Your Highness."

"Right, Guardsman Patrick. As for your question..." He paused, considering. Part of him was tempted by the idea of going back to his rooms, of hiding there, as he had for the last several days. Mostly, though, it made him feel like a coward. After all, he'd been hiding in his rooms like a child tucked underneath his blankets while Diane had been killed. And what point was there in going back, anyway? It wasn't as if he was going to sleep any time soon, not with the image of Diane's body so fresh in his mind.

Worse, he knew that if he did go back, Healer Malden would feel obliged to keep checking on him when the man's talents would be far better used helping someone else, someone he actually *could* help. After all, Matt didn't know what was happening, but he knew that whatever it was, it was beyond Healer Malden's ability to heal.

"No, no, I think perhaps I will walk some," he said.

"Very well, Majesty," Guardsman Patrick said. And then, a moment later, *Great, I get to spend my time babysitting some mad king and trying to make sure he doesn't shit himself.*

The man hadn't said the words aloud, but he might as well have as clearly as Matt heard them. He winced, doing his best to hide his reaction to the man's thoughts, something at which he was getting better. The gods knew he'd had plenty of practice of late. Sometimes, he could go hours without hearing someone's thought or feeling the Green calling him, but at other times their imaginings were like thunder in his mind and the Green seemed not to call but to *pull* at him with a leash to which he was tethered.

He had begun to realize that those waxes and wanes seemed to correlate with how upset he was—the more upset, the louder the thunder, the greater the pull. And he was very upset now, so that the guardsman's thoughts were like a storm raging in his mind.

Why is the bastard just standing there? If we're going to walk, let's walk already. Damned madman.

Matt turned away from the guard, making a show of looking down the hallway to hide his wince, this time not of shame or embarrassment but actual pain as the words reverberated in his skull.

He started walking. He didn't have a destination in mind. He was only focused on moving, on trying to distract himself from the guardsman's thoughts, trying to banish the image of the dead woman from his mind, two tasks at which he failed miserably.

They walked for fifteen minutes or so, Matt focused on weathering the storm of the guardsman's thoughts, thinking about what Valden and Chall had said about Mistress Ophasia's rooms. *Seems like they were looking for something.*

His fingers clutched at the gem hanging from his neck. As he touched it, it seemed to pulse as if with some inner life. Ridiculous, maybe, but he could have sworn he felt it just the same.

When he'd set out, he had thought that he was walking randomly, only moving, not caring about where he was moving *to,* but in time he found himself standing before a door, one he knew led to the king's courtyard.

He blinked, staring at the door, wondering why he had come here. But then it didn't *feel* as if he'd come here so much as been brought. As if the Green had brought him. "I think I will go and sit for a time," he said. "You can remain here."

"Are you sure, Majesty? I can accompany you, if you'd li—"

"No, no," Matt blurted, "that won't be necessary. Thank you, Guardsman Patrick."

No, thank you, the guardsman thought back as he bowed his head, *the last thing I need is more of this shit.*

Matt pushed his way through the door, closing it behind him. Perhaps it slammed a bit, but he was only thankful, as he stepped farther into the courtyard, that the man's thoughts began to recede. A fountain sat in the middle of a profusion of green, in front of which there was a stone bench. Matt moved to it and sat, thankful, for the moment, for the blessed silence, unbroken by the thoughts of others, thoughts he should not hear but did anyway. He focused on slowing his ragged, almost panicked breaths, on letting his mind and his heart settle. As he sat, he found himself removing his necklace and cradling it and the gem attached to it in both hands.

He stared down at that green gem and once again he thought he could almost see the light in it shifting, like clouds moving across the face of the sky. His head began to ache with a familiar pain. Often, after he found himself hearing others' thoughts, his head began to hurt. It was a pain he hated and looked forward to at the same time, for during that time, his mind was his own, and the thoughts of others remained in their own heads where they belonged. As if the gift—or curse, at least to his mind—of being able to read their thoughts needed time to recharge, perhaps.

Sometimes, Matt wondered if he was insane.

Most times, he thought he was.

There was a rustling in the bushes beside him, and Matt's breath caught in his throat. There was a murderer on the loose, one that might well still be in the castle, and he had left his only guard outside. He leapt to his feet, reaching to his hip where he kept his sword and cursing himself as he realized that it wasn't there, not even the wooden one he'd spent so much time practicing with lately.

He tensed, gritting his teeth in expectation, wondering if Guardsman Patrick would hear his cry for help from here as the bushes nearest the path began to move and shift.

But as the figure emerged from the proliferation of green, Matt saw that it was not at all who he'd expected. The newcomer, too, seemed surprised to find him there, at least judging by the startled cry she gave as she stumbled backward.

"Lady Valencia?" Matt asked uncertainly. He had seen the noblewoman when she'd first arrived at the castle—though she'd been sleeping at the time, under the effects of a tea Malden had given her to help her rest. The healer's concoctions might not have worked on Matt, but they'd clearly worked on the noblewoman, for she had not stirred when he'd checked in on her. Still, even though he'd seen her before he found that she was difficult to recognize. Mostly because the once-fine dress she wore was torn on one powder blue sleeve, and much of it, as well as her hands, was covered in dirt.

"King Matthias?" the woman asked, her eyes going wide.

"Please," Matt said, holding up his hands to show that he meant no harm, for the old woman looked beyond terrified, "just 'Matt.'"

Lady Valencia looked around then turned back to him, an expression of surprise on her face. "Are you alone, Majesty?"

"You sound almost relieved," Matt said, offering her a smile.

She returned it, seeming to lose some of the worst of her terror. "Forgive me, Majesty, only...even the old, like myself, can be vain, and I had not thought to be seen in my current..." She paused, glancing down at herself. "Dishevelment. I was under the impression that these gardens were not often frequented."

"You need not worry. My guardsman is positioned outside."

She smiled gratefully. "That is...good, Majesty. Still, no doubt you are wondering why I am in these gardens so dirty."

"The thought had crossed my mind, my lady," Matt admitted. "But it's none of my business."

"Isn't it, Majesty?" she asked, seeming mostly put at ease now. "They are, after all, your gardens, are they not?"

Matt considered that then shrugged. "Are they? The plants and flowers which grow here do not have me to thank but another for their care. I grew up in a small town—a village, really—and it seems strange to me for someone to claim ownership over something they had no part in making or maintaining and that they have had little use of, either good or bad."

"It is the way of the world, Majesty," she said.

"And if some decided they didn't want it to be the way, anymore?" he asked. After all, by the way of the world he was king, a job for which he was not qualified and at which, it seemed to him, he had continually failed.

The old noblewoman gave a small shrug. "They have before, Majesty. Many times, if the histories are to be believed. And what resulted from it... well. In a word, chaos."

"From what I've seen of the world," Matt said, thinking of the dead woman again, "it could use some chaos."

"Certainly, many have believed so over the years, Highness. Believed it so much that they raised armies to bring such change, such chaos about."

"Yes," Matt said grimly, "they call them tyrants."

"Not always, Majesty," Lady Valencia said. "Sometimes...well, sometimes they call them the victor. Sometimes, they call them king."

"I'm...not sure I understand what you mean."

The noblewoman gave a small shrug. "Forgive me, Highness—I do not mean to speak cryptically. A curse of the old, I'm afraid. I only mean that history is decided by the winner. He—and those who serve him—write it down after the fact, write it, *edit* it the same way a bard might a song he's looking to perfect, adding a part here, taking out a part there. Not because he wishes to tell the truth, you understand. After all, the truth can be terribly inconvenient at times. Instead, he seeks to tell *his* truth, the truth that he wishes to be remembered. And is that any great surprise? It isn't as if there is anyone left to argue the point."

Matt considered the woman's words. "You act as if kings have great power," he said.

"Do you not believe it to be so, Majesty?"

Matt shook his head slowly. "Not in my experience, no. Mostly I feel as though I'm being babysat constantly, and from the audiences I have everyone wants me to do something different."

The woman nodded. "I am sure it can be quite...trying. But I would remember this, Highness—some beasts are only caged because they allow themselves to be. Should they choose, they might break free of their bonds easily enough and do what they will."

Matt found himself thinking of the army. Commander Malex had told him that the army was nearly ready to march, but he had picked up from the way the man spoke—and even more from the way he thought—that he believed it was a mistake to send them into the Black Wood. There had been a few incursions into the Fey homeland during the war, but they still knew little about it or what would await such an army. Death, he knew that, for he had heard the stories of the things those few who had survived had seen there when he'd been a child, the same way every boy or girl of the Known Lands had.

And should they squander their army in search of two men—even two princes—then they would be open to reprisal from the enemy, a counterattack that, given the kingdom's current precarious situation, could destroy it altogether. Matt had hesitated, so far, listening to Malex's advice, but what good had that done him? What good had it done the kingdom or his father? "And the beast," he said, meeting the woman's gaze, "what if, by breaking free, by leaving its cage, it might hurt someone else? Maybe a lot of someones?"

The noblewoman looked down at her hands, covered in dirt, then back to Matt. "People always get hurt, Majesty," she said. "It's what we're best at."

"So...what are you saying?" he asked. "That I shouldn't care?"

She seemed to consider that for a moment, and for some reason she looked at her dirt-covered hands once more. "I have lived a long time, Majesty," she said finally. "Too long, some might say. And one thing I have noticed about people is that they always want to believe themselves right, believe themselves *good*. They will go to great lengths to be seen as such, to *believe* themselves as such." She gave a soft, humorless laugh. "I am no better, understand. There was a time, not so very long ago, when I thought myself a good person."

"And now?" Matt asked.

She shook her head slowly. "And now, I realize that society, with all its trappings, exists largely to cover up one simple fact, and that is this—we are not so different, not so very different at all, than beasts. It is, in the end, not so much about good or about evil, not a question of *morality*," she went on, her voice seeming thick with emotion. "Instead, it is about one thing and one thing only—survival. A priest, with all his holy words and holy robes, might think himself good. And, if he is very lucky, he can go right on believing it."

"And if he isn't lucky?"

She gave him a small, humorless smile. "Then the world will decide to prove to him that he is wrong, and he will suffer for it, suffering which will likely be shared by others. It is easy, after all, for the well-fed, well-sheltered priest to give food and water to the poor, isn't it? To care for the little orphans of the world. But what if he has no food to give, has not enough even for himself? What will he do, our charitable priest, when hunger gnaws at his belly like a sack of rats? And then say that one lump of moldy bread falls between him and that starving child. What do you think our charitable, starving priest will do then, Majesty?"

"You're saying that he would take the bread."

The noblewoman raised her eyebrow. "I'm saying that he would be prepared to do far worse than that," she said quietly. "When faced with our own survival or that of another, we do what we must to survive. It is no one's fault—it simply is the way it is."

Matt frowned, thinking that through. He wondered what Priest would have to say on the matter. But then, he was Priest no longer. He was Valden the Vicious once more. "That seems like a terribly lonely way to live," Matt said.

"It is the only way to live, Majesty."

Instead of Priest, Matt found himself thinking of his father. His father who had a reputation for being a brutal warrior. The Crimson Prince they called him, and perhaps they were right to, Matt wasn't sure. He hadn't yet been born when his father had earned the moniker. What he *was* sure of, though, was that whatever else he had done, he had saved Matt's life. Had gone through great danger and trouble and personal pain to do so. He had sacrificed everything so that Matt might live. Perhaps he was a murderer, perhaps he *had* done bad things—certainly he had never disputed that. But he had also done great things and, for Matt, at least, and quite possibly for anyone living and breathing in the Known Lands, he was also a savior.

Matt decided then that he did not agree with the woman, did not think that his father, had he been there, would have agreed with her either. After all, if all men were little more than beasts, if goodness was no more than a luxury that might be given up as soon as it became inconvenient then what was the point of anything? What was all the pain and striving and hurting *for* if not in pursuit of something good, something better? Still, Lady Valencia had been through enough over the last days, and he did not want to be rude. "I...will think on what you said, Lady," he said. She was staring at her hands again. "If you don't mind my asking, Lady, how is it that you got so dirty? Is...that is, are you alright?"

She tensed, looking odd for a moment, almost like a child that was caught at mischief. She gave a soft laugh, one that, to Matt at least, didn't seem genuine. "Ah, I...I am fine, Majesty. Thank you for your concern. It's only...well, perhaps it sounds foolish, but I...that is, I enjoy gardening, working with plants and flowers. From my childhood, I suppose. My mother kept a garden, you see, and it has always given me...comfort."

"I understand," Matt said, and he did. He'd lost his mother far too recently—or at least the woman he thought to be his mother—and he would have done much to have felt close to her again, to feel connected. "Still," he went on, forcing the dark memories back with a smile he didn't feel, "I'm no expert, but don't most people wear gloves when they garden? And clothes that are more..."

"Appropriate?" she asked, glancing down at her dress, one that would have been far more at home in a ballroom than in a garden. She smiled. "No doubt you are right, Majesty, but then my mother always told me that I was a willful child, and just because those days are far, far behind me I see no reason to change. In my experience, what is appropriate is rarely the same as what is fun. Now, with your leave, Majesty, I will go to my rooms. As you have pointed out, I fear that I am in need of a bath."

"Of course," Matt said, and while he couldn't hear the woman's thoughts just then—could barely hear his own with the piercing headache —he didn't need to read minds to see that the woman was eager to leave. Another name, then, to add to the list of people who would rather do... well, just about anything than be around him. Not that he could blame her. Most, he knew, considered him mad, and likely they were right to. After all, what other name was there for a man who believed he could read people's thoughts, who found his sleep—as well as his waking hours—haunted by a force a *presence* he could think of only as the Green?

No sooner had he had the thought than the necklace—which he'd been holding tightly in his hands—seemed to pulse. The feeling was unexpected, and Matt grunted in surprise as the necklace tumbled out of his hands and onto the ground, rolling to a stop at Lady Valencia's feet.

The noblewoman knelt, retrieving it. "Ah, Majesty, you appear to have dropped your—" She paused as she glanced at the stone, and so abrupt was the pause that Matt almost wanted to ask her if *she* felt something too, when she touched it. He hesitated, though, mostly because the kingdom already thought he was crazy, and asking people if gems pulsed in their hands or heated to their touch would just further cement the growing opinion of him as insane.

"My, but this...this is a pretty stone, isn't it?" the noblewoman asked in a distracted way, studying the green gem.

Matt came to his feet, moving forward. "Thank you," he blurted, snatching it out of her hands and draping the chain around his neck once more.

The woman blinked. "Sorry, Majesty, I did not mean to offend you."

"Oh, no, you didn't," Matt said, wincing. "It's just...sorry. It's just been a long day what with...well, maybe you heard about Diane?"

"Diane, Your Highness?"

"The serving girl," he said, "the one that was..." Again he hesitated, this time because he knew that Lady Valencia had recently been attacked at her home as well as Ned's and the last thing he needed to do was to worry the old woman more. But she was looking at him, waiting, and he saw no way of avoiding it now. "She was attacked—killed, I'm afraid."

"I see," the noblewoman said. "That is terrible news...do...do they know who is responsible? Likely another servant, I expect. I have been around enough of them in my life to know that while they might act pleasant enough, *tame* enough, they can often be cruel, malicious creatures."

"As all men can be," Matt said.

"Perhaps you're right, Majesty," the woman said, though she did not sound convinced. "But I believe the gods place us in our stations for a reason, noble and servant alike. But please, you must tell me about that stone—is it an emerald? I have never seen anything quite like it."

Matt realized something then, as he stared at the noblewoman. He didn't like her. At first, he had taken her as a sweet old lady, a victim. Perhaps the fact that she *had* been victimized, had been attacked and nearly killed, might have explained why she would act so callous, but explaining something and excusing it were two very different things. After all, she had seemed more worried about the necklace than a woman's life —*no, not woman*, he thought, *creature. She called them creatures.*

"Perhaps you haven't," Matt said. "Anyway, weren't you in a hurry to get cleaned up?"

The woman looked surprised by the abrupt dismissal, giving a curtsey. "Of course, Your Majesty," she said, glancing once more at his neck where the necklace hung despite the fact that he had tucked it into his shirt, out of sight. "I wish you a good day."

And with that, she turned and left, leaving Matt alone with nothing but his thoughts to keep him company.

It was not pleasant.

CHAPTER FIFTEEN

Maeve, with Emille at her side, made her way through the front door of *Sir Chavoy's Academy of the Healing Arts,* walking through the large entryway past students huddled in small groups and the desk at which a woman sat.

They walked down the center hallway past classrooms with students and teachers engaged in lessons to a door at which stood a guard. Those who attended and taught in Sir Chavoy's Academy, at least on the upper floor, were told—if they were told anything—that the lower level was a place for research, a place where men and women who were chosen as the best and brightest went to work on formulating new medicines, new formulas of healing the sick and hurt.

A complete lie, of course. Those beneath the main level of Sir Chavoy's were not concerned in the least with helping the sick or healing the hurt— quite the opposite, in fact. And anyone "chosen" to be brought down below was not picked based on their empathy or kindness but, in many cases, their complete lack of either.

The guard at the door inclined his head as they approached. "Guild-master," he said quietly. "Lady Emille."

Maeve returned the nod, stepping through the door and starting down the stairs at a brisk walk. Two more guards stood at the base of the stairs.

She recognized them as the same two men who, when she'd first returned to the Guild to discover that Agnes had named her as her successor, had been tearing through her rooms searching for Agnes's diary. Ostensibly, or so Bethesa had told her, to see if it contained any information regarding who had been behind Agnes's murder.

A fool's errand, even if it were true, and Maeve doubted very much if it was. More likely, Bethesa and the other tribunes searched for the diary in the hopes that the words contained within its pages would translate to power or personal gain. Perhaps they would—Maeve couldn't say, for she had only had a brief opportunity to look over the diary before Emille had told her of Chall's injuries, and she'd rushed to the castle to be with him.

What she did know, though, was that if they were looking for who was behind the guildmaster's murder, they would never succeed. Mostly because the woman hadn't been murdered at all, though considering the effort Chall—as well as she and Agnes—had put into the illusion, they might be forgiven for believing so.

What she was not so quick to forgive, though, was that they were, once more, letting themselves into her rooms as if she were a child and they her parents who might come and go into her space as they pleased. They were wrong about that, and Maeve meant to show them just how wrong.

"Guildmaster," one of the men said, bowing. "Good morning. If you will wait here but for a moment, I will let the tribunes know—"

"I'm not waiting to go into my own quarters," Maeve said, "now get out of my way."

The man bowed his head again, stepping to the side, and Maeve walked past him without another word.

Her door was closed. She frowned, glancing at Emille. "Best you wait here—make sure no more uninvited guests show up."

"You're sure, Guildmaster?" Emille asked, glancing worriedly at the door.

"I'm sure," Maeve said. She understood the woman's concerns, but right now Maeve wasn't worried—she was angry. She gave Emille a nod then turned, stepping through the door. No sooner had she done so than there was a hiss from the side, and she spun to see Tribune Silrika there. A knife was in the woman's hands, and before Maeve could say anything the tribune lunged at her, her blade leading.

Maeve barely had time to register what was happening. Thankfully, years of training and decades spent in near-constant battle had left their mark, and while her mind was still trying to understand what was happening, her body reacted.

Maeve pivoted as the woman's knife shot toward her. She kept her forearm tight to her body to give it more power and used it to strike the woman's arm, knocking it wide with enough force that the blade was sent flying from the tribune's hand. Then, before she could react, Maeve brought her left arm swinging backward with a back fist that struck the woman in the face even as Maeve's leg shot out, sweeping her feet from under her.

The tribune hit the ground hard, the air exploding out of her chest in a *whoosh*. She hissed, trying to get up, but before she could, Maeve planted a foot on her chest, holding her down. Silrika pushed against her, her face twisted with rage. Maeve only watched her, calm now that the thing was done. "I would stay down, were I you," Maeve said. "You're not the only one with knives."

"Forgive us, Guildmaster," another voice said, and Maeve glanced to the sitting area of her rooms to see Tribune Bethesa sitting there. The old woman sat with a cup of tea in her hands. "Tribune Silrika did not realize it was you—she meant you no harm."

"Could have fooled me," Maeve said, glancing back at the tribune in question who still lay on the ground, noting the hate in the woman's eyes, the way her upper lip was peeled back from her teeth. "Still could, come to it."

"It is only a misunderstanding, I assure you, Guildmaster," Tribune Piralta—who sat on the second divan opposite Bethesa—said over his shoulder. "The men outside were meant to announce if anyone should seek entrance. Silrika was only surprised by your sudden appearance—as were we all, of course. We do beg for your understanding, Guildmaster."

"I'm not feeling all that particularly understanding just now, I'm afraid," Maeve said. "Nor do I see a need to announce myself when entering what I was given to understand are *my* quarters." She let her gaze travel to Tribune Bethesa. "Or am I wrong about that?"

"*Get your foot off me, y*—" Tribune Silrika began in a growl, one that turned into a grunt of pain as Maeve abruptly put her weight on her left foot, pushing hard on the woman's chest.

"Quiet now," she said. "Grown folks are talking."

"*You bi*—"

"*Silrika!*" Tribune Bethesa shouted. "That is enough."

The woman beneath Maeve's boot didn't seem like she wanted it to be enough, looking like nothing so much as a wild animal, one straining against its leash, eager to rend and tear, an image that was heightened by her bloody nose from where Maeve had struck her. Silrika glanced at the older tribune and, slowly, the feral, wild animal left her eyes and she was a woman again.

"Now then," Bethesa said, "apologize to the guildmaster."

The woman hesitated, and Maeve felt, then, as if she and Silrika were two young children and Tribune Bethesa the patient mother trying to make them get along. Which, she thought, was exactly how Bethesa *wanted* them to feel.

"I'm sorry," Tribune Silrika said, the words nearly as sharp as the knife she'd held and sounding just about as sorry as an executioner with an axe to grind.

"Oh, I wouldn't worry about it," Maeve said. "After all, I'm unharmed." She watched the woman, making sure she understood the implications of what she said, then, after another moment, she lifted her foot from the tribune's chest.

Silrika's face turned a deep, angry red at that, the anger returning to her eyes. Maeve prepared herself, thinking for sure that the woman meant to attack her again.

"Silrika," Bethesa said into the tense silence, "why don't you pick yourself up, come and sit over here, so that we might talk."

The woman hesitated, watching Maeve, and it was unclear if, in her anger, she heard the older woman at all.

"*Silrika,*" the tribune snapped, and Silrika blinked, reminding Maeve of nothing so much as a dog responding to its master's voice.

Finally, the woman gave a slight nod, seeming just as surprised as Maeve was when she didn't attack but instead simply rose to her feet, walking toward the sitting area of Maeve's quarters in a tense, hunched walk.

"I wouldn't get too comfortable, were I you," Maeve said. She was angry, but she was scared too. Anyone who didn't feel a bit of fright at walking into their quarters to discover three of the most powerful assassins in the world ought to check themselves for a heartbeat. But the fact that she was scared only made her all the angrier. "I never agreed to have visitors today. Now, before any more blood is shed, perhaps it would be a good idea if one of you would explain why you are in my quarters without permission."

"Please, Guildmaster," Tribune Piralta said in his weaselly, far-too-eager-to-please tone. "We meant no offense; we only came here because we were worried for you."

Maeve raised an eyebrow, glancing at Silrika where the woman currently sat, sharing one of the divans with Bethesa, her head hung low like a chastised child. "Worried for me?" Maeve asked. "Well, now, you've got a funny way of showing it."

"Yes, of course," Tribune Piralta said, giving an uncertain, tittering laugh, one that grew abruptly silent when Maeve didn't join in. The man licked his lips nervously. "The thing is, Lady Maeve—that is, Guildmaster —that despite appearances to the contrary, well. I mean, that is—"

"What Prattling Piralta is trying to say," Bethesa said in a weary tone, "is that we did not mean any offense by coming here. Circumstances, I'm afraid, left us with little choice. We meant to—"

There was the sound of what might have been something falling from Maeve's study, followed by a muffled curse from the other side of the closed door, and Maeve frowned, holding up a finger. "Quiet," she told the tribune, aware that the woman would take the interruption as offense, and that was alright. Maeve was pretty well offended herself just then.

She let her gaze travel over the three tribunes seated at the divans then turned and started toward the door. She opened it to find two men within her study. One was currently rifling through her desk while the other was casually grabbing books off the bookshelf at the side of her room, rifling through a few pages before tossing them onto the ground in a haphazard pile. He'd emptied about half the bookshelf so far and seemed intent on finishing the job.

"Hi," Maeve said from the doorway.

The two men froze in what they were doing then turned to look at her.

"I'm Maeve—you know," she said. "The guildmaster. What are your names?"

The two men looked at each other uncertainly, then toward the door, no doubt looking for the tribunes.

"Names," Maeve repeated. "You do have them, don't you?"

The man at her desk cleared his throat. "Marcus. My name's Marcus. Guildmaster." He jerked his thumb at the man standing in front of Maeve's bookshelf. "This here's Thomas."

"Thomas," Maeve said, nodding slowly. "I had an uncle named Thomas. He was a bit soft in the head too."

"Guildmaster?" the man asked, clearly confused.

"Well, you are soft in the head, aren't you?" Maeve asked, looking at the man at the bookshelf. "I just assumed you'd have to be, you know, given the fact that you thought it wise to invade my personal quarters and search my belongings without my permission."

The two men looked worried then, as well they might. "Forgive us, Guildmaster," the one named Thomas said. "We did not mean any offense, only Tribune Bethesa—"

"Has no right to my quarters, let alone the right to allow others to do what they will to them," Maeve interrupted. "Unless, of course, the role of tribune outranks that of guildmaster and no one told me."

The man winced. "S-sorry, Guildmaster."

Maeve nodded slowly. "My uncle, I might have been exaggerating before—about him being slow in the head. He might have been forgiven, had that been the case. The truth was, though, that my uncle was a fool. The sort of fool who would do something without thought, and then think that an apology would somehow make it right. But then that's the thing about apologies—they only have value if the person receiving them decides they do. My family decided, for a while, at least, that Uncle Thomas's apologies did. They gave him a second chance, then a third. Until, finally, my Uncle Thomas got drunk—he had a habit of that—and accidentally set my father's stables aflame, killing all of our livestock. It made for some lean years, I can tell you that. And I can tell you, also, that when my father came to Thomas, my uncle apologized—as he always did. He said he was sorry, made promises he had no intention of keeping, as he always did. Only, this time, my father was done hearing them. This time, Uncle Thomas got what was coming to him." She paused, eyeing the two men. "Do you know what all of that taught me?"

"That...that your uncle was a bad man?" the man at her desk, Marcus, asked.

"A worthy effort," Maeve said, "but no. You see I already knew Uncle Thomas was a bad man—everyone did. How could we not? After all, he always seemed intent on showing us. No, the lesson I learned that day, as I listened to the squeals and screams of our animals burning, standing in our field with my family unable to do anything but watch, was a different one altogether. In some ways, I can't even blame Uncle Thomas—he was a fool, after all, and a fool will do foolish things. What I learned was that it was our fault. Ours for giving him a second chance and a third when he never deserved it. When his apologies were as hollow and empty as that burned out barn. Do you understand?"

"I'm...not sure I do, Guildmaster."

"Well, then I'll make it simple. My uncle burned down our barn—that's on him. But it's on us too, for we knew what he was, who he was, and we let him stay anyway out of some idea of false compassion. It was a mistake and one I do not intend to repeat. A dog bites you, you don't keep it around so it can do it again. You get rid of it."

The men tensed at that, glancing at each other, and though they didn't make a move for the weapons sheathed at their waist, they didn't look that far from it. She understood their worry—after all, when someone spoke of getting rid of someone in an assassin's guild there was usually only the one meaning. But while she understood their worry, she didn't care. It had been a long couple of days, with her being named guildmaster, Chall nearly dying, and all the rest, and whatever patience she'd started with was well and truly gone.

"You're done here—both of you. Get out."

"O-of course, Guildmaster," the one who shared her uncle's name said, bobbing his head in a quick bow. "We are sorry. It won't happen again."

"I know it won't," Maeve said. "You misunderstand me. I don't just mean for you to get out of my study. I mean for you to get out of my Guild. Both of you. My father might have believed in second chances, Thomas," she told him, "but I don't."

"Wait, what are you saying?" the man asked. "That you're...*firing* us?"

"There's two options here," Maeve said. "Firing's one of them. I think you'll prefer it to the other, but then it's your choice. Either way, your time in the Guild is done."

"But y-you can't," Marcus said, glancing at Thomas, "she can't."

"Yes," Maeve said. "I can. And as I told you before, I don't care for giving people second chances. So this is your chance—your only one. Get out of the Guild. Now."

"B-but our stuff, in our rooms—"

"Is forfeit," Maeve said. "You will not see it again, not any of it. The price of invading a guildmaster's personal space. Oh, but don't look so glum, lads," she said. "It could be a lot worse."

They frowned, their surprise giving way to anger in their eyes, and Maeve waited. She stood still, and while she did not hold any knives, she was prepared to draw them in an instant. She didn't know if she could take on both the men, didn't know, if they did chose to attack, whether the three tribunes would join in. What she *did* know, though, was that she didn't dare show weakness, not here, not among these people, for to show weakness to such as these was to invite pain and death.

Several tense seconds passed then, as the men thought it over, and she could almost see their minds working. "Make your decision and make it quickly," Maeve said. "Maybe you could take me—two big strong men like you, probably you could. But then I don't think the

Guild would look too kindly on the men who murdered their guildmaster...do you?"

The men frowned deeper at that, and finally the one named Thomas showed more sense than her uncle ever had, bowing. "Forgive us, Guildmaster, for our indiscretion. We...we are sorry."

"You can take your sorry with you," Maeve said. "Go. Now. Before the price goes up."

The two men bowed again, starting toward the door. Maeve stepped aside to allow them past.

"Listen, lads—" Bethesa began.

"No," Maeve told her. "They are not members of the Guild, not anymore, and you have nothing to say to them."

The old woman's jaw tightened at that. Obviously, she was accustomed to being the one to control things, not used to being told what to do. That was alright—Maeve could be a patient teacher, when she had to be.

"Yes, Guildmaster," Bethesa said, and by the look on her face Maeve thought the saying of it cost her more than a little.

The men filed out of the door, their heads down. Maeve waited until they closed it behind them to turn back to the tribunes, all of them, she noted, looking considerably less comfortable than they had when she'd first arrived. Except for Silrika, of course—she hadn't looked very comfortable sprawled on the ground, bleeding from a busted nose.

"Now then," Maeve said, "where were we? Oh yes, you three were getting ready to explain to me why you thought it was acceptable to break into my quarters and, furthermore, why you believed it okay to have your men rifle through my belongings."

"Forgive us, Guildmaster," Tribune Piralta said, "but we did not break in. Only—"

"Are these my quarters?" Maeve asked.

The man hesitated, uncertain. He glanced at his companions, but Bethesa only stared at Maeve, her expression tightly controlled while Silrika sat with one hand pressed to her nose to stem the bleeding. "I...don't understand, Guildmaster," Piralta said.

"Don't you?" she said. "Are these my quarters or not?"

"O-of course, but—"

"And did I invite you into them?"

"I...that is, no Guildmaster, but—"

"Then you broke in," she said. "That's what breaking in is. I'm surprised, given your position within the Guild, Tribune Piralta, that you are not aware of that. It is not so complicated a concept."

The man opened his mouth as if to respond, but he was clearly at a loss as to what to say for no words came out. "Tell me," Maeve said, letting her gaze go over each of them in turn, "what is the going punishment for breaking into the quarters of the Guildmaster of the Assassins' Guild?"

"Forgive us, Guildmaster," Bethesa said and for the first time since she had first offered Maeve the position at Agnes's behest, the old woman seemed uncertain. Likely, she thought Maeve would have been too timid to say anything against them or, more likely still, that they would have been gone and cleaned up before she returned. An eventuality that would have occurred, had Emille not come to warn her. "We meant you no harm," the old tribune went on. "We are only pursuing the investigation as well as we know how."

"What investigation?"

Something flashed in the woman's eyes, satisfaction, maybe. It was gone in another moment but not soon enough for Maeve to realize it had been the wrong question to ask. "Why, the one trying to uncover who was responsible for the murder of Guildmaster Agnes, of course," the old woman said. "I would think, given your new role, Guildmaster, that you of all people would be interested in discovering those behind it. Unless, that is, you know something that we don't?"

Maeve found herself being impressed despite everything else. A trap and one neatly laid. After all, anyone would be frightened to learn upon taking a position that the last person who'd had it had been brutally murdered. Of course, Agnes *hadn't* been brutally murdered, had only appeared to be and that with considerable help from Chall and Emille. But then the tribunes didn't know that. If they had, Maeve would be dead already. "I imagine I know a lot of things the three of you don't," she said, refusing to play the woman's game, knowing that if she lost control of this conversation, she might well lose her life along with it. "What constitutes trespassing, for starters. Anyway, does it normally take three tribunes to investigate a murder? I would have thought there were men and women tasked with such jobs."

She didn't think she imagined the disappointment and perhaps even respect in Bethesa's expression as the tribune tilted her head like a fencer acknowledging a point. "In normal circumstances, it may be that you're correct, but then the murder of the guildmaster is, I think you'd agree, a long way from normal. Of course, there are men and women looking into the guildmaster's murder, but we thought we might look in a different direction."

"And that direction led you here, to my personal quarters."

"I'm afraid so," Bethesa said. "We thought, as before, that we might find something with some clue to the people responsible for the attack on Guildmaster Agnes. The diary, perhaps." Her expression didn't seem to change, but suddenly she was studying Maeve intently with a gaze as sharp as a knife. "I don't suppose you have happened upon anything like that?"

Maeve hesitated for a moment then. Was it another trap? Some might have looked at the old, hunched tribune and been surprised that she still held such a powerful position in the Guild. They might wonder why someone hadn't come along and forcefully retired her, as the woman would certainly not have been able to put up much of a fight. It wouldn't have been the first time someone had decided they wanted a position, saw that it was already occupied, and set about remedying that problem.

But while Bethesa might have not been physically imposing, she was far deadlier than Silrika could ever dream of being. The woman wielded words as skillfully as any duelist his steels, and her mind was as sharp as any blade Maeve had ever seen. Bethesa was watching her again, studying her. The woman was clever, there was no doubt of that, possessed of the wisdom of the old. But then Maeve was far from young herself, and she hadn't survived as long as she had by being a fool.

The woman was trying to make her panic, to catch her off guard. People who were panicked, who were confused or surprised often made mistakes. She was trying to make Maeve make a mistake, but that didn't mean Maeve had to let her. Not good to tell a direct lie, then, and say she hadn't found it. Or, at least, not ideal, mainly because nobody was ever as sure as a liar telling a lie, no one ever so desperate to convince others. The truth didn't need to convince anybody.

"You mean like the diary you spoke of the last time you were here?" she asked, then shook her head. "I've been a bit busy lately, truth be told. I've barely even settled in here, which is maybe just as well. The lack of personal belongings must make it easier on your men when they go rifling through my things."

The woman wanted her uncertain, surprised, and Maeve thought she could play that game well enough. Bethesa, though, was too clever to allow herself to be led from the path. Silrika, however, did not share that cleverness. "She told you, we didn't mean you any harm. We came looking for the diary."

The woman practically growled each word, or at least Maeve thought she meant to. It was hard to tell for sure, what with the broken nose and all.

"Guildmaster," Maeve said. "We came looking for the diary, Guildmaster."

"Listen, Guildmaster," Bethesa said, "what Silrika is trying to say—"

"I don't care what she's *trying* to say," Maeve said, her eyes still on the bloody-nosed woman. "I care what she *does* say. We are, all of us, account-able for the words that come out of our mouths. So," she told Silrika, "let me hear you say it." Some might have seen the look of barely-contained fury on the woman's face, in her eyes and thought Maeve a fool for goading her, but they would have been wrong to think so. Maeve had been around dangerous people all her life, ever since she and all the other people of the kingdom had been chased from their home by the Skaalden. So she knew something about them, knew that some people, like Silrika, let their anger control them, thinking it their greatest strength, a boon. Which it could be, though Maeve had found that, more often than not, it was a curse. Either way, though, there was one thing that answered anger better than any other, and that was fear. Easy, after all, to curse and spit on a serving woman for bringing you the wrong drink—far harder when the serving woman was a man twice your size.

People, despite all their pretentions to the contrary, really were simple creatures.

Silrika's upper lip peeled back from her teeth in a silent snarl, and she shot a quick, almost undetectable glance at Bethesa. Another might have missed that glance, but assassins who missed things didn't live for long—that was another truth Maeve had learned over the years. She did not miss the glance, nor did she like it. It did not seem like the sort of glance that was asking for help. Instead, it seemed like the sort of glance that was asking for permission. "Of course," Silrika finally said, each word sounding like it was being torn out of her chest as she bowed her head, "forgive me. Guildmaster."

Maeve gave the woman the sharpest smile she had. "Of course."

"Now, Guildmaster, if you are satisfied," Bethesa said, "then as I was saying, we did not wish to give offense, only to get to the bottom of what happened to Guildmaster Agnes."

"And so you came here, thinking to find the diary. But then that couldn't be it, could it?" Maeve said. "After all, as I recall, the last time we were all here—when I became guildmaster—you were also searching the rooms. You did not find the diary then. I wonder, what made you think you would find it now?"

"It is not only the diary, Guildmaster," Bethesa said. "There is another matter."

"Oh?" Maeve said her gaze traveling between the three tribunes. "Well, let's hear it. Anything to explain why you and your men were tearing my quarters apart."

"Tell me, Guildmaster," Bethesa said, watching her intently, "when was the last time you saw Amber, your attendant?"

When I killed her, Maeve thought, but she made a show of considering the question. "Well, as I said, I haven't been at the Guild much lately—other matters have drawn my attention away. A few days ago, I think."

The tribunes shared a look then Bethesa nodded slowly. "Yes, that would line up."

"Line up with what?" Maeve asked, surprised that the tribunes had taken it upon themselves to wonder at a servant who'd only been missing for a few days.

"Why, the time of death, of course, Guildmaster," Bethesa said as if it was obvious.

Maeve frowned, feeling caught off guard—a feeling that was depressingly common when speaking with the old tribune. "What time of death? Agnes's?"

"Oh, I'm sorry, Guildmaster," Bethesa said, "I thought you knew. I regret to be the one to tell you that Amber, the guildmaster's personal valet, *your* personal valet is dead."

"Dead?" Maeve asked, taken aback. She knew that Amber was dead of course—she'd been the one to make her that way. She didn't feel any guilt; after all, the woman had attacked her when she had expressed no interest in sharing the discovery of Agnes's diary with the tribunes. But while she didn't feel any guilt or shame, what she *did* feel was worry and more than a little frustration. She had summoned Chall and Emille to her quarters to help her get the body out without anyone being the wiser, and after Chall had left—to nearly get killed at Ned and Emille's home—she and Emille had spent no small amount of time and effort disposing of it. She had thought they had hidden it well, enough that it wouldn't be found for weeks, possibly ever.

Apparently, she'd been wrong.

"I'm afraid so," Tribune Bethesa said. "Someone stabbed her, if you can believe it," the old woman said, shaking her head as if grieved by the thought. And perhaps she was. After all, Agnes had disclosed in her diary that she had known the woman, Amber, worked for one of the tribunes, only she hadn't known which one. If her boss had been Bethesa then Maeve did not doubt that the tribune was upset that her spy had met an untimely demise.

"I can't imagine who would want to hurt the poor old lady," Tribune Piralta said. "Amber was always kind to everyone, and a more loyal member of the Guild I could not imagine."

Loyal sure, Maeve thought, *but to who?* That was the question Agnes had not answered. As for the kind bit, well, Maeve wasn't much on judging people, but she thought that trying to poison someone—and then trying to poke a few holes in them when that failed—wasn't the sort of thing someone expected of a kind person.

"How...that is, where was she found?" Maeve asked.

"An old abandoned warehouse, in fact," Bethesa said, and Maeve didn't miss the way the woman was watching her closely. "Out at the Mournings, if you can believe it."

Considering that she and Emille had been the ones to haul the body out there—a task that had necessitated the temporary theft of a small wagon and mule—she could indeed believe it. What she *couldn't* believe, though, was how quickly it had been found. After all, the Mournings, as they were called, had gotten their name for a good reason. In truth, it was a section of the city—more specifically the poor district—which had been ravaged the worst by the plague that had swept through New Daltenia years ago.

Life was always cheap in the poor district, but never so bad as it had been in New Daltenia during that time, and never so bad anywhere as it had been in the Mournings. A place where, one day, a person might attend the funeral of a loved family member, then the next another and, the third, attend their own. Even now, years after the plague had been eradicated, people still avoided going there unless absolutely necessary. Plagues might fade away in time, but the scarred, painful memories of loved ones lost, of terrible griefs and tragedies suffered were not easily forgotten.

All of this meant that there were dozens, hundreds of abandoned buildings in the Mournings—homes and hostels, warehouses and even churches. It was a big city, after all, and there were plenty of places to live that hadn't once been completely ravaged—in some sections to a man— by plague. Nobody who had lived there wanted to return and no one who hadn't had any interest in trying it. A terrible place to live, then, but a fine place to hide a body you didn't want found.

Or so she'd thought.

"If it was left in an abandoned warehouse, I'm surprised the body was found so quickly," Maeve said, and that, at least, was true.

"No doubt the one responsible would be equally surprised," Bethesa said, her reptilian eyes watching Maeve closely. "And normally you would be right, of course. After all, there are few people that would care to spend any time at all in the Mournings. Only the most foolish or, as the case may be, the most desperate. Fortunately for us—though unfortunately for the people responsible for Amber's demise—" she paused there, only for a moment but long enough that Maeve was sure she hadn't imagined it, "there happened to be two such people on hand when our murderers arrived with the body. Two children, foolish as only the very young can be, and desperate as only the very starving can be. Probably they were searching for something of value in the abandoned warehouses, something to trade for their next meal, likely. Or perhaps just a safe place to sleep for the night. It's dangerous out there."

Dangerous in here too, Maeve thought.

"Whatever the reason," Bethesa went on, "as luck would have it, these two younglings found themselves on hand to witness the murderers dispose of the body."

"That is luck," Maeve said. *Of the worst kind.* "Did they get a good look at them, at least?" She asked the last as casually as she could, but the truth was that her hands were itching to draw one of the blades secreted on her person.

"I'm afraid not," Bethesa said. "Still, I would not worry overly much. We have their trail now. Sooner or later, we will find some track or clue they left to lead us to them."

"Unless they didn't leave anything," Piralta said grimly.

"In my experience," Bethesa said, her eyes still on Maeve, "people disposing of a body are nearly always more focused on speed than anything, more focused on what they're getting away—namely themselves—than what they leave behind. Such people would have likely tried to flee the scene as quickly as possible, hoping that any trail they might leave would be long gone by the time anyone found the body. Don't you agree, Guildmaster?" she asked.

There was that gaze again, those eyes that seemed to see straight through Maeve. "Perhaps," she said. In point of fact, the old woman was exactly right. Emille and Maeve *had* focused more on hurrying than being careful, and Maeve *had* thought, had *hoped* that it would have been weeks, perhaps even months before the body was discovered, any trail to them having long since gone cold. Another proof, then, of the woman's cleverness—not that Maeve needed anymore. She knew the woman was clever —she only hoped it wasn't the *last* thing she knew.

She couldn't keep reacting—that much she was sure of. If she did, if she didn't take control, she wouldn't live very long to regret it. "I'm curious, though, why would the children think to tell you in the first place? About the murder, I mean. It seems to me that the Guild would be the *last* place they would come to share such news. After all, how would they know that the two people—the murderers—weren't there on Guild business?"

"They wouldn't, of course, Guildmaster," Bethesa said. "But as to why they would share it—I suspect in hopes of receiving a reward."

"A reward," Maeve said.

"There is precedent," the old woman said, smiling. "I am old, you see, Guildmaster. I can barely walk, let alone do any running around. And so, some few years ago, I took it upon myself to start hiring out, to let others do the running for me."

"Others like starving orphans," Maeve said.

"Indeed, Guildmaster," the woman said, and if she was at all offended by the implication that she took advantage of desperate children she did not show it. "After all, there are few people more motivated than those with hunger pains gnawing at their bellies."

"Your charity is inspiring," Maeve said.

The woman gave a sharp smile. "It is not charity, of course. Only a trade, one that works for everyone involved. They come to me with any information or news that they think I might find interesting and, in the event that I do, they are recompensed for their trouble with a bit of coin."

Maeve nodded. "Very well. I would speak to the children."

"Ah," Bethesa said, an apologetic expression on her face, one that Maeve didn't believe for a moment, "forgive me, Guildmaster, but I'm afraid that isn't possible. The two children dropped off the information and left."

"I see," Maeve said, frowning.

"Still, I would not worry yourself, Guildmaster," Bethesa said. "We have men looking into Amber's murderers. They are combing the Mournings even as we speak. If the murderers left anything behind, our men will find it. And, in due course, we will find them."

Maeve nodded. "Keep me informed of the investigation—no decisions are made without consulting me first, am I clear?"

Bethesa frowned. "Guildmaster?"

"Forgive us, Guildmaster," Piralta said, "but perhaps it would be better if we were to—"

"It would be *better*," Maeve said sharply, her eyes never leaving Bethesa, "if you did what you were told. I wish to know every bit of what is happening with the investigation—everything goes through me. After all," she went on, giving Bethesa a small smile, "as you pointed out, I am the guildmaster now, and there is no one as concerned with someone out there murdering guildmasters than me."

"We're children then to be overseen by our mother, is that it?" Silrika asked.

"Of course not," Maeve said, turning her gaze to the tribune. "You are not children. I would never hit a child." The woman's eyes went wide at that in a mixture of shock and anger, but Maeve didn't give her time to respond. "Now, leave. All of you," she said. "I am tired and would like some rest." A lie, for she was far too stressed to even consider sleeping, but then they didn't need to know that.

She noted the way Piralta and Silrika glanced at Bethesa, waiting to follow her lead. The old tribune nodded, an appraising look in her eyes as she rose. She gave a slight bow. "Of course, Guildmaster. Come," she said to her companions. "Let us leave the Guildmaster in peace, so that she might get some rest."

Maeve watched the three tribunes as they made their way toward the door. Bethesa at the front, hunched and weary looking but the most dangerous of the three by far, Maeve believed. In fact, she thought it likely that the woman was one of the most dangerous people she'd ever met and that with no small competition. She might not be as physically capable as she'd once been, but then there were many types of danger, and there was a reason the old wolf still ate its fill. Next was Piralta, a weasel Agnes had called him, and Bethesa treated him much the same. But Maeve was not so sure, for she thought perhaps that was what the man *wanted* people to think of him. Beneath that squirming, placating, cowardly exterior something sharp was hidden, something deadly.

Last was Silrika, the woman scowling out at the world past her bloody nose. Maeve did not doubt that she was deadly, but she had little concern for her. After all, blades that were always bared lost their edge and gave way to rust.

Still, as the woman passed her, she kept herself ready, just in case. Rusted blades could still cut, after all. The woman didn't attack, though, contenting herself with a scowl that wasn't even aimed at Maeve's face but at her feet. A lesson learned, then, but Maeve doubted it would stick—they rarely did, even with the best of people, and by her estimation Silrika was far from that.

The tribunes made their way to the door, Bethesa pausing at it to turn back to Maeve. "I'd like to apologize again, Guildmaster. For entering your chambers the way that we did. And I would remind you again about the diary," she went on, watching Maeve again with those eyes that saw too much. "You are sure you haven't seen it?"

"I think I would know," she said. "Anyway, I haven't had much time for reading, I'm afraid."

The woman gave a small smile, inclining her head. "Of course, Guildmaster. I only ask because I think it might prove instrumental in discovering who was responsible for Guildmaster Agnes's death. Until it is found, I feel that no one is safe," she frowned. "Not even, I'm afraid, guildmasters."

"Your concern is touching," Maeve said, "but I wouldn't worry overly much about my welfare. I have been known to take care of myself in the past. I suspect that, just now, Silrika could attest to that. There would be others that might do the same if they weren't all dead."

The woman gave her a smile without humor, something dark seeming to shift across her eyes. "Of course, Guildmaster. No one among us, I am quite sure, doubts your abilities. I only worry. After all, you are one woman, and one woman, however talented, might still fall, if she is not careful."

Maeve returned the woman's smile. "Yes, but then I'm not one woman, am I? I'm the guildmaster. I have the whole Guild behind me...don't I?"

The tribune inclined her head. "Of course, Guildmaster. We are your loyal servants."

Maeve managed to keep from laughing at that but only barely. "Loyal, of course," she said. "Then I would be extra careful, the next time you think to come to my rooms without asking. I'd hate for there to be another misunderstanding." She paused to look meaningfully at Silrika. "One that ends with more than just a bloody nose. Now leave—I will call on you should I have need of you."

Bethesa looked as if she wanted to say something—Silrika as if she wanted to scream it—but in the end the three tribunes left without another word.

When the door closed behind them, Maeve let out a heavy breath, raising her hand and looking at it to see that it was shaking. She had thought, when she'd first walked through the door to find the three tribunes, along with their men, that she was going to die, that today would be her last day alive.

And it still might be, she warned herself. *Just because a snake hasn't bitten yet doesn't mean it didn't intend to.* And the tribunes intended to. There was plenty she was unsure about, but their intentions could not be counted among them, for those, at least, were plain enough to see. They wanted what most people want—power. Status. Money. And like most people they were not concerned with who they had to trample—or stab—to get what they wanted.

She knew she needed to move. There were things that needed to be done, precautions she needed to take, answers she needed to find. They had already discovered the old servant, Amber's, body and that was bad. Maeve didn't *know* that she or Emille had left anything behind that might point to them—a witness who'd gotten a better view of them, perhaps—but she didn't know they *hadn't* either. She needed to retrace their footsteps and make sure the trail was clean, but that presented its own dangers. After all, the only people that tried to hide crimes were those who'd committed them, and if the tribunes got news of her spending time in the Mournings after their conversation she thought that would be as good as a death sentence.

A thousand things within the Guild that needed doing then and thousands more without, regarding Matt and Chall and Priest—she would think of him as that no matter what the man said. It's who he was, that was all. But despite the many tasks looming before her, Maeve only stood with her back propped against the door, giving herself a moment to just breathe. It was a privilege to do, after all, and she didn't think there was a single dead man or woman rotting in their graves that wouldn't happily trade all the maggots and worms and dirt they possessed for the chance to draw even a single breath again.

She breathed. She closed her eyes, letting the worries of the day, of a life wash over her, slide past her without so much as a glance. They would return—they always did. If a person could count on nothing else, she could count on that. But for the moment, she forgot, she *let* herself forget those fears and worries. She did not try to solve the many problems crowding around her, did not even *think* of the problems.

For a brief moment, she allowed herself to forget about the world and to hope, for that brief moment, that it might forget about her. And she simply breathed.

That was when a knock came at the door.

"Guildmaster?" a voice said from the other side. "Is everything alright?"

Maeve noted Emille's familiar voice. No doubt the woman had been worried about Maeve in the presence of the three tribunes—she couldn't blame her. After all, she had been worried about herself. She opened the door.

Emille stood on the other side. The woman had kept herself composed, but Maeve didn't miss the hard set of her jaw or the relief that leaked into her expression upon seeing Maeve standing there, alive.

"Come in, Sister Emille," she said formally for the benefit of the men standing in the hallway. "I would speak with you."

"Of course, Guildmaster," the woman said, bowing her head before entering Maeve's quarters. When the woman was past, Maeve turned to regard the two men standing there. Men who, ostensibly, were her guards. Men who had given her no reason to distrust them since she'd first reluctantly accepted the mantle of guildmaster. But then, Maeve had been part of the Guild long enough to know that the moment a person realized they couldn't trust another was usually the same moment they were sent on an involuntary journey to the afterlife.

"Phillip, isn't it?" she asked one of the two.

The man blinked, clearly impressed that she'd remembered his name. He bowed. "Yes, Guildmaster."

She nodded. "Aside from Sister Emille, I find that I am quite finished with visitors for the time being, Phillip. Should anyone seek admittance to my quarters, I wish for you to turn them away. Forcefully if need be. Understood?"

"Of course, Guildmaster," the man said.

"Good," Maeve said. "Later, we will have a conversation about the two of you allowing unwanted guests into my quarters without my permission."

Phillip and his companion shared a troubled, confused glance. If they were actors, Maeve decided, then they were good ones. But then she thought that when your audience was full of assassins, the bad ones didn't make it all that far. "We wish to apologize, Guildmaster, about...about letting the tribunes into your quarters. We were given to understand that you had asked for them to meet you inside."

"I see," Maeve said. "And who told you that?"

The two men shared another look. "Why, they did, Guildmaster," Phillip said.

Maeve nodded. "They lied," she said. "People do that from time to time and assassins most of all. Going forward, no one is allowed inside my quarters without my express permission. I don't care if they're one of the gods themselves—you let me decide. Deal?"

"Of course, Guildmaster," the man said. "And we're just...that is...we're sorry. Again."

"Sorry's good," Maeve told the man with a smile. "Obedience is better. I believe in second chances, Phillip," she said, aware of how her words contradicted what she had told the two men searching her study, "and— I'm sorry, what was your name again?"

"Joseph, ma'am," the man supplied.

Maeve nodded. "As I said, I believe in second chances—I do not believe in third ones. Understood?"

"Understood, Guildmaster."

Maeve nodded, satisfied that she had made herself clear and that should anyone find their way into her quarters without her permission in the future, they would have no excuse. Not that it would do her much good, of course, for she'd likely be dead. Still, it was something.

"Very well," she said, then she closed the door behind her.

Emille stood on the other side, and on her face was the worry she'd taken pains to hide when she'd still been in the hallway. "Is...is everything alright, Guildmaster?"

"Please, gods, stow the 'guildmaster,' shit," Maeve said. "And no, Emille, to answer your question, I don't think everything is fine. I really don't."

"I was concerned," Emille said, "when you went in alone and they were all in there with their men—"

"That they would kill me?"

Emille nodded.

"Well, they still might yet," Maeve said.

"But you're alive for now," the woman said. "That's good news."

"With plenty of bad to keep it company," Maeve said. "They found Amber."

Emille blinked. "But that's...that's impossible. No one would have stumbled upon her so quickly, not in the Mournings. No one goes—"

"—to the Mournings, yes, I know," Maeve said. "Only the problem is that someone *did*. Two someones, in fact. Or...well. Two someones aside from us. Apparently, two children noted figures carrying something large into one of the abandoned warehouses. They waited until we left, then thinking that perhaps it might be some sort of treasure, investigated the matter. I imagine they were disappointed to discover the body. Certainly I'm disappointed that they did."

"Gods help us," Emille said, moving to the divan and half-sitting, half-collapsing into it. "This is bad, Maeve. Did...did the two children get a good look at..." She paused, glancing at the door. "At who did it?"

"I wouldn't worry about being overheard," Maeve said. "These rooms are soundproof. I should know as I killed someone in here and haven't been caught for it. Not yet, at least. But as to what the children saw, well if they'd gotten a good look at us, I doubt I'd be standing here. You either, come to it. More likely we'd both be in the process of being hauled in front of the tribunal and forced to listen while they—and likely everyone else in the Guild—argued over how they wanted to kill us."

"Well," Emille said, nodding slowly, "that's something, at least."

"Something but not much of it," Maeve said. "Those children might not have gotten a good look at us, but then on the other hand they might have. Bethesa said they didn't, but..." She paused, shrugging. "I don't trust the woman. She's hungry for power, that much I know about her. It might be the only thing I really know."

"Why would she lie about such a thing?" Emille asked. "If it's power she's after, it seems that the easiest way to get it would be to remove you."

"Maybe," Maeve agreed, nodding slowly, thinking it over. "Or maybe she doesn't want to be guildmaster at all, just the power that comes with the role. After all, why be the actor on stage getting pelted with rotten tomatoes if it all goes sour when you can be the person behind the curtain, pulling all the strings and safely out of range of moldy fruit?"

"You paint a grim picture," Emille said.

"I just walked into my quarters to find three of the most powerful assassins in the city waiting on me, along with several of their men who were tearing my rooms apart. I'm feeling pretty grim."

"So what—"

"A moment," Maeve said, thoughts of the men reminding her of what they'd come to find. Her breath suddenly quickening in her chest, she walked toward the study, throwing the door open. The room stood in disarray from the men's search, but she paid the books and papers scattered on the floor little attention as she moved toward the bookcase. She stood in front of it, staring at the books remaining on the shelf then retrieved the diary from where it was tucked between two other, larger books. There were only half a dozen beyond them, which meant that the man would have gotten to it in another few minutes and then couldn't have helped but have found the diary.

She breathed a heavy sigh of relief as she opened it, verifying for herself that it was indeed the same diary she'd found tucked in a hidden compartment of her desk, the same diary that had prompted Amber to try to kill her. She'd thought herself so clever, hiding the book in plain sight, but then that was the problem with plain sight—it was damned easy to see.

She tucked the diary inside her clothes. She took a slow, deep breath then turned and walked back into the sitting room.

"The diary?" Emille asked.

"Safe," Maeve said, patting her waist where she'd tucked the diary.

The other woman sighed heavily. "Good. And the two kids? The ones that saw us?"

Maeve shook her head. "Gone—or so Bethesa said. According to her, the children of the city know to share any interesting news with her in the hopes of getting some coin or a bit of something to eat."

"What a saint she is," Emille said.

"My thoughts exactly," Maeve said.

"Do we know where to find them, at least? Their names, maybe?"

"We'll find them in the Mournings, I'd guess. As for their names, orphans without any family to look after them—what good would their names do anyway?"

Emille winced. "The Mournings are big. It'd take a long time to scour them, with good chances we never find the kids. Even if we do, there's the possibility that they saw no more than Bethesa said. Still, I could go and start searching for—"

"Better if you didn't, I think," Maeve said. She shrugged at the woman's confused expression. "What need do we have of finding the children, of questioning them? We already know who the two figures they saw were, after all. Leave that search to Bethesa's people or those of the other tribunes. We have more important concerns."

"And if they find someone who knows more, who can give our descriptions to Bethesa and the others?"

"Then we're in serious trouble," Maeve said, "just as we would be if the tribunes heard tale of us searching the Mournings for the two children. Anyway, we have better things to occupy our time."

"Oh?" Emille asked.

"We've been on the defensive long enough," Maeve said. "It's time we started putting the tribunes on their back feet for once. After all, one man might burn another's house down, but not if he's busy putting out the flames of his own."

"You want me to look into the tribunes?"

"I do," Maeve said.

Emille considered that for a moment. "I doubt they'd take kindly to discovering that someone was sticking their nose into their affairs."

"I doubt they would as well," Maeve said. "If you want to say no, I will not fault you for it. It will be dangerous."

The other woman gave her a small smile. "As opposed to the cake walk that this has all been so far."

"Exactly," Maeve said.

"What would I be looking for?"

"Anything," Maeve said. "Anything that we could use as leverage against them. It's said that everyone has skeletons in their closet—well, I'd wager that those three have a damned sight more than most. Look for them, find them. We cannot hope to stand long against the three of them working together, so find ways to divide them, to turn them against each other. Do that, and maybe we get to go on breathing for a little while longer. Do that, and maybe we can take back the Guild from the hands of those scheming vultures, maybe use it to help instead of hurt."

"A guild of assassins used to help," Emille said, smiling. "I like the idea, even if it is unlikely."

"Not so unlikely as you might think," Maeve said, thinking of Priest. "I knew a man, once, who was the worst kind of criminal and who changed, who began using his courage and strength to save those around him, to help instead of hurt. If that man could do it, I believe the Guild could as well."

"Sure, but does it *want* to?" Emille said. "Still, it is a good dream, Maeve, one worth sacrificing for. I'll start looking into them, do what I can." She rose then, and Maeve blinked.

"You're leaving now?"

Emille shrugged. "When I was a girl, my mother used to tell me that the best thing to do with a bad job is to do it. The sooner started, the sooner finished."

Maeve thought that was true enough, though she didn't love the idea of them being *finished*. "Good luck," she told her. "And...thanks."

"Sure," Emille said, smiling. "Only, next time when you ask for a favor, how about asking me to fetch you a drink, maybe something to eat?"

"Well, considering that the last servant I had tried to kill me, there's an opening."

Emille laughed. "What will you do?"

Maeve reached into her clothes, removing Agnes's diary from where she'd tucked it inside her waist. "Me? Oh, I think I'll do some light reading."

CHAPTER SIXTEEN

CUTTER HAD ENDURED terrible walks before.

He had marched into war and marched out again, had walked into the bedchambers of his brother's beloved and there betrayed him.

He had walked away from everything he had ever known and everyone he had ever loved, his only company a swaddled babe and a promise made.

He had walked through the Black Wood with monsters hunting his footsteps, had walked what Shadelaresh had called the Path of War, though he thought it fairer to call it what it was—a path of death.

Yet for all the walks, for all the long, wearying hours where death hovered so close that he could feel its breath on the back of his neck, where emotional and physical pain were constant companions, few compared to the endless trudge through the past.

That past crowded around them in all directions. What had started as a few motes of light, only half-glimpsed out of the corner of his eye, had become dozens, hundreds of figures. Figures who had silently walked or fought or loved or grieved, ghosts of the past. Only, according to Door, their escort, in this place, it was the three of them who were ghosts.

Cutter believed the creature—he had no reason not to—but that didn't stop him from feeling haunted. Haunted by those figures living out their lives around them, reliving moments of great pain, great strife. Perhaps there were moments of great love, too, of great beginnings and happy endings, but if there were, Cutter hadn't seen them.

They'd walked for hours—or, at least, he believed they had. It was hard to tell for sure, for they passed no landmarks, and the land around them remained the same. And during those hours, he had learned something—the past had a voice.

That voice had been quiet at first, a single faint shout, quiet enough that he had thought he'd imagined it. But in time, there had been more, the past coming alive around them. Or, according to Door, perhaps it was more accurate to say that it was not the past coming to them but them going to it. And their approach was marked by the increasing volume of the figures around them. But while he could hear them, Cutter could not understand them. Not yet, at least.

It seemed that he should have been able to, but when they spoke or shouted, the voices sounded as if they were in a language he had known once but had forgotten. He had found himself trying to understand at first, their conversations, the grunts and growls of the feylings, the shouts and screams of the few mortals he saw. But he soon gave it up. He did not understand their language, but he did not think he imagined that it was becoming clearer the longer they spent here. He did not know what would happen, exactly, when they understood their words, when those figures around them were no longer vague blurs, but from what Door had said about being trapped in the past, he didn't think he wanted to find out.

For the moment, at least, the faces of those they passed, Fey and mortal alike, remained blurred and indistinct, so that they could have been anyone, anyone at all. And their voices remained unclear, forming into a sort of loud, buzzing in his ears, in his mind, one that made it difficult to concentrate, to think at all.

But then a man didn't need to think to walk, so they continued on, each step harder than the last. Cutter had been haunted by ghosts all his life, the silent specters of those he'd slain and those who, by his actions, he had caused to be killed. It wasn't the type of thing a man got used to, and a quick glance at his brother where he walked beside him showed that Feledias was also feeling the strain.

His brother's face was pale, lines of exhaustion and stress etched into his features, and he walked bent forward as if he marched into some powerful, gusting wind. He did not look around at the increasing number of figures sharing the field with them but moved with his head down, his eyes on the ground in front of him as if each step forward was an effort of will. Which, of course, it was.

Cutter glanced at their escort walking a few feet ahead of them. When they'd started out, the feyling had propped on its hands when it walked from time to time, but now it did not. Instead, as it moved forward, its long, spindly arms gestured this way and that, reminding Cutter of nothing so much as a stage actor pretending to be a wizard casting a spell. Cutter did not know if those gestures were necessary for whatever power the creature wielded that had brought them here and kept them here, or if they were just nervous tics.

As if feeling his eyes on it, the creature turned its long, lanky body to look back at them, checking on its charges, and while Cutter didn't know the purpose—if purpose there was—of the creature's gesturing, he saw, even in its alien form, a weariness to match his and Feledias's own. Door, it seemed, was not immune to the force—the past, Cutter supposed from everything the feyling had told them—pressing in all around them.

Cutter didn't know much about Fey anatomy, but the feyling seemed exhausted, *drained* somehow.

"Fire and salt, what's that?"

It was Feledias's voice, sounding strained and more than a little worried. Cutter pulled himself out of his thoughts, turning to their left where Feledias was staring. He saw at once what had caught his brother's attention—there was no mistaking it. Figures moved in the grass, dozens, hundreds of them, their faces all indistinct blurs, their features uncertain. Yet it was not the figures that drew Cutter's attention.

No more than twenty-five feet away, a strange, geometric pattern of multi-colored light hovered a few feet off the ground. Cutter stared at that light, at once fascinated and repulsed by it as it shifted and changed, almost like a sheet of parchment someone was wadding up in their hands, twisting and pulling this way and that.

"*It is a rift.*"

Cutter glanced to the side and saw that the feyling had made its way back to them and was staring at the shifting lights.

"A rift," Feledias repeated. "Well, that explains it." Yet even his sarcasm —for which, Cutter knew Feledias always seemed to find energy— sounded tired and forced.

"*A confluence,*" Door said. "*A place, a door where the present and the past, where time and space war for dominance. It is here because we have tarried too long. There will be others. We must go.*" Abruptly, the feyling turned and started away, and there was no mistaking the fact that it moved faster than it had before.

Cutter frowned, shooting one more glance at the strange patterns. The way the light shifted and moved, it almost seemed to be reaching for them. Ridiculous, of course, but then it didn't *feel* ridiculous. He shared a troubled look with his brother then followed after the feyling.

It took them several seconds of jogging to catch up with him. "What do you mean the past and present are at war?" Feledias asked. "Should we be worried?"

"*Yes,*" Door said. "*We have tarried over long. It is not safe.*"

"Then take us back," Feledias said. "My past isn't so great that I care to revisit it, at least most of it, and I'm damned sure not interested in reliving the past of a place like this."

"*We cannot return, not from here, at least,*" Door said. "*We must first reach a gate.*"

"What about that thing?" Cutter asked doubtfully, glancing behind them in the direction of the strange geometric pattern of light. "Didn't you say it was a door?"

He turned then grunted in surprise as he saw that the feylling had stopped and its face was thrust forward, so that its large eyes studied him from only inches away. "*You must not touch it or go near it,*" the creature said.

"Why?" Feledias asked. "Have you ever gone near one?"

JACOB PEPPERS

"We have not, but there was another who did," Door said, remaining inches from Cutter but turning its neck so that its eyes studied Feledias.

"What happened to him?"

"No one knows. Perhaps the past took him, or the present. Perhaps he became lost in the in-between. He did not return."

"So really it could be anything," Feledias said. "For all you know, there could have been a beautiful woman on the other side. Or...well, what passes for one in this place."

"I do not think so," Door said.

"Why not?" Cutter asked, curious.

"The screams," Door said, turning its gaze back to him. *"I was a youngling, but I remember well the screams of my broodmate. We were warned by the elders not to spend too long in the past, but we were young and foolish. Come,"* he said. *"There is little time."*

Then they were moving again. As they did, Cutter found himself looking around them. He thought he caught sight of another one of the rifts in the distance, but he could not have been sure. He was still staring at it, trying to determine if that's what it was or not, when something seemed to appear out of thin air. It was fast, darting across his field of view before seeming to vanish into the air after a few seconds.

It was fast, but not so fast that Cutter didn't see what it was—one of the feyling wolf-like creatures that had very nearly killed him and Feledias, that *would* have, had Door not arrived and saved both their lives by pulling them out of the present and into the past.

Cutter frowned, staring at the space. Had his troubled, weary mind simply imagined it? It seemed too much to think so. "Fel, did you—"

"I saw it," his brother said grimly, standing beside him. "Bastards don't give up easy, do they?"

"They are the Unsated," Door said, turning to regard them.

"Unsated," Feledias said. "You said that before. He frowned at the space where the creature had appeared moments ago. "Wonder why they have that name?"

Door turned, regarding him with his strange stare. *"They are called so because they are ever hungry. They feast and yet they are never satisfied, and so they hunt."*

"Right," Feledias said, rolling his eyes at Cutter. "And who knows what they might be hunting?"

"Us," Door said. *"They hunt us. And should they catch us, they will do what the Unsated always do—they will eat."*

"You must be a blast at parties, Door, do you know that?" Feledias asked. Trying for flippant, but Cutter didn't miss the slightest quiver in his brother's voice.

The feyling cocked his head to the side in that way he had, as if Feledias had just said something profound that he was trying to get his mind around. Then, he abruptly turned and began his fast, loping walk once more.

Cutter regarded his brother as they followed in the feyling's wake. "You alright, Fel?"

His brother raised his head from where he'd been studying his feet and let out a sound somewhere between a laugh and the beginnings of a sob. "Well, sure, why not? I'm just sad about my boots, nothing more. They were fine once, you know. Filthy now. Unsalvageable, I shouldn't wonder."

Cutter raised an eyebrow. "I wouldn't worry about it, Fel. When we get home, I'll buy you a new pair, how'd that be?"

That elicited another half-laugh, half-sob from his brother. "Damn my boots," Feledias said. "Damn them and my trousers and my tunic and all the rest. Why not? After all, just look around, brother. *We* are damned already." He waved out at the field around them as if to illustrate their point, but then Cutter thought that some points needed no illustration. It could be said, after all, that they quite literally walked through a world of the damned. After all, those who inhabited it, those who moved through the fields around them, were all dead and far, far beyond saving.

"Would you like to know the truth, Bernard?" Feledias said, regarding him with a tortured gaze. "The truth is, I'm scared."

Cutter hesitated for a moment, trying to think of what he might say to offer his brother some comfort. Before he could say anything, though, Feledias spoke again. "It means to be afraid, brother," he said. "I wouldn't worry about it—it's just something us humans do."

Cutter gave him a small smile. "I know what it is to be afraid, Fel. I'm scared too."

"Are you?" his brother asked. "Because you damned sure don't show it."

"Would it help if I did?" He shrugged. "Okay sure, we might be in the Black Wood, surrounded by feylings that want us dead, and maybe all our friends and those we love are back in New Daltenia—where things weren't exactly going great when we left. And maybe we're walking through some cursed world of ghosts, led by one of the strangest looking creatures I've ever seen, hunted by demon wolves and liable, if we aren't careful, to get stuck in this place. But I don't like to be fussy."

Feledias stared at him for several seconds as they walked then, slowly, a smile crept onto his face as Cutter had hoped it would. "I've got a blister on my heel, too. You forgot to mention it."

Cutter laughed. "Right, and there's that."

They walked on for a few seconds until Feledias glanced back at him. "I'm glad you're here, brother."

Cutter laughed again at that. "That makes one of us anyway."

His brother shook his head slowly. "I mean it. I am. I've always been glad you were there. Even when we were kids. Even when Father..." He paused, clearing his throat. "Even when Father was around, he wasn't often...*around*. Not his fault, of course—he loved us, I know that. But a man, I think, can't be a great father and a great king, too. Or, at least, he can't be a *present* one. Even when he was around, he often wasn't *around*. Do you know what I mean?"

"I know," Cutter said, and that was true enough. After all, most of his memories of his childhood regarding his father were waiting. Waiting outside the audience chamber for him to be done with the head of some guild or some farmer come to be heard by his king. Waiting for his father to come to dinner, dinner which, more often than not, he missed, his time taken by some urgent errand or task. It was, after all, no easy thing to rule a kingdom and rule it well. His father had tried, but with their mother gone and no one with which to share the load it had been a near impossible task.

"Those years, when you were gone into exile," Feledias said. "They...I was angry, of course. I wanted you dead. But they were also the longest years of my life. I was a bad king, I know that. I'd have to be blind not to see it. The kingdom deserved better from me, but without you, without Layna, I didn't know what to do. I didn't know who I was."

Cutter winced. "Fel, all of that—it isn't your fault. It's mine. I did it. This..." He paused, waving his hand around them. "This is my fault. It was my actions that brought us here. My actions that have put the kingdom in such danger."

"And you are the reason the sun sets, no doubt," Feledias said, "the reason orphans roam the streets and starving mongrels limp through alleyways desperate for food."

"That's not...I only meant—"

"I know well what you meant, Bernard," Feledias said. "It might seem like humility to you, but in truth it smacks of arrogance. You cannot blame yourself for all the world's problems. No one, not even you, can do so much. You have played your part, it is true, but then we all have. The world is a dirty, filthy place, I think, and it doesn't take a genius to understand why. Are you aware, Bernard, that there are more servants in castles than residents?"

"Yes," Cutter said slowly, "but I don't—"

"The servants' job is to clean up those messes caused by visitors and residents, and to do that job effectively they have to outnumber them. That tells you two things. One, that it is easier to make a mess than clean it—no surprise there, anyone who has ever spent time scrubbing dishes knows the truth of that. But the next piece might not be so obvious, and it's this: if the world is a dirty place, if the world is a mess—and I don't think any right thinking person could say otherwise—then it is a mess for one reason. There are too many people making messes and not nearly enough cleaning them up."

"You paint a grim picture," Cutter said.

His brother shrugged. "It's a grim world, brother. But...and maybe imminent death has made me a bit sentimental, but I just want to say that it's a little less grim with you in it."

Cutter grunted, surprised by how much that touched him. "The same goes for you, Fel."

They walked on for a few seconds in silence before Feledias spoke again. "Tell me true, brother," he said, "what do you think our chances are of seeing New Daltenia again?"

Cutter pondered that, shaking his head. "I don't know," he said. "Not good."

Feledias winced, nodding.

"But then they weren't good when we first stepped into the Black Wood," Cutter went on. "And yet we're still here."

His brother gave a soft laugh. "Yes, but where exactly is *here?*"

"I don't know," Cutter said. "What I do know is that as long as there's life, there's hope. A friend of mine taught me that."

"Your friend, the priest?"

"My friend the priest," Cutter confirmed.

Feledias snorted. "Priests. Always think they know best."

"A lot like princes in that regard," Cutter said. His brother blinked at that, then began to laugh. A genuine, non-sarcastic laugh, and it did Cutter good to hear it. In another moment he was laughing too as they continued following the feyling into the unknown.

As they walked, the figures on either side increased greater still, indistinct speaking in unclear words. Hundreds, perhaps even thousands of them crowded the field, moving in and out of each other. "Did so many of your kind really used to be here, in this place?" Cutter asked Door.

The feyling glanced to the side from where he walked ahead of them, his long thin arms still gesturing as they had. "*You are not seeing one past but many,*" Door said in that strange, melodic, sing-song voice. "*The new pasts and pasts of old mingle, moving in and out of each other.*"

"Well, sure," Feledias said. "As they'll do."

Cutter gave a laugh at that, but one that cut off abruptly as he noticed another of the colorful geometric patterns that Door had called rifts up ahead of them on their left. So close to the path that they would nearly be able to touch it when they passed—not that he had any desire to do so.

"Damned thing," Feledias said from beside him, his own laughter nowhere in evidence now. "Something about them I don't like."

"I'd be hard-pressed to find something I do," Cutter said, watching the shifting colors as they drew closer. Door had told them that they would likely begin to see more and more of the so-called rifts the longer they remained in the past, just as he had cautioned them not to touch them. On that second, he really needn't have bothered. Cutter thought a man would have to hate himself an awful lot to dare to touch such a thing.

It wasn't just how unusual it was, how strange—although that was certainly part of it. It was also that a feeling, a *hunger* seemed to radiate from it. As if it wished to devour all that was around it. But then he supposed that made sense. After all, the past was always hungry to devour the present. That he knew, for he had seen many men get lost in it—had often gotten lost in it himself.

"It is not much farther now," Door said from up ahead, drawing Cutter's attention away from the strange shifting colors for a moment. Just a moment, an instant in time. But in that instant, something appeared on the side of the path opposite the rift. An Unsated. It was charging at them even as it appeared. Cutter had time to turn, to let out a shout, knocking Feledias out of its path, but no more time than that.

In another instant, the creature leapt, pouncing at him. There was no time to go for his axe. Cutter only just managed to get his hands up in front of him, catching the creature by its front legs but not fast enough to keep its claws from digging into his chest.

He grunted in pain, stumbling backward even as he worked to pull the creature away from him. It was no easy task, for this creature, like those others of its kind Cutter had encountered, was shockingly strong but, more than that, possessed of a wild savagery that made it difficult to keep hold of, let alone pull away from him. The creature's jaws snapped at him over and over again, going for his face, the sharp fangs only inches away.

Cutter staggered backward under the assault, and then with a growl of anger and effort, he didn't just tear the creature's arms free—he twisted both of them, and the bones snapped underneath his grip. The creature howled, its attack forgotten in its pain, at least for a moment—and a moment was all Cutter needed.

He pivoted, slamming the creature into the ground, hard. Then, before it could recover, he brought his boot down on its face. The creature squealed, a terrible, alien sound of pain and fear, and Cutter growled, bringing his foot down again. Something shattered beneath his foot and, this time, the creature was still.

Panting from the brief struggle, his chest aching where the creature's claws had scored him, Cutter raised his gaze from the ruins of the Unsated's face to see that he was inches away from what Door had called the rift. This close, the shifting colors—seemingly of every hue and shade—were entrancing, almost hypnotic.

He let out a slow breath at how close he'd come to stumbling into the rift, then he turned back to check on Feledias and the feyling. He was only halfway around when he heard his brother's shout.

"Bernard, watch out!"

Cutter had just finished turning when something struck him in the chest. He staggered backward, spinning as he struggled with this latest attacker, and so he caught a clear view of the bright, geometric patterns of the rift, shifting and moving in that inviting yet somehow ominous way. A very clear view as he was sent careening into it.

Lights exploded all around him as Cutter and his attacker fell, headlong, into the rift.

CHAPTER SEVENTEEN

VALDEN WATCHED the carriage move down the street, toward where he stood in front of the castle, doing his best to contain his impatience. It was all he could do to keep from running toward it and leaping inside. Still, he managed to suppress the urge, if only just.

He felt helpless. Chall had nearly died while he'd been gone, *would* have died had it not been for Emille. Ned, too. A serving girl *had* died, and yet they were no nearer to finding Catham or Robert Palden than they had been. He had meant to wait for Nadia to get back to him on Catham's whereabouts but given everything that had happened, he decided he couldn't sit and hope that the crime boss found the man and, more than that, decided to share his whereabouts when she did. And so, he would have to take matters into his own hands.

Which meant another visit to Willy. After all, Willy had helped him find Nadia in the first place, so it was possible that the conman would be able to help him find Robert Palden, too. The only reason Valden hadn't asked him in the first place was that he hadn't wanted to give Willy any more information than necessary—information that the conman would, inevitably, try to use to his advantage.

Still, it was a longshot. It was a big city, after all, and Robert Palden had taken great pains to remain hidden. A longshot, but then Valden had been an archer for a long time, and he knew that when a longshot was all a man had, he took it, particularly if he was desperate...and Valden thought he qualified for desperate and then some.

Desperate for some good news, desperate to find some shred of light in the darkness. It felt as if the world were falling apart around him, or perhaps as if the ground were giving way beneath his feet, and Valden found himself grasping for something, *anything* to hold on to. It took the carriage another five minutes of eternity to pull up in front of the castle but finally it did. Ned stared at him from the front seat, frowning.

"You don't look much like a noblewoman."

"Thanks," Valden said.

The carriage driver's frown deepened. "Delilah said I'd be picking up a noblewoman."

"Sorry to disappoint you," Valden said, climbing in the back of the carriage.

Ned regarded him through the open window between the inside of the carriage and where he sat holding the reins. "I'm guessing you don't want to go to a tailor's, then. Pick out a new dress."

"I have all the dresses I need."

Ned sighed. "Ought to have known when Delilah said the customer asked for me specifically."

"You don't have repeat customers?"

The carriage driver shrugged. "A few. Fact is, most people don't care whose back they're lookin' at just so long as we take 'em where they want to go. So," he went on, then paused and raised an eyebrow. "Where is it *you* want to go?"

"I'd like to go to church."

That made the man's eyebrow climb higher. "Church," he repeated.

"That's right. The Grand Church of Raveza's Infinite Grace and Love, in fact."

"Huh," Ned said. "Now that's got a bit of a name on it, doesn't it?"

"It does. Do you know it?"

"Sure, I know it," Ned said. "Wouldn't be much at takin' people places if I didn't know where the places were, would I?"

"No?"

"My question, though," Ned said, "is why you want to go there. No offense, but I was under the impression you were just about done with churches."

"So was I."

"Change of heart, then?" the carriage driver asked.

"Change of circumstances."

"I see," Ned said slowly. "And these circumstances—there a reason why you're tending to 'em without your buddy, Challadius?"

"He's sleeping."

"Sure," the carriage driver said. "And here's me, wondering if that's intentional or not."

"I'm not sure what you mean," Valden said.

"Oh, I think you are," Ned said. "But I won't bust your balls anymore'n I have to. I'm married, after all, and I know just how that feels. But why don't you tell me why it is you want to go to this church, eh? Somethin' tells me it ain't to do a bit of kneelin'. Though, I wouldn't be opposed to you puttin' in a good word or two for me with the goddess, if you had a mind."

"Sorry," Valden said. "But I don't think she's listening just now."

Ned grunted. "Had a bit of a falling out, the two of you?"

"Something like that," Valden said, though the truth was that he was becoming increasingly sure—was all but certain at this point—that Raveza, if she existed at all, never *had* listened. Perhaps the road to peace was taken one step at a time but the road to damnation was sloped, and a man didn't need to walk at all. The world was more than happy to get him started with a good push.

"So if it ain't absolution you're after, why the church? Plenty of folks in a similar spot'll pick a tavern instead."

"Answers," Valden said. "I want answers."

"And you're sayin' church is the answer. Now you're startin' to sound like a priest again."

Valden sighed. "Is there always this much talking before you take people where they need to go? If so, I can see why your customers don't ask for you by name."

"Probably on account of it flits out of their mind when I dazzle 'em with my smile," Ned said. "And to answer your question, no, there's not always this much talking, except when I'm summoned to the castle under false pretenses by a man who, by all appearances, is sneaking out. And choosing, of all places, a *church* to sneak to—not the usual place folks sneak to, I don't mind tellin' you. At least not in my experience."

"Which is no doubt vast."

"I've snuck a time or two. Not since I met Em, of course," he said quickly, glancing over his shoulder as if he expected his assassin wife to materialize out of thin air. "Look," he went on, "I'm the last person to try to mind another's business—it's all I can do to tend to my own. But when you ask for me specifically, talkin' about goin' to church with a look on your face that belongs on a fella goin' to the gallows, I'm goin' to ask some questions. Because comin' back home to my wife and comin' back alive, that *is* my business. Understand?"

"You won't just take my word that you're in no danger?"

Ned barked a laugh. "Fella, the world bein' what it is, I wouldn't take my own word on it. Anyway, trust, that's a two-way street, ain't it? You want me to trust you enough to go? Fine—trust me enough to tell me why."

Valden sighed, seeing that they would be going no farther if the man didn't get some answers. "There's a man there, at the church, a priest. Well, he's a conman, and—"

"Sure, you already said he was a priest, don't got to belabor the point," Ned said, grinning.

Valden nodded. "Anyway," he went on, "this conman, he tends to keep his ears to the ground—"

"Most rats do."

"Just so," Valden agreed. "And I thought to ask him about all that's going on in the city, see if maybe he has any information that could be useful to us."

"I see," the carriage driver said. "And this priest—this conman—you trust him?"

"He's a snake. I trust him to do what a snake does."

"Dangerous?"

"As only snakes can be. It's why I asked for you. Chall is resting—and can barely walk besides. Maeve is gone, so I thought—"

"That you'd have me along, that way if someone takes it in mind to do some stabbin', they'll have an extra target."

Valden was surprised to find himself grinning. "Something like that. Will you help me?"

The man considered that, scratching his chin. "Em's not at the house—gone somewhere with Lady Maeve, accordin' to what I heard. S'pose if she's goin' to be out riskin' her life, I ought to do the same. Anyway, it keeps me from pacin' the floors, frettin' all over the place as Em likes to say."

"Sounds messy."

"Not as messy as getting stabbed, I'd wager," Ned said, raising an eyebrow again. "But aye—messy. Now, I s'pose it's time to stop jawin' and start movin'. If that is, you're sure about this?"

"I'm sure," Valden said. It was a lie, of course, one that, judging by the way the carriage driver turned and clucked at the horses, giving the reins a snap, was convincing enough for him. Valden only wished he could convince himself as easily. The truth was that he was risking himself—and now Ned—with no idea if it would pay off or not. He only knew that it was the only thing he could think to do, and he had to do *something*.

So off they rode, Valden hoping that he was not making a mistake that might cost both of them their lives.

AROUND A HALF AN HOUR LATER, they arrived at the Grand Church of Raveza's Infinite Grace and Love. Valden climbed out of the carriage. Standing in the street, he glanced at Ned still seated at the front. "Coming?" he asked.

"Think maybe I'll stay here," the carriage driver said. He wasn't looking at him but farther down the street, and Valden followed his gaze to see what appeared to be two figures standing in the shadows of an alleyway. It was hard to tell for sure, but he thought the figures were staring at them and the carriage. Two men. They looked young, early twenties, if he had to guess.

"Maybe this was a bad idea," Valden said quietly, watching the figures. "Perhaps we should leave."

"What, on account of them?" the carriage driver asked, glancing at him. "Don't be silly—didn't your mama ever tell you not to jump at shadows?"

"Yes," Valden said, "but then some shadows have teeth and sometimes it's them that jump at you."

Ned smiled. "We didn't come all this way for nothin'. You go on and get some church in ya. Me and the ladies'll be fine," he said, patting one of the horses on its haunch. "We're not scared of a couple of shadows."

Valden frowned, glancing back at the two figures. He knew that Ned could handle himself—he'd seen him do it and that more than once—but he still didn't like the idea of leaving him alone. "I can come back later."

"Yeah," Ned said. "You can. Or you can quit being a pain in the ass and go in, throw some money in the plate, do some kneelin' and some chantin', talk to your conman priest, and then come on back. But if you're gonna do it—and you are—then I'd just as soon you did it soon. The thing about shadows, Valden, is that they gather."

Valden frowned, glancing around the street. He could still only see the two young men looking no more than twenty years old, if that, but with the hard look of men who had done violence before and who meant to do it again. Valden knew that look—how not? He'd seen it on others often enough over the years, had seen it on himself often enough.

Ned frowned at his hesitation. "Look, you're the one that wanted to come here, right?"

"Yes, but—"

"And have the reasons you wanted to come changed in the last half hour?"

"Well, no, but—"

"Then get in there already and stop wasting time," the carriage driver said.

Valden paused for a moment but only that, then he gave a single nod. "I'll be fast."

The carriage driver nodded, watching the two figures again, continuing to hold the reins in his left hand even as he patted the seat beside him where, Valden saw, sat a length of steel about a foot and a half long.

"I'd be more comforted if it were a sword," Valden said.

"Wouldn't have fit so easily in the seat, though," the carriage driver said, giving a wink. "Go on, now. I'll see you in a bit."

"See you in a bit," Valden said.

The last time Valden had come to the church there had only been a dozen or so people scattered about the pews, their heads bowed in prayer or speaking quietly with one of the priests or nuns in the church.

Now, it was early morning, and more than fifty men and women sat ensconced, listening to the words of a man standing on the raised dais. Valden was in a hurry, though, so he paid the man's voice little attention, still hearing enough to recognize much of what he was saying. Words of encouragement, of hope. They were words Valden had heard plenty of times, words he'd *said* plenty of times...back when he'd believed them.

He looked around, noting a woman at the corner of the room whose clothes marked her as a nun. No doubt the woman stood close so as to be available should any of the parishioners need assistance. Valden wasn't exactly a parishioner, but he *did* need assistance, so he walked along the edge of the room to where she stood.

The woman noticed his approach and smiled as he drew close. "Good morning, sir," she said. "How may I help you?"

"Good morning, Sister," he said. "I would like to speak with the high priest, please."

"Forgive me, do you mean High Priest Aledran?"

Valden frowned. He supposed that could have been Willy's last name —the fact was he had never known it. The *other* fact was it could just as easily be a lie. He couldn't see a reason for the conman to lie about his last name, but then a man like Willy didn't need a reason to lie any more than a snake needed a reason to bite. It was simply what it did. "I... maybe?" he said. "He's short, the man I mean. Dark hair. First name William?"

The woman smiled, inclining her head. "Yes, sir. That is indeed High Priest Aledran. But I'm afraid he is not present for service just now. Perhaps I might be of assistance?"

She was young, the woman, in her early twenties if he had to guess, and possessed of a certain innocence that made him think she knew little to nothing of murderers and criminal organizations. Valden could only hope the world allowed her to keep that innocence. "I'm afraid the question I have is for him specifically," Valden said.

"I see," the woman said, nodding, still smiling, but curious, too.

"Willy and I go way back," Valden said by way of explanation.

She blinked at that. "Willy?" she said, grinning as if they were two young children and he had just whispered a curse word. "I have never heard High Priest Aledran called so. I could not imagine doing it," she went on, shaking her head. "I would not even dare call his grace 'William.'"

"Not so graceful as you might think," Valden said. Her smile faltered at that, but he waved a hand dismissively. "Yes, well, as I said, the two of us go way back."

"I do not mean to pry but were you old friends?"

Enemies was far closer to the truth, but then he didn't think saying so would help speed things along. Neither did he love the idea of lying to the kind young woman while standing inside a church, a sermon being preached behind him. "We have known each other a very long time," he said, smiling, hoping that she would take that as agreement.

Thankfully, she did. "Of course, sir. And, forgive me, but who may I tell the high priest has come calling?"

Valden hesitated at that. Whatever he'd led the woman to believe, he and Willy were far from close friends, and his name was just as likely—more than, really—to make the man avoid him than bring him forth. Still, refusing to give his name would seem odd and would even more readily ensure that Willy didn't come. After all, the man hadn't survived as long as he had without any martial prowess by luck. He was careful. "My name is

Valden," he said. "If you will tell him that it is important that I speak with him, I would appreciate it."

She inclined her head. "Of course. If you would like to wait here, I will return with word as quickly as I can. Perhaps," she went on, waving her hand at the pews, "you would like to listen to the sermon."

About as much as I'd like to drive nails into my skull, he thought. A grim thought, but a true one. After all, nothing hated the light so much as shadows, and no man who hated talk of virtue and peace more than a sinner. Still, there was no use telling the woman as much, so he only nodded in return. "Thank you," he said. And with that, the woman gave him another smile then turned and walked toward the door at the back of the church, the one which, Valden knew from the last time he'd visited, led to the priests' quarters as well as Willy's own.

While he waited, Valden busied himself considering the many problems they faced. It wasn't hard to find one to consider, that much was sure, for anywhere his mind turned there was one waiting to be worried over. Plenty of problems with so few solutions. He could only hope that Willy might have one for him.

The young woman returned in a few minutes, an apologetic expression on her face. "Forgive me, sir, but I'm afraid that High Priest Aledran is indisposed at the moment."

"Indisposed?"

She winced. "Yes, sir. The high priest is at table."

"He's eating?"

"Yes, sir."

"And did you tell him it was Valden? That it was important?"

"I did, sir, yes." She shifted, clearly uncomfortable. "Perhaps...perhaps you might return tomorrow?"

Tomorrow. Tomorrow would have troubles of its own and then some —that Valden knew from experience. He was just about to speak, to try to convince her of the importance of his errand, when a voice came from behind him.

"Ah, hello again."

Valden and the woman with him turned to see the old priest, the one who he had spoken with the first time he'd come, moving toward him, his crutches tucked underneath his arms. "Valden, wasn't it?" the man asked, giving him a friendly smile.

"It was," Valden said, inclining his head. "It's good to see you again, Brother Elmer."

"And it's good to be seen," the man said. "Meeting with the high priest again, I take it?"

"Trying to," Valden said. "I don't hold out much hope."

"Where there is life, there is hope," the priest offered.

Valden grunted. "Well, apparently the high priest is busy."

"Busy?" the man asked, glancing at the woman. "Is this true, Sister Sabrina?"

The woman inclined her head. "Forgive me, Brother Elmer, but the high priest is taking a meal and said that he does not wish to be disturbed."

Brother Elmer glanced at Valden. "Our high priest often is busy, I'm afraid. Coincidentally, that business tends to coincide with certain...shall I say, less than desirable tasks."

"Same old Willy."

The old priest smiled at that, turning to the woman. "If it is alright with you, Sister Sabrina, I will help our visitor here."

"Of course, Brother Elmer," she said, bowing her head. Then she turned and moved away.

"Now then," the old man went on when she was gone, turning to regard Valden. "Your meeting with the high priest—it's important, I take it?"

"Yes. Very."

Elmer nodded. "I suspected as much. It didn't seem likely that you came for the pleasure of the high priest's company." The priest watched him for a few seconds, his gaze seeming to grow almost painfully sharp. "I have been a priest for a long time, have learned much in the years—still a fool, but one that has had the privilege, over the course of his life, to learn from men far wiser than myself. Yet for all those lessons, I find that one of the greatest truths I know is one I learned back when I was just a child, taught to me at the hand of a drunken, violent father. It is this—suffering, often, leads to salvation. Words he spoke to me often, words almost always accompanied by fists."

"Suffering leads to salvation," Valden repeated.

"Just so," Elmer said. "My father, in his drunken, staggering stupor, stumbled upon what I believe to be a universal truth, stumbled upon it the same way a man walking in the cold darkness might stumble into shelter through no effort of his own but pure luck. Of course, he did not mean it the way I have come to believe it, meant it only, I expect, as a taunt, a sort of mockery. But then truth, like anything else, does not stop being what it is simply because the one holding it does not recognize it."

"He sounds like a cruel man, your father," Valden said.

The old priest nodded sadly. "He was. The truth is I pity him. The *truth* is I pitied him, even then. Still, you did not come to speak about my father. I only mention him because you have come to see the high priest, the high priest who, it seems, has little interest in seeing you."

"It's important."

"So you've said, and so I believe," the priest said. "I only want to make clear, that I, like all servants of Raveza, the Goddess of Peace, abhor violence except in extreme circumstances."

"I didn't come to hurt Willy. I just need to talk to him—that's all."

"Good," the priest said, "that is good. For, as I said, suffering often leads to salvation. This church..." He paused, glancing around. "It has an... interesting history. And there are some things that happen here which I do not, strictly, agree with. But that does not change the fact that its existence has helped hundreds of the city's people, and while it is true that, perhaps some of the coin always seems to vanish from the collection plates, what remains has fed and clothed many of the city's most unfortunate souls."

"Suffering leading to salvation," Valden said.

"Just so," the old man said, inclining his head. "The church has been a boon to many, and I would protect it, if I could."

"So would I," Valden said.

The priest watched him for a moment, as if gauging his sincerity. Then, in another moment, he nodded. "I believe you. Come—I will show you to the high priest."

Like last time, Valden was led to the door at the back of the church but, unlike last time, the priest did not show him to Willy's study. Instead, he led him into a dining hall that had clearly been made to accommodate several dozen people at a time. Not that it did just then, for as they stepped through the door and into the room, Valden saw that the only person seated at the tables was Willy. Before the man was a spread of food and drinks worthy of a king's feast. Willy took note of Valden and Brother Elmer as he was taking a drink of wine from a goblet in his hand, and he sputtered, spilling wine over the front of his priest's robes, a stain to go with the others of food and drink already marring the once-fine clothes.

"Good afternoon, High Priest," Brother Elmer said, his tone completely devoid of any of the disgust Valden felt staring at the man in his grease-stained robes.

"Brother Elmer," Willy said, frowning. "I told Sabrina I wasn't to be disturbed."

"Ah, forgive me, High Priest," the old priest said. "*Sister* Sabrina said as much, but I thought she must have been mistaken. After all, I knew that you would not wish to turn away any who came seeking your aid."

Willy frowned, the sour expression on his face making it obvious that he knew well the trap he was in. "Of course," the fake priest said. "I meant to seek out Brother Valden as soon as I was finished here."

"And now, High Priest, it seems that you will be saved the trouble," Brother Elmer supplied, the old man giving him a smile that appeared completely genuine.

"So it seems," Willy said, clearly annoyed. "You may leave, Brother Elmer."

"Thank you, High Priest," the old man said, bowing his head.

Willy watched as the man went to the door and closed it behind him. Only then did he hiss. "Old bastard," he said. "Thinks he's better than me."

"Oh, I wouldn't let it bother you, Willy," Valden said. "He *is* better than you."

The conman frowned. "Is there something I can do for you, Vicious? Or did you just come to interrupt my dinner and insult me?"

"I didn't come to interrupt your dinner, nor did I come to insult you, Willy. I came looking for your help."

"My help," Willy said, and Valden could see the twinkle in the conman's eyes. "Twice in as many days. What am I, a charity?"

"Well, you are a priest," Valden pointed out. "Or at least pretending to be one at the moment."

Willy frowned. "And just what sort of help are you needing, Vicious? If it's absolution you're after, you'd be better off kneeling out there with the rest of those pitiful bastards."

"Not absolution—information."

"Ah, I see," Willy said. "Now that is a lot harder to come by, I'm afraid. Still, seeing as we are old friends, why don't you tell me what it is you want to know."

"I need your help finding a man. A few men, actually."

"Now, Valden, it seems you might not be looking for a church but a brothel. I know of one that might fit the bill, I suppose..." He laughed then, but when Valden only stared at him the laughter quieted, and he cleared his throat. "Anyway, these men you're looking for," the conman went on, "do they have names?"

"They do. Catham, you know—"

"That slippery bastard?" Willy said, then grunted. "Good luck finding him if he doesn't want to be found. Easier to steal a nun's virtue than to lay hands on Catham the Cautious."

"I suppose you'd know," Valden said.

"And the other?" Willy asked.

Valden hesitated, wondering if this had been a mistake, wondering if he would make that mistake all the worse by telling Willy the second name. Still, if he'd had a better option—which meant pretty much any option—he wouldn't have come in the first place. "Robert Palden." He watched the man closely, trying to see whether or not he recognized the name, but then whatever else he was, Willy was a chameleon, a liar with a lifetime's worth of practice, and in the end Valden couldn't have said if he recognized the name or not.

"Robert Palden," Willy said, as if trying out the name.

"That's right," Valden said. "Do you know him?"

"Should I?"

"The Wolves are back," Valden said, "and he's the one leading them. Anyway, I need to know where he is, where they *both* are."

"Want to have a nice chat with them, that it?"

"Something like that," Valden said.

"So Catham and this Robby fella—"

"Robert. Robert Palden."

"Right. Anything else?"

Valden considered that for a moment then nodded. "I want you to keep an ear to the ground, see if you hear anything about someone talking about murdering serving women in the castle."

The conman blinked. "A murder in the castle? What with all those stone walls? All those guards just waiting to poke a hole in someone?"

It was a taunt, and one that Valden didn't bother responding to.

Willy frowned, disappointed. "Say that I do find these men for you, say that I figure out who might be going around killing serving girls—what's in it for me?"

And there was the question, the only real question, Valden thought, that the conman ever truly considered. *What's in it for me?* If the man had a motto, that was it. "I can pay you."

The conman shrugged. "I'm sure you can, but then I'm not doing terribly bad on coin just now. You'd be surprised just how giving people can be when they come here."

"You mean the money you steal from the offerings."

"Appropriating. I wouldn't really call it stealing, if—"

"Everyone else would."

Willy gave him a small smile. "It's a trade, really. They do something they're ashamed of, come to church, drop a bit of coin in the plate, and then they can let go of whatever guilt they brought in with them. At least until they do the next thing they're ashamed of, that is."

"Not everybody is like you."

"Aren't they?" Willy asked. "I don't tend to sit in on many of the confessions—they bore me. But I've listened to enough to know that even the sweetest looking grandmother can do some of the cruelest things. It seems to me, Vicious, that they *are* like me. Only, most people just aren't as good at it."

"You are one of a kind," Valden said. Based on the way the man smiled, he took it as a compliment, but Valden certainly hadn't meant it as one. "Anyway, if you don't want coin, what *do* you want?"

"These Wolves—this Robert Palden and Catham, guess you're wantin' 'em pretty bad, huh?" Willy asked, licking his lips.

Valden didn't bother saying anything to that.

"And you, Vicious," the conman said, "you work for our young king, don't you? Which means that if *you* want the Wolves, so does he. Am I right?"

"Say that you are," Valden said, though the truth was he wasn't sure if Matt had even given the Wolves much thought lately. The lad had more than enough problems of his own, after all.

"I can see how they're a problem for you, for the king," Willy said, his eyes dancing with greed. "A big problem. Which means that the fella who solves them, well, he'd deserve a big reward, wouldn't he?"

Valden turned and made for the door. He had no intention of going through it, of course, but then conmen could be conned too.

"Alright, alright," Willy blurted, rising and bringing his hands up in front of him as if to say he meant no harm. "Just take it easy, Vicious."

"This is me taking it easy. I don't have a lot of time to waste, Willy," Valden said. "If you have something to say, say it."

Willy sighed. "I want a lordship."

Valden blinked. He wasn't sure what he'd been expecting, but that certainly wasn't it. "Sorry?"

"You heard me," the conman said. "I want to be made a lord. Given some land, a castle—it doesn't have to be the best. And the title, of course."

"You," Valden said. "A lord. Lord Willy."

"Oh, don't look so shocked," Willy said. "It's not as if I'd be the first to get his lordship through...unconventional means. Why, I wouldn't even be the worst this kingdom's seen. Shit, look at their own princes. One a bloodthirsty psychopath that'd just as soon split a man open with that great axe of his as speak to him, and his brother little better."

"I'd be very careful, Willy," Valden said. "Prince Bernard is a better man than you'll ever be, and I won't listen to you demean him, do you understand?"

The conman licked his lips nervously. "Alright, Vicious, alright. I don't mean any harm. But if it's help you're after, then the price is a lordship."

Valden considered for a moment. He didn't love the idea of Willy being a lord, of course—didn't love the idea of the man having any influence at all. But then if something didn't change and soon, there wouldn't be a kingdom for him to be a lord *in*. "Okay."

"Okay?" Willy asked, his eyebrows climbing to his hairline.

"Okay," Valden said again.

The conman looked shocked, then, slowly, his wide grin gave way to a frown. "Wait a minute—just like that? Without even asking His Royal Majesty?"

"King Matthias trusts me," Valden said, although the truth was he was not sure of that. "He knows how important it is that we find the Wolves. You help us, and you'll get your lordship."

"That a promise, Vicious?"

"That's a promise."

"Guess I'm just to trust you then, that it?"

"It seems funny to hear you of all people talk about trust," Valden said. "I am many things, Willy, but I am no liar."

"I've said similar things myself," Willy said.

"I'm not you," Valden countered. "That's the best offer you'll get—take it or leave it."

The conman considered then, finally nodded. "Alright, Vicious. I'll look into these two fellas you mentioned—Catham and, what was the other? Tolbert?"

"Robert," Valden said, frowning. "Robert Palden."

"Right, right," Willy said, tapping his head. "Got it."

"Good," Valden said. "Send word to me at the castle when you find anything." He turned and started toward the door, pausing and glancing back. "And Willy? That priest, Brother Elmer, he is a good man. If anything happens to him, if he so much as stubs his toe because he brought me back here, I'll be...upset. Am I clear?"

"Clear," Willy said, frowning. "Always a pleasure, Vicious."

Valden grunted. "Wish I could say the same," he said, then he walked out the door, closing it behind him.

In the nave of the church once more, Valden moved past the rows of pews toward the door. As he did he passed by Brother Elmer seated beside a parishioner, speaking in quiet tones. The old man noted him and smiled. "Everything come out alright, I hope?" he asked.

"Too early to tell, I'm afraid," Valden said.

The old man nodded. "It will," he said. "Be well, Valden, and remember the path to peace is taken one step at a time. Good luck."

"Thanks," Valden said. *I'm going to need it.* He gave the priest a nod before turning and walking out. Despite his worries for Ned, the carriage driver sat the same as he had before with his left hand holding the reins of the two horses hitched to the carriage and his right arm propped casually on the top of the seat.

"Everything alright?" Valden asked as he drew closer.

"All good here. You get what you came for?"

"No, but there's still hope yet." He glanced back at the alleyway where he'd first spotted the two young men. "And our friendly neighborhood shadows?"

"What's that?" Ned said, following Valden's gaze. "Ah, them. Hard to say. Fled, I s'pose. You know, the way shadows will."

"Fled," Valden said.

"That's right."

"And did they have any help with that, I wonder?"

"Hard to say."

He nodded slowly. "Hurt your hand, did you?"

Ned glanced down at his right hand, the knuckles scraped bloody, then grunted. "Huh. What about that?" He shook his head as if in wonder. "Dangerous world we live in, a fella just sittin', mindin' his own business and ends up with some bloody knuckles. Must have scraped 'em on somethin', I s'pose."

"Dangerous world indeed," Valden observed. "Though I imagine there are some people suffering more than some bloody knuckles just now."

"Might be the case, sure," Ned said. "It's a big city, after all, a big world."

Valden leaned over the carriage, eyeing the small, stout length of steel that still lay as it had. It didn't look as if it had been moved, and there was no blood or hair or anything else on it that might indicate that it had been used in a fight, but then the carriage driver didn't strike him as the type of man that believed in leaving messes. "Do I need to worry about the city guard being called on us?"

"Why?" Ned asked. "You do somethin'?"

"I was more worrying about you," Valden said, "about the two men who were lurking in the alleyway when we arrived."

"Worrying about others. Might be you're still a priest after all. Anyway, I wouldn't concern yourself with those two. We had a little chat is all. Reckon it left 'em all tuckered out. They're takin' a bit of a nap, but they'll wake up soon enough, maybe with a bit of a headache but in my experience few of life's lessons come so cheaply. Soon enough, they'll be right on back to lurkin'—though, I suspect, not around this church."

Valden watched the man for several seconds. What he was saying—or, rather, what he was taking pains *not* to say—was that he'd just handled two criminals and save for some bloody knuckles he didn't have so much as a scratch on him. More than that, though, he wasn't upset or put out in the least. Most people—even criminals—tended to get worked up over such things, yet there the carriage driver sat, as calm and collected as if he'd just woken from a pleasant nap. "You know what, Ned?" Valden said slowly. "I think that maybe you're one of the most dangerous people I've ever met."

"Might be you ought to get out more," Ned said. "So. Time to leave?"

"Time to leave," Valden agreed.

They started away then, but had barely begun to move when a figure stepped out into the street in front of them. At first, Valden thought that it would be one of the two young men who'd been skulking in the shadows of the alley mouth, perhaps not as tired out from their chat as Ned had thought. But as he peered at the figure he saw that he was wrong. The man standing in the street was older and while Valden did in fact recognize him, it was from somewhere else altogether.

"*Excuse us, fella,*" Ned called. "*Just lookin' to get by.*"

The man standing in the street didn't move, only stood as he had, staring at Valden. Ned grunted. "I tell ya, Priest, folks just don't seem to have any manners anymore." He sighed. "Stay here—I'll be right back."

He started to rise but Valden grabbed him, stopping him. "I think you've had enough chatting for one afternoon, don't you? And I told you—I'm not a priest."

Ned raised an eyebrow. "What can I say? I'm a people person. Anyway, you're out here, visiting churches, worried over men that'd be all too happy to stick a few new holes in you, if they thought any coins would fall out... seems awful priestly to me."

Valden frowned. "I'll be right back."

"If you say so," Ned said. "I'll just take a load off, get comfortable. But not *too* comfortable, understand?"

Valden did. The man would wait, but he wouldn't wait forever. "I'll be right back," he said again, then he was climbing out of the carriage, moving to the figure in the street.

"Aubrey, isn't it?" he asked as he approached.

"Don't much care for the way you say it," Nadia's man said.

"How do I say it?"

The man shrugged one shoulder. "Like it's a girl name."

"It's a guy's name too," Valden said, repeating what the man had told him before.

"Damn right it is," Aubrey said. "Been lookin' all over the city for you—you're a hard man to find, you know that?"

"How *did* you find me?"

251

The man glanced over Valden's shoulder at the church in the distance. "Let's just say I prayed about it, how'd that be?"

Which meant that there was someone in the church, possibly a parishioner but more likely a nun or priest, who worked for Nadia. They'd been watching him. No great surprise there. He had made a deal with Nadia, after all, and the thing about criminals—crime bosses in particular—was that they pretty much always had trust issues. He wondered if Willy was aware that one of those who served in his church worked for the crime boss and decided he doubted it. If he had, Willy would have likely been running away just as fast as his feet would carry him. He was known for his cleverness, not his courage.

"I see," Valden said. "Well. You found me. What now?"

"Now you should come with me. The boss wants to see you."

"What about?"

"On account of she's putting together a card game and we're one short. Why the shit do you think? You had a deal, remember?"

Valden blinked. "Wait...do you mean. It's Catham? She has him?"

The man glanced around. "Keep your damn voice down," he said. "Most of the city guard are in our pocket, but that don't mean all of them are. Anyway, I find it best not to test the loyalty of the patently disloyal. As for your question, yeah, sure, we have Catham. At least...most of him."

Most of him. That sent a stab of worry through Valden. He had no love for Catham—the bastard had tried to have him and Chall killed and had very nearly succeeded and that was before he'd tried again at Ned's house, nearly killing Chall. Still, while he didn't have any love for Catham, he *did* have questions. "He's alive, though?" he asked.

"Was when I left him," Aubrey said, "though, if I were you I wouldn't fuck about. I know you and the boss go back, so I imagine you know that when it comes to revenge, she tends to skip the pleasantries and get right down to it."

"Right," Valden said, glancing back at Ned. "And my friend?"

"Will still be your friend later on, but he ain't comin'. Afraid my invite is for you and you only."

Valden sighed. He'd figured as much. "Just a minute."

He turned and moved back down the street.

"Have a nice chat, did ya?" the carriage driver asked as Valden approached.

"Well, my knuckles aren't bloody anyway," Valden said.

Ned gave him a small smile as he glanced past at Nadia's man still standing in the street. "He's got the look of a fella who means to stab someone and ain't all that particular."

"I'd say that's a fair assessment, given what I know of him," Valden said, remembering the first time he'd met the man and the crossbow he'd held trained on him and Chall.

"What's he want with you then?"

"It might be better if you don't know."

"Might be better if I was a fat merchant dressed in soft silks. Or maybe if I'd have been clerk like my ma always wanted." Ned shrugged. "But I'm not—I'm here, and in my experience a fella is always better off knowin'. Assumin' he wants to keep on breathin', that is."

Valden winced, knowing that the man wouldn't be put off easily. "It's about the Wolves," he said. "That man there, his boss might have a line on them. They have Catham."

"Alright," Ned said instantly. "Tell him to hop in—might as well save the boot leather while we're goin' to that boss of his."

"I'm going alone."

The carriage driver barked a laugh at that. "Sure, why not? 'Cause everybody knows that's the best way to go see a bunch of criminals—alone. I never knew priests could be so funny."

"I told you," Valden said, "I'm not a priest. And I'm not joking."

Ned watched him for several seconds. "You're right," he said finally. "You're not a priest. You're a fool. Leastways, you are if you're thinkin' about goin' by yourself. Even if you could trust this boss—which you can't—there's Catham to think on. Maybe the two of you go back, but I've seen enough of him to know that he's a slippery bastard. Dangerous."

"You'll get no argument there," Valden said. "But that doesn't change the fact that I have to go alone."

"And I'm to do what, exactly?" Ned asked. "Just sit on my hands? Maybe take up sewing?"

"I was going to ask for a favor."

"Of course you were."

Valden winced. "Listen, Ned, I know that I'm asking a lot here, and I know that I haven't given you any reason to trust me, but—"

"It's not you I don't trust," the man said quietly, looking at Nadia's man still standing in the street.

"But there isn't any choice," Valden finished. "They won't take us both, it's as simple as that. Either I go or none of us do, and we won't get any closer to finding Robert Palden and figuring out what the Wolves are up to."

"Won't get a whole lot closer if you're dead either," Ned countered.

"It's a chance I have to take."

The carriage driver studied him for a moment. "You know," he said finally, "for a man who acts like he lost his faith, you sure do seem to have plenty to spare."

Valden gave him an expression somewhere between a wince and a smile. "In my experience, sometimes desperation can look like faith, from the outside."

"Easy to get those two confused, sure," Ned said. "But not just from the outside. From the inside too. Might be you're more of a priest than you think."

"I'm sorry, Ned, but that—"

The carriage driver held up a hand, forestalling him. "Never mind that. You keep on tellin' yourself whatever you need to to get through. Meantime, what's this favor you're wantin'?"

Valden let go a sigh of relief. He had been afraid—and more than a little certain—that the carriage driver would refuse to let him go alone. "I need you to go to the castle," he told Ned. "Chall's there, Matt too. I need you to look after them for me."

"I'll look after your mage—shouldn't be too hard as he can't hardly walk just now. But what about Lady Maeve? She's with him, ain't she? She's a damn-sight better of a guardian than me, I'd wager."

"Maybe," Valden said, though the truth was he wasn't so sure. "But she's not there. She was called away on business by your wife."

Ned frowned. "That'd explain why she wasn't at home. And here I thought maybe she'd went to the market."

"I'm afraid not," Valden said. "There's trouble at the Guild."

"You mean the guild of insane murderers and back-stabbing sons of bitches of which they're a part?"

"That'd be the one," Valden said.

Ned sighed, shaking his head. "I swear by all the gods, that if me and Em make it out of this, I'm goin' to take up farmin'."

"I hear it's hard work."

"Sure, but then so's bein' killed, I imagine," Ned said. "Anyway, I ain't ever heard of a man gettin' stabbed sloppin' out pig shit."

"Will you go?"

"I'll go," the man said.

"Thank you."

Ned grunted, glancing back at Nadia's man in the street. "We'll see if you're so grateful when one of those sons of bitches decides to see what you'd look like with a knife stickin' in you."

Valden gave the man a small smile. "Good luck, Ned."

"If I had any to spare, I'd let you borrow it as I think you need it more than me," Ned said. "Good luck, Priest—try not to get yourself killed, eh?"

With that, the carriage driver clucked at the horses, giving the reins a snap, and the carriage started forward, directly at Aubrey, and the man let out a shout of indignation as he was forced to jump out of the way to avoid being trampled.

"*Sorry, fella, didn't see you there,*" Ned called.

"I told you," Valden said in a whisper as he watched the man ride away, "I'm not a priest." He walked back to Nadia's man as Aubrey picked himself up off the ground.

"Your friend's a bit of a bastard, ain't he?" he said, making a show of dusting off the front of his tunic.

"Funny," Valden said, "he said the same thing about you. Now come on —let's get this done."

255

CHAPTER EIGHTEEN

HE HIT THE GROUND HARD, landing on his back with enough force to knock the wind out of him, but Cutter didn't let that distract him, for to do so would mean a quick, brutal death. It took all his weary strength to keep this latest attacker at bay, its slathering fangs snapping shut again and again only inches away from his face.

But as wildly savage as the beasts Door had called the Unsated were, their greatest danger was in their numbers. One was no match for Cutter, even in his weakened, exhausted state. He switched his grip on one of the creature's forelegs and growled as he gave it a savage twist, breaking it. The Unsated squealed, its attack momentarily forgotten by the shock of pain. Cutter let go of the creature's other foreleg, instead grabbing the back of its furred head in his left hand and wrapping his right around its snout, forcing its jaws closed.

Then, with another growl, another savage twist, he snapped the creature's neck. Its wild struggles stopped at once, and its body fell limply atop him, surprisingly light. Grunting in disgust as the creature's blood seeped onto his face and chest, Cutter shoved it off him. He lay there for a moment, wheezing and struggling to get his breath back. Then, when he felt just about as good as he thought he was going to feel, he sat up, wincing at the fresh pain in his chest and arms.

He looked at his arms first, taking stock of himself, seeing how badly he was wounded. The cuts were painful, but thankfully none were so deep as to be fatal. Those on his chest were even less deep. He put a hand on the ground and winced as he hoisted himself to his feet.

He didn't know what he expected when he rose—to find himself in some hellish, unreal landscape, perhaps. He was more than a little surprised, then, when he looked around and saw that the place in which he found himself looked, at least at first glance, identical to the one he'd been in before falling into the rift.

The path upon which they'd walked was still there and so, too, were those figures on either side, milling this way and that, different figures from different times all converging within the past. In fact, as Cutter looked farther down the path, he was shocked—and more than a little relieved— to see that Feledias and the feyling, Door. They were still walking on the path as they had been, no more than twenty-five feet ahead of him.

"*Fel!*" he shouted. His brother continued to walk as if he hadn't heard him, though Cutter couldn't imagine how that was possible.

He started toward them at a slow jog. "*Hey, I'm here!*"

But Feledias and the feyling still did not turn, only continued forward as they had. Cutter reached them in another few seconds. He grabbed his brother's shoulder. "Hey, is everythi—" he began as he forced him to turn, but as he did and Cutter got a good look at him, he staggered back with a hiss of surprise and disgust.

The man before him was Feledias—he knew that, could see it in ever part of him. In the width of his shoulders, his clothes, even in the way that he walked. It was Feledias. Only...it wasn't. For the face that stared back at Cutter was not that of his brother. In fact, he wasn't sure if it qualified as a face at all. The features were blurred and indistinct, as if he stared at a reflection in a muddy pool. Or, perhaps, as if his face was clay in the process of being worked by some sculptor.

His brother—or whoever the figure was—finished turning to face him straight on. As he did, the feyling turned to regard him, moving just as Door had, but as the feyling finished turning Cutter saw that, like Feledias, its features were blurred and indistinct. "Fel," Cutter said, "are...are you... okay?"

He wasn't, of course—Cutter could see that at a glance just as he could see no definitive mouth with which his brother—or whatever the thing before him was—could answer even if it had a mind to.

Cutter frowned, trying to understand, wishing Door was here to explain what was happening to him. But the Door before him, if it was the feyling at all, didn't look in any danger of explaining or doing anything just then save silently regarding him. And while Cutter couldn't have said exactly *why*, he was under the distinct impression that the way in which they regarded him was hostile.

As he stood there, trying to understand what was happening, he realized something. The fields around him had gone completely, deathly silent.

He glanced around, expecting to see that the figures on either side of the path had vanished, for the buzz of unintelligible words and growls and screeches was gone. But when Cutter looked he saw that the figures remained, only now they did not move. Instead, they were completely still, all of them facing in the same direction—at him.

Thousands of figures, stretching on as far as he could see, and each of them regarding him with the same silent hostility as Feledias and Door. Only, Cutter noticed something as he regarded those faces. While most had the same ill-defined look as Fel and Door, as if someone had stuck their hand into their features and stirred them around, some of those in the crowd looked as real and as normal as a person or creature met in the real world.

Which was strange.

Stranger still was that Cutter recognized them. Feyling and mortal alike, he knew them, and how not? They were his ghosts, ghosts which still bore the wounds he had given them. Here was a giant of a man, nearly eight feet tall. He had been the leader of a band of bandits. Senshin the Savage, they'd called him. That had been nearly twenty years ago now. The man's teeth, Cutter remembered, had been filed to points, and he'd kept his eyebrows shaved, both of which had added to his menace. He was as ugly now as he'd ever been. Uglier, in truth, for his face was split open by the wound that had felled him, an axe blow to the face. Senshin had been strong, incredibly so, but all the strength in the world didn't stop an axe to the face. He had been a terror then, his name whispered in hushed tones in taverns. Cutter had gone to meet him, not because he wanted to save the people but because then, like always, he'd simply been spoiling for a fight.

Feledias had counseled diplomacy, but then Cutter had never been much for diplomacy. They had fought, and even now it had been one of the most brutal fights Cutter had ever been in, one which had taken him a week to recover from. Senshin had been as powerful, as strong as the stories had claimed. Fast, too. So great a warrior that many had thought him invincible. As it turned out, though, that part, at least, had not been true.

Less than ten feet away from the dead bandit stood the gretchling he'd killed when he and Matt had first entered the Black Wood, the one which had presented itself as a young girl and had very nearly killed Matt.

There were others. Countless others, each felled by his fist, his axe. The men who he had fought outside Brighton, staining the white snow red with their blood. On his other side stood the mayor of Two Rivers and, nearby, the feyling regent who had very nearly brought down the kingdom. Cutter let his gaze sweep over them, recognizing them, knowing them as he did, until he noted a figure standing not on either side of the path but on the path itself, only a short distance away.

This one, too, he recognized. "Yeladrian," he said, his voice little more than a whisper. The Fey King looked much the same as he had in life. He stood like a man and, as in life, he was as tall as Cutter himself. But while Cutter was broad and muscular, the Fey King was thin and graceful, a willow to Cutter's oak. His pale gray skin, so light as to be almost translucent, stretched over compact, wiry muscles. Staring at him, at the way he managed to somehow stand gracefully, Cutter felt, as he had so many years ago when they'd first met, like some bumbling, awkward creature. An ox standing next to a unicorn.

Cutter remembered when the feyling had come to the castle and so many of the noblewomen and serving girls had swooned over his ethereal beauty. At least, that was, until Cutter had put an axe through it. The Fey King looked identical to how Cutter had last seen him save for one thing—his head was still attached to his shoulders, though along his neck was a gruesome scar where Cutter's axe, the same axe the Fey King had gifted him, had cleaved off his head.

Cutter noted that the Fey King held his signature sword down and at his side. No mortal working, this. The sword—long and slender like its bearer—was composed of thousands of thin, intertwining strands of what looked like saw-grass. An odd weapon, one that barely looked like a weapon at all as much as a piece of art. But while Cutter didn't know what magic held the blade together, he knew well its efficacy, for he had felt its touch when he and Yeladrian had fought. As light, as thin as the sword appeared, he knew it possessed the strength of steel, able to parry even the Breaker of Pacts, and its edge was as keen as any blade forged and honed by a human smith. Likely keener.

Cutter frowned, regarding the Fey King. He had not thought to see him again. Most of the time, when he killed someone, they stayed dead. Except, that was, when they visited him in his dreams.

The Fey King said nothing, only studied him with his strange, alien gaze, one eye as bright blue as the sky on a sunny day, the other a verdant green so dark it was almost black. He did not speak, did not even seem to so much as breathe.

He did not move...

Until he did.

Yeladrian burst into motion, moving with a speed that would have been shocking had Cutter not fought him before. He had often wondered, in the years since his fight with the Fey King, whether it had been luck or skill that had been the reason for his victory. After all, Yeladrian was an accomplished warrior, and the swing that had taken his head had certainly felt, at the time, like a surprise to Cutter.

But it seemed that now he was going to find out, one way or the other. He drew the Breaker of Pacts, hefting it in front of him, then lumbered forward to meet the quickly darting Fey King. Yeladrian sped straight at him until he was nearly within weapon range, then he pivoted, abruptly leaping several feet to the side with an agility and grace that no mortal could hope to match, barely slowing before he lunged at Cutter from this new angle.

The blow was aimed at his midsection, and so as his axe was already near that position, Cutter only had to shift it a few inches to knock the questing blade away. Even still, he barely managed it, the blade's tip only an inch or two away from his flesh before he batted it aside.

Yeladrian used the momentum of the parry to carry him into a sideways, somersaulting spin where his entire body left the ground. He turned like a dervish in the air, and his feet had barely touched the ground again when he was coming at Cutter once more. This time the Fey King opted not for a lunge but for a diagonal slash that moved with the speed of crashing lightning.

Cutter had expected such a blow though, so even as he'd parried the Fey King's first attack he'd already been stepping away which meant that he was out of range of the follow-up strike. Yeladrian didn't seem bothered, though, darting forward once more, and then they were at it in truth.

Cutter didn't think, in those seconds, for if he had stopped to think he would have died. He let his instincts take over, the axe moving with a mind of its own, placing itself in the path of the questing blade again and again as Cutter waited for his opening.

The Fey King spun away only to pivot, launching himself off his back foot into another lunge. Cutter had expected a similar move, and so here, then, was his chance. He stepped to the side, the green blade cutting through the air only inches from his midsection, then let out a roar as he brought his own axe down in a two-handed blow.

Positioned as he was, his legs wide, committed to his lunge, Cutter was confident that the Fey King would not be capable of avoiding the blow, that even his superhuman agility and grace would not be enough to see him clear. On this, at least, he was right, for the Fey King did not manage to get out of the way of the strike. The axe cut down with inevitability, but when it struck the Fey King in the space between his shoulder and neck, there was no more resistance than there had been as the axe head cut through air. The blade passed through the Fey King as if he was a ghost in truth, blurring his form the way an image reflected in water might blur as a ripple ran through it, only to reform a moment later once his axe was through.

Like a mirage seen in the desert, he was no more real than a man's desperate desire for water in a place that had none. But while Yeladrian's form might not have seemed real, the sword that came flashing back at Cutter was real enough. He took a staggering step away, bringing his axe up in a parry, and even through his surprise he almost managed to knock the blade away without being harmed.

Almost.

Cutter hissed as the blade cut a line of agony across his upper arm before his axe caught it. He lashed out with the Breaker of Pacts again, more out of instinct than any thought to do real harm. Yeladrian somersaulted away but not before Cutter witnessed his axe pass through the Fey King's midsection with no more of an effect than it had the first time.

The Fey King backed away, circling him slowly, in no hurry. But then, why would he be? After all, a fight to the death lost a lot of its threat if you couldn't die. Cutter's first fight with the Fey King had been difficult, one of the hardest fights of his life, and Yeladrian had not been invincible then. *But this is not Yeladrian,* he told himself. After all, Yeladrian, the *real* Yeladrian, was dead, his head separated from his shoulders.

The creature before him might share Yeladrian's appearance, might wield his sword, but he was not the Fey King. "Who are you?" Cutter said.

The figure said nothing to that, only continued to slowly circle, flicking its blade this way and that in lightning-quick flourishes, something Yeladrian had done as well. Suddenly, the figure stopped its circling and raised its sword, the tip pointing directly at Cutter.

Cutter stopped as well, lifting his axe. It hadn't done any good the first time, but the obsidian weapon would, at least, manage to keep the creature's own blade at bay...for a little while. In a fight where one of the fighters couldn't die and the other could die all too easily, the outcome was never really in doubt.

Suddenly, Yeladrian burst into motion, spinning and pivoting on one foot, leaping to the side, his blade spinning and twisting in the air. Yeladrian—or, at least the creature who had taken on his appearance—was incredibly graceful, and even as it rushed toward Cutter he found himself thinking that it turned the ugly, bloody work of combat into something approaching art.

The Fey King glided across the ground toward him, his feet seeming to hardly ever touch the earth, then leapt over six feet into the air, his blade held up and over his shoulder, pointing at a downward angle toward Cutter.

Cutter bared his teeth, moving his axe into line to parry the blow...but the blow never came. Frowning, he stared at Yeladrian as the figure seemed to float in the air, stuck like an insect in amber. "Huh," Cutter said quietly. "That's new."

"*You cannot defeat it,*" a woman's voice said, "*not with the weapon you carry.*"

"Worked well enough the first ti—" Cutter cut off as he turned to the side and saw the woman standing to his left.

She wore a long, flowing white dress, the same dress she had worn the first time he'd seen her, and she studied him with the same sad eyes that had stared at him as he had walked out of her life and his own, carrying her son, *their* son, with him.

"*Layna?*" Cutter breathed, feeling as if Yeladrian's blade had pierced him after all.

"*Layna is no more,*" the figure said. "*I am only a memory. A ghost.*"

It was her voice. He knew that voice, had heard it countless times in his dreams. Dreams where she had told him again and again that they had made a mistake, that they were damned for what they had done. Dreams where she asked him to watch after her son, to watch after *their* son. Dreams where, as in life, he failed.

Out of all the pain, all the shocks Cutter had suffered over the last days, over his life—and he had suffered more than his share—few rivaled how he felt seeing her there. "You...you're not real?"

"*The past is always real to those who lived it,*" she said.

263

Cutter glanced back at Yeladrian. "And he?"

"*Will remain. For now. But the past will not be kept at bay for long—there is little time.*"

In Cutter's experience, there was always little time. "Makes a man wonder who's spending it all," he said. She said nothing to that, only watched him, so he spoke on. "What about them?" he asked, nodding his head at the hundreds lining either side of the path, all still staring at him. None had moved yet save Yeladrian, but that didn't mean they wouldn't.

"*You have no need to fear them,*" she told him.

"You sure about that?" he asked, his gaze traveling over the figures and forms. Figures and forms he knew, figures and forms who had been cut down by his axe at one time or another. Figures who had no love for him, of that much he was sure.

"*They are your memories,*" she said, "*your ghosts. They have no more power over you than you allow them, can do nothing more than you let them to do.*"

"You're saying I allowed him to stab me?" he asked, glancing back at Yeladrian.

She followed his gaze to the figure still frozen in the air, his eyes roaming wildly in their sockets. "*He is different,*" she told him. "*You brought these others here, and so you are their guide, their master. He was here already, and so is beyond your control.*"

"I don't understand," he said.

"*Truth does not require understanding to exist. It exists beyond the ken of Fey and mortal.*"

He nodded. "Listen, Layna, I...I just want to say, about...about all of it, I'm sorry."

"*I know,*" she said, and Cutter didn't think he imagined the sadness he heard in her tone. "*Now, you must come. The present beckons.*"

He loved her.

Over the years, Cutter hadn't been sure of that, had begun to doubt. He had thought that what he had felt could only have been lust or, perhaps, some symptom of his cruelty that he might covet his brother's chosen. That he, being ugly, might have seen the beauty of the two of them and wanted, *needed* to ruin it.

Now, though, he realized that that wasn't true. Or, at least, that wasn't all of it.

He loved her.

But then what difference did that make? What difference *had* it made? Only the near-ruin of an entire kingdom, a betrayal of his brother. But then was that any real surprise? After all, a hog might love some painted masterpiece, but should it come into its possession, it would do the only thing it could do. Ruin it, trample it underfoot, for the hog knew nothing else. And yet, the hog, being a crude beast, still dreamed of something better as all living creatures did. It did not deserve it. Would almost certainly never have it...

But still it dreamed.

"I have tried," he told her. "I have tried to make up for...for all of it. I have tried to look after him...our son."

"*I know,*" she said. "*But it is not finished yet. Come—you must return to the present.*" She glanced back at Yeladrian. "*Some ghosts are more powerful than others. He will not be held for much longer.*"

"I've beaten him before."

"*Not like this,*" she said. "*The present holds no danger for the past, while the past is ever a threat to the present. You should know this better than most. Now, will you follow me?*"

Cutter glanced around at the figures surrounding the path, watching him. He looked, too, at Yeladrian. "Yes."

"*Good,*" she said. "*Come. It is not far.*"

He thought that she would turn and begin down the path, but she did not. Instead, she stepped off the path, into the crowd of feylings and men, all of whom parted around her like a curtain, creating an aisle through which she walked.

Cutter followed her, his gaze traveling from one side to the other where those memories, those ghosts regarded him. They did not move, did not speak, yet he could see the hate in their eyes, and as he walked he felt his shoulders tense, expecting that they would charge forward at any moment and attack.

None did, though, and soon she stopped. Cutter walked up to stand beside her, frowning. Another rift stood a few feet ahead of them, its geometric patterns shifting and changing in seemingly endless combinations.

"Why do I get the feeling you're going to tell me something I don't like?" he said.

She turned to him, catching him in her gaze, and for a moment he found it difficult to breathe. *"You must step into the gateway. It is the way back."*

"Didn't work out so well the last time I went through one of those things," he observed.

"Did it not?" she asked, and he didn't think he imagined the slightest twinkle in her eye.

He watched her, a confusing storm of emotions inside him. His brother's betrothed. The only woman he had ever loved. "How can you speak?" he asked.

"I do not understand."

"You said that the others," he went on, waving his hand at the gathered multitudes surrounding them, "that they couldn't speak because they were my ghosts. Because they had no power except what I gave them. So if you're my ghost, why can you speak?"

She studied him then, her gaze so deep that it seemed she could see right into him, could see further past a life of pain and hurt and hate then he could see himself. *"Because I am not yours,"* she told him in a sad voice. *"I never was. Now go, while there is still time."* Suddenly, she turned to regard the path from which they'd come, a panicked expression on her face. *"You must go,"* she said. *"The barrier is broken, the past comes again. He comes. For you."*

Cutter followed her gaze and saw Yeladrian's ghost sprinting toward them, moving so quickly his feet didn't seem to touch the ground. "I've never been keen on running from a fight," he said.

"And what of death? Will you run from that? Your people need you."

Cutter turned to her then. A thousand things he wanted to say, but there was no time. There never had been. He stepped toward the rift.

"Goodbye, Bernard."

He turned back, watching her, aware of Yeladrian rushing toward him out of the corner of his eye. "Goodbye, Layna," he said, then he stepped into the rift. As he did, he heard her voice following him.

"Take care of our son."

THE TRIP through the rift was disorienting, a confusing shifting of colors and patterns that made him feel as if he were being assaulted. Then, suddenly he was stepping onto solid ground. Even as he did so, he heard a roar from a familiar voice.

He spun to look in the direction from which the shout had come and saw, in a moment, that he was in the field once more, less than two dozen feet from the path. And on that path, he saw Feledias and the feyling, Door. The two were not walking as they had but were instead standing back-to-back, fending off what appeared to be nearly a dozen of the wolf-like creatures Door had called the Unsated in a desperate defense.

Cutter didn't hesitate. His axe was in his hands, and as he had for his entire life, he ran to the fight. Several of the creatures were in between him and his two companions. As Cutter drew closer, one of the Unsated spun from its attack on his brother to face Cutter, racing toward him and covering the few intervening feet between them in an instant.

Which was fine, for in that instant Cutter was not idle. He brought his axe down in a two-handed blow so that even as the creature leapt through the air at him, the axe's blade caught it on the top of the head, driving it into the ground with enough force to send dust billowing out in a small cloud.

A cloud through which Cutter walked, his axe flashing to the left and right, cutting down another creature, then another. By the time he reached Feledias, his brother was on his back, his swords lying near him on the ground. Not that he was in any danger of retrieving them any time soon. An Unsated was crouched atop him, snarling and biting as its claws raked at him. Cutter's brother had hold of its front legs and was doing his best to keep it at bay.

Their struggling was fierce, and Cutter did not dare use his axe so close to his brother. Instead, he tossed it to the ground, grabbing the creature with both hands and, with a growl of effort, lifted it off his brother. The creature thrashed wildly, not caring who it caused pain to or how it caused it, just so long as it did. Cutter grunted, pivoting and hurling it away.

The Unsated twisted in the air, landing on its feet the way a cat might and launching itself back at him with hardly a pause. There was no time to go for his axe, so Cutter didn't try. Instead, he braced, bending his knees slightly and bringing his hands up in front of him. The creature hurtled through the air at him, and Cutter caught it. Its claws raked at him, but he waited until the creature opened its mouth to lunge forward and try to sink its fangs into him. Then he let go of his hold on the creature's forelegs and grabbed the top of its mouth and the bottom of its jaw in either hand. Before the creature could respond or do anything, including take advantage of the fact that its claws were now free, Cutter roared and pulled the creature's jaw apart. Muscle snapped and bone broke as he tore the top of the creature's jaw and face off, throwing it to the ground in disgust.

He looked around, ensuring himself that the Unsated he'd killed had been the last, then Cutter turned, scared of what sort of shape he might find Feledias in, for he had not been able to see much of his brother past the beast's writhing form.

Feledias lay on the ground staring up at him with something like shock. "Bernard?" he breathed.

Cutter offered his hand, and his brother took it. He pulled him to his feet. "Okay?" Cutter asked.

His brother continued to stare at him in shock for a second then, abruptly pulled him into an embrace. "Stones and starlight, but it's good to see you," Feledias said.

Despite his exhaustion, despite all the pains clamoring for attention, Cutter found himself smiling. "You too, Fel."

His brother leaned back, looking at him. "I saw you go through that damned portal, and I thought...I thought you were dead."

"Come on," Cutter said, giving him a small smile. "It'll take more than some twisted magic of the darkest part of the Fey realm to kill me."

Feledias stared at him for a second then grunted what might have been a laugh. "Bastard," he said.

"What about you?" Cutter said. He glanced around them at the dozen dead bodies littering the ground. "Seems you haven't lost your talent for making friends while I was gone."

"Sure," Feledias said, nodding his head at the nearest. "That one there is Spot. Spot likes long walks, playing in the bath and ripping people's throats out."

"Charming," Cutter said.

"You have the touch of the deep past on you."

Cutter and Feledias turned to regard Door. The feyling bore dozens of scratches and cuts, all of which leaked blood of a strange blue-green color. But what drew Cutter's attention immediately was that one of the feyling's hands was gone, a bloody stump in its place. The creature had seen better days. They all had, of course, but as bad as his and his brother's wounds were, their escort was far worse. "Door," Cutter said. "Are you alright?"

"We will make it to the gate," the creature told him. *"It is not far."*

Cutter frowned. "That's not what I meant. Your hand, we have to see to it."

"See to it?" Feledias said, sounding sick. "I don't see it at all."

The feyling looked over his shoulder, beyond him, then regarded him with its large, alien eyes. *"There is no time. The Unsated come."*

Cutter and Feledias turned, and his brother let out a hiss of fear. Not that Cutter could blame him for a few hundred feet away he could see dozens, perhaps hundreds of the wolf-like creatures all charging toward them.

"Come," Door said. *"We go."*

And with that, the feyling was moving again in his loping walk with the stub of his missing hand tucked against his chest, his free hand dancing in those strange, intricate patterns that it had before.

Cutter and his brother had to move at a fast jog to keep up with the feyling, which was fine with Cutter, for he knew that while they had a good lead on the creatures following them, they could not hope to keep it. That was true even had they not all been wounded and exhausted.

"So...Bernard," Feledias panted as they ran after the loping Door, "are you going to tell me...what happened?"

"When I fell through the rift, do...you mean?" Cutter panted back.

"No, when you...ah, shit on it, of course that's what I mean," Feledias said back, apparently too winded even to engage in his usual sarcasm.

Cutter considered that, considered what he might say to his brother. He saw no reason to tell him that he'd seen Layna—some wounds never really healed, only scabbed over, scabs that might be torn free easily enough to expose a wound that was just as bad as the day it had been received. Cutter thought probably his brother's love and loss of Layna was one such scar, and with everything around them wanting to cause them pain he saw no reason to add to it.

"I saw...Yeladrian," he said.

"The Fey King?" Feledias asked, clearly surprised. Cutter understood— he'd been pretty surprised too.

"That's right."

"Huh," Feledias said. "Not everyday a man gets to talk to someone he killed nearly two decades ago."

"He didn't do much talking," Cutter said, remembering all too well the shocking speed of the feyling.

Feledias looked as though he would ask more—given what Cutter had told him, who wouldn't?—but before he got a chance, Door spoke.

"*We have come to the gate.*"

Cutter had been so focused on marking the progress of those Unsated chasing them that he'd paid little attention to where they were going. So, as he stepped forward to stand beside the feyling he was surprised to see that while he'd been expecting a rift similar to the one he'd fallen into, this one was different. Not a shifting mass of multi-colored geometric patterns, this, but a gate in truth, one that still bore the rainbow of hues the rifts had but which did not shift or move but held steady.

"*This will lead you back to the present,*" the feyling said, turning its large circular face and massive eyes on Cutter. "*But take care, for while a creature might leave its present and cling to its past, leaving the past to return to the present is no easy task and is fraught with danger. Do not stop, for if you do, the past will have you. Keep hold of each other,"* the feyling said. *"Keep hold of yourself, and you will see your present again."*

"You mean 'we,'" Cutter said, frowning. "You're coming with us, aren't you?"

The feyling glanced back at the trail behind them, where the Unsated were charging forward. They would be on them in a minute, two at the most. *"We remain here,"* it said. *"To hold them while you make the journey. But you must hurry. The Unsated have your scent, and they will come. It will take them time, but eventually they will find you again."*

"Bullshit," Feledias said. "You're coming with us. Or do you want to die, is that it?"

"There is no death," Door told him, *"only a returning. Still, we do not wish to cease. We wish to live."*

Feledias let out a snort that sounded very close to a sob. "You got a funny way of showing it."

"To stand against wrong," Door said, turning to regard Cutter, *"to pick one's moment, to act according to one's purpose, is this not life? Is this not living?"*

Cutter considered that, and as he did he heard Layna's last words to him ringing in his ears. *Protect our son.* It was his purpose, had been his only purpose for a long time. He nodded. "Let him be, Fel," he said.

"Bernard, you can't be serious," Feledias said. "They'll kill him," he went on, gesturing angrily at the approaching creatures. "And that's before you consider that we have no idea where we're *going.*"

"All know the way out of the past," Door said, *"only not all possess the strength or will to make the journey."*

"Whatever *that* means," Feledias said.

"It is time," the feyling said. *"We will hold them for as long as we can, but do not tarry and do not stop, for the Unsated will do neither."*

Cutter nodded. "You heard him, Fel. Let's go."

Feledias watched him for a moment then turned and regarded the creatures rushing toward them. Close now. Too close? Cutter wondered.

Then, finally, his brother nodded. "Okay...it...okay. You lead, brother—I'll follow."

Cutter nodded, glancing back at Door. "You're sure?"

"*We are ready,*" the creature said, inclining its head.

"Good luck," he told the creature, then, knowing that time was not on their side—as it so rarely was—he moved toward the gate.

He looked back to make sure that Feledias was following and saw that his brother had stopped in front of the feyling. "Thank you, Door," he said in a quiet, tortured voice. "For everything."

"*You are very welcome, Feledias Stormborn. Live well.*"

"Fel," Cutter said, glancing at the creatures barreling toward them. "We have to go."

His brother nodded and moved up to step beside him. As he did, he saw that there was a tear winding its way down his dirt-stained cheek. "Same time?" he asked.

Cutter nodded.

"Once more into the fray, then?" Feledias asked, giving him a small, pained smile.

"See you on the other side," Cutter said. Then, with that, they stepped through the gateway traveling, as all living men did, into the unknown.

CHAPTER NINETEEN

EMILLE SIGHED, sitting back and rubbing her eyes. It would be dark soon—in truth, it might well have been dark already. Ensconced in the small, windowless room as she was, there was no way to know for sure, and so no way to be sure just how long she'd been here.

Hours, she thought. Maybe days. She would not have even been surprised had someone told her a lifetime. It certainly felt like one. A lifetime spent poring over this ledger or that requisition order. Yet still she had not even scratched the surface of what there was to look at since she'd had the fool idea to come to the Hall of Records.

It had seemed an innocent enough thought—sift through the Guild's recent record of events with an eye toward trying to understand what the tribunes had been up to, to find some leverage Maeve might use against them, if she needed to. And, considering the three tribunes as Emille knew them, it wasn't really a question of *if* she would need to, only *when*.

It had seemed a good enough idea—perhaps even a clever one. It did not seem so now. She had thought to herself that there could be nowhere better to find a record of the tribunes and their activities than the Hall of *Records*. And she'd been right...at least as far as it went. In the time since she'd come to the hall, she'd already stumbled on dozens of orders the tribunes had signed off on. Their activities were recorded, there was no doubt of that. The problem, though, was that it seemed as if whoever was in charge of the records—a small army, she had to think—recorded not just the tribunes' activities, but *everything*.

Everything from orders for food from the kitchen, supplies for the healer's academy above, to assassination orders and confirmed kills. All of it stored in the same place with the same meticulous record-keeping, none of it given anymore importance than the other.

She felt like a miner looking for diamonds deep in the earth. Maybe they were there—likely there were. The problem was that those diamonds were buried underneath a *lot* of dirt.

There was a knock on the door to the small office in which she sat and Emille looked up from the most recent paper she'd been glancing at. "Come in," she said, aware of the eagerness in her voice, relief at even the chance of a brief respite from the endless slog through this report or that account.

A woman opened the door, stepping inside. She looked like the world's grandmotherliest grandmother. But then in a guild of contract murderers, few things were as they seemed. Still, she had been nice enough so far, aiding in Emille's request. But then that was the thing about people and beasts with teeth. They were nice—until they weren't.

"I have some more papers for you, Sister Emille," the woman said, carrying a stack of papers in that was large enough and no doubt heavy enough that it might have been used as a weapon to the table where she set it down.

"Thanks," Emille said, trying not to sound like she wanted to stab the woman. After all, the woman was only doing what she'd asked.

"Forgive me, Sister," the old woman said, "but I might be better able to aid you in your search if you told me what it was you were looking for."

"I wish I knew, Sister Pauline," Emille said, eyeing the latest stack of papers regretfully. "I truly do."

"Very well," the woman said, bowing her head. "I'll go and see if there is anything else."

Fire and salt, don't let there be anything else, Emille thought, but she gave the woman the best weary smile of which she was capable. "Thank you," she said.

And then she was back at it, forcing her blurry eyes and equally blurry mind to pay attention, lest she miss what it was she'd come to find and all her suffering be for naught.

She wasn't sure how much time had passed when there was another knock on the door. "Come in," she said. *Please, no more,* she thought. *Anymore, and I'll drown.* But while it was Sister Pauline who stepped through the door, Emille saw, to her great relief, that the woman wasn't holding any papers. "Can I help you, Sister Pauline?" she asked.

"Forgive my interruption, Sister Emille, but Tribune Silrika's valet came by. The tribune has requested your presence in her chambers."

Emille blinked at that. She could count on one hand the number of times she'd been summoned to the private quarters of a tribune—mostly because the number was zero. She glanced down at the stacks of papers in front of her. Somehow, they must have already discovered, or at least become suspicious, that she was looking into something they didn't want her to. Which meant that she was on the right track. Some small consolation, at least. "*That was quick,*" she muttered.

"I'm sorry, Sister?" the old woman asked.

Emille shook her head. "Nothing, never mind. Very well, I will go to her now."

Anything, she thought, *even a visit to the tribunes, will be better than this.*

She was wrong about that, but she did not know, at least in that moment, just how wrong.

CHAPTER TWENTY

NADIA'S MAN took Valden to the same butcher's shop where he'd met her before. This time, though, the butcher said nothing as he opened the door, only moved to the side to allow them entry, giving Valden a nod as he passed. Aubrey led Valden to the back room which held the trap-door then stood still, regarding him. Valden glanced at the closed door then at the man.

"If it's a formal letter of invitation you're waitin' on, you're goin' to be disappointed," the man told him.

"You want me to go ahead and go down?"

"You'll find it more difficult to talk to the boss if you don't, but I don't give much of a shit either way. I was told to bring you here, and you look pretty damn here to me."

Valden glanced at the other man in the room who sat at a table nearby, looking relaxed, but he thought that would change in a hurry if anyone came in without permission. "Alright," Valden said.

He started down the ladder. He had no sooner stepped onto the first rung than he smelled the blood. A cloying, sweet-sour scent that filled his nostrils and mouth. He reached the bottom of the ladder in another moment. As he did, he noted a figure moving toward him out of the flickering orange light provided by a lantern hung in the center of the room.

"Easy, Frederic," a voice that he recognized as Nadia's said.

Valden glanced around the small cellar. Nadia sat at her desk as she had before, a desk with sheaves of paper on it—apparently running an underground criminal enterprise was not without its paperwork. But other than that, everything else shared little similarity to the last time he'd been here.

There were the two men for starters—Frederic and another Valden didn't know. Both of them big, powerful men that looked like they could beat a mountain into submission if they took it in mind to do so. And their scraped, bloody knuckles were proof that they had indeed taken it in mind to beat on something, only that something hadn't been a mountain.

Instead, it had been the last figure in the room, one who sat slumped in a chair at the room's center, his arms bound behind him with a rope, tightly enough that Valden could see that they'd scraped his wrists bloody. And that was far from the only blood staining the man's skin and clothes.

"Ah, Valden," Nadia said. "And here I was beginning to think you wouldn't show—at least not in time. Come on then—don't just stand there like a lump. I'd offer you a chair, but I'm afraid there's only one spare, and it's taken at the moment, isn't that right?" she said, turning to regard the bound man.

Valden glanced at the man closest to him then moved forward, walking along the edge of the cellar and around toward the desk so that he was at the front of the man in the chair. He knew what to expect—after all, criminals were not known for their mercy regarding the innocent, even less those who had wronged them.

Still, even expecting it, he found himself wincing at the bloody mess of the bound man's face. One eye was swollen shut, his lip had been split open, and his nose was a red, mashed ruin on his face, the entirety of which was covered in blood. He had been beaten, badly, so that he barely looked like a man at all anymore. "Catham?" he asked, his voice little more than a whisper—he could not manage much more just then.

"In the flesh," Nadia said, and if Valden had ever found himself

277

tempted to like the no-nonsense older woman then her casual shrug was enough to kill that temptation. "Or, at least, most of it."

The figure—who might have been Catham or anyone, so beaten and unrecognizable were his features—raised his head with what appeared to be a monumental effort, blood and slobber dripping from his mouth as he did. *"Hey...Vicious. Long...time."*

The voice was gravelly and pained, but it, at least, was recognizable to Valden. It was Catham, then. Of that there was no doubt.

"Suppose that's enough of a break," Nadia said. She nodded at the man nearest Catham. The big man stepped forward, his expression bland, almost bored as he reached out and punched Catham in the face.

The bound man cried out in pain as his head rocked backward by the blow, blood and sweat flying as he did. Valden knew that Catham had tried to have him and Chall killed, had tried, on a separate occasion, to kill Chall and Ned—and come damned close. He knew that the bound man had colluded with Robert Palden, had caused and *planned* to cause unknown damage to the kingdom. Yet staring at him bound there, bloody and broken, he could not help but feel pity.

"Fire and salt, Catham, just answer her questions," Valden said.

The man raised his head to regard Valden with the one eye that wasn't swollen shut, letting out what sounded like a mixture of a whimper and a laugh. *"What...questions?"* he managed.

Valden frowned, turning to look back at Nadia, the old woman sitting at her desk as calmly as could be. "You haven't asked him anything yet?"

"Haven't we?" Nadia asked, glancing at the two men, a mock expression of innocence on her face. "I'm sure I *meant* to...oh well," she finished, shrugging. "I'm old. I suppose I lose track of what I'm doing sometimes."

"So you're, what, beating him just for the fun of it?" Valden said.

"Oh, and what fun it's been," Nadia said, baring her teeth in what might have loosely be considered a smile. "You may look at me like that if you wish, Vicious," she said. "You might have left this world behind, gone and pretended to be something else, something better, so perhaps you have forgotten. Let me, then, remind you. You walk among wolves, here. Here, there are no rules except those you carve out in flesh and blood, no 'right' except that which the one still standing when the killing is done decides. Here, you will find no sheep." She paused, glancing at Catham and smiled again. "At least no living ones. Go on, then—you have questions? Ask them. Me and the boys, we can wait...for a little while."

Valden was repulsed by the woman's casualness, by how easy it was for her to hurt another person, even one guilty of what Catham was. Valden had killed before, of course, but only when he'd had no choice, the same as a man putting down a mad dog. Not because he enjoyed it, but because it had to be done, because such a creature had no business in a world with innocent children and defenseless babes. This, though, this was different. He wanted to walk out, to express to Nadia, in no uncertain terms, the level of his disgust.

He wanted it badly. The problem, of course, was that while he wanted to express his repulsion, what he *needed* were answers. He moved to stand in front of Catham, aware of the eyes of the other three tracking him as he did.

"*Vicious...*" Catham said, pausing to hack and cough out a goblet of blood onto the already stained floor in front of him. "*How you...been?*"

"Catham, I need to know where he is."

"*Who?*" the man asked, but by the twinkle in his one good eye Valden was confident he knew well who he meant.

"I need to find him, Catham," he went on, "to learn what he's up to. Why has he re-established the Wolves? What is Robert up to? What does he want?"

Catham stared at him for several seconds then slowly shook his head. "*You...still...don't get it. You talk of him like a...man, but he is no...man. Maybe he was...once...but not anymore. Anyway...you don't find...the bogeyman, Vicious. When it's...time...he finds you.*"

"What does he want?"

The man bared his bloody teeth in a macabre grin. "*He wants...what he always wanted. To destroy those he believes are...evil. People like...that cold-blooded bitch there,*" he said, jerking his head at Nadia. "*But not...just her.*"

Valden followed Catham's gaze to glance at Nadia who shrugged one shoulder as if to say that she didn't plan on arguing with the label, then he turned back to the bound man. "Who else? Who is he after?"

Catham let out a sound somewhere between a grunt of pain and a snort of laughter. *"Don't...you get it, Vicious? He's...after...everyone. Well... everyone...human, at least."*

Valden frowned. "What does that mean?" he said.

"It means...what it means. You tell me, Vicious. If you meant to...rid the world...of all evil, and there was no...morality stopping you...what would you do?"

Valden suddenly found it difficult to breathe, let alone speak. If what Catham was saying was true, then Robert Palden wasn't reforming the Crimson Wolves to take on the criminals of New Daltenia but to take on— to *destroy*—New Daltenia itself. A goal that sounded ridiculous, impossible, that might have been laughed away. After all, how could one man hope to bring down a kingdom? Impossible. But then, if what Nadia had told Valden was true, Robert Palden, whatever he had once been, was not just a man any longer. And then, of course, he was not alone. Others were working with him—just how many Valden had no idea. *Too many,* he thought. *You know that much.*

"Never have been...a man of faith...Vicious, not like you," Catham said, interrupting his dark thoughts. *"But...I'll tell you this for free...that bastard says he will bring down the kingdom and...and you know what?"* Catham met Valden's gaze with his one good eye. *"I...believe him."*

That sent a shiver of cold dread through Valden. Just the barbed jabs of someone who knew he was going to die, or was Catham telling the truth, at least the truth as he saw it? There was no way to know for sure, so Valden set it aside. Time enough to think on it later. For now, he needed to focus on the problem before him. "What is he?" Valden asked. "Nadia said that when he attacked Flo's he was struck with a sword and arrows and wasn't hurt. How is that possible?"

Catham grinned a bloody grin, glancing over Valden's shoulder at Nadia. *"Heard...about that. Wish I'd have...been there...to see it. To see you... run."*

Nadia said nothing, only watched him with her cold, reptilian gaze, but while she might not have shown any reaction, Valden knew enough of her to know that she would exact a price for that comment soon enough. But then, Catham was no fool—whatever else he was, he was not that—and so the man was no doubt aware that he was not leaving this room alive, so what did he have to lose? "But how did he do it?" he pressed.

Catham turned his attention back to him, his one good eye regarding him. *"You ask...how it's possible. It isn't...not if he's...just a man. But he's...not."*

"What does that mean, that he's not just a man?" Valden asked. "What else could he b—" He cut off then, his eyes going wide as realization struck. He should have gotten there sooner, he supposed, but with everything that had been going on of late it had been all he could do to focus on the many problems at hand. How could a man who, according to Ned had been a quiet, shy clerk who had never picked up a blade, let alone wielded one in anger, gone from that to a man who took on a room full of hardened criminals and sent them either running or to the grave?

He couldn't, that was all. At least not without help. "The Fey," Valden said, staring at Catham. "He's working with the Fey."

It wasn't a question, not really, but Catham answered it anyway. *"Those bastards drive a hard bargain, I don't mind tellin' you that,"* Catham said. *"But it was one...he was happy to make."*

"Traitors," Valden said, finding himself angry now. "Both of you."

"Sure...today," Catham said, shifting his shoulder in what might have been a minute shrug. *"Tomorrow...something else."*

"Tomorrow, you'll be a dead man," Valden said, finding that he had considerably less pity for the man now, any man who would side with the Fey against his own people. "I don't know what your plans are," he told the bound man, "what *his* plans are, but I will stop them. *We* will stop them."

Another bloody grin, and this time something dark and loathsome, the *real* Catham, shifted in the other man's good eye. *"You don't get it...do you? It's done already. All this—"* he moved his head as if to indicate the room— *"all* any *of it is, is the death throes of a corpse too stupid to know it's dead. But it will...soon."*

"What are you talking about?" Valden said. "Taking on a brothel is a long way from taking on a kingdom. I doubt he'll find it so easy."

281

"*Easier,*" the other man said, grinning.

"Lies," Valden said. "The idle threats of a man who knows he's dying."

Catham did the most worrying thing he could have done just then—he laughed. A grating, pained sound but one that was genuine for all that. "*We're all...dying, Vicious,*" he said. "*And while I might beat...you and the others to the grave...it won't be...by much. Your king...he will die. And your kingdom will fall.*"

"Hard job to take on while you're here, bleeding out with your hands tied behind you."

"*It would be...if I were the one intending to do it. I die here—we both know that.*"

"If not you then who?"

"*Oh, Vicious. You still...think that you have time...that it can be fixed...but there is no fixing it, not now...and no time to do it even if you could. You want an answer...how about a question instead. Tell me, Vicious...have you and your pet king taken in any strays lately?*"

Valden frowned. "Strays? What does that mean?"

"*Didn't...remember you being...such a fool. Haven't you wondered, Vicious... how an old woman who can...barely walk, made it away from...me and my men?*"

And there it was, the answer to why a sinking feeling had been growing in Valden's stomach as they spoke, that he felt had been growing in his stomach for days now. He was on his feet in a moment. "I have to go," he told Nadia. "Now."

"*Run as fast as you like, Vicious,*" Catham said. "*A man can't run from his fate...and neither...can...a king.*"

The words followed him up the ladder as he took the rungs two at a time, barely slowing even as he struck the trapdoor and threw it open, leaping into the back room of the butcher's shop. So abrupt was his entrance that the man set to guard stepped in front of him.

"Get out of my way," Valden said.

The man frowned, and Valden was just prepared to make him when Nadia's voice came from below.

"*Let him go.*"

The man moved, and so did Valden, rushing out of the butcher's shop and into the street. He wished that Ned had come now, for if he had there'd be a carriage he could take, or a horse he could leap onto and ride to the castle with all the haste he could muster. But Ned was gone, at the castle already, he expected. Valden had sent him, asking him to watch over Chall and Matt, and while he did not doubt the man would do just that, he could not possibly expect that the danger was coming from Lady Valencia.

They couldn't know the danger, not any of them, unless Valden made it there and warned them.

He was running then, sprinting through the city streets, streets which, with full dark no more than an hour away, were cloaked in shadow.

A man must always mind his surroundings. Valden knew that. He had learned it long ago, during his early criminal days, and that lesson had been reinforced during his time as a scout and archer for the army of the Known Lands.

For death, almost always, claimed those who did not see its approach until it was too late. He knew this, and yet, he was so stunned by the shock of what Catham had told him, his own terror for Matt, that he allowed himself to become distracted. Not for long, only for a few minutes, but then Death, when it came, never needed much of an opening.

Had he not been distracted, had his thoughts not been consumed with his fear, he might have noticed something, had some instinctual reaction that things were not right, that something was wrong. He'd had such instincts, such feelings before, as all men had, and listening to them had saved his life and that more than once. Instinct. It was the name men gave to the mind's understanding that something was off when they couldn't explain *how* it understood it.

But if his instincts spoke just then, the storm of worry in his head was too loud to hear them, so he was unaware that anything might be wrong, that any danger might lie ahead, until, like the hare noting, at the last moment, the movement in the tall grass, it was too late.

He was halfway down an alleyway, sprinting in the direction of the castle, when two figures stepped out of the alley's other end. Valden came up short, caught off-guard by their appearance. The two figures moved closer and, as they did, in the failing light he could see that he recognized one of them who walked to the side and slightly behind the other.

"Willy? What are you doing here?" he asked, but even as the question was out of his mouth he knew its answer. What did the unexpected appearance of a conman mean? Nothing good.

He had not met the other man before, but his slight frame and bookish appearance were enough for Valden to know who he must be even before he spoke.

"Hello," the man said. "It's Valden, isn't it? Otherwise known as Priest?"

"Just Valden."

"I see. A crisis of faith then, is it?" the man asked, sighing softly. "I understand—I have experienced something similar myself, some years ago." He shrugged. "But when one belief fails, sometimes a man must find another. As I did."

"And some might say that changing beliefs when it suits him means that a man didn't have beliefs to begin with, only whims at best and excuses at worst."

The man gave a small smile. "Willy said you were clever. Still, in this world of shadows, cleverness isn't enough. Neither, I'm afraid, is altruism."

"I'm not feeling particularly altruistic just now."

The man nodded, glancing around. "Where, I wonder, is your friend? The carriage driver? Neddard, isn't it?"

Valden felt a stab of fear for Ned at that. There were few things worse than meeting a devil in some shadow-laden back alley, but he supposed that discovering that the devil in question knew your friend's name was up there.

"I just realize I've failed to introduce myself," the man said. "Forgive me for that—it has been a trying few weeks. My name is Robert Palden."

"I know who you are," Valden said. "You have a lot to answer for."

"As all the living do," the man said. "I know something of you, Valden, something of your past. You are, by all accounts, a formidable warrior, a man others admire. You need not die here in some filthy back alley where the scum of society—scum like Willy here—will pick over your body like vultures."

"Hey now," Willy said, "that's not—"

"Join me," Robert Palden said as if Willy hadn't spoken, as if he didn't exist at all. "I could use you. Join me and change the world."

"Destroy it, you mean."

The man considered that then slowly nodded. "Yes. But sometimes, that is what is needed. Sometimes, a man must tear something down so he can build it back up, and a phoenix cannot rise until it has first fallen."

"And you fancy yourself the instrument of that falling, that rising?"

He shrugged. "Someone must be. The world is sick—anyone with eyes can see that much. And like a patient with some terrible terminal illness causing him anguish, must be put down. In such a situation, the healer would not be called cruel or mad. It would be considered a kindness. You know this, I think, don't you?" he asked. "After all, why else would a priest lose his faith except that he comes to understand the truth?"

"What truth is that?"

"Isn't it obvious?" Robert Palden asked. "That we are all crude beasts who can only destroy. It is not even our fault—it is simply within our nature. The world, like the patient, suffers, and so I mean, out of kindness, to do what the healer must– to end it. Or do you disagree?"

In fact, Valden didn't. If the world wasn't broken, he thought it was probably just about as bent as it could be. Bad things happened to good people while good things happened to bad people. There was no denying that. "So your answer to suffering is to destroy everything?"

"Not everything," the man said. "The world will still exist, of course. But without us contaminating it like some malicious virus, it will have a chance to heal, to regrow."

"You mean to kill everyone."

"Do you know of another way to put an end to all the suffering?"

"And what of joy? What of love? Of hope?"

"Lies we tell ourselves to make the unbearable bearable," he said. "People are not capable of loving others—they cannot even love themselves. Just look at Willy here. A grasping, pathetic excuse of a man, if man he might be called. A man who would do anything to anyone if he thought it would give him what he wanted. A man like that cannot love anyone else. He cannot even love himself. And, I'm sorry to say, Valden, but we are *all* like that."

"You're insane," Valden said. He'd thought as much, of course, from all that he'd seen, all that he'd heard. But thinking it and *knowing* it were very different things. And he wasn't just insane—he was dangerous. Dangerous not because he could, according to Nadia, absorb arrows and sword thrusts as if they were nothing. Dangerous because to Valden it seemed that the man's thoughts, his way of viewing the world, were what waited at the end of the path Valden himself had started down.

"Insanity is looking for goodness in a world that has none," the man said.

"Look," Willy said, "I don't much care to be ridiculed. You wanted my help finding Vicious, well, here he is. Now, if you'll give me what was promised, I'll be on my way, leave you gents to it."

"Oh yes," the leader of the Crimson Wolves said, still staring at Valden. "I did make you a promise, didn't I, Willy? Very well. Then come and receive your reward."

He reached out with one hand, grabbing the back of Willy's hair in a casual, almost bored sort of way.

"Hey," Willy said, "what the fuck, man?" He tried to pull away, but the other man had a firm grip of his hair and seemed able to hold onto him with ease. In no hurry, taking his time, he pulled Willy toward him. The conman hissed, trying and still failing to break free of his grip as he pulled his head down in front of him.

"Let go of me, damn you," Willy said, "this wasn't the deal."

"Oh, but you're wrong, Willy," Robert Palden said, still looking at Valden, "this was always the deal." With one hand still on the back of the conman's head, he grabbed underneath Willy's chin with the other. Willy cursed, reaching into his belt and retrieving a knife, burying it in the other man's chest. But if it bothered him at all, the leader of the Crimson Wolves didn't show it. With a casual ease, he twisted Willy's neck.

There was a *tearing, ripping,* then a *snap* as the conman's neck broke.

Still, the other man continued to twist his grip, a bored expression on his face as blood spurted over his hands and chest and face. Then, with Willy's head turned all the way around to his back, Robert Palden let the body drop to the ground.

"As I was saying," he said, not even out of breath and seemingly not disturbed in the slightest by what had just occurred, what he had just done, "it is a fool who looks for hope in a hopeless world. Surely you must see that."

Valden fought back his rising gorge, fought back fear at the man's casual brutality. He found himself thinking of Brother Elmer, the old priest he'd met when visiting the church. "There is still goodness in the world, and where there is life, there is hope," he said.

"Hope," the man said, sniffing. "Hope of what? A brief respite from pain? Don't you see, Valden? That is what I offer. Only the respite I offer is not brief but permanent. Not a respite at all, really, but an ending. One that is long overdue. So, will you join me? Will you help me to put this poor patient that is our people, our kingdom, out of its misery?"

It wasn't Brother Elmer that Valden thought of in that moment. Instead, it was Prince Bernard. Prince Bernard who people believed loved to fight, loved violence. Prince Bernard who even believed it himself. The Crimson Prince, they called him, and the man did not argue it. But even if he had been that—and Valden wasn't sure—he was not that man any longer. Valden had spent enough time with him of late to know it. The prince did not spoil for a fight as many thought, but neither did he run from one. Valden meant to do the same and like his prince, he decided to waste no more words than were strictly necessary. "No."

The man standing in the alleyway over the corpse sighed, wiping his bloody hands on his tunic. "I cannot change your mind?"

Valden didn't answer, at least not with words. Instead, he let his actions answer for him, drawing his sword.

"A shame," Robert Palden said. He didn't draw a blade, but then Valden supposed when you could twist a man's head around backward as if it were nothing and take on an entire brothel full of criminals you didn't need to bother yourself much with weapons. "I hate to kill you,

287

but I can't let you and your friends get in the way of my plans any longer."

"I hate to die, but while I may not be a priest any longer, even I know that a man who doesn't stand in the way of evil is no man at all." He raised his sword.

The other man glanced at the blade pointed in his direction, then gave a small smile, his eyes slowly going to his chest where Willy's knife was still lodged. He withdrew the blade, looking at the length of metal curiously. "Funny," he said. "I used to be so afraid of weapons like this, of the damage they could do. Seeing a man carrying one was enough for me to break a sweat. And now...they seem, to me, such crude instruments."

"Let's see if we can't change your opinion on that," Valden said.

Valden had done his fair share of close-in work when he'd been younger, but since joining the prince and the others, he'd grown to prefer the role of scout and archer, a role for which he had shown a fair share of natural aptitude. Beyond that, he had become a priest, embraced the idea of helping instead of hurting. Before recent events, it had been some time since he'd raised a blade in his own defense, but he raised it now as he watched the man—who stood more than six inches shorter than his own six-feet—walk calmly closer. Not that he thought it would do much good.

Barring a miracle, he was going to die. He was going to die and there would be no one to warn Matt and Chall of what was happening, no one to tell them that the danger they feared wasn't coming—it was there already, in the castle with them.

If only I had not stopped believing in miracles, he thought as he watched the man approach.

"Well?" the man asked, stopping a few feet away from him. "Are you just going to stand there? I only ask because I have other appointments to keep—with Nadia, for instance."

"You mean to get Catham," Valden said. "You won't save him—it's too late."

The man grinned widely. "That's alright. He has served his purpose. As I've already told you, I am not here to save anyone. Now, best we get on with it. Things to do and all that."

He moved forward then, swinging a punch at Valden. It was a careless, casual blow with seemingly no force behind it, but Valden took a step back anyway. An easy blow. So Valden was surprised, then, when the man's fist struck the brick wall of the alley and brick shattered as he punched a hole into it, shards exploding out in a hail.

If the blow hurt at all, the man didn't show it, only glancing at his fist, then at the wall and, finally, at Valden himself, letting a confident, easy grin spread on his face. "I was never a strong man," he admitted in a confidential sort of voice. "I always fancied myself an intellectual, a *thinker*. As most weak men will. As if an absence of something—strength, in this case —meant that that lack must be made up for somewhere else. I used to loathe those brave warriors with their wide shoulders and incredible strength." He shook his head. "Now look at me. Like most men, it seems I have become what I hate. And you know what?" he asked. "It feels good."

"You are no warrior," Valden said. "You are a traitor who has sold his loyalty to the Fey, who has turned against his own people. You are cursed."

Robert Palden nodded slowly at that. "Funny," he said. "I don't *feel* cursed." He grinned. "I feel great."

Then he came forward again.

Valden knew that the man had been given some power, likely by the Fey, one that made him difficult, perhaps impossible to kill, one that made him incredibly strong. So he had been counting on his greater speed and experience to give him an advantage, but as the man came at him, swinging this way and that, his punches almost too fast to follow, Valden realized one inescapable fact. Whatever power gave the man his strength, it also gave him speed. Speed that meant that he moved in a near blur, and Valden was forced to leap away from his blows several times, narrowly avoiding being struck by a fist that, if the alley wall was any indication, would have punched a hole straight through him.

He could not look to his speed, then, and that left only his experience in battle. Experience that, just then, was telling him that unless one of the gods—who he was not sure existed at all, and if they did, if they had any interest in helping—chose to perform a miracle, he was in very bad trouble.

An idea that was reinforced as Valden's sword lashed out again and again but with no discernible effect. He struck the man several times. He *knew* that he did, for he felt the resistance, saw the blood. Yet no sooner had his blade created a wound than that wound healed in a fraction of a second, before he managed to bring his blade back for a follow-up attack.

The man growled, apparently frustrated that Valden was evading his blows, and moved forward to grab him. Valden responded by taking a leaping step back then pivoting and lunging forward, his blade piercing the man's chest, driving through it and into his heart.

Robert Palden froze, staring down at the blade, and Valden had a brief moment in which he thought that he had done it. But that hope was dashed a moment later as the other man looked up at him and smiled. The leader of the Crimson Wolves grabbed the blade in one hand, apparently unconcerned by the sharp metal biting into his flesh, and pulled it *through* him until Valden, pulled along by his grip on the sword, found his face less than a foot from the man's own. He tried to wrest the blade free, but he might as well have been a child struggling against a grown man for all the good it did.

He had the thought to abandon the blade altogether, but before he could the other man reached out and grabbed the front of his tunic. Valden tried to break free of his grip, but his opponent shifted, and the next thing he knew, Valden was hurling through the air. He struck the wall of the alley hard enough that he heard something—either the wall or him, he couldn't be sure—*crack.*

The air exploded out of his mouth along with some blood as Valden lay there on his stomach, gasping, feeling like he'd been struck by the fist of a god. A cracked rib, that was sure. Maybe more than that. It was difficult to separate the many pains and agonies clamoring for his attention just then.

"Before we finish things up here," Robert Palden said, drawing his attention as he walked calmly toward him, not out of breath or put out in the least by their exchange, looking the same as he had before save that his shirt was cut in several places with no matching wounds underneath. "Maybe you can help me. I've been looking for an old friend of mine I think you know—Neddard. I wonder if you might tell me where to find him."

Valden said nothing, an easy enough thing to do when all he could manage just then were some desperate, wheezing breaths as he watched the man, watched his death come.

"*Hyah!*"

The shout came from behind him, and it was accompanied by the sound of horse hooves on cobbles. Valden turned from his place on the ground, craning his neck and was shocked to see a carriage racing toward him from the opposite end of the alley.

He rolled to the side, narrowly managing to avoid the carriage as it careened past him, the horses galloping as fast as they could, the wagon itself shaking and rattling against the cobbles. He followed its path as the horses ran toward Robert Palden, who stood there with a perplexed look on his face, then ran *over* him, knocking him to his knees in time for the carriage itself to strike him and explode in a shower of wood and debris.

The two horses were somehow knocked free of their traces by the impact, and they continued their wild gallop off into the night, leaving the shattered wagon—and shattered man lying somewhere beneath it—behind them.

Valden stared at the wreckage of the carriage, wondering how he was still alive, wondering where it had come from. He was still wondering when a voice spoke from behind him.

"That was...significantly more dramatic than I had anticipated."

Valden turned, expecting to find Ned there—the only reasonable explanation for the carriage's appearance in the nick of time that he could think of being that the man had followed him against his wishes. But when he turned to regard the figure, it was not Ned who stood there.

"Brother...Elmer?" he wheezed.

"At your service," the old priest said, leaning on his crutches as he walked toward Valden, offering him a hand. Valden blinked at it for a few seconds, surprised to be alive and even more surprised to find the old priest standing before him. He took the hand, careful not to overbalance either of them as he rose.

"What...how did you get here?"

"How?" the priest asked, smiling. "Well, I walked most of the way.

Rode that carriage for a bit, though I will say it was in considerably better shape then."

"No, I mean...how...why did you..."

"Sometimes, the gods guide our steps," the priest said.

Valden blinked, trying to find something to say to that but before he could, the priest spoke on. "And *sometimes* we might overhear a certain head priest speaking with a certain ne'er-do-well regarding an ambush and decide to come and check it out for ourselves."

"Ah," Valden said. "And here I was thinking it was a miracle."

"What greater miracle is there in all the world," the old priest said, "than a man hearing what he needs to hear when he needs to hear it, or a man being right where he needs to be right when he needs to be there?"

Valden nodded at that. "Well...whatever the case...thank you. You saved my life."

"Not I," the priest said, watching him. "Or, at least, not alone. And the head priest?"

Valden glanced back down the alley. He couldn't see Willy just then, not for all the wreckage of the wagon, but then he didn't need to, for he remembered the horrific sight of his head turned round on his body easily enough. "Dead," Valden said.

The old priest nodded slowly. "I was afraid of that. I am sorry to hear it."

"I would not worry overly much," Valden said. "Willy was not a good man."

"And who among us is?"

There was a groan then, and they both turned to regard the pile of rubble the wagon had left as it shifted slightly. It seemed that being run over by horses and a wagon could be included on the list of things that would not kill Robert Palden. "Listen, Brother Elmer—"

"You need to go," the priest finished for him.

"I do. And you—"

"Need to go as well?" the old priest asked, giving him a small smile.

Valden nodded, glancing at the man's leg where half of it was missing beneath the knee. "Oh, I wouldn't worry," the priest said. "I can move fast enough when I need to. I'll be long gone before our friend here extricates himself from the remnants of the wagon. Go and do what you must. I will be fine."

"You're sure?"

"I'm sure."

Valden nodded. "Thanks. Again." He started down the alleyway, his arm cradled against his broken rib.

"It is not me you should thank but Raveza. Miracles are her purview, not mine."

"Let's hope she has one more left in her," Valden muttered, then he started away at a shuffling jog, and as he did, he did something else, something that he had not done for what felt like a lifetime.

He prayed.

CHAPTER TWENTY-ONE

I‍T WAS LATE. Matt knew that. The time when most people—at least those people who weren't cursed with dreams that felt more real than the waking world—would be sleeping. Or, at least, preparing to. He was surprised, then, to hear a knock on the door.

"Yes?" he called, clearing his throat.

"Forgive me for the interruption, Highness," Guardsman Vorrun called from outside his door, "but you have a visitor."

Matt blinked at that. Likely it was Healer Malden. The man came by often to check on him, recommending they try some new tincture, some new solution. Matt ignored him most of the time, unable to stomach the thought of getting his hopes up again only to find them dashed once more as whatever was happening to him continued to grow worse.

"*Tell Malden I'll speak with him tomorrow,*" Matt called back, knowing it was a lie even as he said it. Malden couldn't help him—he knew that now, had known it for some time. The healer couldn't help him—no one could.

"*Forgive me, Highness,*" Vorrun called, "*but it is not Healer Malden. Lady Valencia wishes to speak to you—she says it's urgent.*"

Matt grunted. Now that *was* a surprise. He hadn't spoken with the noblewoman since they'd met in the courtyard following Diane's death. He couldn't imagine what she could possibly need to tell him that would be urgent unless she had remembered something about the attack on her and the others, something that might help them find the Crimson Wolves. And even if she had nothing so important to share, still Matt thought he would be glad for the distraction. Better that than staring at his ceiling, waiting for sleep that likely wouldn't come.

"*Thank you, Vorrun,*" he said, rising from the bed. "*Please, let her in.*"

He'd only just stood when the door opened, and the guardsman bowed. "Yes, Majesty. I present Lady Valencia."

The old noblewoman walked in sheepishly. "Th-thank you, Majesty, for seeing me so late."

"Of course, my lady," Matt said. He nodded to Vorrun. "That will be all, Vorrun, thank you."

"Yes, Highness. We will be right outside, if you have need of us."

A moment later the door closed, leaving him and the noblewoman alone. For a second, the two of them just stood there awkwardly, then Matt made a move to the table where a silver decanter had sat, untouched, since a servant had brought it earlier in the day. "Sorry, Lady Valencia, but would you like some...wine, I think?"

The woman seemed to hesitate for a moment, looking surprisingly nervous to Matt, then she gave him a shaky smile. "O-of course, Majesty. Thank you."

She moved into the room as he poured. "Please, have a seat," he said, gesturing to one of the two chairs at the table. "Is everything alright?"

She sat, giving him another smile. "Not yet, Majesty," she said. "Not yet, but I think it will be soon. Actually...that's what I came to talk to you about."

THERE WAS A LOUD *THUMP*, then another, and Maeve's head jerked up. She looked around her, confused, and realized in a moment that she'd fallen asleep at her desk at the Assassins' Guild. Agnes's diary lay in front of her, still opened to the page she'd been reading when she'd fallen asleep. And no wonder, really, considering that in the entry in question Agnes had chosen to describe, in excruciating detail, her dislike for corn. Its texture and taste, apparently even the color gave her offense.

Another loud *thump* reminded her of what had woken her.

"*Lady Maeve, open the door.*"

Maeve frowned. She was used to being called "Lady" of course, but not here. Here, she was always "Guildmaster." She rose, moving out of her study and into the sitting room. "*Who is it?*" she called back.

"*It is Tribunes Bethesa and Piralta, Lady Maeve,*" the voice—whom Maeve now recognized as Piralta—called back.

She frowned. Still no "Guildmaster" anywhere in evidence. She wondered at what that might mean—nothing good, of that much she was confident. She was still wondering when Piralta shouted again.

"*Open the door, Lady Maeve,*" he called, "*or we will break it down.*"

Well, whatever small hope Maeve had been entertaining that maybe she'd read more into the man's lack of her title than was there vanished. She considered her options, looking around the room. The problem, of course, was that, by and large, she had none. There was no way out of her quarters save the door at which Piralta and Bethesa apparently stood. She patted her clothes, reassuring herself that her knives were well in place, then moved to the door. She took a moment, taking a slow, deep breath, and nearly jumped as there was another loud thumping knock.

"*Lady Mae—*" the man's voice cut off as Maeve swung the door open.

As she did, she saw that, indeed, Tribune Piralta as well as Tribune Bethesa stood in the hallway. And they were not alone. Maeve counted six others in the hall, men and women with grim expressions, not staring at her the way one might expect the member of a guild to stare at the master of that guild but instead the way one might expect a murderer to stare at the soon-to-be-murdered.

"What's going on here?" Maeve demanded, doing her best to keep her fear out of her voice.

"What's going on, Lady Maeve," Bethesa said, giving her a smile that was a sharp as a dagger, "is that you are to be detained."

"Detained?" Maeve asked. Whatever she'd been expecting, it was not that. "Detained for what?"

"Firstly," Tribune Bethesa said, "for suspicion that you were involved, directly, with Guildmaster Agnes's murder and that you carried that murder out so that you might take her position as head of the Guild."

"That's ridiculous," Maeve said, "I'd never—"

"Also, for the murder of Amber, the guildmaster's servant who, we believe, knew too much and so, to ensure her silence, you killed her as well. Which, of course, is just the beginning of your crimes."

"That's not—I didn't—"

"Already, we have captured and detained your co-conspirator," Tribune Bethesa said, her eyes dancing with something like evil glee. "Now, will you come peacefully?"

She almost sounded as if she hoped Maeve would not, and based on the amount of swords and knives she saw sheathed around the waists and backs of the six in the hallway it didn't take much to guess what would happen if Maeve resisted.

"I wonder how the Guild will react when they learn that you've wrongly imprisoned their guildmaster," she said.

Bethesa smiled again at that. "The Guild has been made aware of your treachery. You are to be detained until a trial may determine your guilt or innocence in the matters at hand."

Maeve didn't like the sound of that, not at all. "A trial. And who is to judge my guilt or innocence?"

"Why, Tribune Piralta and myself, of course," Tribune Bethesa said. "Presiding over such trials is, as you know, one of the primary functions of the tribunal. True, normally the guildmaster is seated at the head, but considering that it is you who is under investigation, I suppose I must fill that role."

Maeve snorted. "With much reluctance, no doubt. And where is the third of you, then? I'm surprised Silrika isn't here to gloat."

Piralta sneered. "As if you don't know. It is your *minion* who murdered her, after all."

"Murdered? What are you talking about?" Maeve asked, truly shocked. "What minion?"

"Oh, I would not worry overly much, Lady Maeve," Tribune Bethesa said. "You will be reunited soon enough." She motioned to the man at the front. "Bind her hands. You," she said to a second, "check her—Lady Maeve is quite famous for the knives she secrets about her person."

Maeve stood in shock as the men did as they were told, one stepping forward to pat her down and begin retrieving the knives she kept hidden. He was at it for a few minutes, Piralta's eyebrows climbing further and further up his forehead with each knife the man removed. Eventually it was done, and they bound Maeve's hands in front of her before they began leading her down the hallway.

Surrounded by assassins, an uncertain future ahead of her—or, perhaps, one that was all too certain, for the Assassin's Guild was not known for keeping prisoners and certainly not for long—Maeve found herself thinking of Chall.

Chall who had told her not to come, Chall who she had assured that she would be fine, that she had to go. Chall who, likelier than not, she would never see again.

Please, gods, major and minor both, look after him, she thought, glancing at the hard-faced men and women on either side of her. *I do not think I will be able to anymore.*

CHALL STARED AT HIS HAND. A shitty one and not the first—his coin purse, considerably lighter than it had been when he'd first arrived, was proof of that. As he tossed the cards away, folding, he wondered—also not for the first time—why he'd bothered coming to the guardsmen's barracks in the castle. He'd been invited to play cards with the guardsmen several times since coming back to New Daltenia after his nearly two-decade absence, but this was the first time he'd accepted it. He'd ignored that invitation up to now for several reasons. Partly because he used to play cards a lot— right around the time he'd been drinking a lot, womanizing a lot, too.

He knew that it wasn't so for everyone, but for him cards meant drink and smoke, and drink and smoke meant women, meant foolish nights and shameful mornings. He knew that, for he had lived it far too often. That was the biggest reason. There was also the fact that Vorrun had warned him that Guardsman Patrick—one of the three men seated around the table opposite him—was a liar and a cheat and while Chall hadn't actually *caught* him at it, the man sure did seem to win a damned awful lot.

Yet he had come anyway, and he knew the reason for that well enough, too. Partly, it had been because Guardsman Dalton had been so insistent but mostly Chall had come because Prince Bernard was gone, Matt was in trouble, Valden was not Valden anymore and—and this most of all— Maeve was gone.

Even that thought sent a shiver of supernatural dread through him. *Not gone,* he told himself. *Not gone, only not here.* But then, that was little consolation. After all, the place she *was* was a guild full of professional murderers. If a man walked into a cave of hungry bears, he *might* not get eaten, but it'd be a far greater surprise than if he did.

"Thinking maybe you'll play a hand tonight, Chall?" Guardsman Patrick asked.

Chall frowned. He really didn't like the man, nor did he like the way the abbreviated, familiar version of his name sounded coming out of the man's mouth, but then considering that he'd told them to call him "Chall" instead of the socially-awkward Sir Challadius when he'd first come, he could hardly complain.

"Oh, leave him alone, Prisshy Patty," Guardsman Randall said. Or slurred, really. Based on the sound of him, Chall thought he was well on his way to shit-faced if, that was, he hadn't already arrived. "Let the mage play how he wantsh to play." This one Chall liked more than Patrick, but then that wasn't saying all that much. He was friendly, though, even if his friendliness translated to far too much arm-around-the-shouldering and close, drunken breath for Chall's liking.

"I've asked you not to call me that," Guardsman Patrick said, frowning.

The other guardsman laughed, clapping Patrick on the back—he was a big shoulder clapper too, this one—but Chall thought he might not have laughed so much if he'd seen the look of pure hatred Guardsman Patrick shot him.

"Oh, lay off it, Randall," the third man, another guardsman said. "You know he doesn't like it."

"You asksh me," the drunken Randall said, "Prisshy Patty here doesn't like anyshing."

"Nobody did ask you," Guardsman Patrick snapped. "Now, mage, are you in or out?"

Chall glanced at the pile of coins in front of the guardsman. "I can't help but wonder how you can be so upset when you're doing so well," Chall observed. "I suppose everyone has their talents."

The drunken Randall guffawed at that, and even the youngest of the three, Guardsman Dalton, cracked a grin.

Chall knew he ought to stop there. The problem, though, was that while he seemed to at least have the part of a man's brain that told him to stop doing something foolish, based on years of evidence he seemed to have been left without the part that actually *did* the stopping. "Perhaps that's why they don't call you Smiling Sammy."

Another loud guffaw from Randall at that. "Shmiling Shammy. That'sh...that'sh a good one."

Chall looked at his cards, frowned at his cards, then discarded his cards. The other three started to play the hand while Randall went on grinning, and Patrick went on scowling. The two men were consistent if nothing else.

Chall sighed inwardly. He figured that, before the night was out, one of them was going to end up bloody. Likely both of them, considering the way these sorts of things often went. And while Chall did not much resemble the man he'd once been, this much they had in common—he preferred to be long gone before the bleeding started. "Well," he said, "I guess I'd better be going."

"Really?" the youngest asked, sounding almost panicked at the thought. "So soon? Surely you can stay a little longer."

"Oh, let him go, Dalton," Guardsman Patrick said. "It's late."

"Late?" Dalton asked. "What time is it, would you say?"

"Gettin' pretty damn close to *that* time," Randall said, then turned his drunken gaze on Chall. "Know what I mean?"

"I'm...I'm not sure," Chall said.

Another drunken grin, another far-too-heavy slap on the back.

"Anyway," Chall said once he'd recovered from what the man might have considered friendly camaraderie but what he was pretty sure any judge would consider assault, "I'd best be going. If I lose much more, I'll have to start betting my clothes. Trust me, no one wants that."

"Just a few more games," Dalton said. "Come on—I'll stake you. Why the hurry?"

That was a fair question. It wasn't as if Chall had anything to get back to, not with Maeve gone. Leaving just meant that he'd go back to his quarters and lie, sleepless, in a bed that was far too big in a room that was far too quiet. He shrugged. "Well. I suppose I can't say no to free money."

They played on.

They were three more hands deep, the night crawling on toward morning, when the door swung open to reveal another guardsman, this one appearing to be in his early twenties. "Oliver?" Guardsman Patrick asked, his voice sharp. "What do you think you're doing here?"

"What I should have done a long time ago," the guardsman said.

Patrick frowned. "You know I'll have to report this—you're supposed to be posted at the king's quarters."

"Fuck the king," Oliver said. "And fuck you too. I'm tired of listening to your orders."

"I don't know what's gotten into you," Guardsman Patrick said, rising, "but you'll regret those words."

"I won't," the new guardsman, Oliver said, "and I won't regret this either, you son of a bitch." To that point, one of the guardsman's hands had been behind his back which was a little odd, slightly off-putting, at least so far as Chall was concerned. What was considerably more odd, considerably *more* off-putting was the crossbow he produced as he moved his hand around in front of him, and even more so the way he pointed it directly at Patrick.

"Listen here, Oliver," Guardsman Patrick said, "I don't know what it is you're playin' at, but—"

But whatever else the man was going to say, he never got a chance to finish as the newcomer chose that moment to interrupt him. Not with words but with the pulling of a trigger and the releasing of a crossbow bolt which flew with deadly purpose. The bolt punched into Patrick's throat, and the man staggered backward, staring at it protruding from his neck with a surprise and shock that Chall shared.

The man gurgled out an unintelligible sound that could have meant anything as he pawed weakly at the crossbow bolt in his neck before collapsing to the ground.

"*Hey,*" the drunken guardsman, Randall, said as his gaze—considerably more sober than it had been a moment ago—traveled between the newcomer and Patrick. He rose, drawing his sword from his waist. "Protect the mage, Dalton, I'll get this basta—" But he, too, cut off. Not to a crossbow, though, for the newcomer only stood, watching him, a small smile on his face.

No, it was not a crossbow that silenced Randall but a knife, and not one held by the newcomer but one, instead, clutched in the hands of Guardsman Dalton. He stepped up behind his fellow guardsman and dragged the blade across the drunken Randall's throat from behind, opening a deep rend in his neck from which blood sluiced like a fountain.

Chall had been in deadly situations before—often it felt as though he'd been in little else. Yet for all that he'd seen, for all that he'd experienced, he found himself shocked at the sudden, terrible violence. One minute they'd been playing cards, and the next two men were dead. He staggered out of his chair, knocking it onto the floor as he did. Not that he paid it any attention. All his attention was on the guardsmen. Or, at least, the two that were still standing while their counterparts bled out on the floor, dead or well on their way.

"What...I don't understand," Chall said.

"Surprise," Guardsman Dalton said, smiling as he wiped his blade clean on the table at which they'd sat playing cards only moments ago.

"But...why?" Chall said. "I thought...that is, they were your friends."

Dalton considered that for a few seconds then shrugged. "Yeah, maybe. But then I can make new friends—I always have been a pretty amiable guy. Far easier to make friends than to make the kind of fortune that's waiting for me once we finish up here."

"Wait...someone paid you to kill your friends?"

His grin widened slowly in a way Chall didn't like, and the two guardsmen shared a look, laughing. "Not quite," Dalton said. "Turns out, you're the man of the hour."

Chall found his gaze traveling between the two men. He hadn't brought a weapon with him—true, there'd been a murder in the castle, but then he'd been playing cards with a bunch of guardsmen. What could be safer? Anyway despite evidence to the contrary over the years, Chall was no fighter, no warrior to wield a blade in battle, and in truth he had just about as much chance of taking his own life as someone else's. Or at least that was the thought that he'd had at the time, a thought that might well lead to his death.

"You killed your friends...for money?" Chall said.

"No," Dalton said in a bored voice, "We killed our friends because they were in the way. *You* we're going to kill for money."

"But...I trusted you. How could you betray your people like that?"

The two men shared another look. "It really was a lot of money," Dalton explained, showing no remorse for what he'd done or what he planned to do. "Now then," he said, "best we be getting on with it—a couple of hours from now I mean to be countin' coins 'til my fingers cramp." He started forward then, the knife in one hand as he drew his sword in the other.

"The king will hear of this," Chall said, trying to buy time to think of some way out of this. "You won't get away with it."

Another knowing smile. "The toddler king has his own concerns, believe me," the guardsman said. "I think he'll be far too busy being dead to get any revenge for you."

That sent a shiver of terror through Chall. Whatever they were doing, whatever they had planned, according to the guardsman it didn't end with Chall's death but with Matt's. Terror roiled through him at the thought but then, a moment later, there was something else, crashing through him in a wave that easily eclipsed the fear which had come before it...anger. Anger that these men would kill two guardsmen without showing even a speck of remorse, anger that they would betray their kingdom for coin promised them, no doubt, by Robert Palden. Anger, most of all, that they would think to harm Matt, a young man who had only ever tried to help others the best he was able, who had been more of a king to the people of the Known Lands in the brief time that he'd been in the role than anyone had been in a very long time.

The people finally had hope. Sure, things were bad, but then they'd always been bad. What was new was that now, for the first time in a very, very long time, the country's king actually cared about making them better. And the two men standing in front of him meant to take all that away, all so that their pockets would jingle a little more when they walked.

The guardsman continued forward, likely thinking that it was fear that gripped Chall. Most times, he would have been right. But not this time. Likely he thought that Chall would run or, at least, try to—not that he'd make it very far. Malden had done a fine job caring for him since the attack, but a crossbow bolt in one leg and a knife in the other weren't the type of things that were cured by a bit of foul-tasting medicine and a night's rest. Wounds like that took time to heal, time that Chall had not yet had. Time that, if these men had their way, he would never get.

The guardsman continued forward, and Chall waited until he judged him close enough. Then he reached over and snatched one of his crutches off the wall from where he'd propped them when he'd sat. He grabbed it in two hands, pivoting and, before the guardsman could do more than grunt in surprise, he swung the long length of wood at the man's face.

Chall was not known for his strength like Prince Bernard. He was no warrior. But he *was* motivated. He swung hard. The end of the crutch struck the guardsman in the face and blood and teeth flew as the heavy wooden crutch broke. The guardsman screamed, staggering to the side against the wall, the sword and knife falling from his hands as he brought both to his face. *"My fashe,"* the guardsman slurred, his voice sounding mushy, *"what did you do to my face?"*

"Oh, you haven't seen anything yet," Chall said. Then he did what was likely one of the most foolish things he'd done in a life full of little else—he charged. Or, at least, he tried to. Two wounded legs made for a pretty poor charge. Really more of a limping, aggressive shamble. Still, what he made up for in speed and strength and all around menace he compensated for—or at least tried to—with sheer desperation. He knew that he had to finish the man quickly, for the second guardsman was still at the side of the room with his crossbow, and it was too much to hope that he'd only brought the one bolt.

Chall struck Guardsman Dalton—still too worried about his ruined face and teeth to think of much else—as hard as he was able in a tackle that sent the man slamming against the wall. In a fair one-on-one fight he thought it likely that the guardsman—just like nearly anyone with a pulse —could take him, so Chall did his best to endeavor to make sure the fight was as far from fair as it could be. He punched the guardsman in his already bloody mouth, making his head rock back against the wall, then again.

He was going back for a third when Dalton let out a growl and charged forward in a tackle of his own, driving Chall backward. Chall tried to resist, but he was off-balance, and they continued backward until he fetched up against something and a sharp pain in his lower back told him that they'd struck the table.

"*Kill you*," Dalton growled, bloody spittle flying from his mouth as he leaned over Chall—who was bent backward over the table—and wrapping both his hands around Chall's throat, proceeded to do his best to make good on the promise.

Chall struggled and growled and spat, grabbing the man's wrists and trying to wrest his hands free. But the guardsman was atop him, and he had all the leverage. Try as he might, Chall couldn't break his grip. His vision began to darken, shadows creeping along the edges of his sight, something he didn't need Malden to tell him wasn't good.

He was just beginning to think this was the end—that it was finally over—when the strangest thing happened. A crossbow bolt seemed to sprout from the guardsman's chest as if by magic. Chall was surprised by that. After all, the other guardsman was no more than a dozen feet away—pretty damned hard to miss. But as surprised as Chall was, Dalton was even more so. He loosened his grip, stepping back and staring at the crossbow bolt in surprise equal to that Patrick had shown. "How…" he began, but managed no more than that before his eyes rolled back in their sockets, and he fell backward.

Chall lay there for a minute, gasping and hacking, each cough a special anguish of its own as his throat felt as if someone had gone at it with a handful of sanding paper and a whole lot of determination. He was still lying there trying to get his breath back when a figure appeared above him.

Chall winced, tensing as he expected the second guardsman to finish what his companion had started. He was shocked, then, when he saw that the figure was not the second guardsman at all but a man he recognized.

"Chall," Ned said, "you alright?"

"*Great,*" he wheezed, coughing again. "I was…just…about to…take him."

"Of course you were," Ned said. He offered his hand, and Chall took it. A moment later, he was standing, rubbing at his sore throat as he turned to regard the second guardsman, realizing as he did that he needn't have worried. The guardsman with the crossbow had, apparently, come down with a sudden case of sword-through-the-chest.

He found his gaze traveling between the two dead men. They'd meant to kill him, *would* have, had Ned not shown up when he had. Which begged the question: "Not that I'm not grateful, but why are you here?"

"Valden sent me," Ned said. "To look after you and—"

"Matt," Chall said, his eyes snapping wide as he remembered what Dalton had said about Matt. "We have to go. Now!"

———

As he traveled through the gate, what Door had described as a bridge between the past and the present, Cutter was assailed by hundreds, thousands of images, flashing by so quickly as to be almost—but not quite—unrecognizable. Images from throughout his life, including the alleyway back in Daltenia where he had first tasted his own blood and nearly died, including, also, his last sight of his homeland from the deck of one of the ships upon which he and his people had fled the Skaalden's invasion. He saw their arrival on the shores of what would become the Known Lands, saw his battles with the Fey, his killing of Yeladrian, and on and on it went.

But it was not just the sights—it was the sounds, too. Voices, some speaking in whispers, others in screams. Voices from his past, all clamoring, demanding his attention, demanding that he stop and look at them, pay them heed.

But Cutter did not stop—he did what he always did. He kept going. He put one foot in front of the other, each step a monumental effort of will as he kept his gaze forward, not looking at the colors and images that swirled around him but only ahead. It would have been easy to get lost in the past, as easy as it always was for a man to be consumed by his past successes or his past failures. But Matt did not need him in the past—he needed him in the present. So he walked on.

He walked on until, finally, he took a step that did not feel like he was hindered by thousands of pounds of weight tied to him. Suddenly, the images were gone, the voices too. He stood not in that strange in-between place of color and flashing light through which he'd traveled, but in the present in truth.

Cutter took a slow, deep breath as he looked around. He stood in a field as he had while traveling with Door and Feledias, but something was different. For one, there were no translucent, ghostly figures crowding the area around him, but that was not what struck him the most. He saw that the field in which he stood was not green like the one he'd left, but white. Not fields of grass at all but snow. His breath plumed in the air in front of him in a great cloud, and his exposed fingers and face felt numb with cold.

He pulled his hood over his head, blocking it from the driving snow. He looked around, trying to figure out where he was, for he had not seen snow in some time, not since first entering the Black Wood. As he swept his gaze around him, he noted another difference between the field in which he stood and the one through which he and his brother and their escort had traveled. A short distance ahead of him, no more than fifty feet away, was a line of trees that stretched to the left and right as far as he could see. And not normal trees, but by their size and the alien menace that seemed to radiate from them even to where he stood, trees that, he knew, marked the border of the Black Wood.

He frowned at that, trying to understand where the gateway had taken him, was still trying when he heard a gasp from behind him. Cutter spun, one hand going to the axe handle sticking up over one shoulder, but he paused as he saw a figure seem to appear out of thin air, stumbling out of nothing into the world in front of him. What's more, it was a figure he recognized even as the newcomer fell to his hands and knees, hacking and gagging.

Cutter let his hand drop, moving forward. "Fel?" he asked.

His brother raised his head, studying him with a groggy, pained expression. "Bernard?" he said, running a forearm across his mouth.

"You alright?"

"Sure," his brother said, clearing his throat. "Never been better. Remind me not to go through any doors from the past again, will you?"

"You got it," Cutter said, offering his hand. His brother took it, and he pulled him to his feet.

"Where are we?" Feledias asked, glancing around.

"I'm not sure," Cutter said, but as he took a moment to look around them he realized that wasn't true. There was the Black Wood nearby, fields of snow beyond, and to the north were giant peaks of mountains reaching so high their tops were shrouded in the clouds.

"Those are the Barrier Mountains," Feledias said, clearly shocked.

"Yes," Cutter said.

"And that," his brother went on, jabbing a finger at the tree line in the distance, "is the Black Wood."

"Yes."

They turned to regard each other then, grins slowly spreading on both their faces. "We made it," Feledias said. "We made it out."

"I...I guess so," Cutter said in surprise. Part of him, a very large part, had not thought he would ever see the Known Lands again, yet here they stood. He knew this place, for he had walked it before, long ago with Matt as they'd fled Brighton.

"Fire and salt but we made it," Feledias said again.

Cutter was opening his mouth to respond when the air was suddenly pierced with an alien howl. First one, then another until there was a chorus of what might have been hundreds, perhaps thousands of creatures all raising their voices in unison. He wondered for a brief moment what was making the sound, but as a wave of figures appeared out of the Black Wood, rushing toward them, he knew.

The Unsated had found them. The Black Wood, it seemed, was not quite ready to let them go.

Cutter watched that great tide of creatures rushing out of the tree line, hundreds of them, thousands of them, and more coming all the time.

"*Stones and starlight, how can there be so many?*" Feledias breathed from beside him.

"I don't know," Cutter said, no trace of the grin they'd shared a moment ago on either of their faces now.

"How many are there...do you think?" Feledias asked, still watching.

"I don't know," Cutter said, but then that wasn't exactly true. He knew exactly how many there were.

Enough.

"What do we do?" Feledias asked.

Cutter knew the answer to that one, too. He remembered this place, knew it well, for he had lived much of his life since his exile in the north, and so he knew that the nearest settlement was hours away. Hours they didn't have, and even if they had a settlement of no more than a hundred people couldn't have stood against the number of Unsated pouring out of the tree line. There was nowhere to go and no time to get there even if there had been.

He drew his axe.

Feledias sighed. "Well," he said. "At least we get to die here, in our lands, instead of that damned cursed place," he said, pulling his swords from their scabbards.

And then the two brothers stood side by side, their weapons in hand, as they waited for death to come.

Cutter did not think they would have to wait for long.

HER ESCORT of assassins led Maeve through the guild halls where several people stopped to watch the procession. By their hateful expressions, it was obvious that Bethesa and the other tribunes had been busy spreading lies about her already. Eventually, they reached a door guarded by two men. A door which, Maeve knew, led to the dungeon.

The two men bowed to Tribune Bethesa and again to Tribune Piralta.

"The other prisoner?" Bethesa asked.

"Unchanged, Tribune," one of the guards said.

The old woman nodded. "Come," she said, giving Maeve a cruel smile. "Let us show our guildmaster to her new quarters."

The men opened the door and, a moment later, Maeve was being led inside. The dungeons were not large—after all, assassins weren't, as a general rule, fans of taking prisoners. Sometimes, though, such prisoners were necessary, as were the answers that they would eventually give if asked long—and hard—enough. The dungeon existed for just such eventualities.

Three cells waited against the wall, iron bars at their front. Inside the cell on the left, Maeve saw a figure she recognized. *"Emille?"* she asked, feeling a mixture of fear and anger, for the woman lay on her side, her knees brought up to her chest in the fetal position, her eyes closed, her body unmoving. "What did you do to her?" she demanded, rounding on Bethesa, an abrupt movement which one of the old woman's guards took as ample excuse to strike her a backhanded blow. He hit her hard, and Maeve cried out, staggering and nearly falling, *would* have fallen had one of the men not caught her in a rough grip, jerking her back to her feet.

"Oh, don't worry," Bethesa said in a soft voice as if nothing had happened. "Your little pet is alive—at least for the moment. Though for how long I dare not say...after all, we are a guild of assassins, aren't we?"

The old woman nodded her head to Maeve's escort, and they dragged her roughly toward the middle cell, shoving her in hard enough that Maeve cried out again, stumbling and falling to the hard-packed earth floor on her hands and knees.

She was hurting and scared, but she refused to give them the satisfaction, so she rose even as the iron door slammed shut behind her, and one of the guards locked it.

Bethesa smiled as if she knew well what Maeve was thinking, then waved a hand at the guards. "Leave us."

"Tribune?" the man asked. "Are you sure?"

"Of course I'm sure," the old woman said. "She can offer us little harm from behind bars. Now go."

The men shared a look, then a moment later they filed out of the room until only Bethesa and Piralta remained.

"You won't get away with this," Maeve said. "The Guild will not stand for it."

"Oh, I think they will," Bethesa said, smiling. "Particularly when they discover that you ordered your pet to kill Tribune Silrika."

"Emille didn't do that, and you know it."

"And yet," Bethesa said, smiling, "there are half a dozen people who will swear that they saw her enter Silrika's chambers, saw her leave with a bloody knife like the one we found on her."

"You did this," Maeve said.

"That is not what the evidence suggests, I'm afraid" Bethesa said, smiling. "You see, Silrika, she was a fool. A dog, a beast who might be useful sometimes, but who, when it refuses to obey, must be put down. For the good of everyone."

Maeve growled in anger. "Why? Why are you doing this? What do you want from me?"

The tribune sighed, shaking her head slowly. "Oh, Lady Maeve, you still do not understand, do you? But do not worry...you will soon enough. There is a new world coming, Lady Maeve, and you will help us bring it to fruition. Anyway, it is not I who wants anything from you, Lady Maeve."

"Then who?"

Bethesa only gave her that vulpine smile, then glanced at Piralta beside her. "Come, Tribune. Let us allow Lady Maeve to get used to her new... accommodations. It is a long, busy night, and there is much yet to do." They turned and started for the door.

"Who?" Maeve called after them. "Who's behind this?"

They didn't even turn this time, and in another moment the door closed behind them. "Emille?" Maeve asked. "Are you alri—" She cut off, though, as the door opened once more. She thought that it must be Bethesa or Piralta returning, likely to do some more gloating, but when the figure stepped into the light of the lantern hung on the wall, Maeve felt her breath catch in her throat. "What..." she said, staggering back in shock. "It can't...why...*Agnes?*"

Agnes, the previous guildmaster, flashed her a smile as sharp as a dagger cut. "Hello, Maeve."

CHAPTER TWENTY-TWO

MATT FOUGHT BACK the urge to yawn. He was tired. But then, he was always tired now, a product of the fact that he rarely slept ever since the Green had come into his dreams, his mind.

"And that's how my husband and I met," Lady Valencia finished, wrapping up the third story of her past she'd told since arriving in his quarters claiming that she'd needed to see him.

Matt knew from the last two times that if he didn't speak soon, she would begin another story and another ten minutes or longer would pass with the telling of it. "Forgive me, Lady Valencia," he said, "and I mean no disrespect, but, may I ask what it is that brought you to see me?"

She winced. "I've spoken too much again, haven't I? A habit of mine, I fear, one that my husband often scolded me about."

"It isn't that, Lady, only when you arrived you seemed...distraught. As if something was troubling you.'"

She nodded, glancing at the window. "It is getting late, wouldn't you say, Majesty?"

"Near midnight, I'd wager," Matt said. "Perhaps a little after now."

"A little after," she repeated, nodding slowly. "As for why I came...I suppose it is just that I'm frightened. My rooms—those which you were so kind to lend me—while beautiful, felt very...empty. Very...lonely. Does that make sense?"

"It does," Matt said. After all, he knew well the feeling of loneliness she was describing for he felt it too, constantly.

She gave a soft laugh. "You must think me a silly old woman," she said, shaking her head.

"Not at all," Matt said. "I understand loneliness."

She gave him a warm smile. "I hope I do not overstep, Majesty, when I say that you are a greater king than ever your uncle or brother could have been. It is very kind of you to take the time to comfort an old lady, for I am sure you have much more important matters to be about. Just as you no doubt did when you were kind enough to speak with me in the courtyard before and to show me that pretty necklace of yours, the green one. It is quite something, isn't it?"

Matt blinked, surprised by the abrupt change of topic. "It is a fine necklace," he said uncertainly which, of course, was just about the biggest understatement he'd ever made. Since he'd discovered it, the necklace had become a sort of focal point for the strange feelings he'd dealt with over the last days and weeks. A sort of physical representation of what he'd come to think of as the Green. He found his hand straying to his shirt where the stone Mistress Ophasia had given him even now hung around his neck.

She nodded. "Oh, but I do wish I might see it again, Majesty. Perhaps one day."

Matt's initial response was a sort of jealous defensiveness, and he found his fingers clutching the necklace as if to protect it. Then he realized what he was doing and gave the old woman a smile. "Of course," he said. Yet despite his words he still found himself hesitating as she continued to watch him, a smile on her face.

"Majesty, if you do not wish to show it, I understand. Only—"

"No, no," Matt said. "No, it's, it's fine." He took the necklace out, offering it to her.

The woman took it, and by some trick of his weary mind it almost seemed to him that she snatched it. Just his imagination, though, just as he was sure he imagined the greedy look of satisfaction that swept across her gaze. Not a reflection of her own inner thoughts, he was sure, but his, for the truth was he was loathe to let the necklace go, even for a moment.

"It really is quite beautiful, isn't it?" she asked, staring at the green, cloudy surface of the gem.

"I...suppose so," he said.

"Funny," she said in a quiet voice that made him think she wasn't talking to him at all but to herself, "funny that something so small could be so important. But then...I suppose that's the way of it."

Matt frowned. "I'm not sure I understand what you mean, lady."

Lady Valencia started, giving herself a shake. "Forgive me, Majesty. Sometimes, my mind wonders. A curse of the old, I fear. I wonder, might I have some of that water, there?" she asked, indicating the pitcher of water by his bedside.

"Is the wine not good?" he asked, glancing at the goblet in front of her.

"Oh, it isn't that," she said. "The wine is quite good, Majesty, only too much, and I will make an embarrassment of myself."

Matt nodded. "Of course." He rose, glancing at the necklace still held in her hands before turning and starting toward the bedside table where the pitcher of water sat.

He was pouring into a waiting cup when suddenly there was a knock on his door. Only, it wasn't really a knock so much as it was a thundering bang.

"*Matt, are you in there!?*" A voice, one that he recognized as Chall. Which was surprising, just as it was surprising that the man had called him "Matt" not "Your Majesty" and that he'd knocked on the door like he'd meant to break it down.

But out of all of it, what struck Matt the most was the panic in the man's voice. He sounded afraid. Matt turned to the door and let out a grunt of surprise as he saw that Lady Valencia stood right behind him, less than a foot away.

"Lady Valencia, is everything alright?" he asked.

She glanced down at her hands. "I'm afraid not, lad," she said. "I'm afraid not." Matt followed her gaze and saw that she still held the green necklace in one hand. It was her other hand, though, that grabbed his attention, for it held something too.

Not a necklace, this, and Matt just had time to realize what it was before the woman thrust her hand—and the knife it gripped—forward.

Green exploded in Matt's mind, in his vision for a moment, gone the next, and time seemed to slow to a crawl. He watched the knife moving toward his stomach, inching closer. He wanted to dive out of the way, to knock the blade away, and tried to do just that, but while the world seemed to have slowed down, he had slowed down, too. All of him, that was, except his thoughts which had done the opposite, speeding up to a frenetic pace.

There was panic and fear and shock as he took in the knife, took in, also, the old woman's face, which he had thought grandmotherly before, but not now. Now, it was twisted with hate and something like hunger.

But it was not the woman, not even the knife that his gaze settled on. Instead, it was the necklace, the gem that she held in her other hand. It was not beautiful, as she had said. It was an answer. Or, at least, the beginnings of one. The answer to a question he had not even known until that moment.

What is the Green?

Even as he had the thought, he felt it, that force, that power, rising up in him. He'd felt it before, when unintentionally hearing the thoughts of others, or when he dreamed, dreams that felt realer than the reality he would always wake to, bathed in cold sweat, panting for breath.

And he felt it now. But now he felt it far more powerfully, not a wave crashing over him but a wave crashing over the entire world, a force that could not be hidden from or stood against, that could not be endured. A force that would sweep over anything it came against. A force that swept over him.

And in that wild storm of green, in that emerald maelstrom, he found that it was not himself he thought of. It was not the old woman before him or the slowed-down thundering knocks as Chall and whoever else tried to bust their way into his rooms. It was not even the knife.

A WARRIOR'S OATH

Instead, he thought of his father.

His father who had always been there for him, even when he'd been a child, watching over him silently. His father who was not perfect, it was true, but who had sacrificed everything, who would have braved anything, even the Black Wood itself, to protect him.

His father who was miles and miles away, gone into the Black Wood where Matt had sent him. His father who was far too far away to help him now, to protect him. And yet...Matt found himself wishing for him anyway. Wishing that he were here, that he was with him.

A silly child's wish, but one that, standing within that maelstrom of green, that storm of emerald, had power. A wish that had, within it, an answer to the question.

What is the Green?

It was him. *Matt* was the Green. He knew it in that moment as much as he knew anything, as much as he knew that he wanted, desperately, to see his father again.

Even as he had the thought, there was a *shifting*, a movement within that storm, something purposeful, intentional. The Green surged forward, toward him, *through* him, and Matt was carried along with it.

"*MATT!*" Chall yelled. Then, suddenly, he felt a surge of power, immense, magical power from somewhere inside the room, and he, along with Ned and the guardsmen in the hallway, were suddenly thrown backward by some invisible wave of force.

"Damn," Ned said. "What in the name of the gods was that?"

"I don't know," Chall said as they picked themselves up off the floor. He winced at a fresh pain going through his leg as he rose and turned to Vorrun. "We need in that room. Now."

"You heard him," Vorrun said, turning to the other guardsmen—nearly twelve in all—crowding the hallway behind Ned and Chall. "Who's got an axe?"

"I got one, sir," a voice said, and then an axe was being handed forward.

"You'll want to back up," Vorrun told Chall and Ned, then without preamble he began chopping at the door. Three swings at the handle made short work of it, then he gave the door a savage kick, and it flew open. They rushed inside, Chall's heart in his chest.

He had seen some terrible things in his time, but the thought of finding Matt—the kindest, *best* person he'd ever met—dead was more than he could take. As he entered the room, he saw Lady Valencia standing near the bed, facing them. She stood with a stricken expression on her pale face, a knife held loosely, almost forgotten in one hand, a familiar necklace, of a match to the one Chall had seen Matt toying with often of late in the other.

"V-Val?" Ned asked, shocked. "It...it's you?"

"Where is he?" Chall demanded. "What have you done with him?"

"He's...he's gone," the noblewoman stammered, staring at the knife in her hand then back toward the bed.

Chall cast his gaze about and, sure enough, he didn't see Matt anywhere. "Take her," Vorrun said, and two guards moved forward, the noblewoman standing, apparently stunned, as they took the knife and necklace from her.

"What would you have us do with this, sir?" the guard said, holding up the necklace.

"I'll take it," Chall blurted, for he felt something coming from the necklace. A tiny bit of magic, a whisper-thin leak, but an undeniable one just the same.

Vorrun nodded. "You heard him."

The guard handed the necklace to Chall who took it, pocketing it.

"He's not here," Ned said, frowning around the room. "Think she put him somewhere?"

"Where, her pocket?" Chall asked, shaking his head. He looked around the room, trying to determine what had caused that powerful surge of magic, one of the most powerful uses of the art he'd ever felt. But there was nothing to explain it. The necklace he held contained some sort of magic, it was true, but whatever had caused the surge, the necklace was not it, for the magic leaking from it was only a trickle, nowhere near what he had felt.

"Okay, then where is he?" Ned asked. "Where's the king?"

Chall stared at the necklace in his hand, frowning. "I...I don't know."

HE GRIPPED the Breaker of Pacts in two hands, and he fought after his name's sake, swinging again and again. He did not take aim, did not pick a target, for there was no need. The creatures were all around them, a great wave of death which would sweep over them any moment.

Cutter and Feledias stood back-to-back against that tide of teeth and claws, cutting down one Unsated after the other. In the end, though, he knew it would make no difference, for there were plenty more to replace those they killed.

Still, he fought on. It was what a man did. Sometimes, that man would win, and he would celebrate. Other times, like now, he would lose, *must* lose, but in the end, he thought it was not the winning or the losing that really mattered—it was the fighting. The standing.

And so Cutter stood. He fought.

He was still fighting when there was a *pop* in the air, a sort of static charge like that which sometimes came before a powerful storm. Several of the Unsated cried out, being hurled away as if thrown by some invisible force. That force struck Cutter a moment later, and he grunted, staggering as he spun in the direction from which it had come raising his axe, expecting to discover that some new feyling had joined the fray.

Indeed, a figure had appeared as if out of nowhere among the Unsated who had all been thrown a dozen feet by whatever power he'd felt. But as Cutter stared at that figure he was shocked to see that it was not another feyling after all, nor was it an Unsated. Instead, standing before him, looking as confused and shocked as Cutter felt, was Matt. His son. "Matt?" he breathed, his voice hoarse from shock.

He was so stunned by this sudden appearance that he forgot, for a moment, all about the creatures surrounding them. At least, that was, until something struck him hard in the side, and he was sent tumbling, rolling onto his back. He tried to rise but didn't get a chance before one of the Unsated pounced on top of him, its teeth going for his throat.

"*Stop!*" a voice thundered. It was Matt's voice, but it seemed to ring with power, like the command of some ancient god. The Unsated, too, seemed to notice it, for it did stop. "*Leave him alone!*" Matt roared.

And, to Cutter's great surprise, the creature did, its mouth shutting at once, climbing off of Cutter who was left panting.

He climbed to his feet to stand beside Matt and Feledias, watching in stunned silence as the hundreds, likely thousands of Unsated which had surrounded them suddenly turned and started away toward the Black Wood.

"How...how is this possible?" Feledias asked.

Cutter, though, could think of nothing except for his son standing before him. "Matt, is...is it really you?"

"Father?" It was his voice. There was no denying that. Cutter sheathed his axe and stepped forward, pulling his son into a tight hug. "How...how are you here?"

"I...I don't know," Matt said. "I think...I think maybe the necklace...or..."

"What necklace?" Cutter asked. "You know what? It doesn't matter. I don't care. You're here."

He felt tears gliding their way down his cheeks as he held his son, felt his own shoulder growing damp from Matt's tears. "Father...I'm sorry about...about what I did. It was Emma, the feyling. She was in my mind, making me do things, making me send you here and—"

"Never mind that," Cutter said, leaning back. "Are you alright?"

"I'm...I'm fine," Matt said.

"Are you sure?" Cutter asked.

"Why...why wouldn't I be?"

"Your eyes, lad," Feledias said, moving to stand beside Cutter. "They're...they're green."

Matt frowned. "I don't...I'm not sure what you mean," he said, and even as he spoke his eyes—which, to that point, had been a complete, vivid green, pupil and all—slowly returned to their normal color.

"Well, I don't know where you came from, nephew," Feledias said, stepping forward and clapping Matt on the shoulder, "but I'm damned glad you're here." He glanced at the retreating forms of the Unsated as they disappeared into the distant tree line. "How'd you do that, anyway?"

"I don't know," Matt said honestly. "I...don't think I did anything."

"Oh, you did something alright," Feledias said. "Felt like you were talking inside my mind. Funny," he went on, turning to Cutter. "Door said they'd never stop, no matter what."

Cutter frowned at that. That wasn't exactly true, though, and he thought Feledias knew it. The feyling hadn't said the Unsated would never stop. He'd said that they would only stop if ordered to by a member of the Fey blood, their versions of royals. "Shadelaresh must have called them back for some reason," he said.

"Perhaps," Feledias said, staring at Matt.

Cutter frowned, dismissing his brother's unspoken words—that he could hear as clearly as if he'd said them aloud—and turning back to his son. He put a hand on his shoulder. "I don't know how you got here," he said. "But I'm glad you did."

"So am I," Matt said, and then they were embracing again.

"I don't mean to ruin this moment," Feledias said, "but while I enjoy a good family reunion as much as the next guy, I'd just as soon not freeze to death to see it, and this snow doesn't seem to be letting up anytime soon."

Cutter stepped back from Matt, glancing around him and up at the sky. "You're right—there's a blizzard on the way. We should get moving."

"Great," Feledias said. "Is there somewhere close, somewhere we might be able to get some horses, maybe? I'm just about all walked out."

Matt glanced at Cutter. "Is this...?"

"Yes."

The young man nodded, looking around. "There's a village a couple of hours' walk northeast. Windam. We could go there, perhaps find some horses, if we're lucky."

Cutter nodded. "Very well," he said, thinking. "Horses. Then we'll be on our way."

Feledias shook his head, a smile on his face. "Damn, but it'll be nice to go back home. I never thought I'd see New Daltenia again. What about you, Bernard? What will you do first? Drink? Some whoring?"

"I'm not going back," Cutter said, staring north, at the distant Barrier Mountains. "At least not yet."

"What do you mean you're not going back?" Feledias demanded, then followed his gaze. "Wait a minute...shit. You're thinking about what the Gray Man said, aren't you?"

"What Gray Man?" Matt asked. "What did he say?"

Cutter turned to his son. "He said that the key to defeating Shade-laresh, to ending this war, lies to the north, in the mountains."

"Yeah?" Feledias said. "So does a lot of damned snow, Bernard. And death, likelier than not. There's a reason why they're called the Barrier Mountains and not the Pleasant Stroll Mountains. They're *famous* for being impassable."

"Maybe," Cutter said, "but I have to try. If there's a way to end this war, I have to find it."

Feledias hissed, clearly frustrated. He turned to Matt. "Can you speak some sense into your fool of a dad, nephew, before he ends up getting himself killed?"

"The answer to defeating Shadelaresh, to ending the war is in the mountains?" Matt asked, glancing at Cutter.

"Yes."

Matt nodded. "I'm going with you."

"Matt, no," Cutter said. "It's too dangerous."

"Before I appeared here," Matt said, "an old woman tried to kill me. I would have been the third corpse in the castle in less than a week. Trust me, Father, I'm safer here, with you, than I am in New Daltenia. Besides," he went on, "what sort of king would I be if I saw a means for ending the war, protecting our people, and did not try?"

Cutter watched his son for a second, saw the worry in his gaze at the prospect of venturing into the mountains. But more than that, he saw resoluteness. He saw steel. "Okay," Cutter said. "Alright."

Feledias shook his head. "Fools, the both of you." He sighed. "When are we leaving?"

"Wait, you're coming?" Matt asked, surprised. Cutter, though, knew his brother, and so he was not.

"Well, sure," Feledias said. "Foolishness runs in the blood, after all. So?"

Cutter looked at the two of them, grinning as he turned back to the mountains in the distance, shrouded by clouds. "How's now suit?"

And now we have come to the end of *A Warrior's Oath*. I sincerely hope you enjoyed this latest adventure in the Known Lands. The next book will be coming your way soon.

In the meantime, I've got a few other series you may want to give a shot.

Want another story of an anti-hero in a grimdark setting where a jaded sellsword is forced into a fight he doesn't want between forces he doesn't understand?
Get started on the bestselling seven book series, The Seven Virtues.

Interested in a story where the gods choose their champions in a war with the darkness that will determine the fate of the world itself?
Dive into The Nightfall Wars, a complete six book, epic fantasy series.

Or how about something a little lighter? Do you like laughs with your sword slinging and magical mayhem? All the world's heroes are dead and so it is up to the antiheroes to save the day. An overweight swordsman, a mage who thinks magic is for sissies, an assassin who gets sick at the sight of the blood, and a man who can speak to animals...maybe.
The world needed heroes—it got them instead.
Start your journey with The Antiheroes!

If you enjoyed *A Warrior's Path*, I'd really appreciate it if you'd take a moment to leave an honest review. They make a tremendous difference, and I would love to hear from you.

If you want to reach out, you can email me at Jacobpeppersauthor@gmail.com or visit my **website.** You can also give me a shout on **Facebook** or on **Twitter.** I'm looking forward to hearing from you!

TURN THE PAGE FOR A LIMITED TIME FREE OFFER!

Sɪɢɴ ᴜᴘ ꜰᴏʀ ᴛʜᴇ ᴀᴜᴛʜᴏʀ's ᴍᴀɪʟɪɴɢ ʟɪsᴛ and for a limited time receive a FREE copy of *The Silent Blade*, prequel to the bestselling fantasy series *The Seven Virtues.*

Go to https://www.JacobPeppersAuthor.com to get your free book now!

NOTE FROM THE AUTHOR

Once more, dear reader, we have reached the end of our adventure. Cutter has finally found his way free of the Black Wood and now travels to the Barrier Mountains in the hopes of finding a means of defeating Shadelaresh and ending the war. What's more, thanks to a power he does not understand, Matt has evaded an assassin's blade and father and son are reunited at last.

But in New Daltenia the troubles are far from over. An assassin runs free in the castle while a man possessing seemingly super-human abilities is on a rampage of murder. Meanwhile, Chall is wounded, Maeve is imprisoned, and Valden, who has lost his faith, struggles to find it again. The question, then, is if he will find it in time.

I want to take this chance to thank everyone who has made this book —and all my books—possible. First, as always, I want to thank my wife, Andrea, for her unending support and for taking care of the important stuff so that I can spend my time sitting around making things up.

Thank you, also, to my children. In a life full of blessings, you are the best of the lot.

And, of course, I want to thank my beta readers. Whatever straight paths my readers travel in my books, they have you to thank for them. You who have gone before, hacking away at a host of problems to clear the way and make my books, if not *worth* the read, then certainly *possible* to read.

And last, I want to thank *you,* dear reader. I have all the props—the stage and magician's hat. Maybe even a rabbit or two. But it is you, when you come and take your seat, it is you who brings the magic. So thank you, for that. Thank you for all of it.

We've been on quite a journey so far, but then it isn't finished yet. The Barrier Mountains await. The only question is—are you ready?

Happy Reading and until next time,

Jacob Peppers

ABOUT THE AUTHOR

Jacob Peppers lives in Georgia with his wife, and his children, Gabriel, Norah, and Declan, as well as their two dogs. He is an avid reader and writer and when he's not exploring the worlds of others, he's creating his own. His short fiction has been published in various markets, and his short story, "The Lies of Autumn," was a finalist for the 2013 Eric Hoffer Award for Short Prose. He is the author of the bestselling epic fantasy series *The Seven Virtues* and *The Nightfall Wars*.

Printed in Great Britain
by Amazon